The Catskills

Revised Edition
By Adam Cornell

Jade, Hudson & Steele Publishing
Watertown, New York

ISBN: 978-0-9853165-3-2

For Belinda.
You and me against the world.

Always.

The Catskills

Revised Edition
By Adam Cornell

Jade, Hudson & Steele Publishing
Watertown, New York

Author's Foreword

I first published *The Catskills* in the spring of 2012, after spending months in the writing and editing process. It was an amazing feeling; creating characters and dreaming up scenarios through which they would need to struggle to survive.

As is the case with many writers, the characters and situations began to wrest away control and dictate which direction the story went. Not in the sense that they actually took over like in an other worldly, supernatural possession type of way, no. Rather, as a writer becomes intimately familiar with each character, it becomes apparent that each character, in order to stay true to themselves, will act and react to the stimuli to which they've been exposed. Some of those actions and reactions got away from me at times.

That said, the initial publishing of *The Catskills* included situations, language and scenarios which, though they may have been appropriate for the characters as I imagined them, in hindsight, created a book that I just couldn't take pride in. I found myself apologizing for the language or the violence I had included. I dusted off my old On-Air Radio name Adam Speed and used it as my pen name in an effort to distance myself from the work. Needless to say, it caused confusion and even more need for explanation.

I did some soul searching over the summer of 2012 and came to a realization: I needed to release an alternate version, a revised edition. I would take the time to add a bit more to a few scenes, carve a few scenes up, and remove any expletives. Additionally, I added the first two chapters from the upcoming sequel *Hollow Pointe*, as well as some of the sketches I created while I was writing the novel over the course of several months.

When I write I will often times sketch the characters or perhaps a scene. I placed the sketches at the back of this edition as they are not meant to be illustrations and fit next to certain sections of the manuscript, though a few of them are very scene-specific. Rather, I sometimes will thresh out a scene or character in my head on paper first, then write about it,him or her respectively. I thought you, the reader, might like to see some of these sketches as an added bonus to this revised edition. Perhaps I'll include sketches with each of my future books, perhaps not.

Additionally the book has been reset and the layout has been improved for better legibility and easier conversion to digital format. This will provide a similar experience to the reader whether you have the paperback version in your hand or an eReader.

Lastly, if I was going to write, I wanted to be proud enough of what I wrote to put my real name on it, and now I am.

Without further delay, I humbly give you *The Catskills* as I feel it should be presented. I hope you enjoy the trip, as much as I enjoyed charting it.

Respectfully Yours,

Adam "Speed" Cornell
December, 2012
Watertown, NY

Epigraph

. . . and the earth became filled with violence.

Genesis 6:11, NWT

I shall raise my eyes to the mountains.

From where will my help come?

Psalms 121:1, NWT

Introduction • Spring 1933

It was nearly midnight when he finally pulled into the gravel parking lot of the Lexmore Hotel, a light spring rain still splashing against the windshield of his 1930 Lincoln Model L. The car was a beautiful maroon and black with custom tan leather interior. It was his second automobile and one in which he took great pride. David Josephson put the vehicle in park and switched off the ignition. The red and blue neon lights of the hotel sign refracted through the dancing raindrops that streamed down the windows as he sat for a moment, weary from the long day and thankful to finally be home.

Josephson stepped from the Lincoln, walked to the rear of the vehicle and retrieved two bags from the trunk. They were black leather satchels and far heavier than they looked. He walked up the steps through the front door of the hotel and was conscientious to wipe the rain and mud from his shoes before heading back behind the front desk to his office. He set the satchels down on his desk, with a thud and metallic jingle, and went back out the front door to grab two identical bags from the trunk. They were just as heavy as the first, weighing nearly sixty pounds each, and he felt his arms weakening from the exertion.

It was finally done. He took a large book off his bookshelf and opened it. A metal flask was nestled in a hollowed out, flask shaped compartment in the center of the book. Slipping out the flask, he loosened the cap and took a pull. As he sipped at the illegal gin, he contemplated what he should do with the contents of the bags. It had to be hidden, but where and how were the questions he was now forced to ponder. He'd thought about the dilemma for the duration of his six hour drive upstate from New York City.

There were two reasons why he had over forty-five thousand dollars worth of gold coins evenly divided into fifty-five drawstring bags of ten, one-ounce coins each, per leather satchel. The first was that President Roosevelt had abolished the gold standard in an attempt to breathe life into the economy. Executive order 6102 required all U.S. citizens to deliver any gold coins, gold bullion or gold certificates to the Federal Reserve in exchange for $20.67 per troy ounce. The order was meant to prevent gold hoarding during the current economic depression. May 1st was the deadline for all such transactions to be completed, a deadline that was now two weeks old and one to which Josephson did not plan to adhere. He was the last living of his father's sons, and he and his wife had not had any children. The family wealth had fallen to him. He wasn't about to trust a bank with it. He knew he was running a risk by keeping the gold, but he didn't imagine that the law would stand for very long. People would fight it and it would be overturned. It was one of the things he loved about this country, injustices could always be undone. He thought of this as he looked at the flask in his hand. He remembered the other reason he'd gotten the gold out of the New York City lock boxes and took another drink.

The second reason had to do with a new trouble that

had cropped up. Since prohibition had begun, more and more of the big city criminal element had been making its way into the quiet villages and provincial towns of the Catskill Mountains. Over the previous summer the Coopers Hollow Bank had been robbed and it took nearly an hour for the county Sheriff's department to respond. In October Federal Agents stormed a mob-owned moonshine operation on the outskirts of town. Then, just a week ago a taxi driver turned up dead on the doorstep of the Lexmore Hotel, sixteen bullet holes in his body. The Delaware County Sheriff's department had sent up a deputy to investigate, and it made front page news in *The Mountain Star*. He was from New York City, Brooklyn to be exact, and had been traveling upstate on an apparent vacation. He had decided to stop at the Lexmore for the night, but never made it inside. Josephson and his wife had thought that some of the local kids had gotten a hold of firecrackers and lit them off on their doorstep. When he rushed to see what was going on, Josephson saw the poor man slumped on the ground, halfway out of his taxicab, and a black Ford sedan driving away in a cloud of dust.

He had met with the village board the following day and suggested that they form their very own police department. Everyone on the board agreed, though none of them knew how they were going to pay for such a position. Josephson had volunteered to pay for a new police car and one year's salary, thus the need for retrieving his gold. Bernie Bindman, owner of Coopers Hollow Bank, pledged to pay for two additional years' salary. The board voted unanimously to entrust the responsibility of hiring the first Coopers Hollow Police Chief to Bindman, who was a

board member, and Josephson, since he had made such a
gracious donation to get the program started.

After the board meeting Josephson and Bindman met
again in Bindman's office on Main Street. They had been
friends for years, so when Josephson told the other man
about his gold problem, he knew that the information
would be kept in the strictest confidence. Bindman suggested going down to the four banks in New York City
where the gold was being kept in safe deposit boxes and
retrieving it all. There was rumor that in just a few weeks,
Federal Agents would start raiding banks to search boxes
in their hunt for gold hoarders. It was just a rumor, but
where there was smoke. . . well, wise men knew better than
to wait around for the flames.

They also spoke about the new position of village
police chief and who they felt would be the best fit. They
wanted to make sure of the fact that, whoever it was they
selected, he had no ties to the mob. Additionally, they
wanted to ensure that he couldn't be easily manipulated or
fired by the village board members after the three years of
promised salary ran out. So, they devised a plan to build a
trust fund that would be responsible for the $2400 annual
salary as well as an operating budget of $1000 annually.
Bindman would setup a legal foundation for the trust and
would oversee the funds, choosing wise investments with
the money so as to guarantee the fund's existence for decades to come. Josephson for his part would give Bindman
ten thousand dollars worth of gold coins for the fund
in exchange for helping him convert his additional gold
holdings into cash whenever he needed to. Bindman had
more than enough contacts in the banking world to be able

to quietly move gold to the appropriate buyers. The only thing Roosevelt had done with his new gold standard was drive the trading underground, just like prohibition had done with alcohol.

Bindman knew people in the banking industry who knew people in Washington D.C. The word was that after Executive Order 6102 had been thoroughly implemented, the Federal Reserve was going to revalue a gold troy ounce at a higher rate for international trade. This had the potential of doubling the value of Josephson's gold almost overnight. The only problem would be moving that gold so as to realize the value. Bindman could help, but Josephson had to make it worth his while. With a police chief in town, the Coopers Hollow Bank would be much less of a target. Bindman couldn't afford to make a commitment to the new police chief's salary on his own, and the village did not have the funds to get the program up and running. Josephson could help with the salary and providing funds for the trust, Bindman could help move the gold when Josephson needed to, and the new police chief would keep them safe from any more bank robbers or encroachment by any mob elements. It was a sound partnership.

Josephson finished off the flask and returned it to the book on his shelf. He took two of the satchels and headed up the stairs to room 213. He rarely let out the room, due to superstitious travelers, and he knew that there was a gap in the wall between rooms 213 and 212. It was going to take all night, but he was going to create a hole in the wall where he could store the gold. The plan that had formulated in his mind involved moving the bed to the center of the room and cutting a hole in the wall near the floor, where the head of the bed had been. Then he would put the satchels of gold into the empty space between the two rooms. To cover the hole he would use a decorative air grate, there were a couple of extra ones in the basement. Then he would move the bed back into place, covering access to the grate. No one would ever look for the gold there, it would be safe.

He returned to his office and retrieved one of the other satchels. The fourth satchel was to be delivered to Bernie Bindman the following morning. Thinking he heard a noise outside, he froze on the steps. He stood there for a few moments, his arm aching from the weight of the single bag. After a time he decided it had been nothing and continued up to room 213. It took him another twenty minutes to gather the necessary tools and bring them up to the room as quietly as possible. There were no guests in the hotel for the evening, and that was a rare occurrence, especially this close to summer. Josephson wasted no time and set to work on his project.

He finished his chore by four o'clock in the morning and wearily climbed into bed next to his wife. She hadn't heard a thing, he knew, as she regularly wore earplugs due to his snoring. Even though it was just for a few hours, he slept as soundly as he had in ages.

It was a few days later that the phone rang at the front desk of the Lexmore Hotel. His wife, Sarah, answered in her normal cheerful voice. He heard her address Bernie, and he came out to take the call.

"Hello, Bernie," he said.

"I took care of your package you brought by. Just

wanted to let you know. Also, I have someone I would like you to meet. I think he would be the right man for the position of police chief," Bernie said on the phone.

"Who is it?"

"David, you just have to meet him. Come on over around ten o'clock, I will have him here at the bank then."

"Certainly, I will stop over at precisely ten." Josephson hung up the phone and looked at his wife.

"What's that about?" She asked her husband as she dusted the front desk.

"Bernie wants me to meet a prospect for police chief. I'm going to head over in about an hour or so."

"Hmm. Okay, well say hello for me." Sarah reached up and kissed her husband on the cheek. She continued humming a song to herself.

The appointment gave Josephson an excuse to drive his beloved Lincoln across the small town of Coopers Hollow. The village was established over one hundred years earlier, in 1828. It received its name from the barrel making business that had been founded in the valley. Eldridge Cooper, a fourth generation barrel maker from Germany who had taken the last name of Cooper after emigrating to the United States, had settled into the lush valley at the headwaters of the Delaware River because of the copious amount and robustness of the oak trees in the area. It was easy for him to create his barrels and float them down stream to Hobart and the upper dam where the saw mill was located. Cooper would pay a penny per barrel to the children of the saw mill owner to fish his barrels out above the upper dam and roll them down Main Street in Hobart past the lower dam and drop them back into the water. They would then float down to Delhi where they would be pulled out and filled with various dry goods and sold to the farmers and individuals in the county.

Despite the village's name, barrels hadn't been made here for nearly thirty years now. The main mill in town had converted to manufacturing wooden crates that were shipped by truck to the local towns and some even down to New York City.

Josephson had moved up to Coopers Hollow and had taken over the Lexmore Hotel nearly fifteen years ago. The hotel was only two blocks from the railroad station, and had long been a favorite destination for many of the Jewish families that would take their holidays away from the hustle and bustle of New York City life. Josephson and his wife had stayed at the hotel several times and had commented that if Mr. Lexmore ever wanted to sell, they would be interested. In the summer of 1918, while the war was still raging in Europe, Josephson received a telegram that informed him that Mr. Lexmore had taken ill and wished to move to a warmer climate before winter set in. Josephson was on the next train to Coopers Hollow with his check book in hand.

The town had only changed minimally since they had bought the hotel. The Main Street still housed a bank, barber shop, grocery store, hardware store, several churches, two boarding houses and many of the homes of the more well-to-do residents. The railroad station was off Main Street on the appropriately named Railroad Avenue. There were several warehouses and old stables along Railroad Avenue where farmers would bring in their goods to ship back to New York City on the trains. Now that automobiles had begun to replace train travel, fewer folks were arriving by rail via the Ulster and Delaware Railroad. The boarding houses were not nearly as full. Nor was Josephson's hotel, these days.

As he drove through the small town, enjoying the rumble of the eight cylinders under the hood, Josephson waved to a few of the local people whom he considered friends. He parked the car on Main Street and strode up the granite steps into the Coopers Hollow Bank Building.

When Josephson finally walked into Bindman's office, he wasn't expecting what was waiting for him. Bernie introduced them, and when the man stood to shake hands, Josephson almost audibly gasped at his sheer size.

"This is James McIntyre. Mr. McIntyre, this is David Josephson," Bernie said. He couldn't help but smile at his friend's reaction. McIntyre reached out to shake with a hand that was nearly twice the size of Josephson's.

McIntyre stood at six foot six inches tall. He had broad shoulders and a frame that was pressing the limits of the simple brown suit which he wore. He had fiery red hair, blue eyes and a round face with a deep cleft in his chin. His features gave him something of a boyish look.

"Pleased to meet you, Mr. McIntyre. Where are you from?" Josephson took a seat, setting his hat on his lap.

"I was born in Dublin, Ireland. My father and mother came to America when I was just a boy. My father was on the police force in Boston until he was killed in twenty-two. I was on the force until last month, which is when I resigned." Josephson shot a glance at Bindman, who was just smiling.

"And why was that," Josephson inquired. McIntyre sighed heavily. He looked over at Bindman, who nodded.

"I killed a man," McIntyre said.

"Well that seems like it might happen in your line of work," Josephson replied. The thought of killing didn't sit well with him, having just seen the body of that poor taxi driver not weeks before. He shifted uneasily in his seat.

"It was the police captain's brother-in-law," McIntyre shrugged. "He was caught up with some booze runners and I didn't know who he was when I shot him. I told him to stop. Gave him plenty of time, but he didn't listen. I can't take it back. He's dead now and I'm out of a job. Mr. Josephson, I'm a proud Irishman. I never took a bribe in my life and I will fight to the death to protect the people of this fair town." The intensity in McIntyre's eyes was unmistakable. Josephson liked a man of conviction and this looked like one of them. "Being a policeman is all I know. It's what I was born for. All I'm asking for is a second chance here. I'll make you both proud."

"Are you married? Any children?"

"No. Not yet. I mean, I hope to one day, but I haven't met the right girl yet," McIntyre said sheepishly. Josephson sat in his chair contemplating the man for a moment.

"I trust you're handy with a pistol," Josephson said.

"I'm as good a shot as there is, but I don't expect there will be much call for it up here."

"I should hope not," Bindman chimed in. Josephson and Bindman exchanged slightly worried glances. They both hoped there wouldn't be any more gunplay in the area, but the whole reason they were looking for a police chief was to discourage anyone from that exact type of activity. It was the whole point of the exercise, really.

"Well, if Bernie vouches for you, I'm satisfied," Josephson said, finally. He reached over and shook the big man's hand again. The shake was a bit more vigorous this time.

"Thank you very much, Mr. Josephson. I certainly won't let you down. But there's one more thing," he said, giving pause.

"Yes?"

"Mr. Josephson, I was hoping you could let out one of your rooms to me for the time being. As I understand it, you've offered to pay for my salary for the first year, so perhaps we could come to an agreement on a room. I thought about one of the other boarding houses in town, but a chief of police in a boarding house, well it just doesn't seem right."

"No, it doesn't," Josephson said carefully. "I think we could come to an agreement. If you'd like, I'll put you up for half price this evening. We can get the board together this afternoon and have you meet with them. Welcome to your new home, Mr. McIntyre, and congratulations."

"Okay, Mr. Josephson. Thank you, sir. Thank you Mr. Bindman."

The village board approved the hiring of James McIntyre as the first police chief, with the board chairman swearing him into service using an oath he borrowed from the Sheriff's department.

It was a bright and sunny Wednesday morning when "Pip" Gianni and "Two Finger" Sanzone walked into the Lexmore. Sarah was busying herself sweeping the lounge area. She welcomed the gentlemen and scooted back behind the front desk to wait on them.

"We need to see Josephson," Pip said. He always did the talking. He was the talker, Two Finger was the muscle.

"Oh, okay," she didn't have an evil bone in her body, and was naïve about the badness in the world around her. She didn't ascribe bad motives to anyone, and didn't even think to warn her husband that the two men asking for him looked a little shady.

David Josephson walked out from his office and saw the men standing at the counter. Wearing long coats and expensive looking fedora hats, the two of them were dressed far too sharply to be anything but from the mob. Josephson steeled himself for what was about to happen.

"Gentlemen, can I help you?"

"You the Jew that owns this joint?" Pip didn't like Jews very much. He didn't like most people very much.

"I'm the owner, yes," Josephson bristled. "What can I do for you?"

"We just want to make sure that you're smart. That you don't go opening your mouth to nobody about things you seen and you don't go stickin' that Jew nose of yours into nobody else's business. You got that?" Pip leaned forward across the desk, staring straight into Josephson's eyes.

"I think you boys need to leave," Josephson said. No sooner had the word's left his lips when McIntyre came down the stairs from his room. He stopped mid-flight as he saw the men at the front desk. He was wearing his gun belt and the new uniform that he had purchased. They were still making a badge for him, so he didn't quite look completely official yet. His hand instinctively went to his revolver, but he just rested it there, he didn't draw his weapon. Slowly, he descended the remaining steps.

"Is there a problem here?" McIntyre asked.

"Nothin' that concerns you," Two Finger said.

"They bothering you, Mr. Josephson?"

"I don't know. Are you bothering me, fellas?"

"Guess you ain't so smart after all," Pip said. He slid his hand inside his jacket.

In a flash McIntyre was across the room with his revolver out. He cracked Two Finger across the bridge of the nose, breaking it. The big man crumpled to the floor. Before Pip could react he had a revolver jammed in his mouth.

"I don't know where you came from, or who you work for, but you need to make sure you understand: this is my town now. If I so much as see your shadow come across the welcome sign on the outskirts of town again, I'll put a bullet in your head. Do you get me?" McIntyre was bending down, face to face with the much smaller man. Pip nodded compliance.

"Now, if you don't mind, I think I'll keep your weapons just to make sure you don't walk out that front door and suddenly forget our little talk." McIntyre reached inside of Pip's coat and pulled a large revolver from his belt.

He set it on the desk and slid it down towards the registry book. Next he reached down and grabbed Two Fingers' gun out of his belt. Blood was gushing from Two Finger's nose, turning his white shirt a deep crimson.

"Get your friend outta my sight, little man, and don't you ever come back to Coopers Hollow again." McIntyre shoved his gun in a little further to make sure his point was made. Pip nearly choked on it. As swift as lightning, McIntyre holstered his gun, grabbed the two hoods by their collars and dragged them out the front door, tossing them down the front steps.

Pip and Two Finger sat on the concrete of the sidewalk for a moment in stunned disbelief. Nobody stepped to them in such a fashion. Nobody. Pip walked to the black Ford they'd driven up in and ripped open the passenger door. He reached under the seat and grabbed a sawed off shotgun and a pistol. He tossed the pistol to Two Finger, who was called such because he could shoot just as well with either hand, thus having two trigger fingers. They headed back up the stairs and into the Lexmore lobby. McIntyre was waiting.

Before either of them could get a shot off, McIntyre put a bullet between Pip's eyes, blowing his hat and the back of his head off. He was dead before he hit the ground. Two Finger raised the pistol and fired. Just as he did, he took one of McIntyre's bullets in the arm, sending him to the ground once again. Another bullet caught him in the stomach, but he managed to get his pistol into his other hand and fire off a few shots of his own. The next bullet hit him in the throat and severed his spinal cord, killing him instantly.

McIntyre held his gun on the two men, watching to make sure they were both dead. When he was sure, he approached them and took their weapons. Suddenly there was a shriek behind him. Sarah was cradling Josephson on the floor, his white shirt blossoming with crimson. He was coughing up blood as well. He was trying to speak, but McIntyre couldn't hear him over Sarah's screaming.

Josephson reached for the big man, and McIntyre came closer. All he could make out from the dying man were three words made in a barely audible whisper.

"Gold. . .room. . .great."

David Josephson was dead.

Chapter 1 • Present Day

A shower of sparks erupted in the side mirror of the van, as the cigarette he'd tossed out the window bounced along the highway behind him. He took the wheel with his now empty cigarette hand and played with the radio in an attempt to find the game again. All he received for his effort was static. As he crested the next hill he caught the commentator yelling "Touchdown!" The descent down the other side brought the return of a garbled hiss, making the all important fact of who scored the touchdown impossible to decipher. Rain began to splatter against the windshield, but it was a thick and icy rain.

Stinkin' mountains, he thought to himself. *Not even real mountains like back home, just annoyin' stinkin' hills that make it impossible to listen to the game!*

The signal had been crisp and clear from about Scranton, Pennsylvania and then north through Binghamton, New York. But as soon as he followed the interstate highway into the rural hills, the station faded into scratchy noise. He didn't take disappointment well and cursed under his breath as he continued to play with the radio knob. The fifty bucks he'd put down on the game was weighing on his mind. He really didn't have the money to spare, but it wasn't like he had a girlfriend anymore who would ride his back about losing the dough.

Not that he couldn't have had a girlfriend if he wanted one. He wasn't ugly, but he wasn't no Brad Pitt neither. Brown eyes and a protruding nose were from his mother, though there was no telling if he resembled his father at all, as he had no idea who the man was. His chin extruded slightly, but he hid that feature with three days worth of stubble. He shaved about once a week, or when it started to get scratchy. Black hair came down to his collar, and he liked to wear it slicked back. A scar started just above his left eyebrow and stretched up two inches towards his scalp. He'd caught a beer bottle in the head in a bar room fight when he was nineteen. It gave him character, he thought, and he liked it. Chicks liked tough guys, especially where he came from.

He rolled the window down and cursed his cheap, penny-pinching boss for not at least springing for power windows on the one ton van. No CD player, a radio that didn't pick up anything but static, and no power windows – cheap. Despite the air freshener hanging from the rear view mirror, the smell of his cargo was getting up into his nostrils and added to his already grumpy mood. The taste had gotten into his mouth. He snorted mightily and spit out the window.

His boss had told him not to smoke in the van while he still had the cargo, but his boss wasn't here at the moment and he wouldn't even get the chance to sniff around the van once he returned, as it was a rental. Not that you could smell the cigarettes over the animal stench.

Whatever! He doesn't have to deal with this god-awful stink, he thought as he reached for another cigarette. He popped in the lighter on the console and waited for it to heat. It seemed to take forever, but eventually it popped and he brought the glowing orange end up towards his face. Touching it to the end of the cigarette, he ignited it just enough to get a nice ember. The relaxing fragrance hit his nose, blocking the foul stench that seemed to get worse with each mile.

He drew in against the cigarette and felt himself relax slightly. He needed to relax, as this was going to be an all night drive and it wouldn't do any good to get himself all worked up and tire himself out. A contact would be waiting to make the transfer of cargo just over the Vermont border at seven in the morning. He took a moment to glance at the clock display, and cursed again. It was already nearing midnight, which meant he'd have enough time to fuel up and maybe grab a coffee, but not really get too much sleep. The forecast wasn't promising either. Right now it was just a light rain, but before he lost the radio signal, the weather guy had said that higher elevations could get some substantial snow.

Snow in stinkin' October! Why the heck would anyone put up with that?

His trip had started in southeastern Ohio earlier in the day and he should have had plenty of time to allow for a little shut eye, but he pulled off at one of those roadside massage parlors in Pennsylvania and spent a little too much time and far too much money. Now he was behind schedule and, whether it snowed or not, he had to make up time.

It really made him mad that he was on this trip at all. It was supposed to be Colby's run, but he had gotten sick, or so he said. Colby was about as reliable as a cop was at minding his own business. The boss had offered double pay to get him to agree, but not until he pissed and moaned a bit. He'd been driven by his boss over to the rental place and they paid with cash along with a heavy security deposit. He'd signed the name Davis, even though his real name was John Thomas Bartlett, or just Tommy to the rest of the guys. They always used fake names and stuff because moving this type of cargo around wasn't exactly legal.

It wasn't like it was drugs or anything, though he had made some deliveries in that particular trade as well. They were just moving rare animals around for rich old dudes with private zoos and hunting grounds. He'd sneaked a look at some of the paperwork back in the office and couldn't believe some of the prices people were willing to pay for zoo animals. As soon as he'd figured out what kind of money was changing hands, he demanded a raise. He wasn't an idiot, after all.

Perfect, now it's snowing.

It was as if someone had flipped a switch in the sky, and changed the precipitation from rain to the white stuff. After just a few moments, Tommy realized it was sticking to the road. He had to slow down but figured he still had an hour of cushion. It would be no problem. That hour of cushion soon evaporated in his mind as the snow really began to pile up and he could no longer see the lines on the road. He was down to a crawl when he rounded the corner and saw all the flares and flashing lights. He slowed the large van to a stop and rolled down the window, cursing his cheap boss again.

"What's goin' on, officer?" He used his best,

non-accented, non-southeastern Ohio English. But he knew that the cop could smell that he was a southerner. He'd been born in Virginia but had grown up in a small town in Ohio just over the West Virginia border. He couldn't help but pick up his mother's drawl. He wondered momentarily if northern cops disliked southerners the same way that southern cops despised northerners.

"Pretty bad accident up ahead. We're closing down the highway. You have to get off this exit here." The officer was eying him up and down, and wrinkled his nose when the animal smell hit him.

"Okay," Tommy said simply. Hoping that he could end the conversation, figure out a side road to take, and try to stay on schedule.

"What are you hauling there?" The nosy cop asked, briefly flashing his light into the back of the van.

"Dogs," Tommy said, surprising himself at how easily he fabricated the story on the spot. "I'm a breeder. I've got some Siberian Huskies I'm taking up north to a racing camp. They're going to be sledding dogs. Sorry about the smell."

"Sledding dogs, huh? Well you may end up needing them before the night is out. They're calling for eighteen inches. Be careful, buddy." The officer waved him on and returned to his lonely highway vigil.

Tommy breathed a sigh of relief and struggled to get another cigarette in his mouth as quickly as possible. He fished his cell phone out of his pocket to see if he'd gotten any calls, but the phone was blank.

Dead. Perfect. This kind of garbage always happens to me. This is that loser Colby's fault. I should be home right now watching the game.

But when he looked at the clock again, he realized that the game had probably ended over an hour ago. He was losing too much time slowing down for the snow!

The road he was taking as a detour ran parallel to the highway, so he was relatively sure that he was heading in the right direction. While his road climbed the side of the valley, he could look down on the Interstate and he spotted the flashing lights surrounding the accident scene. A big rig was sideways across both lanes, with a minivan jammed violently under the trailer. Bright lights illuminated the scene, and though he couldn't see any bodies, white sheets were draped over the windows of the minivan, so he knew what that meant.

A brief, morbid thought about what the passengers looked like in the twisted wreck crossed his mind. He envisioned the blood and the gore, and felt himself shudder just as the rear tires on his vehicle lost traction for a moment, and the back end of the van fishtailed. A shot of adrenaline coursed through his veins, and he gripped the wheel even tighter. He'd driven in snow before, but not a stinkin' blizzard. He slowed even more, and almost thanked God when he crested the hill and saw a town with a burger joint, gas station and one of those huge SuperShopper stores. He needed a phone charger and more cigarettes.

Rolling to a stop at the SuperShopper, he checked the time again; after one in the morning. In dry conditions he'd only be three and a half hours away. With snow, it might be double that, or worse. He thought about just calling his boss in the morning and telling him he couldn't make it through because of the snow, but he thought better of it. He had the contact's cell number, so he could just call before seven in the morning and let him know he was running a bit late is all. It would work out, but it was going to be a pain in the neck drive, that was for sure.

Tommy exited the van, and was surprised at just how cold it had gotten. He thought about the animals in the back, but figured he was just going to be a minute or two. Besides the cell phone charger and cigarettes, he would purchase a map just in case the road he was following veered off too much from the Interstate. The sooner he could get back on the better.

He trudged through the parking lot snow which already totaled nearly half a foot. He stomped the snow off his boots when he got in the door and squinted at the brilliance of the fluorescent lighting. He ended up having to walk almost the entire store to get what he needed. Cell phone chargers were back in the electronics section while the road atlases were up by the magazines clear on the other side of the twenty four checkout lanes.

The girl behind the checkout counter looked like she was going on empty and could have climbed up on the counter right then and there to go to sleep. He tried to make small talk, but she caught the smell that had penetrated his clothing, and shut him down quickly. He grabbed another six-pack of air fresheners and threw them onto the moving conveyor. The checkout girl smirked slightly as she pulled them across the scanner, but didn't make eye contact. She had to call her manager over to open the locked cabinet to get him his cigarettes, so they stood there for a few moments in uncomfortable silence. When she finally scanned the two packs, he thought she had screwed up somehow. The total for everything came to nearly fifty dollars. He couldn't believe how expensive cigarettes were in New York State. He asked her to put one of the packs back. He would just have to make each cigarette last.

Finished with his shopping, he headed back to the van and noticed it was moving.

Great, they're awake. Now it will smell AND sound like a zoo. At least it will be a bit easier to stay awake.

Tommy started the engine and cranked up the heat. It had gotten decidedly colder in the van since he had left. Some of the animals that were in the back were from tropical climates and didn't do well in the cold for extended amounts of time. He circled through the all night burger joint and got a burger, coffee and the biggest cola they had. He ate the burger in just a few bites and sipped the piping hot coffee. It burned his lips and he cursed again. He grabbed the cola and sipped that to cool his lips, but it tasted horrible, like they'd forgotten to replace the syrup in the machine. It was quickly turning into the worst delivery run he'd ever made.

He'd consulted the map as he drove, and saw that he could cut across the mountains on Route 23 popping out on Interstate 87 just south of Albany. Once he made it up to Albany, it wasn't but another hour or so to the meeting point. As he drove, he tried the radio again but was rewarded with nothing but static. The chirps, squawks, mews, caws, yelps and general animal chatter from the back of the van kept him awake enough, even as it seemed like the snow was getting heavier and heavier on the road stretching out before him. A sign on the side of the road told him that Coopers Hollow was twenty-three miles away and Catskill was seventy-five miles away.

Huh! There's a Coopers Hollow in New York too. What are the chances of that?

He had grown up in Coopers Hollow, Ohio, and still lived there in a small apartment over a garage owned by an elderly couple. It wasn't much of a town, but it was home.

He checked his cell phone and saw that it was charging just fine, but there wasn't a signal to be had. Even if he slid off the road he wouldn't be able to get any help. Rubbing his eyes, he tried to focus on the road, but it was now just a white strip between the guardrails. There was no telling where the lines were, and there weren't even any tracks to follow. It was like driving blind.

The van started up a hill, and he felt the rear wheels struggle to keep traction. He kept his foot light on the accelerator and eased the vehicle to the top. As he crested the hill, and the lights shone on the road ahead, he realized that he was probably going to have an accident. It was a steep downward grade with a curve to the left.

He pumped the brakes as gently as he dared, but felt the van immediately begin to slide. He tried to aim for the center of the road, but it was no use, he was going into the guardrail. The impact shattered the passenger side headlight and made a sickening scraping noise along the entire length of the van.

So much for the security deposit, he thought in frustration as he struggled with control of the heavy vehicle.

He managed to regain control of the van and get it back
into the center of the road. It was much more difficult to see
with just one headlight. The van shimmied a little and he felt
the steering wheel give a bit of a wiggle in his hands.

*The front wheel must have been knocked out of alignment
a little, but it seems like it's still okay to drive.*

He was only going about twenty miles per hour now.
At this rate, he'd never make it to the meeting point.
Slowly, he got braver and applied more acceleration. Before
he knew it, he was approaching thirty-five, then forty and
he still had pretty solid control. He paid attention to the
signs warning of curves ahead and slowed to navigate them
successfully.

Up the hill to the right he saw, what looked like, a car
headlight bouncing through the trees. Then he noticed
another and another, all following each other in a disjoint-
ed dance of follow the leader. He couldn't make out what
they were until they started heading down the sloping hill
towards the edge of the road. They were three snowmobiles
out on the trails at three in the morning. He'd never seen
such a thing. The riders stopped their vehicles at the edge
of the road as he drove past, and in his rear view mirror he
saw them cross the road and head down into the field on
the opposite side.

You wouldn't catch me out in this weather unless I had to be.

Double pay wasn't sounding as good as it had this
morning. He checked the clock again and couldn't believe
he'd only gone about twenty miles in the last hour. Despite
all of his efforts to increase his speed, he wasn't making
any headway. In fact, he was falling even further behind

schedule.

The white of the snow coming down in streaks in front of his one headlight was mesmerizing. He slapped himself to stay awake now, but felt himself fading. He took long pulls from the cola he'd bought, despite the nasty taste, and then lit another cigarette. Nothing was helping. He was in danger of falling asleep at the wheel with no place to pull off.

His mind drifted back to the conversation he'd had with his boss about the animals. Some of them were going to private zoos and roadside menageries. Others might end up as prey for some rich guy's private hunting preserve. Still others would be killed and cut up for their parts. Tiger bones and genitals were said to contain the powers of sexual prowess. They were worth so much, though, that traders and dealers would sometimes fake the truly expensive parts by substituting them with parts from other animals like the cougar. He had also told him that they made wine out of tiger bones. They would put the whole tiger skeleton in a giant vat and ferment wine from it. And people drank it up like it like it was some type of magic potion or elixir.

It is one sick, messed up world, he thought to himself. He couldn't imagine who would believe that drinking wine made from animal bones or eating animal genitals in an effort to get rid of impotence would actually work.

He was lost in thought, not really paying attention, when the right front tire blew out. Part of the bumper had been pushed back into the tire when he'd hit the guardrail and slowly, like a lathe, peeled off sections of the tire until there was a catastrophic failure. Had it been on dry roads, had he perhaps been slightly more alert, he probably could have gotten the vehicle under control. But the blowout came at precisely the wrong moment.

In one hand he held his lit cigarette and loosely gripped the steering wheel, with the other hand he had grabbed the giant cola and leaned to take a sip from the straw. *Bang!* The tire blew out and pulled him towards the edge of the road. He dropped the soda and the cigarette and grabbed the wheel with both hands, but it was already too late.

The van slid off the road, smashed through a road sign and ran up onto the guardrail. He was going just fast enough to get the heavy vehicle up off the wheels on the guardrail, and then gravity did the rest. The van lurched to the right and began to roll. It was a gently sloping embankment down into a creek bed, and, had he been on all four wheels, it probably wouldn't have caused too much damage. The van wasn't on all four wheels, however. It was rolling onto its side out of control. Everything seemed to move in slow motion for Tommy.

The van was not built to be upside down, and the weight of the vehicle itself, as well as its cargo, pressed the body out of shape and popped the rear doors open. The crates in the back crashed against each other. The steel cages held, but the larger wooden crates burst open. As the van continued its roll, some of the smaller cages flew forward and struck Tommy violently in the back of the head. He was knocked out cold and became a rag doll in the driver's seat.

The van finally came to rest back on all four wheels in the creek, water lapping up against the sides. All was quiet for a few moments, until the animals began to test their enclosures. Several were free immediately, some had been killed instantly. Still others were scratching at the cages to get out, and putting up a pretty serious cacophony in the process.

Tommy had not been carrying any paperwork for the animals, as was the norm for his particular company. If, for some reason, they were pulled over, he was instructed to just take the heat and whatever fine was handed out and keep his mouth shut. He wasn't going to be the one talking, though. The impact from the metal cage had cracked his skull and his brain began to swell. The whipping action on his neck, caused by the rollover, herniated a disc in his vertebrae. The pressure in his spinal column pinched the nerves and made his lower body go numb.

He regained consciousness briefly and was confused by what he saw. The road sign he'd hit was lying out in front of the van, reflecting its message back to him, illuminated by the single headlight. It said "Coopers Hollow 2 miles". He suddenly felt calm. He was only two miles from home, he imagined. The pressure building on his brain sent him into unconsciousness once again. His last, blissful thought was that he was almost home.

The van had come to rest in the creek and water found its way into the cabin of the vehicle. It only came up a few inches, but it was enough to submerge Tommy's boot clad feet. Because his lower body was already numb from the spinal column trauma, he didn't even feel it. The frigid water had a detrimental effect almost immediately. His body temperature began to drop, and hypothermia set in.

Had it been in the middle of summer, he would have easily survived, but the temperatures would stay below thirty degrees Fahrenheit for the entire night. The steel of the van began to radiate cold, and his thin leather jacket was not nearly enough thermal protection. Add to it the fact that he was unconscious and no one would discover him or the wreck for another five hours, and it meant one tragic conclusion: Tommy was going die from hypothermia sometime around sunrise.

Chapter 2

One would think that a vehicle as large as a one ton paneled van off the road due to an obvious accident would draw almost immediate attention, but that wasn't the case. The snow fall had totaled sixteen inches, a few less than forecast. The plow trucks had gone through and piled the snow up to nearly three feet on both sides, completely obliterating any trace of where the van had left the road. To top it off, the wreck was on a curve, and a good fifteen feet below the road level. And frankly, a white van covered by eight inches of snow is somewhat difficult to notice anyway.

It was actually a school bus driver on her way in to the bus garage who spotted the wreck. She reported the accident location and then headed out on her bus route, picking up all the disappointed kids who had hoped for a snow day but only received a two hour delay. It took another thirty minutes for the village patrolman to pinpoint the accident. He drove past it twice, but finally saw it.

Patrolman Jack McMurphy Jr. did not really feel in the mood to go trudging through the snow just to record a license plate number and the Vehicle Identification Number from the registration sticker. He kept his lights on and left the motor running, as per procedure. He'd already prepared for the day by switching from his normal patrol boots to his over the calf snow boots. They weighed quite a bit more, but he didn't think he'd be in any foot chases any time soon.

Jack was just thirty years old and was a third generation officer of the law. His grandfather, Frank McMurphy had been a New York City cop who had moved the family up to the Catskill Mountains after his wife was struck and killed by a city bus. He made a good life for his two kids, Jack Sr. and Judy, and remarried after four years as a single father. Jack Sr. had gone to the police academy and planned to go back to the big city and maybe try to become a detective. But Frank had gotten himself hired as the Chief of Police of Coopers Hollow after a heart attack claimed the life of the previous one. Once hired he knew he needed a few patrolmen he could trust, as the ones that were on staff at the time had become thoroughly corrupt. He talked his boy into staying upstate and it turned out to be a pretty good decision.

Jack Sr. married his high-school sweetheart, Beatrice and they had one son, Jack Jr. When Frank retired, Jack Sr. put in for the job and was hired with a unanimous vote by the village board. By that time, Jack Jr. was entering high school with aspirations to play football professionally, but those dreams were never realized. He had a few chances to come off the bench in college, but no scouts recognized his talent, and he didn't have much of a game tape as a resume either. The Giants were going through a major overhaul and held some tryouts in Albany, but it turned out to be just for show; a publicity stunt to sell more tickets during another lackluster season.

Jack McMurphy Jr. resigned himself to the fact that he was going to be a cop and a good one, too. He had already gained years of experience before he was even ten years old by listening to his father and grandfather retell their old cop stories. He was a pretty fair shot, and had a sharp mind for details. He'd worked two homicide scenes in cooperation with the Sheriff's department in the ten years since he was made a patrolman, and now had thoughts of maybe becoming the chief of police himself once the old man decided he'd had enough.

Jack Jr. had tried his hand at marriage, but wasn't really any good at that. He'd dated Anna for two years, and had gotten serious about marriage only after she was hurt in a car accident. It scared him that she could be taken away from him like that. Yet, after they had been married for a few years, he was so focused on the job he didn't even notice when she'd left him. He'd been sleeping on the couch those days, working double shifts over night to help out his dad. The note on the refrigerator was there for two days before he realized she was gone. Some big city detective he would have made.

Jack Jr. shared his father and grandfather's square-jawed good looks. He had steel blue eyes and reddish brown hair that he kept closely cropped. He'd noticed a gray hair two days after his thirtieth birthday, but pretended it was just a really blond one. When he didn't shave for a few days, some of the whiskers had begun to carry a strange resemblance to a shade of gray as well, so he made sure that he was always clean shaven. He stood at six feet even, and had a fairly muscular build. He had never been a gym rat, which may have been why he didn't go further with his football career, but he did try to keep himself in shape by jogging and doing some occasional weight lifting, leaving him more wiry than bulging with muscles. Mostly he kept busy working on his motorcycle and classic car in the summer, chopping wood in the fall, and in general, just staying active. He wasn't one of those cops you'd find in a donut shop. He was more likely to grab a banana and granola bar than a pastry.

"Dispatch, this is Patrolman McMurphy, I'm leaving the cruiser to check out an abandoned vehicle off the road on Route 23, just past Emilio's garage. Over."

"Copy. Over," crackled the reply over the CB radio. They had cell phones for some communications, but up in these mountains, where the cell towers were sparse, the CB radio was still needed.

He exited the white patrol car, which was emblazoned with red letters on the doors that read Coopers Hollow Police, and went around to the trunk to retrieve his insulated over coat.

No sense freezing to death over a snow-banker, he thought to himself. Every year they would have what they called "snow-bankers", people who would bury themselves into a snow bank so severely that they had to abandon the vehicle there. Usually nobody was hurt, it just became a hassle to extract the vehicles once the plows had gone by and packed up feet of snow on the side of the road.

He buttoned his jacket, pulled the wool gloves out of the pockets and started to climb the snow bank. The first few steps he found to be rather firm, but as soon as he made it over the crest, he sank into snow up to his crotch.

Great. I'll have wet pants for the rest of the day. Nothing beats a day of work in wet pants.

He half swam, half crawled through the rest of the bank and got down the hill a bit more to where he could walk a bit better. As he approached the vehicle he saw that it was in worse shape than he had initially believed. The snow had covered the damage. The back doors were open with the glass broken out of them. The whole vehicle was askew somehow, and he figured it had probably rolled at least once. He looked back towards the road and calculated. It may have rolled twice and then come to rest in the shallow creek.

He called out, but did not hear any reply. There was some noise coming from the back, so he started there first. Pushing the doors apart further, he was struck by the smell of animal feces and blood. Cages and crates were tossed about the back of the van, and it looked as if most of them were dead. A bird in one of the cages flapped its wings then steadied itself on the crooked bars of the cage.

"Hey, are you okay?" He could see through the mess, what looked like a figure slumped over in the driver's seat. Hustling around to the driver's door, he tried to open it, but it was locked. Suddenly he broke through the thin ice of the creek and sank into knee deep freezing water. The water went over the tops of his boots and filled them. His toes began to ache immediately. He banged on the window, but there was no movement. He peered in through the glass and saw frost on the man's slightly bearded face, and his chest wasn't moving. Blood had streamed down from the back of the man's head and soiled the collar of his shirt and jacket. Jack quickly moved around to the passenger door to try it, slogging through the freezing creek water, but it too was locked.

The passenger side window was cracked badly, so he grabbed the glass breaking tool from his belt, held it firmly in his fist and punched at the window. It shattered into a million pieces immediately and provided him access to the manual lock. It took a couple of yanks, but he got the door open and stepped up out of the water. Animal mess had run up into the front of the vehicle and had begun to mix with the six inches of water that had seeped into the van. The smell was potent. Jack climbed further into the van to check the victim. His feet felt like he had cinder blocks strapped to them, his boots filled with water as they were.

Pulling off a glove, he grabbed the man's wrist to feel for a pulse. The victim was ice cold. He was dead. It didn't look like he'd bled out, so McMurphy's best guess was that he had been knocked out and died from the cold. The county medical examiner would be able to tell.

"Dispatch, this is Patrolman McMurphy. I need you to send out an ambulance and fire rescue with a sled to my location. Tell them to take their time. Over." The confirmation came back to him. "Also, see if there's a DEC officer nearby who could check out the scene. I've got some caged animals that may have survived, over."

With backup on the way, Jack hunted around for the man's identification. He found the wallet with an Ohio driver's license. The town said Coopers Hollow, Ohio. This gave McMurphy pause, surprised that there was another Coopers Hollow out there someplace. He also found a couple of receipts floating in the water on the floor, soaked in animal urine. He looked at the time stamp and did some calculations in his head. He put the receipt onto the dashboard and pulled out a notepad. He wrote down his estimated time of the accident, wrote down the man's name and license number and returned the wallet. Sometimes it was easier to keep everything with the body. He slid out of the van and went around to the license plate to record it. They were Utah plates, but with the Ohio driver's license, he guessed that it might be a rental vehicle.

Jack climbed back up the hill, and over the snow bank, his feet feeling like they were about to freeze off from the cold water sloshing around in his boots. He wiped his gloves off in the snow to remove the urine smell from when he'd picked up the receipt, though he knew they would need to be washed. After he made it back to the cruiser, he sat in the driver's seat and emptied the water out of his boots onto the roadside. He had shoes over on the passenger side, but then they would just get wet too. After ringing out his socks, he sat in the driver's seat with the heat blasting his bare feet for a few minutes to warm up. Despite his efforts to dry them out, his socks would be wet for the rest of the morning. Finally, after he could feel his toes again, he put the wet boots back on, walked to the back of the vehicle, popped the trunk and retrieved a small fold-up shovel. He started digging into the snow bank so the ambulance team could get one of their sleds down to the wreck.

It wasn't long before the fire and rescue team showed up and started setting up for a vehicle extraction. Most of the guys on the F&R squad were good guys, volunteers all of them. Sometimes one of them would get a little too big for his britches, but most of the long timers kept the newbie's in line. On a call like this, the newbies did the grunt work while the long timers sipped coffee from insulated mugs, chit chatting with the officers and tow truck drivers on the scene. Jack looked longingly at the steam rolling up from the travel mugs clutched in gloved hands that weren't his.

"Hey Jackie," Copper Owens, the volunteer fire chief, called out as he walked towards Jack.

"Hey Copper," Jack said, shaking the man's hand. "Far as I can tell, he went off the road a little after three in the morning. That was right in the middle of the storm. I think it rolled a couple of times and he got himself knocked out. Froze to death, poor fella."

"Jeez, probably didn't feel anything, but still." They stood quietly for a moment looking down on the wreck. "Want a cup of coffee? When you told dispatch that the ambulance should take their time, I figured we'd be pulling out an ice cube. I filled up just before I left."

"That's why I like you, Copper, always thinking ahead." Jack slapped the older man on the shoulder as they walked back towards Copper's SUV. Copper had been friends with Jack's family for years, and had been fire chief for nearly twenty years. He was one of those figures in town that everyone knew and everyone liked. Each year, as the leaves began to turn into their radiant rainbow, he would stand out in the middle of the road in front of the fire department with a big rubber boot, slowing vehicles down and asking for donations for the station. It was rare for a car to not slow down and toss in at least a buck or two.

Copper poured the steaming coffee into a paper cup for Jack and returned the Thermos back to his SUV. Jack sipped at it as they walked back over to the snow bank to watch the Fire and Rescue team extract the body from the van and strap it to sled. They covered it with a blanket as they didn't have body bags.

"No matter how many of these accidents I work, seeing the body get pulled out still gives me a chill right down my back," Copper said.

"I hear you," Jack echoed, trying to stifle a shiver. He figured it was probably just because his feet were still damp.

The DEC officer arrived forty-five minutes later. The DEC, or Department of Environmental Conservation, was tasked with protecting the natural environment of New York State, which included water, timber and animal life. If you were hunting without a permit, it was the DEC that came down on you. They also investigated illegal treatment of endangered animals. It only made sense that they would be contacted if illegal animal trafficking was suspected.

It was now a little after ten in the morning, and the coffee was cold. Everything was cold. The body had been pulled up the hill on the sled, put into the back of the ambulance and taken to the county medical examiner in Delhi. They would start an autopsy once the next of kin were notified. McMurphy took the DEC officer, Davidson he'd said his name was, down to the van and showed him the animals. Davidson let out a whistle.

"This guy was an exotics trader," Davidson said after a few moments. "That's a squirrel monkey, there's a Macaw, there's – was this guy a local? I mean, some of these animals are legal some aren't. Unfortunately it looks like most of them are dead. Let's get the few living ones up to my vehicle. I think we're going to lose them all to hypothermia, though."

"Uh, okay." McMurphy was just going to burn the gloves. The smell was never coming out. "I don't think he was local. Ohio license, rental truck, all the different species, I was thinking he was transporting them somewhere. There was no paperwork in the vehicle, so I'm thinking he was not part of a legit operation. Is this something you would investigate?"

The two of them struggled up the hill with cages of animals that looked like they were in distress. Davidson opened the back of his SUV and placed in two cages. He took McMurphy's and stacked them on the others.

"Well, not really. My jurisdiction has to do with protecting the wildlife. You know, hunters without licenses, illegal dumping, et cetera. Also if these animals were taken across state lines it knocks it up to a federal investigation. It looks like a few of them could be on the endangered list. So, it would probably be a U.S. Fish and Wildlife Services investigation and would have to go to a federal prosecutor to get charges."

"Really?" McMurphy was a bit incredulous. There was no way a federal prosecutor would waste his time with some low-end animal trafficker. They headed back down to the van to see if there were any other animals still alive.

"You said that he didn't have the proper paperwork, so you could give him a citation for that. You'd have to look up which ordinance it broke, I don't remember off the top of my head," Davidson said, shrugging his shoulders.

"He died in the accident," Jack said.

"Oh, well, I guess that's out then." Davidson was crawling into the back of the van even further, trying to avoid getting his uniform soiled in the process. "What was in the big crates here? Did you already take the animals out?"

"Uh, no. I don't know. I was the first on the scene and there was nothing in those crates. Do you think something got out?" That would be a whole different scenario.

"Well based on the size of the crates and the scat left behind, I'd say they were fairly large animals." Davidson was stooping down to get a closer look at the animal feces when McMurphy heard his name being called. He looked up the hill and saw a New York State Trooper giving a short wave.

Perfect. At least I don't have to worry about jurisdiction anymore. Surprised the Sheriff's department hasn't already sent up a deputy to pull rank just to prove they can.

When the state troopers rolled up, they took over the investigation. It was one of those things that his father and grandfather had talked about when they had gotten together for poker nights back in the day. Grampa Frank had been gone now for almost fifteen years. It was tough to believe it had been that long now. Needless to say, there still wasn't much professional courtesy between the troopers and the Coopers Hollow Police Department.

"Patrolman McMurphy, Officer Adams, nice to meet you," the trooper extended his hand to shake.

"Yeah, same here. What's up?" Jack took off his gloves to shake, though he thought about leaving them on just for spite.

"Well I just got done working the cleanup down on I-88 and wanted to follow up on a hunch," Adams said.

"Yeah, I heard about that one. I guess it's been a rough night for all of us. First snowfall of the year is always a treat," McMurphy replied.

"Well I was on detour duty early this morning and sent a white van driven by a male off the interstate. I just wondered if it was the same guy," Adams said.

"The driver didn't make it. They already took him away. Poor sap froze to death, at least that's my theory."

"How did the dogs fare?"

"Dogs?"

"He said he was transporting Siberian Huskies to be trained as sled dogs. I kind of have a soft spot for dogs, I just wanted to see if they made it okay."

"Hey, Davidson," McMurphy called down to the van. To Adams he said: "Come on down to the wreck."

They made their way down the well worn path in the snow. Davidson had pulled most of the animal cages out and placed them outside the van in the snow. The animals were all dead.

"Davidson this is Officer Adams, he says he spoke to the driver." McMurphy paused to let Adams complete the revelation.

"He said he was transporting Huskies, for dog sled training," Adams said.

"Well, it might be dogs. Huskies, especially, have large feces," Davidson said, looking back at the crates in contemplation.

"There were a couple of large crates that were empty," McMurphy said. "We were a little worried something got out that, uh, shouldn't have."

"He seemed like a shady character, but he really didn't look like he was lying about the dogs," Adams shrugged.

"Maybe he wasn't." Davidson brushed his hands together as he exited the van. "I mean, we could send out the scat to find out what exactly we're dealing with, but to my eyes it looks like a bunch of dog crap."

"Nice. Well, Adams, I appreciate your coming out here. I'll mention your cooperation in my report," McMurphy said with a bit of a laugh.

"Listen, we'll have to check each of these animals for disease, it may take a few weeks for all of the reports to be complete," Davidson said. "And by the way, thanks for giving me stacks of paperwork for the next three weeks."

"The benefits of the new era of collaboration," McMurphy said, garnering a chuckle from the others. "Listen, maybe we can grab breakfast sometime, my treat. We'll compare notes and talk shop."

"Sounds good," said Adams.

"I never turn down a free breakfast," Davidson replied.

Adams headed back to his cruiser while McMurphy helped Davidson haul the rest of the cages up to the road

side. A DEC pickup truck showed up, and they loaded the
dead animals into the truck bed. Things started moving
along pretty quickly at that point. The wrecker showed
up to pull the van out, and Davidson and the other DEC
officer departed.

Within thirty minutes the wreck was on the flatbed
tow truck and except for a few last notes left for him to
scribble down in his notebook, McMurphy was ready for
a break. He took off his insulated coat and tossed it, along
with his gloves, into the trunk. He reported in to dispatch
and then drove into town for a little lunch. It was just after
noon now, and he was exhausted.

Chapter 3

Not much had changed in the village of Coopers Hollow during the thirty years of Jack McMurphy Jr.'s life. A convenience store which sold fuel and some groceries called Stewart's had gone in on the corner of Main Street and Route 18, which headed north out of town. Mike's Garage still sold gasoline at the other end of town, but received most of its income from fixing the pickup trucks and tractors of the old timers in the area. Most of the new folks preferred taking their vehicles to Emilio's just on the outside the village limits, near where the accident scene had been.

One of the larger boarding houses on Main Street, along with the rest of the houses on that block, had been torn down when he was just a kid and a Grand American supermarket, along with its huge parking lot, had been built in its stead. This forced the old grocery and butcher shop, which had been on Main Street for close to seventy years, to go out of business. It reopened a few years later as a specialty meats shop, but that hadn't lasted. It now sat dormant, a faded 'for sale' sign in the window.

The Coopers Hollow Bank was bought out in the seventies and subsequently closed down. As a last gesture of goodwill towards the town, the huge international bank, RB&T, which had made the purchase, sold the old

building to the village. RB&T erected a new bank building on the corner of Railroad Ave and Main Street where
an old warehouse had once stood. It was just one of nearly
one hundred twenty branches in the Upstate New York region. The old Coopers Hollow Bank Building became the
new Coopers Hollow Police Station. They even converted
the old bank vault into a single-bed prison cell.

The old barrel factory which had long ago been converted into a crate factory had been converted once again
into a small furniture manufacturer. They made barstools
and tables from the local hardwood and sold them all over
the world. One of their biggest customers was a Native
American casino which was partially owned by a former
native of Coopers Hollow whose father had once worked at
the factory. All of the barstools and restaurant tables in the
entire casino had been made right in Coopers Hollow.

Numerous eateries and other businesses had come and
gone over the years, inhabiting store fronts for a few years
and then disappearing. All in all, however, the structures
hadn't changed too much. The hardware store was still
there, though they had purchased the building next door,
knocked a hole through the adjoining wall, and expanded
into a small electronics store as well. The post office was
still in the same place on Railroad Avenue. Right next to it
was the former train station, which had fallen into a state
of temporary disrepair after it had been abandoned by the
railroad company. After a few years of abandonment, it
had been purchased, fixed up and renovated by a wealthy
couple who now used it as their eclectic mountain retreat.
During the summer months you could always tell when

they were in town because a new Aston Martin would be parked in the freshly paved driveway.

The Peachy Keen was a diner that had stood on Main Street in the small town for as long as Jack could remember. McMurphy liked the fact that it still had the old counter and the swivel stools just like when he was a kid, when he had come here regularly with his dad. In Jack's mind, the old lunch counter was reminiscent of that glimpse of Americana that had been captured by artists like Norman Rockwell. It gave him a strong sense of nostalgia.

"Hey, junior." The man behind the counter had called him junior for as long as he had been coming in, which was just about the entirety of his thirty years of life. Everyone knew the owner of the Peachy Keen as "Seemo", which was short for Simonopolis. He was Greek by heritage and had become a U.S. citizen nearly forty years before. He'd run the Peachy Keen for thirty of those forty years. Even though it had all the makings of a run of the mill diner, Seemo put together some exceptional Greek dishes. This guaranteed that the place was always packed. Of course you could still get a burger, which is what McMurphy ordered: Cooked medium, tomato, pickle and just a swipe of mayo. Hold the onions.

"Hey, Seemo. How's it going today? Been busy?" McMurphy took his traditional seat at the counter, closest to the television which was perched up on a shelf above the milkshake machine.

"Oh, it's always busy, ya know. People come, people go. We had three snowmobilers in here at five this morning. I had just turned on the lights when they pulled up. Then

Mrs. Graves come in. She talk about her daughter coming home for the weekend." Seemo still had a bit of broken English to his dialect, and still talked to himself in Greek when he was cooking in the kitchen. When he was a little boy, Jack had thought the man to be crazy because of the foreign language he was using.

"Oh, Starlett's coming home for a visit? It's tough to believe she's off to college already. I remember when they first moved up here. Has it really been that long?" Jack accepted the cup of coffee from Seemo.

"Just a few months after 9/11. She always look so lonely. Poor woman. She needs a man to make her happy. Cheer her up a little." Seemo cared about everyone. He was as good hearted as they came. "Tubby came in for his Frosted Flakes. He don't seem right lately. Maybe you talk to him. He likes you."

"Yeah, alright." McMurphy made a mental note to stop and talk with Tubby if he saw him. He was a dim-witted kid who still lived with his insane mother in an old house up one of the side streets in town. She had about a million cats and never came out of the house. He'd do odd jobs for people around town and stayed out of trouble. He was quiet but generally liked by most people in town. He got a check every month from some sort of settlement and that's what they lived on. As Jack thought about it he realized that Tubby wasn't a kid anymore, he was probably pushing past thirty years old now.

The door chime jingled, and a man walked in. He was tall, over six feet at least, probably in his fifties. The stranger had graying hair, dark eyes, a day or two of unshaved growth on his chin. He wore a rather expensive looking black leather jacket. McMurphy met his gaze, and received a nod of acknowledgement. The man sat down at the opposite end of the counter.

"Morning, Mr. Cooke," Seemo said cheerfully. Then he looked at the clock and realized it was now well past noon. "Or I should say, good afternoon."

"Afternoon, Seemo." Mr. Cooke said. Then, turning to McMurphy, "Officer."

Jack put down his coffee and came down to shake the man's hand.

"Jack McMurphy Jr. with the village police department."

"Michael Cooke. Nice to meet you."

"New to town?"

"Kind of, yeah. I bought the Johnson's old place. They called it Eagle's nest," Cooke said. "Finally decided to move up for good."

"Well, welcome to town. What do you do for work?" Jack grabbed his coffee and slid down to be two stools away from the newcomer.

"Retired. I was a New York City cop."

"No kidding. Small world. My grandfather worked as a cop in New York before he moved up here to become Police Chief," Jack said. As he appraised Cooke, he noticed that the man was still young enough to be on the force. "What squad? Why did you give it up?"

Cooke smiled for a moment, as he sipped his coffee. He pursed his lips then replied.

"I was a sharpshooter on the ESU. I did it for nearly

twenty years after Sniper School. Why did I retire? Well, sometimes it's just time." He sipped from his coffee again as McMurphy's food was brought out by Seemo. Jack was sizing him up with a bit more attention now. You had to respect a man who could shoot.

"That's why my grandfather retired. He'd worked an accident involving a family we knew. Little girl was killed. A week later he retired. It was just time," Jack said. He started into his burger and the conversation died off as they watched the weather man go on and on in excited breathlessness about the snow fall totals across New York State and how this was so unseasonal for the month of October. He must have said unseasonal about twelve times.

The door jingled again, and in walked Paula Schumann, the local reporter for the small weekly paper. She immediately spotted McMurphy and sat down next to him, taking the seat separating him from Cooke.

"Why hello there Jack, I was wondering if I could ask you a few questions about the accident this morning," She said, sliding out her cell phone and placing it on the counter. She'd gotten him about a year ago with this little trick. She had a voice recorder app in her phone that she used for interviews. He'd said something he thought was off the record not realizing that she was recording the conversation and it ended up in print. It wasn't the type of thing that anyone would get fired over, but it made it sound like the village police department and the mayor weren't seeing eye-to-eye on a few things. Which they weren't, but the whole world didn't need to know about it.

"I'm eating, Paula. Call my office later and I'll give you a statement," Jack said over a mouthful of burger.

"I would, normally, of course, but we're going to press tomorrow for this week's issue, and, well, I wanted this to be the lead story. We've already got the pictures. I just need some details about the accident itself." She was tenacious when she really wanted something.

"Listen, let me finish my lunch and then we can talk, okay?" Jack hadn't even filled out the reports yet.

"Okay. I'll join you then," she said finally. "Seemo, can I get a BLT on rye and a diet cola?"

"Excuse me," Cooke said to Paula. "I don't want to seem rude, but you kind of interrupted a conversation I was having with Jack, here. So, if you would, kindly excuse us."

Paula gave him a withering glare. Cooke gave it back to her. His dark eyes were piercing and from McMurphy's perspective, he could tell that the man had no problem looking through a scope at another human being and pulling the trigger when he received the go-ahead.

"Seemo, could I get that to go, please," she asked. Then she turned to McMurphy. "My deadline is six pm, Jack. I just need fifteen minutes for some questions."

"Paula, as soon as I'm done I'll swing by your office and give you ten minutes. Deal?"

"Deal." She paid for her lunch and received a brown paper bag and foam cup from Seemo. As she headed out the door she gave Cooke the stink eye again. McMurphy shot a look at Cooke to gauge his reaction and smiled.

This is one cool customer, Jack thought to himself. But he doesn't know who he's messing with. Paula will eat him alive.

"I think that's the shortest conversation I've ever had with Paula," Jack said aloud with a chuckle.

"That girl is like a pit bull," Seemo chimed in with a warm smile. "Once she bite into something, she never gonna let go."

"Sorry. Making people disappear is a talent, I guess," Cooke said, looking a little embarrassed for acting as a bit of a jerk to a woman he didn't even know. As the words left his lips he realized he probably could have phrased it differently. "That doesn't sound too good from a guy who just told you he was a sniper, does it?"

"As long as you were one of the good guys," McMurphy said. He finished his burger, took another drink from the straw and put a ten dollar bill next to his plate.

"Hey, Junior! Your money's no good here. I don't take money from cops," Seemo said with a laugh.

"And I don't take bribes in the form of food. Clean up this dump, Seemo," McMurphy said as he stood up. "Mr. Cooke, nice meeting you. I'm sure we'll bump into each other again."

"Take care," Cooke acknowledged.

Jack exited the Peachy Keen diner and headed down to his squad car. The sun was out and the whole town had a feeling of being clean and new. People were still clearing sidewalks from the snowstorm, but the temperature had risen above freezing, so the melting had already begun.

It seemed like every year there was that first snow that packed a wallop, and then the temperatures jumped back up in time for Thanksgiving. It was like nature was warning everyone what was coming so they could prepare. The sun felt warm on his face, while the air still held a crispness that invigorated him. He decided to walk the three blocks up the hill to *The Mountain Star* office and keep his promise to Paula.

Across the street he noticed Tubby heading into the Grand American grocery store. He made another mental note to take the time to see what was troubling him. Seemo wouldn't have brought it up if he wasn't really concerned. It was kind of nice to be in a small town where people cared about each other.

As he passed the library, Mrs. Graves stepped out, carrying an arm load of books. She would come into town once or twice a week, do her shopping, return books and check out new ones, then head back up to her lonely home just outside of town. She always had a nervous quality about her. She wasn't unfriendly, but she was less than social. Jack wasn't sure what it was about her, she just seemed to not want to get too close to anyone.

"Looks like you got plowed out okay this morning," Jack said conversationally. Gloria, or Mrs. Graves, she would correct if you just called her Gloria, seemed a little jumpy this morning. She recoiled slightly when Jack spoke to her.

"Yes. Emilio was up with his plow. He tells me I'm always the first one he plows out," she paused on the sidewalk momentarily. By the way she glanced around nervously, it looked as if she was trying to figure out a way to escape. Jack always thought she was a pretty woman, even when she first moved up, back when he was still married.

She had brownish blond hair, almond brown eyes and a nice figure. She was probably about five feet, six inches if he had to make a guess. She'd seem taller if she wore different shoes, but she was usually wearing flats in the summer or her boots in the winter, like she was now.

"I was talking with Seemo and he said Starlett might be coming home for a visit. That sounds exciting. Hard to believe she's already off to college."

"I don't like it. I really can't wait until she gets this out of her system and comes home," she said. She started walking towards her car, trying to end the conversation.

"Well, someday the chicks have to leave the nest," he replied.

"You never did," she said, as she opened the door to her silver Volvo and climbed in. She quickly pulled on her seatbelt and started the engine.

Well that was a heck of a thing to say on such a beautiful day. Being cooped up in that house is slowly killing her. The poor girl needs a few friends or maybe a good vacation to knock it out of her, get her back to living life.

He continued on his way to the newspaper office and knocked the snow off his boots before he entered. It was an old building, but the office looked fairly modern. Back in the day the building used to be a pretty nice hotel. That was back when the trains would run from New York City on the Delaware and Ulster line from Kingston. The rail line cut across the Catskills all the way to Oneonta with a stop right here in Coopers Hollow. Once the automobile became popular people stopped taking the train up to the Catskills for their vacations and started taking their cars all over. Now the old building, which still had the old rooms on the upper floors, was home to the small weekly newspaper called *The Mountain Star*.

Four people worked at *The Mountain Star* full time, and they had a couple more people help with distribution each week. Paula Schumann was the editor and lead writer, Harry Osterhaut was the sales manager, Trudy Osterhaut, his wife, was a sales associate, assistant writer and book keeper, and Toby Gunter was the graphic designer, webmaster and assistant writer. The paper was partially owned by another paper out of Kingston, NY. The weekly edition would be sent electronically and would be printed in Kingston and then trucked back that evening. The peak circulation was during the summer months when all the out-of-towners stayed at their summer homes. Circulation numbers remained strong through the holidays and then dropped off substantially during the harshest months of winter. Overall, it was a small operation, but they did a very good job of keeping a finger on the pulse of the small community.

The Mountain Star had once been a daily paper back in the late 1800's and early 1900's. Back then, every small town had its own paper, and Coopers Hollow was no different. It was housed in an old brick building right on Main Street that was now a thrift store. As the years went by, fewer and fewer people called Coopers Hollow home. The paper mill closed and then the sawmill shut down as well. The death blow came when they finally shut down the rail line that kept the town connected to New York City. The entire area sank into a depression that didn't start to shake free until the advent of high-speed internet.

It was as if people had rediscovered all the little towns in the Catskill Mountains once they had high speed internet. A person could be physically in the middle of nowhere and still connect with the rest of the world. It made the small towns seem much less secluded.

Something similar had happened back when they first strung the telegraph lines and then again when the telephone eventually made the telegraph obsolete. It used to be that the Catskills were only for farmers or outdoorsmen, but when the businessmen of the big city could still get off a telegram or later receive a phone call, it became a convenient and practical escape from the city without giving up the connectivity.

The Mountain Star printed a weekly paper now, but it also kept an online version that featured news stories, links to other local websites and a pretty extensive classified section. It had gone from non-existent to a thriving local business that kept the community connected. It wasn't an easy job to establish the paper again, and it was due mostly to the tenacity of the editor, lead writer and re-establisher, Paula Schumann.

Paula's mother, Ashleigh Schumann, was a wealthy magazine publisher from New York who provided her daughter access to the family fortune with relatively loose purse strings. Paula had come up to the Catskills with some of her friends when she was just eighteen and had laid eyes on the old hotel which was up for sale. She begged her mother to give her the one hundred thousand dollars to purchase the property and another seventy-five thousand to renovate the entire first floor and convert it into a modern office space.

Paula had planned to house her then boyfriend's dot
com startup business in the floor space she had made,
but he ended up blowing all of the investment capital by
partying and doing everything but build a company. He
also decided that he would rather have an exotic dancer as
a girlfriend rather than her. Grade A jerk.

She was left with a great business location without
the business. She found herself reading about the history
of Coopers Hollow in the old newspaper archives in the
library when she realized that there was no reason she
couldn't restart the paper. There was no way it could be
a daily, but a weekly could easily survive, especially if she
backed it with a solid online presence and offered exclusive
content that no one else was offering.

She made herself something of a local celebrity
with the new paper, and even the most skeptical of the
townspeople had to admire her spirit and tenacity. At
twenty-eight years old she had run the paper successfully
for five years when her mother's purse strings were pulled
shut and the money she'd been pouring into her personal
project stopped cold.

Her mother, Ashleigh, had lost most of the family
fortune in a Ponzi scheme. She was one of the many who
got caught up in one of the biggest swindles in the history
of the world. She had been one of those who got in early,
but got complacent and left her money in the scheme for
too long until it was too late. Gone were the funds used to
support the family yacht, the house in the Hamptons, the
apartment on the upper east side of New York City, and
the bungalow in the Bahamas. All the properties had to be
put up for sale to pay off the bills. Ashleigh had to move

into a small apartment with comfortable but somewhat Spartan furnishings. It lasted for three months before she swallowed a bottle of pills and half a bottle of wine and drifted off to a permanent slumber.

Paula was shaken by the death of her mother, but she was also thrown into a panic over the financial realities of the newspaper she owned. If they could reduce the printing costs, and raise the advertising rates slightly, the paper could continue and actually be profitable, not just break even. She decided to enter a partnership with *The Kingston Chronicle.* They would take partial ownership in exchange for a reduced rate for weekly printing.

The lawyers for *The Chronicle* had put in specific language in the agreement that gave them 51% ownership if Paula didn't meet certain advertising goals. *The Chronicle* exercised that part of the agreement on the first of the year, wresting away control of the paper she had created from nothing. They had promised her nothing would change and so far, they had kept their word.

Jack knew the whole story because he and Paula had been friendly once upon a time, and they still talked, sometimes at length. But only occasionally.

"Paula, I'm here. You've got ten minutes," Jack said. This wasn't one of those occasions. Jack had too much work on his plate at the moment.

"Okay, let's make it worth it," she said. "What was the name of the man driving the white van?"

"We're not releasing that until we've notified next of kin."

"Of course. Around what time did the accident occur?"

"Between three and four this morning."

"Were there eye witnesses? How can you pinpoint that time? The autopsy hasn't started yet has it?"

"Our investigation revealed that the driver had purchased food in Oneonta around two this morning from the Burger Barn. Based on weather conditions, it probably took him about forty-five minutes to get to where he was found. That's the best we've got."

"And where was he from?"

"He had an Ohio state license, so we assume he's from Ohio, but again, we haven't even had an opportunity to contact relatives."

"What type of animals were involved? Domestic animals? Farm animals? Were any harmed?"

"Where did you hear about that?"

"Police scanner. I heard your call come in this morning for the DEC officer. Oh, and Toby drove out to get pictures."

"Okay, I guess I missed him. Well, long story short, it looked like the driver was transporting some animals. We don't have many details. Most of the animals were killed in the accident. I will get a full report from DEC once they're done cataloging the full contents."

"Did any animals get free, and if so, what kind?" She was good at the rapid fire questions. Jack thought about how he should answer this. He was ninety-nine percent sure that some sledding dogs had gotten lose, but there was that lingering one percent.

"I don't really know if anything got lose. Again, I'm

waiting for the DEC report. It may take a week or so. Maybe I'll have more for you next week. Do you need anything else?"

"How about dinner tonight?" She asked with a hopeful smile.

"Not a chance," he said. "We tried it once, remember?"

"Can't blame a girl for trying. Again," she said, mocking disappointment. "One last thing, what was the name of the DEC officer you worked with?"

"I've got to go. I've got about eight hours of reports to fill out. Can't wait to read the new issue." He walked towards the door to head back out into the sunshine. He stopped and turned. "Davidson. Officer Davidson was his name. Didn't catch his first name, sorry."

After a leisurely walk back to his car, Patrolman Jack McMurphy Jr. headed into his office to finish up paperwork and make some phone calls to see if he could dig up anything else on the traffic accident victim from Ohio.

Chapter 4

Her morning had already been hectic. There was always something else to do on a day like today. The dinner party had to be perfect. The Goldbergs, Boldts and Hartzells were coming, and she knew her husband had to make a good impression if he had any chance of advancing in the firm. She still had to run out for a few things: fresh greens, several more bottles of wine and the cheesecake for dessert. Other than that little bit of shopping and running past the dry cleaners to pick up her dress, her day was free. Not bad for a Tuesday.

It was a beautiful sunny day, so she grabbed her sunglasses along with her keys as she headed for the door out to the garage. Driving across town would take some extra time, but they always had better salad greens at the other grocery store. If she played it right, she could meet up with Deborah for lunch, pick-up the dry cleaning, be home in time for the bus, and have the dinner table set all before Philip even came home.

She had the key in the ignition and did a mental recheck making sure she had everything she needed. She didn't want to have to back track at all today. It was just too important a day to forget something.

Oh! The ticket stub for the dry cleaning!

She hopped out of the car and ran back into the

kitchen and snagged the ticket from behind a magnet on the fridge. One of Starlett's crayon drawings floated to the floor. It was a picture of the three of them, Starlett, Philip and her on a picnic. Gloria couldn't remember when they had last gone on a picnic, but then again, the picture was several months old. She rehung the drawing on the fridge with the rainbow magnet, and headed for the door to the garage. The phone rang.

I'm never going to make it out of the house at this rate. I can just leave it for the machine to pick up, she thought as it rang again.

No, it might be Phillip needing me to get something else for this evening.

She grabbed the cordless receiver and checked the display for the caller ID number. Sure enough, it was Phillip.

"Hello, sweetheart," she answered.

"Oh, thank God I got through. I've been trying for the last hour, but the lines have all been busy. Something bad has happened, Gloria."

"Phillip, what is it, what's wrong?"

"There's a fire. There was some kind of explosion. Gloria, we're trapped, we can't get out."

"Phillip where are you?"

"I'm at work, there was an explosion about an hour ago, and the stairways are all blocked. The smoke started pouring up. Gloria it's a nightmare."

Gloria ran into the living room and turned on the television. The news had a camera trained on the Twin Towers of the World Trade Center, where Phillip worked. Smoke was pouring out of both of them. The news crawler across the bottom said that a plane had struck the North Tower just after 9am and a second struck the other tower a half hour later. She looked at her watch. It was five minutes to ten.

"Phillip, oh my God! The news says that airplanes flew into the building. You have to get out of there!"

"We can't! We're stuck here. We've put wet towels and jackets under the door, but the smoke is coming in anyway now. We tried to stay on the floor, but it got too hot. Listen, Gloria, I don't think I'm going to make it out of here."

"Phillip, no! You've got to try! No. No. No. No!" She was sobbing now, having collapsed down to the floor by the couch after watching the news report. They were replaying the video of the second plane striking the South Tower.

"I can't, this is it. We both need to be brave now. Listen, Gloria. I love you. I love Starlett too. She's not going to understand all of this. You have to be strong for her. You've got to be strong."

"I can't. I need you, Phillip, I need you." She could hardly breathe. Her chest hurt and she felt as if she was going to vomit. It didn't seem real at all. It was like a nightmare from when she was a little girl. She'd dreamed that her parents had been sucked up into a tornado. She remembered it so vividly that even years later it seemed like a real memory and not just the dream that it was. The roof had been ripped off the house and they had run into her bedroom to save her and then they just floated up into the air. She had tried to reach out to them, but they floated out of reach until they disappeared into the funnel cloud. She awoke believing it had really happened. She was so scared she couldn't even scream. It was all just a dream, but for days afterwards she was shaken by it.

"I want to wake up, I want to wake up." She was sobbing, hoping and praying that this was all just a bad dream as well.

"Gloria, shhh. Baby its okay. I'm okay. Everything will be fine. I love you. I'll always love you."

"I love you too. Tell me we're going to be okay." She looked at the television and saw a huge plume of smoke and debris flowering out around the buildings. She couldn't tell what happened.

"Phillip!"

"Something just happened. Everything's shaking. I don't think I'm going to be able to talk much longer. The smoke is too thick. We're going to break down one of the windows for fresh air. Gloria. I love you! Tell Starlett I love her too. She's not going to understand this."

"Pray with me, Phillip."

"Okay, Gloria. Okay. Our Father who art in heaven, hallowed be thy name. Thy kingdom come. Thy will be done on earth as it is in heaven. Give us this day our daily bread, and forgive us our trespasses, as we forgive those who trespass against us, and lead us not into temptation, but deliver us from evil. Amen."

"Amen," Gloria said through tears streaming down her face. "Again."

"Okay, Gloria, baby. It's okay. Our father, who art in heaven. . ."

•   •   •

"Say 'goodbye old house'," Gloria had on her brave face as she waved. She had been strong for her little Starlett at the funeral and afterwards. They tried to avoid the media as much as possible, but every once in awhile another young reporter would show up, hoping to get a comment on how she was doing. They had no comment. It became Gloria's job to shield Starlett from all of the fallout from that horrible day in 2001. No morning shows. No interviews with the local paper. No names on lawsuits. They handled the matter privately with their closest friends and family members.

After the insurance paid out completely, they decided to sell the house and move out of New Jersey. Gloria's realtor had found an amazing deal on a house in the Catskill Mountains of New York, just outside of the small provincial town of Coopers Hollow. It was gorgeous. A twenty-four hundred square foot, ranch style house built in the early 1990's. It was on fifty-five acres and included a six stall horse barn that was fully powered and plumbed.

"Mom, I don't want to go," Starlett said. At eleven years old, she was just starting to establish stronger social bonds with her friends. She was one of three kids in her school that lost someone they were related to on September 11th. Months later, everyone's curiosity about how she was coping had been satisfied. Now she had to go make all new friends and answer all the same questions all over again, relive that day where she was pulled out of class and told to wait for her mother in the nurse's office. The kids had heard about what had happened already, and she thought they were going to go to the hospital to see her dad. That he had just been hurt, but he would be okay, like the time grandpa fell off the ladder.

"Starlett, honey. You know this will be the best thing for us. We'll have more space. We'll get to finally have horses of our own. We'll only be forty-five minutes from Grandma and Grandpa."

"I know, mom. I just -" She trailed off and looked out the window as they pulled away from the house. A moving company was going to pack and move everything up to the new place, so they were going to go on a mini vacation. It just didn't seem right. It was like they were trying to run away from the memory of dad. She knew that everything in the house reminded her mom of him. On more than one occasion she found her mother sobbing because she felt guilty after having had to move something like his golf clubs, wishing she hadn't given him such a hard time about golfing on Saturday mornings instead of being with the family. Starlett knew this was going to be better for her mother, but it was the last thing she needed right now. She needed the support of her friends. Now she was losing not only her dad but everything else that mattered to her as well. It wasn't fair, but Starlett understood it. Life wasn't fair. It was a tough lesson for an eleven year old.

"Listen, don't tell anybody that dad died in the attacks, okay?"

"Why not?" Gloria was surprised that her daughter would say something like that.

"Because, I just want to be normal. I mean, I want people to treat me normal. If we tell them about it, they'll treat us different."

"Differently," Gloria corrected. "And no they won't," Gloria said, though she understood what her daughter was saying. Everyone spoke a bit softer to her when they found out. They then had to tell her the story of what they were doing when they heard about the attacks. Then some would even proceed to ask for more details culminating in downright morbid questions. Which building was he in? Did she get to talk to him? Did they find the body? It took a strong person to deal with all of it. But that was the promise she'd made to Phillip in the last seconds they had together. She would be strong.

"Mom, you just don't get it sometimes," Starlett rolled her eyes and looked out the window as New Jersey slid by.

• • •

"I'm so proud of you, honey." Gloria had on her brave face again. Her heart was breaking in her chest. "I know you'll do great here."

"I love you, mom." They hugged for what seemed like an eternity. It's funny how some moments in time seemed to last forever, and yet whole decades can slip by in the blink of an eye. High school was a blur, and graduation day seemed like it came and went with such velocity that it hadn't really happened. They spent years building up to this momentous occasion and then it was gone and they had to reset their goals and keep going.

They had toured about twelve colleges before Starlett had settled on Binghamton University. Gloria had tried to convince her to go to Oneonta, so she could live at home and commute everyday for classes, but Starlett's persistence and stubbornness won out. It was only an extra fifty minute drive, and it wasn't a big city like Syracuse or Albany, or, God forbid, New York City.

"It will be fine, mom. This is the right thing for me. You'll see. It's you I'm worried about," Starlett pulled away from the hug and looked at her mother. Gloria seemed a little worn out. She'd always been so strong, but now she seemed smaller, weaker.

"Me? Honey, you don't have to worry about me. I'll be fine. I've got the horses to keep me busy. They're a full time job." She tried to hold back the tears, but no one was that strong. They came in streams now, and mother and daughter embraced again.

They had packed up Gloria's Volvo and Starlett's Ford sedan and brought down everything she could possibly need for her dorm room. She would be on campus for the first year, then probably make a few friends and move to one of the many rentals available off campus. Binghamton had enough to keep life interesting, but it wasn't a notorious party school, so Gloria felt pretty secure that there would be some actual learning going on.

"Listen, I'm only an hour and a half away, so if you need anything, don't even hesitate to call me." Gloria was struck by the fact that these words should have been coming out of her mouth, not her daughter's. They were strong together. She didn't know how they would do on their own.

"I'll be fine. You'll be fine. This will be good for us, I promise," her daughter continued. "And now that I'm out of the house you can bring your boyfriend home for a romantic night."

"What? I don't have a boyfriend," Gloria said, shocked. Then she saw her daughter's smile and realized she was being teased.

"You should. You need to start living again mom. Dad's dead, you're not." Starlett smiled and hugged her mother again. "I love you mom. Be safe."

"You too, baby. You too."

• • •

"Mom, I need to come home for a bit." Starlett sounded as if she'd been crying.

"Sure, honey, what's wrong?"

"Well, I think I'm in some trouble and I need advice, but I don't want to talk about it over the phone," Starlett said. Gloria's mind immediately started to swim. Her little girl was in trouble and her protective instincts kicked in.

"Okay, do you need me to come down? I can leave right now," Gloria said. The quiver in her voice was unmistakable.

"No. No it's fine. I just need some advice, is all. I'll leave this afternoon. I should be up before the snow starts." Starlett was a sensible girl.

"Okay, but if it starts snowing too much, pull off and get a room. Put it on the credit card. They're saying we're going to get a foot or more up here, but it's not supposed to start until after midnight. I love you baby girl, be safe."

"I love you too mom. Don't worry too much. Everything is going to be fine. I just need some advice." Starlett broke off the phone call, and left her mother in a state of absolute nervousness.

For the first few months, while her daughter was away at college, she had held it together. It didn't take long to start to unravel, though. She was constantly in a panic that something had happened to Starlett. She would read a news article about an accident and have to call her to make sure she was okay. When there was a shooting in Binghamton at one of the gas stations clear on the other side of town, she called to check on her daughter. Finally, she went to her doctor and asked for something to help with the anxiety.

Her doctor had prescribed one drug after another, but none of them seemed to help. She became more reclusive and didn't talk to the people in town like she used to. She found herself minding the horses, watching television and reading to while away the days. Her doctor suggested trying to make friends in town. Volunteer at the old folk's home. Visit her parents for a week. Go on a cruise and get away. They all sounded like great suggestions, but she could see the inherent problems and obstacles with each venture, so she just stayed home. Her daughter's words kept coming back to her: Dad's dead, you're not. The problem was, she didn't feel alive inside, at least not unless her daughter was around.

Starlett came home for the holidays, and the mood of the house was immediately brightened. She had a new boyfriend who came up to spend a few days as well. He was a bright young man named Dalton Beckman. His family was from New Jersey and his father worked in New York City. They seemed quite wealthy, since Dalton had driven up in one of the new Mercedes SUVs. He was suave and kind and Starlett was head over heels in love with him. Gloria was worried that her daughter would get swept away with her emotions, and not focus on finishing school and achieving her goals. Boys were sometimes very good at making a girl forget her goals.

After the two of them had left, Gloria fell back into a state of depression. She'd brighten up for visits from her daughter and she was very careful to hide just how truly desperate she'd become. It seemed like every day she woke up to relive the loss of Phillip, and it was just more than her poor heart could take. But she soldiered on and summer break came and Starlett was home more.

They spent their days riding trails and then going swimming in the new pool that Gloria had installed. The money she'd received from the settlement had been very well invested, and their family wealth had grown over the years. Gloria would never have to work again, and Starlett's college education was already taken care of. Gloria should have felt relieved, but she was still filled with angst.

Fall semester rolled around and Starlett was back to school, but this time she would be off campus with two

of her friends. It was an old house on the north side of
town. It was a longer commute, but the rent was better
and the neighborhood was safer, so Gloria approved. Her
daughter seemed so much more grown up each time she
saw her. They would talk regularly on the phone, and they
even setup the internet camera phone so they could see
each other. This small change had made a difference, and
Gloria finally felt like she was coming out from under the
dark cloud that had been looming over her for years. Her
doctor had prescribed a new medication that seemed to be
helping as well, taking the edge off at least. She'd enrolled
in a pottery class in town, taught by a transplanted artisan
from Soho. She began going into town more, socializing a
bit more, even getting involved in some volunteer drives for
the fire department. Her life felt worth living again. Dad's
dead, you're not. Maybe her daughter was right.

The phone call from her daughter had shaken her. The
way Starlett and Dalton were getting along, she just knew
what it had to be about. She had tried to have a talk with
her daughter about being careful and making sure that she
was protecting herself and her future properly, but maybe
she had danced around the subject too much and the point
hadn't been made. The family had never really been too
open about sex, even though the mother-daughter relationship was healthy.

Gloria had abstained from any relations after Phillip
died. It wasn't that she didn't find men attractive. If she
had to be honest, she was afraid of caring for someone as
strongly as she had with Phillip, and then losing him. She
couldn't deal with that again. She could see how her lack
of enthusiasm about dating, her self-imposed celibacy,

may have put a damper on any conversation about sex she might have had with her daughter other than the initial nuts and bolts talk. She blamed herself for this mess.

Now, the phone call had come. Starlett was in trouble. Hopefully Dalton was man enough to step up and marry her. The problem was, if he did marry her, Starlett may forever wonder if he did it because it was the right thing to do or because he truly loved her. The inherent issues swirled around Gloria's head like a maelstrom. Something was different this time, though. Even just a year before she wouldn't have been able to control the panic and would have been out the door and on the road to see her daughter. But now she was able to deal with the situation more calmly. She thought about it some more as she made herself a cup of tea.

Maybe it wasn't as big a deal these days. Single mothers survived just fine. There were a lot more resources now for helping with a baby. Then too, Starlett could transfer to Oneonta and Gloria could take care of the baby. She suddenly became excited by the prospect. She had gone from the depths of despair to the pinnacle of elation in just moments. A baby!

It was about 9pm when Gloria's phone rang again. She looked at the caller ID and saw Starlett's cell phone number. She had hoped her daughter would have been home well before then, but obviously she had gotten tied up. Gloria actually hoped that she was calling to say she was going to wait to come up, as the snow was threatening to start already. It probably wouldn't be bad down on the interstate yet, but flurries were already fluttering down from the sky, bright white in the area lights mounted on the garage.

"Hey, mom."

"Hi, honey. Tell me you're waiting to come up until the storm blows through."

"Yeah, I think that's what I'm going to do. Things have calmed down a bit here. I'm thinking I'll come up Thursday and stay for the weekend if it's okay."

"Sure. Are you sure you don't need to talk before then?"

"Well, not really. But I've got responsibilities that I have to take care of. I think I was a little rash in calling you like I did. I just kind of panicked."

"Starlett, whatever you want to talk to me about, whatever it is, I promise, I won't judge you. I'm here for you. You're an adult now, and adult problems aren't easy to deal with on your own. Believe me. So whatever you need from me, you've got it."

"I love you, mom."

"I love you, too."

"See you Thursday."

"See you then. Bye-bye."

She stayed up late watching an old movie. It was a classic Alfred Hitchcock directed thriller with James Stewart and Kim Novak. It wasn't just the movie, but the music that captivated her; an eerie melancholy soundtrack that seemed to take on a life of its own. She felt herself nodding off, so she turned off the movie and went through her nightly ritual before bed. She took a glimpse out the window and she could see the snow starting to accumulate. There was already a few inches on the ground and the weather report had called for at least a foot if not more in the upper elevations. It was one of her favorite times of the year: The first snow.

After brushing her teeth, she looked at herself in the mirror. She took a long moment to take in her reflection. The good looks were still there, at forty-four she still looked like a woman in her thirties. She had taken good care of herself physically, but the stress of the last decade and the loss of her husband had left its toll in worry lines. She smiled at herself, pulled her brownish blond hair back, put it up in a hair tie, and began to wash and moisturize her face. The secret was the moisturizer.

She headed to the bedroom with a fresh glass of water that would stay on her bedside table for the night. She climbed between the flannel sheets, and reached over for her sleeping pill. It was the only thing that helped her not wake from nightmares. She'd needed the pills ever since she'd lost Phillip. It frustrated her to know that something that happened so long ago still had such a hold on her life.

She put all worry out of her mind and turned off the light, drifting off to sleep in short order. The snow outside continued to fall gently. She dreamt about that day, the day she lost Phillip. She dreamt that she had missed his call. That Starlett's colored page hadn't fallen from the refrigerator. That she never got to say goodbye. She was suddenly there with him, in the smoke filled room, huddled in the corner of his office with three of his co-workers. He kept dialing the home number, but it just rang and rang. The machine would pick up and he'd curse, hang up and try again. Finally he just clutched the phone to his chest and cried. She reached out to touch him, she stroked his face. He looked at her and put his hand on hers. He pulled her closer and hugged her to his chest. They were both crying now. They both knew what was about to happen.

"We don't have much time," he said.

"I know."

"I love you."

"I love you too."

"You need to stop this thing that you're doing, it's been long enough," he said to her.

"I can't, Phillip. I miss you so much. I can't let go of you."

"You need to baby. You need to go live life. You've done your duty for me. You turned Starlett into the woman I always wanted her to be. I'm proud of her. And I'm proud of you."

"I love you so much. I always will."

"It's time."

"No, can't we stay together for just a moment longer," she sobbed, running her fingers through his hair.

"It's time."

Suddenly the floor dropped out from beneath them and they fell. The roaring of the building coming down all around them was deafening. They held hands as they fell into oblivion. It seemed like an eternity as they tumbled through the office debris.

"Let go," Phillip yelled. "Let go."

He released his grip on her hand, and they drifted apart as they fell into darkness. The bodies rained down around her. Men in suits clutching briefcases, women in skirts and high heels, all flailing and clutching out at the empty air. She yelled for him, but he was gone. They were all falling and then suddenly, she was alone. The buildings fell around her, but she wasn't being hurt. She was watching it on television, sitting in her living room in her new house in the northern Catskill Mountains. Another crash and rumble occurred.

She awoke with a start. Her heart was beating hard, and her face was streaked with tears. She heard it again; a bang and rumble outside. It took her a moment to realize that it was a snow plow on her driveway. Emilio would drop the blade of the plow and then push the snow off the driveway with a rumble. She looked at the clock and saw that it was six-thirty in the morning.

Her doctor had told her that getting up in the morning was the first step to fighting depression. If you got up, got moving, you had your first victory. You had to keep track of your victories throughout the day.

The floor was cold on her bare feet, and it sent a shiver through her body. She walked out to the kitchen and started the coffee maker then headed back to the bedroom to put on her clothes. She had to get the horses fed, shovel out the side walk, clean off the deck, and then clean up the edges of the driveway with the snow-thrower. She was going to have a busy morning, then perhaps a quick trip into town for an early lunch at the Peachy Keen and a stop at the library for some new reading material.

She finished dressing and pulled her hair back into a pony tail. She walked out to the coffee maker and poured herself a steaming cup and looked out the kitchen window. The snow on the railing of the deck told the story of the previous night's storm. There was at least fifteen inches out there. It would take a few hours to do all of her chores.

Gloria pulled on her snow boots, slipped into her heavy coat, wrapped a scarf around her neck, pulled on a hat and gloves, and headed out the door. She'd positioned the shovel by the door the previous night, so she was able to start shoveling a path right away. She started with a path down to the horse barn, tossing shovels-full of fluffy white snow. After she'd gotten halfway to the barn, she stopped. Something was different.

She looked around her and noticed that there were still some light flurries falling from the sky, like diamonds floating to the earth. As she stood there, under the brightening gray sky, she felt alone. Very alone. For a long time after she'd lost Phillip, she would still hear his voice helping her through the day, as if he was standing there, giving her instructions on how to accomplish her tasks.

"We need to get the walk shoveled, then feed the horses," he would have said in her mind. But he wasn't there this morning. He was gone. She leaned on her shovel for a moment and thought about how that made her feel. He was dead, she wasn't.

The sun was creeping over the mountains and the clouds were now spotty above her. She looked up at the sky and watched her breath drift away.

"Goodbye, Phillip."

"Hello, Mrs. Graves," Seemo said as she opened the door to the Peachy Keen.

"Morning, Seemo," she said.

"Your usual?"

"Um," she thought for a moment. "No, let me see a menu."

"Okay, Mrs. Graves."

"Just Gloria is fine."

"Really?" Seemo was surprised. She was always so closed up, so quiet, so precise. He'd never understood why she had insisted on being called Mrs. Graves rather than by her first name, and he'd never asked. Everyone in town knew something had happened to her and Starlett before they'd moved into the area, but they never told anyone. He had guessed that maybe it was her defense mechanism for not getting too close to people. It had worked very well.

"Okay, Gloria. Let me know when you decide. I get you coffee."

"Thanks, Seemo." She looked around the little diner and smiled. She remembered bringing Starlett here numerous times. She'd tell her daughter to sit still, but the swivel top stools at the counter were too much of a temptation for a child, even one who was practically a teenager when they'd first arrived. Starlett would spin around when she thought her mother wasn't looking. Nothing had changed in the diner, except for the television perched on the shelf above the milkshake machine. It used to be a small older model, but the color had gone, so Seemo went out and bought one of those small flat screen LCD televisions so he could get the games in high-definition on Saturdays and Sundays.

"You're smiling this morning," Seemo said as he returned with the coffee.

"I was just thinking about when I used to come in here with Starlett. She's coming home this weekend for a visit. I think we'll come down one morning for breakfast while she's up," Gloria said.

"I'd like that," Seemo responded. "I'd love to see her again. It's been nearly a year since she was last in. Have you decided what you'd like?"

"I think I'll go with the gyro wrap today with fries on the side."

"Okay, I'll have it up in just a minute." He took the menu back and walked back towards the kitchen. His cook was already working on a few burgers for a couple of the other restaurant patrons. Seemo dropped the fries down into the fryer as he spoke to the man known in town as Poppi. Most people in town thought they were brothers. Those who knew they weren't brothers thought they were gay. Really, though, they were just good friends. They'd escaped from Greece with their lives after a transaction they'd been involved with had gone terribly wrong. The men owed each other their lives. They were probably closer than brothers.

"Mrs. Graves is here, and she wants a gyro wrap, and get this, she say I should just call her Gloria," Seemo said.

"Really? Wow." Poppi and Seemo knew each other so well that very rarely did they surprise one another with any news, but this was indeed a surprise. They knew everyone in town and would comment on just about every person who came in. They had a pretty complete mental catalog of the entire community. They could tell you who was married to whom, when someone's child was born or graduated from high school. Between the two of them they never forgot a face and didn't miss a thing. If it came through the front door, or happened in the diner, the two of them would remember it forever.

"Maybe whatever dark cloud that been over her all these years has finally moved on," Seemo suggested.

"Gyro, huh? Not a Rueben?" Poppi contemplated the change for a moment. "Maybe you right."

Gloria ate her early lunch while watching the television. The station in Albany had picked up the story about the accident on the interstate from overnight. Two people were killed in the minivan, after they ran into the jack-knifing eighteen-wheeler. Normally a news story like that would send Gloria into a depression that would last for days. She'd withdraw into a shell and think about Phillip. But today it didn't touch her in the same way. She felt bad, but it didn't emotionally cripple her.

She finished up, paid the check and left a nice tip. She said goodbye to Seemo and made the door chime jingle as she opened the door to leave. It was a short walk up the sidewalk to the Coopers Hollow Public Library, and the sun felt warm on her face. The steps up to the library were shoveled off and rock salt had been thrown down to melt away any left over ice. The brilliant sunshine had pushed the temperature up over the freezing mark, so the sidewalks that had been shoveled or blown free were just wet.

Gloria wiped her feet as she entered the library, and opened the fabric bag she'd been carrying so as to retrieve the three books she wished to return. She put the books into the return bin, and noted that Francis Luft was not behind the desk at her normal station. She headed over to the fiction section and began to browse the new books which had just recently come in.

The library was part of a group of libraries in the county, and they would rotate new releases and coordinate their overall catalog of books between all the branches. Deliveries were made every Tuesday at this branch, so the new books were usually out on display by noon. Francis was very good at requesting an excellent selection of fiction that kept Gloria busy, as they shared the same tastes in literature.

As she looked through the newest mysteries and political thrillers, she heard Francis talking to someone a few aisles away. Gloria selected a book and wandered through the other aisles, aware that it was a man speaking with Francis. As she rounded a corner, she came face to face with the man to whom Francis had been conversing.

He was about six-feet, two-inches tall. He had dark hair with a touch of gray and dark eyes, brownish-green. She had found herself gazing into his eyes, but then realized it and looked away. He smiled warmly.

"Excuse me," he said. "I didn't mean to startle you."

"Oh, Mrs. Graves, how are you?" Francis smiled sweetly. She was one of the few people in town who considered herself a friend to Gloria, and vice versa.

"Oh, Francis, just call me Gloria, please." The look

of surprise on Francis' face was enough to let the stranger know that something was afoot. "Aren't you going to introduce us?"

"Hello, Gloria. I'm Michael Cooke. I just moved into town," he said with a warm smile. He extended his hand, and Gloria took it for a momentary shake. Francis looked just as surprised at the handshake as she had at the offer to change how she could address Gloria.

"I'm Gloria. Pleased to meet you, Mr. Cooke."

"Michael. Or Mike, whichever you prefer. Find anything good?" He indicated the books she had in her arms.

"I'm not sure. I've read this author before. He tends to be a little too visceral for my liking, but he always puts together a good story." Michael craned his neck to see what she had and then nodded in agreement.

"Well, Francis was nice enough to help me pick out a few things for the week." He showed her the books he had picked out. They were both non-fiction, one was about a sniper from World War II, the other looked like a travel book.

"Interesting choices," Gloria said. "Well, it was very nice to meet you Michael. I'm going to keep browsing. Enjoy your day."

"I can get you setup with the library card and get these books checked out to you, Mr. Cooke," Francis said as she led him away to the front desk. Gloria caught herself watching him as he walked away, and turned quickly when she realized what she was doing.

She could hear the two of them talking in hushed voices, but she couldn't make out what they were saying. She found herself trying to eavesdrop, and then felt slightly guilty for it.

Moments after he left, Gloria emerged from the bookshelves and brought a small stack of four books up to the desk.

"Well, he seemed like a very nice man," Francis said.

"Yes, he did," Gloria found herself saying. He smelled nice too, she didn't say. She didn't quite understand what had come over her. She knew that she'd started a new medication for anxiety several weeks back. Perhaps that was it. Or maybe it was just time to start living again.

"He's single. His wife left him when he was overseas in Iraq," Francis informed her friend, with a glint in her eye. "He was a soldier in the first gulf war and a cop in New York City after that."

"I see. And why are you telling me all of this," Gloria asked.

"Oh, I don't know. Just thought maybe you might be interested," Francis said, looking down at what she was doing with the books.

"He did seem nice," she said finally.

"Have a nice day, dear." Francis handed over the books and they said their goodbyes.

Gloria found herself thinking of the man she'd just encountered as she walked out of the library. She was looking around to see where he'd gone. She suddenly felt a wave of guilt come over her. She felt like she was doing something wrong, even entertaining a thought of another man other than her Phillip. But as soon as the feeling came upon her, it was gone again. She saw Patrolman McMurphy walking along the sidewalk.

"Looks like you got plowed out okay this morning," he said.

"Yes. Emilio was up with his plow. He tells me I'm always the first one he plows out," she paused, thinking about the horrific dream from which she had been startled awake by the scraping of the plow. She suddenly felt a wave of panic set in. She looked around and realized that she had to breathe, that it was all just in her mind.

"I was talking with Seemo and he said Starlett might be coming home for a visit. That sounds exciting. Hard to believe she's already off to college," McMurphy said to her as he walked past. She was a little shocked that Seemo had said anything to the Patrolman, and it irritated her slightly.

"I don't like it. I really can't wait until she gets this out of her system and comes home," she heard herself say. It came out differently than she intended, but she was thinking of the phone call she'd received and the trouble her daughter was in.

"Well, someday the chicks have to leave the nest," he replied cheerfully.

"You never did," she shot back and immediately regretted saying it. She wished she had said that he didn't have to leave to recognize that where they lived was beautiful and they had everything they needed here and it didn't make sense for someone to want to leave. She saw him recoil like he'd been slapped in the face. After she had closed the door, buckled her seatbelt, and started the engine to the car, she paused and looked at herself in the rear view mirror feeling regret for having been so sharp tongued.

These people are just trying to be nice, Gloria. *You don't have to act this way.*

She put the vehicle in drive and headed back home for an afternoon of reading and relaxing. As she pulled up to the lone red light in town, she saw Tubby McIntyre walking along the sidewalk. He seemed oblivious to the traffic around him. He walked right out into the road as a minivan slammed on the brakes and had to swerve to miss him. He absentmindedly continued across the street to the corner convenience store.

The driver of the minivan yelled out the window, but Tubby was oblivious.

That boy is going to get himself killed.

Chapter 5

Mama, what's my daddy's name?" The boy brought his gaze up from the sales catalog he was looking at while sitting at the kitchen table. The picture in the catalog was of a father and son working on a house built from miniature logs. They looked so happy. Some children might have thought that it was the toy making the child happy, but he knew it was because the child was playing with his father.

"Thaddeus Cornelius McIntyre, what would make you ask a question like that? You know you're from the Lord and he is your father." She was a large woman, both in physical size and faith in the Lord. Everything in her life was because of the Lord. There were not coincidences, there was no choice. It was all the Lord's bidding.

"Oh," he said simply. He was a simple boy, already two grades behind in school, and getting all the remedial help available in the rural school district, which wasn't much. A settlement check came like clockwork every month, and that's what they survived on. Apparently the doctor that had delivered him had been drinking a bit before he was called to the hospital and he dropped the baby in the delivery room. In Mama McIntyre's mind it was the Lord's doing, as now they got plenty of money for food and cable television every month. They had brought the cable through town just over the summer of his eighth year of life, and Mama McIntyre took some of the money out of the back room and paid the man who knocked on their door asking if they wanted to sign up.

She had lived in the house her entire life, it having been in her family now for three generations. When she died Thaddeus would get it. Her grandfather had bought it a few months after he'd moved into town. Her grandfather had been the first Chief of Police. Her father had been the town drunk. After she'd become pregnant with Thaddeus she swore never to have a drink again and gave her life over to the Lord. She spent her life going to church, watching television and taking care of all of her cats. It didn't leave much time for taking care of the house or helping Thaddeus with his schoolwork, when he was in school. It wasn't like he was going to amount to anything anyway. The drunken doctor had made sure of that when he dropped him in the delivery room.

Thaddeus had trouble saying his own name when he was younger. He had trouble with the "th" sound and he would substitute b's for d's, so it sounded like he was calling himself "Tabbeus". Of course the other children thought it was just too perfect a fit that the dim-witted, overweight kid with the speech impediment who already called himself Tabbeus shouldn't be called Tubby-us. This label changed over a short amount of time and settled to simply "Tubby".

Tubby didn't mind the name, as he never liked the name Thaddeus much. He found the name much too complicated for someone like him. Sometimes he wished he was just a Bill or Joe. As a name, Tubby would do, he supposed. Even if they were making fun of him when they called him Tubby, at least they were talking to him. After a few years, even his teachers started calling him by the less than flattering nickname.

He never graduated from school, he just stopped going. One day, he just decided that he wanted to stay home and watch television instead of going to school. Nobody told him he couldn't, so he never went back. Everyone around him just understood that he was done with school, and no one bothered to even bring it up to him. People around town were always friendly to him, and he was friendly back. He didn't have any ill will towards anyone, not even Mama, even if she wasn't nice to him.

She would call him stupid all of the time. She'd hit him if he spilled his cereal bowl on the carpet when he was watching television. That's why he started going to see Mr. Seemo for his Frosted Flakes. She would tell him he smelled like a dog if he hadn't bathed that week, and she told him that the Lord was going to send him to hell if he looked at women in those magazines or on the movie channel late at night. He didn't want to go to hell, it sounded like a very bad place, so he wouldn't look at the magazines that were sold at the gas station in the middle of town, or stay up and watch the movies on the cable television where the women got naked.

Tubby had worked for quite a few of the people in town. He was very good at raking leaves or moving heavy branches. By the time he had turned twenty, he had grown into a large man, topping out at six feet four inches tall and weighing nearly three hundred pounds. He could move heavy things no problem.

One time he had been sitting at the counter at the Peachy Keen and someone had run in saying that a child had been hit by a car and was stuck underneath. Everyone ran outside, and some people tried to get to the poor child under the car. He was stuck, and crying that he hurt. Tubby put his shoulder in under the roof of the car where the driver door was and stood up, lifting the car onto two wheels. They dragged the boy out, and got him to the hospital where he got better.

Tubby got a shiny award from the mayor and got to ride on the fire truck during the Thanksgiving Day parade that year. Mama told him that he was able to lift that car because the Lord wanted that little boy to grow up and be somebody important. So he didn't feel like people should be telling him how good he was for doing it anymore because it was really the Lord who should have gotten the credit. So, if anyone asked him about how he did it, he would tell them that Mama said that it was the Lord who did it, really. But riding on the fire truck was a lot of fun, and Tubby was happy that he helped that little boy.

The house they lived in was huge, with plenty of rooms, which was good because they had a lot of cats. The Lord and cats were what Mama loved most. She'd tell them that she loved them. She didn't tell Tubby that she loved him, though. Every time she told the cats that she loved them and that they were her special gift from the Lord, he hated them a little bit more. He was never jealous when she said she loved the Lord, though. He got nailed up on that tree to die for everybody, so you couldn't be jealous of him, but you could hate cats just fine.

There was one room in the house that Tubby wasn't allowed into. It was the back room, off the kitchen. Mama kept all of her important things there. She had money in there, he knew, and other stuff too. When he was sixteen he sneaked in just to look around, and she caught him and made him kneel in the corner praying to the Lord, asking for help to not be such a rotten, vial dog anymore.

Tubby never got a hair cut or trimmed his facial hair, so he looked like a cross between Grizzly Adams and a sasquatch. He showered rarely, and only wore flannel shirts and blue jeans. To any one new in town, he looked like a brute. To those that had watched him grow up, he was more of a big unkempt puppy dog, harmless and, to an extent, lovable.

When Tubby turned twenty-one, a couple of the local guys decided to take him out for a few drinks to celebrate. It was then that Tubby discovered what he loved most: Beer. Beer from the tap, preferably. In a small hole-in-the-wall dive called Taylor's Taproom, Tubby learned that he not only liked the taste of beer, but he loved the way it made him feel. Especially when he was buying drinks for others, everybody was his friend when he was drinking.

Tubby's daily routine became: wake up, go to the Peachy Keen for Frosted Flakes, walk over to the grocery store, walk back home with groceries for Mama, walk over to the Peachy Keen for lunch, then walk down to Taylor's Taproom for drinks for the rest of the day. He was there so often that he became a fixture in the bar. The proprietors of Taylor's even went out and purchased extra large mugs that would hold nearly two pints. They affectionately named them "Tubbies".

Mama didn't like that Tubby was spending more money, but now that he was twenty-one, all the checks were officially his. He didn't need a cosigner and he didn't have to give her a cent. Of course he didn't know that, so she continued to give him the money he asked for without complaint, only warning him that drinking alcohol would lead him to hell. Tubby reasoned that Jesus drank wine, so beer couldn't be all that much worse.

The more he drank, the bigger he got. At twenty-three he was tipping the scales at three-hundred fifty pounds. He lumbered like a mountain as he walked, but the walking was what probably kept him away from the four hundred pound mark.

A couple of the local guys convinced him to join the bowling league. They even got him a special ball with holes drilled out to fit his enormous fingers. He didn't so much as bowl, as he did hurl the ball at the pins. It was done with such violence that he broke a few pins during his league games. He would average about 180 per game, and for the team, he wasn't the worst bowler. Of course the bowling alley had beer. Bowling and beer were now his two favorite things in life. He could not be separated from them. When he talked, it was all he talked about.

If he had a best friend, it was Rusty Anders, another local who had grown up a few doors away from Tubby and the man who had introduced him to bowling. They had played together as kids and even went to high school around the same time, despite Rusty being a few years younger.

Rusty was, what one would call, a born loser. He didn't do well in school, and any time he got into any mischief he got caught. He was a horrible liar and could never think on his feet. He'd been arrested for vandalism when he was just thirteen, underage possession of alcohol when he was fifteen, again when he was sixteen, then possession of marijuana when he was seventeen. On his eighteenth birthday, he went out drinking, stole a car in town and totaled it in a head-on collision which killed a hunter from New Jersey who was up for the weekend.

Rusty went away to prison for seven years. When he got out, the only guy who treated him exactly the same as before he went in was Tubby. Rusty got a job with a local logging company and eventually got married and moved into a mobile home on the outskirts of town. When he was asked to join the bowling team sponsored by the logging company, he jumped at the chance. When it came to the first night of league play, one of the loggers didn't show. They had fifteen minutes to get another player or they would forfeit. Rusty jumped in his Camaro and sped across town to drag Tubby out of Taylor's Taproom and into the bowling alley. From that point on, Rusty and Tubby were together Thursday nights for bowling.

Rusty would talk about his plans for him and his wife, how they were going to move to Florida and Rusty would open a tattoo shop. Rusty would draw on the bar napkins, making interesting designs like tribal bands and animal spots. He would try to draw hot rods as well, but he wasn't as good at that. Art school would have helped, but he didn't even dream about how much that would cost.

"How much money does it cost to move to Florida?" Tubby asked one Thursday night around the fifth frame of their first game.

"Oh, I'd say I'd need at least five grand to do it right. We could get another trailer down there and I could setup shop," Rusty said. He took a swallow from his beer and stood to take his turn. Tubby thought about that and wondered if he could help his friend with the money. It just seemed like so much money. Tubby only got one hundred dollars a week. Almost all of it went to beer and food. He would buy a comic book sometimes if it was a really good one.

"Maybe I could help you," Tubby said. "I could save up and give you some money to help you and then when you start making lots of money with your tattoo shop, you could pay me back, or maybe help me move to Florida too."

"Tubby," Rusty said, taking a swig from his beer bottle to accentuate his point. "You could never leave your mama."

Rusty wasn't being mean when he said this, he was just stating a fact. Tubby didn't take it as an insult at all and sat contemplating the point for a few moments, until he was told to get his Neanderthal butt up and bowl. It was a thought that troubled Tubby for a long time.

It was a thought that he woke up with the day it snowed sixteen inches in October. He realized that he couldn't leave Mama, or that she wouldn't let him leave. It frustrated him and he was suddenly very angry at her. It was still early in the morning, and she was still sleeping. He rolled out of bed and quietly went down the stairs, at least as quietly as was possible for a three hundred fifty pound man.

He went to Mama's back room where she kept the money and other stuff he wasn't supposed to get at. When

he opened the door, he saw all the shoe boxes stacked
on the shelf. He knew that each of them was filled with
twenty dollar bills, as his mother never cashed checks for
anything bigger than twenties. He opened one of the boxes
and grabbed a handful of the bills. He stuffed them into
his pants pocket. He stopped and listened for Mama, but
she still was sleeping soundly. He took more and more,
until both of his pockets were bulging. He had no idea
how much money he had, but he figured it was probably
five hundred dollars at least. He was going to give it to
Rusty, and maybe do the same thing the next day. There
were fifteen shoe boxes on the shelf, so Tubby figured there
was enough money to get Rusty the five thousand dollars
he needed. And after the tattoo shop was a success, Tubby
could move to Florida with his friend.

He was about to leave when he realized that Mama
might have hid more money in the room. He searched
through other boxes, but they were full of pictures and
trinkets and jewelry. In one box he found a gun and a gun
belt like the one that Old Man McMurphy, the Police
Chief wore, and his son too. There was also a book in that
box that had the words Police Chief McIntyre written on
it. Tubby grabbed the book up and opened it. It was a journal written in the scratchy writing that he couldn't read
good. It was too big for his pockets, so he slid it into the
waistband of his pants and cinched his belt tighter to hold
it in place. Maybe Rusty would read some of it to him.

Tubby continued to look around the room, digging
through the boxes. Mama's cats came to investigate, and
began meowing loudly for him to get food for them. As
soon as one started, they all did. He'd finished with the

shoe boxes, surprised at just how much money Mama had been hiding in them. There must have been like a zillion dollars in that room. The only other thing left in the room that he hadn't looked in was the big white chest freezer. Then he wondered why there was even a large freezer like that in the back room.

He tried to lift the lid, but it was locked. He looked around to see if there was something to help him pry it open, because he was now sure that Mama had hid even more money in the huge freezer. He knew there was a metal pipe in the basement that he could use. Quietly he crept down the basement steps, pushed some boxes out of the way and got the pipe. He was back upstairs in the back room in just a few moments, jamming the pipe under the handle of the freezer, trying to pry it open.

Giving it everything he had, every ounce of strength, the lock finally gave, snapping loudly. The pipe fell out of his hand and clanged on the floor. He didn't mean to drop the pipe, it was just that the lock gave so quickly and violently he had lost his grip on it. He slowly opened the freezer and looked in.

He didn't move for what seemed like an eternity. He couldn't move. He was transfixed. His concentration was finally broken by a voice from behind him.

"What do you think you're doing?" The clanging pipe must have waked Mama, as she was standing in the doorway to the back room in her nightgown and slippers. Tubby didn't say anything. He couldn't. Instead, he ran at her, anger in his eyes. He pushed past her and ran right out the front door.

By the time he got to the Peachy Keen, he was sweating, even though it was chilly out and he didn't have his coat. He sat at the counter, ignoring the three snowmobilers who were stuffing their faces and chattering on and on about their night ride.

"Morning, Tubby," Seemo said cheerfully. "You're up early. If you're looking to make a few dollars, you could borrow my shovel and go shovel off the walk in front of the church."

Tubby reached into his pocket and pulled out a wad of twenty dollar bills and left it on the counter. He didn't say a word, just stared at the counter in front of him. Seemo looked at the money and realized he'd never seen Tubby with that much cash before. He got a bowl of Frosted Flakes for Tubby and took one of the bills over to the register to get Tubby his change.

Tubby just looked at the bowl of Frosted Flakes. He stared at them until they had gotten soggy. He never even picked up the spoon.

"Tubby, are you okay? What's wrong?"

Tubby stood up, took the cash back off the counter, stuffed it into his pocket and walked out the door. He meandered over towards Taylor's Taproom, and sat down on the bench outside, as it wouldn't open until noon, and it was just now eight in the morning. He put his head in his hands and for the first time in his life, prayed to the Lord.

Anton Oleksandr had emigrated with his wife and daughter from Ukraine in the late 1960's. He had first lived in New York City amongst others of their nationality, but he did not want to raise his daughter in the city. He bravely moved the family up to the Catskill Mountains where they didn't know a soul and barely spoke the language. He bought a small home behind the school in Coopers Hollow, and made a modest life for his family creating jewelry to be sold at the local stores. At the time there was a jeweler on Main Street. The old man who owned the shop had started to get Parkinson's and his hands trembled so severely that he couldn't manage some of the repairs that he used to. Anton helped with the repairs and kept the shop in business for a few years until the old man died and his sons, who had moved away long ago, simply closed up the shop and left it empty. Anton continued to do repair work on his own, but not many people knew him because of his steady hand or sharp mind. In town, he was known for something else entirely.

Just about every morning, Anton would dress in a suit, put on his hat, a heavy jacket and gloves in colder weather, and walk up and down the streets of Coopers Hollow engaging people in Bible discussions. He believed strongly that he had found answers to the riddles of life within the pages of the Bible and he shared them every morning with anyone that would listen.

At first he was regarded with curiosity, and on occasion, contempt. But soon he was just another staple character in the small town who everyone could count on being there. Rain or snow, heat or cold, Anton would be walking each morning with his black Bible under his arm and a charming smile on his face.

He was never antagonistic, and never pushed people to talk to him if they clearly didn't want to. He was simply a good man trying very hard to share positive messages with his neighbors.

So it wasn't a surprise when he appeared that morning, as Tubby sat on the bench outside of Taylor's Taproom, and asked if he could have a seat. Anton was now nearly eighty years old. His walk had slowed quite a bit over the decades, but his blue eyes still twinkled with kindness, and his broken English was still endearing.

"Bad day, Thaddeus?" Tubby looked up at the old man who wasn't even half his size.

"Yeah."

"What troubles you?"

"I can't say. It's bad." Tubby looked at his boots and kicked at the already melting snow on the sidewalk. Anton considered this for a moment and sat back without saying anything. He watched the cars go by, and the people clearing off their sidewalks and cars from the night's storm.

"Well, in the country I come from, Ukraine, I see bad things. Many bad things. When I live there, they kill a man in front of his family just for having this book." He held up his Bible. "I do not tell people here about such things. It make people very sad. I tell people about good things to come. It make people happy."

"But why do bad things happen?" Tubby looked over at the old man and had the look of a frightened child on his features. "Why do people do bad things?"

"Ah. That is the question. The big question. Where does evil come from? I tell you the answer. Evil come from two places," Anton said, holding up two fingers.

"The devil, and man's heart. The devil start it all, he lie to woman, woman take what is not hers, she get man to do the same and they become sinners. It is what put evil into man's heart. But then man's heart grows more and more evil. Every day it get worse and worse. Maybe little by little, but still worse. Until here we are, where bad things happen all the time."

"We can't fix it?"

"No, we can't. We just keep trying. Only God can fix it. Do you pray?"

"I just did, just now," Tubby said, almost hopefully.

"Can I ask what you pray about?"

"I asked that the Lord help me know what to do. I don't know what to do."

"Well, Thaddeus, keep asking. Keep asking and he will show you the answer. But," Anton paused for dramatic effect. "You need to pay attention. When big decisions come, we sometimes have two choices. Pay attention to make the right choice. The easy choice is usually the selfish one. The hard choice is the one that takes courage. But in the end courage always is better. The Lord had courage, and it was better."

"Mama, talks about the Lord alot," Tubby said.

"Ah, your mamma," Anton said. "Your mamma, if you excuse me for saying so, uses the Lord like a club. She say the Lord say this or the Lord say that but only when it suit her. You are better to read it for yourself. Learn it for yourself. Never take another person's word for what the Lord says!"

"Mister Anton," Tubby said sheepishly. "I can't read so good."

"Ah," Anton laughed. He put his arm around the wide shoulders of Tubby and patted him heartily. "It's okay. It's okay. When I come to this country, I do not know only two words. Where job? But I learn! I learn to read the whole Bible in English! I tell you what. I have a plan. I will teach you to read. You can come to my house and help me with chores so I have the extra time, and then we will help you learn to read! Then you can see what the Lord has to say and you don't take no man's word for it no more!"

"Thanks Mister Anton!" Tubby stood up and decided not to drink today.

"It's okay," Anton said. "You a good boy, Thadeus. You just remember to make good decisions. And come see me so we can start your lessons!"

"Okay," Tubby said. "Bye!"

He was going to go try to make things right. With his head down, he trudged down the sidewalk thinking about how he was going to make things right. He decided to go back to the Peachy Keen and do some thinking.

Seemo got him another bowl of Frosted Flakes but didn't charge him. He watched Tubby carefully. It looked like his lips were moving, like he was talking to himself, having a conversation.

"Are you okay, Tubby?" Seemo was concerned. He'd known the simple man for much of his life, and he'd never seen him in a stupor like this before. Tubby didn't reply, as he was deep in thought. "Okay, well if you need anything else, you just let me know. Okay?"

For nearly three hours Tubby sat at the counter and barely moved. He did finish all of his Frosted Flakes, and then had two big glasses of orange juice and then a cherry and cheese danish from under the glass display. It was after he finished the danish that he finally perked up.

"Mr. Seemo, I need to move something heavy. I need to move it out of Mama's house, but I have to move it someplace where it can be plugged in again, and then leave it there. Where could I do that? Where could I plug it in?"

"What is it you're trying to move?" Seemo was puzzled by the question and why it seemed to be bugging Tubby so much.

"I need to move a freezer because we don't have enough room for it, but I want to keep it, but Mama don't want it in the house anymore, it's not good for her."

"Okay," Seemo seemed to get the idea. He knew that Tubby went hunting from time to time and probably stored some of his meat in the freezer, and knowing his Mama, she probably told him he couldn't keep it in the house anymore. "Well, you could rent one of those storage garages down on East End Ave. They're only about six or seven blocks from your house. You could rent one of them and plug it in there."

Tubby thought for a moment and nodded his head. He could do that. It made sense. He dug one of the wadded up twenty dollar bills out of his pocket and put it on the counter to pay for all of the food he ate. He stood up and walked out the door, jingling the bell as he did so.

First he went to the hardware store to see if they had one of those hand trucks. The owner told him that they would have to order one because they just sold the last one to the grocery store. Tubby knew the people at the grocery store, so he thought maybe if he asked nicely they would let him borrow it, so he walked over to the store and asked the owner if he could borrow the hand truck. The owner of the grocery store wanted to help, but they needed the hand truck today to unload a shipment, but the convenience store by the stop light had one that they used for moving around the milk crates, they might let him borrow it.

He walked up to the convenience store and didn't even notice the minivan that almost hit him. The manager told him he could borrow the hand truck, but not until after three o'clock in the afternoon. That was fine, as it gave Tubby time to walk back over to the storage garages and talk to the owner, Mr. Street.

Mr. Street was another old timer who had called Coopers Hollow his home for his entire life. He owned a few interests throughout town including a floral shop, video rental store and the storage garages. If you wanted to talk to him directly, you had to go to the floral shop, as he spent most of his day working on the flowers and plants in the green house.

"Hello, Tubby. What can I do you for?" Mr. Street said as he helped out a customer. It was a man he didn't recognize, probably someone who was new to town. He was buying a bunch of flowers. "You here to buy your mama some flowers?"

"No. Not today," Tubby replied. "I want to talk to you about a storage garage."

The other customer thanked Mr. Street and headed out the front door.

"Okay, what would you like to know?"

"Can I plug something in?"

"Sure, I have a few with outlets. So are you looking to rent one for awhile?" Mr. Street studied Tubby with a skeptical eye. "Does your mama know that you want to rent one of my garages?"

Tubby shook his head, "No."

"And I bet you don't want her to know either," Mr. Street continued.

"No."

"Okay, well listen. I've got a couple available, I charge thirty dollars a month for the small one, but that doesn't have electricity. For sixty dollars a month you can get a medium sized one with one outlet. And for a hundred dollars a month you can get the biggest I have, and it has three outlets, one on each wall."

"I want the middle sized one," he said. "Is this enough?" Tubby pulled out the wads of money in his pockets.

"Well, well. Let's see." Mr. Street began unraveling the bills and flattening them out on the counter. When he was done, he saw that Tubby had brought in about six hundred dollars. "I'll tell you what. You've got enough here, if you want to pay in advance, for the whole year. How's that sound?"

"Good."

"Good. I do have to get some paperwork together to have you sign, but you can do that the next time you come in, okay?"

"Okay."

"If you want to, you can go and start moving in whatever you want to. It's garage number three. Can you remember that?"

"Yeah. Number three."

"Okay. Now, I won't tell your Mama about this, okay? Just so you know."

"Okay," Tubby said. He felt good, suddenly. He felt like he was planning something big, and it was all working out. He nodded one last time and then turned to leave.

Tubby still had to buy a lock for his new garage, some rope to tie up the freezer so it wouldn't open, and to tie it to the hand truck, and pick up the hand truck itself. It was going to be a busy afternoon.

When he arrived home after he'd done his shopping, which included a beef stick at the convenience store, he realized that Mama wasn't home. Tubby had to think about what day it was. It wasn't a bingo night, and it wasn't a bank day, so he was confused why she wasn't there. Maybe she was mad about what he'd seen in the freezer, maybe she left because she was so angry.

Tubby didn't think much more about it. He set to work getting the freezer tied up so the top wouldn't open, then he got it up onto its side and got it onto the hand truck. He tied it tightly so it wouldn't fall off. Then, at last, he pulled the plug and the freezer motor went silent.

It was a heavy freezer, but it wasn't too heavy for him. He managed to get it out of the back room, through the kitchen, down the hallway, out the front door, down the front steps and onto the sidewalk. He then started walking with it towards the storage garage. It took about a half hour of walking, and by the time he got there, he was tired.

The storage garages were painted white with black spots to look like a black and white cow. The name on the garages was "Mooovers Delight Storage Facility". Tubby didn't think Mooovers was spelled right, but he wasn't very good at spelling stuff.

He opened garage number three and moved the freezer into place. He plugged it in right away, and the motor started right up. He untied it from the hand truck and set it down gently. He thought about taking off the rope that had kept the lid closed, but then decided that it didn't matter as long as it was out of the house. He dragged the hand truck behind him, and closed the garage door. He bought the best lock that he could at the hardware store. He clamped it onto the latch and pulled out the keys. Tubby had never had keys to anything before in his life, and now he did! They were his and no one else's, not even Mama's.

He returned the hand truck to the convenience store and walked back home. He was tired and thirsty. But he decided to go home first to see if Mama had come back.

When he walked in the door, he could see she was standing in the kitchen with the back room door open. As he approached her, she jumped with a fright and turned to see who it was.

"What happened, Thaddeus? What did you do with the freezer?" She was wearing her Sunday dress that she wore for church. Her face was pale and her eyes were big. Tubby thought she looked scared.

"Why are you dressed up, Mama?"

"I went in to church today to do some praying. The Lord needs to help this family. Now, tell me what you did with the freezer."

"I took it away," he said simply. He didn't want her to know that he got the garage and the keys to the lock.

"You did? Did somebody help you?"

He shook his head.

"Did anybody see you?"

He shrugged his shoulders.

"Okay, well good. Maybe this is how the Lord has answered my prayers. I think maybe, if somebody saw you or they find out about it, you should know what to say."

She told him about what was in the freezer and how it had gotten there.

Chapter 6

It was suddenly aware that it was awake and cold air was blowing on it. Its enclosure was open enough to squeeze through, and suddenly it was out in the open into the snow. The smell of blood was in the air, but it was the smaller of the two large animals in the back of the van. They were both male and both highly territorial, so it stretched its legs in a quick run through the snow. It was up onto a hard surface and in one leap was back into the soft snow.

Despite its captivity, pangs of hunger triggered instincts that were hard wired into its brain. It needed to eat. It had been malnourished during its most recent captivity, and now it would hunt. Almost immediately it caught the scent of potential prey. The valley was relatively clear of trees and small brush, so it would have to approach with stealth. Slowly it crept towards the scent and then froze.

There was movement on the ground just ahead. The large animal got close to the ground and crept nearer. The prey was unaware of the threat as it hopped through the snow slowly. The snow coming from the sky suddenly grew heavier, and a wind blew it sideways. The small animal paused, and it was the last mistake it would make. The attack came with lightning quickness, and the powerful jaws clamped down. Its neck was broken in an instant, and it quickly became a meal.

The large predator was known as Puma Concolor Couguar, or the North American Cougar. A subspecies had once had a strong population in the Catskill Mountains region and had been called a Catamount locally. But hunting and the mass clearing of land for farms and homes had pushed the native population into non-existence hundreds of years earlier.

This particular animal had experienced a long journey to arrive at this place. It had been just a cub when it was taken from its mother's den in Colorado and sold for a few hundred dollars to a private zoo just outside of Omaha, Nebraska. As it grew into a full grown adult, it changed hands two more times, eventually ending up in the ownership of Ohio Exotics, Inc. located about a hundred fifty miles outside of Cincinnati, over near the West Virginia border. Marcus Higgs was the owner of Ohio Exotics and traded, bartered and sold exotic animals all over the country. He would import from overseas and even broker animal exchanges between parties.

Acquiring the cougar was part of a three way deal between a private dealer who wanted a black bear, a zoo that was looking to replace a pair of spider monkeys they had lost to disease, and Higgs who was just looking for a way to make a little cash and pick up something that had some value. The cougar was healthy and fit the bill perfectly. In fact, he already had a buyer before he closed the initial deal. One of his better clients located in Vermont was known to purchase large cats and destroy them for their parts which were used for mostly Asian medicinal concoctions and sold on the black market in New York City.

The animal had no concept that it had escaped a death sentence when the driver of the van had wrecked. It also had no idea that it was the first cougar to be stalking the region in nearly two centuries.

The area was ripe for the return of large predators, as the forests had been allowed to grow back and fill in. Fewer and fewer farms were in operation in the Catskill region, and the forests were thicker than they had been in two hundred years. The number of hunters actively harvesting wildlife in the region had also begun to decrease, which meant that some of the animal populations had exploded. White tailed deer specifically were more numerous in the region than they had been in two centuries. That meant that there were more auto accidents involving deer and more human deaths related to deer strikes than ever before. Many of the local law enforcement officers had discharged their weapons in the line of duty more than any other officers in the rest of the country because they had to put down the poor animals that were injured but not yet dead.

All this meant that the cougar should not have had a problem finding food. However, it had been in captivity for most of its life, so it wasn't used to the need of an extended hunt. Rather than naturally learning the ambush tactics common to the rest of its species, it had become a predator of opportunity, taking advantage of the feedings that gave little resistance, like the live chickens that were tossed into its cage once a week. It had been fortunate to find a rabbit out in the storm. The next meal would not be as easy. Weak from malnourishment, a sustained chase was outside the range of its abilities for the moment. It would need several easy meals and several weeks of exercise to acclimate to the rigors of life in the natural world.

It was a beautiful animal. Nearly seven feet in length from nose to tail, which was about average for a cougar its age. It would not grow much longer, but with a more natural diet, it would gain more weight in a short amount of time. Its coat was a golden brown and its ears were tipped in black. It was built for stalking and ambush, but it could reach high speeds for short sprints.

Because of its life of captivity, it did not exhibit the normal habits of cougars in the wild. It had experienced humans for most of its life, and therefore was not afraid of people. It also was fed regularly during the day, and it adapted to being awake during the day and sleeping at night rather than being the nocturnal hunter it would have been had it stayed in the wild. Cougars were territorial, but it would take some time for it to establish its territory.

It finished its feast in short order, and then naturally began to seek shelter to rest. All along the creek that ribboned through the valley there were rock out-croppings and small caves that would make for more than suitable shelter. It meandered down to the waters' edge and took a drink. It then followed the stream east looking for a place to spend the rest of the night in a safe shelter from the storm.

Chapter 7

The phone rang at four-thirty in the morning. It took a moment for him to realize what was going on, as he had been sleeping deeply. He grabbed the receiver on the second ring and hit the talk button.

"Hello," he grumbled into the phone.

"Rusty, it's Quinn." It was his boss with the logging company. "Just wanted to let you know we're not logging today. The snow from Tuesday has made everything a mess. We're calling off today and tomorrow and we hope to get back to it on Monday. Sorry I called so early, I just wanted to catch you before you left home."

"Okay," Rusty said groggily.

"And that means no pay. Sorry. I just wanted to let you know."

"Okay," he replied though he wanted to tell his boss to go play in traffic. They worked through the snow for two days and were pushed to hustle as quickly as possible to get the trees on the truck. Rusty should have seen it coming that his boss would work them hard for three days then blow off the last two days of the week. Twice the work for half the pay.

"Alright, see you Monday."

"Okay," Rusty said again. He pushed the hang up

button and rolled back over to get some more sleep.

"Who was that?" The call had woken up his wife, Heather.

"Work. They're calling off today and tomorrow because of the mud from the snow."

"We needed that money," she said. She knew he knew that, but she said it anyway.

"I know. I can see if I can work with Bubba hanging sheetrock. Not sure what he's up to, but I can usually get a day or two out of him," he said. "But it's too early, I got a couple hours before I can call."

He rolled away from her and closed his eyes to try to get back to sleep. It wasn't half an hour before Libby was up from her bed in the other room. He heard her little feet pitter patter down the hall to their bedroom. She always went around to her mother's side to climb in. Ten seconds later, ice cold feet were thrust onto his bare legs. Had it been Heather's he would have grumbled, but his little girl was his life, so he squished her cold little feet between his calf muscles and warmed them up.

Heather had to be up at five anyway, as she was helping open the convenience store this morning. It took her ten minutes to get there and twenty minutes to get ready, so she was cutting it close to be on time for five-thirty.

Rusty tried but couldn't get back to sleep. He thought about the two-hundred-fifty bucks he was losing out on by not being able to work. It was going to make everything tight for the next couple weeks. If he could hang sheetrock, he could make up half of that. Tonight was Thursday, bowling night, and he certainly wasn't going to be able to drink as much as usual.

Maybe Tubby will buy drinks tonight like he did a few weeks back. Tubby'll be good for it. He lives for drinking and bowling, that guy.

It seemed like just a few moments before Heather's alarm went off and she rolled out of bed. Libby curled up closer to him and went back to sleep. He listened to his wife use the toilet and then shower. You could hear just about everything through the thin walls of the trailer.

He longed for the day when he could give them a better life, better than he ever had. For now, though, this was the best they could do. They did have satellite television, and two cars, and enough spending money for going out to dinner once in awhile and going drinking with the boys every now and again. It wasn't a bad life, it just wasn't the life he had hoped for when he was little. He wanted bigger things for himself. Rusty hated working for someone, but for the moment that was all he had. He wanted to have his own tattoo shop someday, it was a dream he had, but deep down inside he knew he wasn't a good enough artist.

Heather was done with the shower, so he eased himself out of bed trying not to disturb Libby. He walked to the bathroom and caught her just drying off. She was definitely heavier than when they got married four years before. But she had carried a baby, and he knew that women rarely sprung back to where they were before they got pregnant. Even still, he didn't mind the extra pounds. He liked the way she felt soft against him when they laid in bed at night.

He tried to kiss her, but she turned away.

"Ew, morning breath," she said. He breathed on her again just to tease and she made a gagging noise. He went over and lifted the toilet seat and relieved himself while she dried her hair with the electric hair dryer. After she had dried it thoroughly, she pulled it back into a ponytail. As she pulled on her under-things, he reached over and gave her a pinch.

"Rusty, I don't got time. I'm gonna be late," she said. "When I get home, baby."

He quickly brushed his teeth and splashed some cold water on his face as she went into the bedroom to get dressed the rest of the way. He looked in the mirror and didn't like what he saw. He was nearing thirty years old, and he could tell he was losing more and more hair. He tried to compensate for it by growing facial hair, but he didn't think it was helping. He flexed in the mirror and frowned at his developing gut. He'd always been that skinny strong kid in school, and then when he had to do time, he couldn't keep weight on. Now he was starting to pudge up a bit and he felt old. He turned from the mirror, clicked off the light and headed out to the living room to get breakfast and watch television.

Heather came through in a flash of jacket, purse and keys as she headed for the door. She leaned over and kissed him and left. He felt so alone when she left for work. It reminded him of being a kid when his mom would leave for her job at the bar at night. He and his brother would have to put themselves to bed, which was kinda cool, but some nights he just wished that his mom would come home and read to them until they fell asleep like she did when they were little and their dad had still been around.

That was one thing he had promised himself. No matter how bad it got, he wasn't going to leave the family like his old man did. He was going to make sure his little girl had a daddy. He even gave up smoking after she was born. It made it easier that they didn't let you smoke in the bowling alley or even in the bar anymore, but that's not what made him do it. His mom had died when Libby was just a year old. Forty-nine years old. Dead. Lung cancer. He didn't want to leave Libby behind like that.

There wasn't much on the television this early. No real sports to speak of, as the baseball season was done for the year, at least for his team it was. Football wasn't on until the weekend, and hockey and basketball weren't his thing. He switched it over to one of the Albany stations whose broadcast went out over the satellite signal. They were showing a story about the snowstorm from a couple of days ago. He turned up the volume to hear the news lady talk.

"The storm from earlier this week that left much of the capital region drenched in wet snow actually claimed three lives in the Northern Catskills in two separate incidents. The first happened on Interstate eighty-eight, around Oneonta, when a tractor trailer jackknifed on the snow covered road, blocking both lanes. A minivan driven by William Tuttle slammed into the trailer, shearing off part of the roof. Tuttle and a passenger, his wife Juliet, were both killed. They were both fifty-nine. The driver of the tractor trailer was not injured and was not ticketed for the accident.

"The other incident is something of a mystery. John Thomas Bartlett, twenty-six of Coopers Hollow, Ohio was found dead in a rental van on route 23 west of Coopers

Hollow, New York Tuesday morning after the storm. Apparently Bartlett was struck in the head by items in the van during the roll over crash. He succumbed to hypothermia before the wreck was discovered. He was carrying exotic animals in the van, most of which died in the accident. There were a few lucky survivors, however, a Macaw parrot, and what were believed to be two Siberian Huskies that were being transported up north for dog sled training. The Macaw parrot is doing fine, but the Huskies are nowhere to be found. They were fortunate enough to make it out of the wreck, but animal control has been unable to locate them.

"Pretty sad news," she said to her co-anchor.

"Indeed. A very sobering reminder to be careful during snow season when you're out driving. But what are the chances of being from Coopers Hollow, Ohio and getting in a fatal accident outside of Coopers Hollow, New York?"

"Strange and a bit ironic," she replied, looking mildly annoyed at her co-host's mindless bantering.

"Well, it looks like we may have another storm looming on the horizon. We'll get to that and more when we return," said the male co-anchor, Bob something or other. Commercials came on, and Rusty got up to get a bowl of cereal. He was pouring the milk when he felt a tug at his shorts. He turned to see Libby rubbing her eyes.

"Hey baby girl, you can go back to sleep," he said, picking her up.

"Where's mommy?"

"Mommy had to go to work today, it's Thursday."

"Do you have to go to work? Am I going to Miss Sally's house?" He thought about this for a moment. He really should call Bubba to see if he could work in with his crew hanging sheetrock. His heart was torn. It didn't happen too often that he got to spend time with his little girl, just him and Little Bitty Baby Libby, as he called her.

"Nope, today it's just me and you. We'll play all day." She stopped rubbing her eyes and leaned into him, putting her arms around his neck and her head on his shoulder. He grabbed the bowl of cereal with one hand and carried her with the other back out to the couch. He laid her down and pulled a blanket over her. She snuggled in to sleep a bit more, while he crunched on the cereal and watched the rest of the news.

After about a half hour, Libby woke up again and wanted breakfast, so he made a bowl of cereal for her. That's when he noticed that Heather had left her cell phone plugged into the wall.

If her head weren't screwed on, she'd leave that behind too.

It was only about a ten minute ride into town, so it wasn't a big deal, but it meant now that he had to get dressed and get Libby dressed and get on his way so Heather could have her phone. He watched some more television while Libby poked at her cereal and sang a song he hadn't heard her sing before. It was something about popsicle noses and teacup ears.

Whatever. At least it's not that stupid dinosaur song she was singing last week.

"Come on, honey bear. We've got to get dressed and take mommy her phone," he said. She hopped down off

the kitchen chair and skipped to her bedroom. He followed
her down the hall and continued on to his room to throw
on a tee-shirt and jeans. He came back down the hall
and saw that she had gotten distracted with her dolls and
hadn't even attempted to get out of her pajamas.

He picked out some clothes for her and told her to
strip. He got her into the fresh clothes, and out to the living room in just a few minutes. He put on her shoes, coat
and hat before starting on his own.

"Can I go outside to say hi to Sparkplug?" Sparkplug
was their old Black Labrador.

"Yeah, okay. Don't go off the porch," he said. She ran
to the door and opened it by herself. She slammed it hard
enough to make the windows rattle. Rusty pulled on his
socks and shoes and was going to grab his jacket off the
peg when Heather's phone rang. He picked it up off the
charger and saw that it was the convenience store. He
flipped it open to talk.

"Hey, I was just about to bring it down to you,"
he said.

"Oh. Sorry, I left it. I thought maybe it was in my
purse and I just couldn't find it."

"Nope, you left it on the charger. I'll bring it down."

"Did you call Bubba? Are you going to be able to work
today?"

"Na, Bubba didn't have anything for me," he lied. "He
said maybe tomorrow."

He heard something outside, and suddenly Sparkplug
started barking aggressively. He could hear her scratching

the deck, pulling at her chain.

"Hey, something's gotten into Sparkplug, I gotta go. See you in a few minutes." He closed down the phone, grabbed his jacket and flung the door open. He was about to scold Sparkplug for barking so much but he was stopped short.

What he saw didn't seem to make any sense. It looked like a giant short haired house cat dragging a doll across the muddy driveway. Sparkplug was going nuts. It took him a moment to realize that it wasn't a doll, but it was Libby. Some kind of mountain lion had gotten hold of her and was dragging her into the woods.

"Hey! Get away from her! Get away from her!" He grabbed the nearest thing he could, which was a snow shovel, and launched off the deck into the yard. The big cat dropped Libby and hissed at him. He swung the shovel and connected. It leapt back and coiled like it was going to attack at him. He swung again, and this time it jumped clear and then launched at him, with claws and teeth bared.

He dropped the shovel in reaction, and grabbed at the attacking animal. It scratched him good across the chest and bit hard into his left arm. Suddenly the adrenaline kicked in and he went full speed on the cat. He threw it to the ground, ripping open his arm in the process. He then kicked it hard with his work boots and connected solidly. It backed away, and turned to look quickly at Libby, who was now trying to crawl away, bloodied and sobbing.

"Don't even think about it!" He then let out a guttural roar that was so primal and ferocious that the cougar backed down. It paused, and then fled off into the woods. He rushed over to Libby to see if she was okay.

She had blood streaming out from under her pink coat. It looked like the cougar had grabbed her from behind and tried to get at her neck. Her puffy jacket had caused it to miscalculate and it just gouged her, but it didn't look like it had punctured anything vital.

Rusty, on the other hand, was losing blood, and he was starting to get light-headed. He looked at the injury to his arm, and it was bad. It had ripped away flesh right down to the bone. His chest was streaming blood as well. He stumbled back to the house with Libby under one arm.

He almost fell inside. His legs were weak, and he felt like he was going to faint. He grabbed a tee-shirt off the laundry basket and wrapped it around his arm. Then he pulled down a scarf from the rack and started a tourniquet to stop the blood flow. Fishing his wife's phone out of his pocket, he called the convenience store. It rang five times before someone answered.

"Hello?"

"This is Rusty. Tell Heather to call an ambulance now. Something attacked us. I think Libby's okay, but I'm losing a lot of blood. I think I'm going to faint."

"Oh my god, Heather! Heather! It's Rusty. He's hurt!" He could hear the girl tell his wife. The whole room started to spin. He had to sit down, but instead he kind of just crumpled. He dropped the phone and could see it in front of him on the floor, but he couldn't seem to remember how to make his hand move over to get it. Things weren't making too much sense.

Libby came over and picked up the phone and said hello.

"Mommy," she sobbed. "Something bit me and then it bit daddy too. I think he's taking a nap because he had to fight it."

Darkness started to close in on his vision. Libby bent down and rubbed his head.

"It's okay, daddy. They're going to come and help. I'm right here. It's okay, daddy."

Blackness.

McMurphy got the call from dispatch just as he was pulling into Stewart's convenience store for a cup of coffee. He threw the vehicle into reverse and turned on the lights. He knew exactly where the trailer was that was reported in the call, and gave the car all the gas he could around the twisting road out of town.

He figured he'd beat the ambulance there, as he had just seen the crew going into the Peachy Keen not five minutes earlier. They'd be sprinting out to the ambulance right about the time he was leaving the village limits.

Jack knew that Rusty was a local kid who'd had a bad string of luck, but had seemed to straighten himself out after he got out of jail. Last he heard the kid got married and had a kid of his own. They moved out to the old Wilcox trailer. Jack had gone on many a call out there for domestic disturbances when the Wilcox's owned the place. Lots of drinking and lots of fighting.

He made it to the trailer in six minutes flat. He parked on the road, not blocking the driveway and leaving the lights on so the ambulance would have no trouble finding the place. He popped the trunk, grabbed his first-aid kit and sprinted towards the trailer.

The door was open so he went right in and saw immediately that things were bad. The little girl had blood all over her, and a pool was starting to form around Rusty. Jack put down the first aid kit and quickly pulled on his blue latex gloves.

"Are you okay, sweetie?" He looked her over quickly, pulling down the back of her bloodied pink coat to see the lacerations on her back. They were already clotting and didn't look deep.

"Daddy fell asleep," she said. She was rubbing his head gently.

Jack felt for a pulse and at first thought there wasn't one. Then he found it, ever so faint. He saw the gash on the arm and the loose tourniquet. He went back to the first-aid kit and retrieved a latex band and put it around the arm to make an even stronger tourniquet. He then pealed back the tee-shirt and saw that the injury was severe. Jack flopped the piece of flesh back into place and then put on a couple of fast clotting sponges. He wrapped it quickly and tightly with a gauze bandage. Pressing his fingers against the man's neck, he felt for a pulse again, and swore it was stronger this time. By the time he had gotten the bandage in place, the ambulance crew was coming through the door.

"He's bleeding fast. I did the best I could to stop it," Jack said.

"Grab the stretcher," Mikey Wilbur yelled to his partner. "Jeez, Jack, what did this?"

"It was a lion," Libby said.

"Really, honey, a lion? Are you sure it wasn't a doggie or maybe a bear?" Jack took another quick clotting sponge and put it on her back as the ambulance crew brought in the stretcher and carefully lifted Rusty onto it. They gave him oxygen, and then strapped him down.

"Where's daddy going?"

"We're going too," Jack said, lifting her up and walking out with the crew. He over heard them say that the pulse was steady, but weak. That was a relief, but the nearest hospital was a thirty minute drive to the north. One of the dangers of living this far away from a hospital was the chance that you would die en route. Every year someone died in the region because they didn't reach the emergency room in time.

"We can take her too," Mikey said.

"I think she'll be okay," Jack said. He realized that Rusty might bleed out on the way, and that would be a very scary thing for a little girl. "I'll follow right behind you. Be careful driving, guys."

"You too," Mikey said. "Let's roll!" The ambulance pulled out of the driveway with full lights and sirens. Jack took Libby over to his car, pulled a blanket out of the trunk and wrapped her in it. Even though it was against the law, he sat her in the front seat and buckled her in.

"Have you ever ridden in a real police car," Jack asked, hoping he knew the answer that was coming.

"Nope," she said.

"Okay, well we're going to go pretty fast and I'm going to turn the lights and sirens on, okay?"

"Yeah," she said, and she looked a little excited about the prospect of such an experience.

"Do you want to turn the siren on?"

"Yeah!"

"This button right here," he showed her on the dash mounted control panel. She pushed the button and immediately the whooping of the siren began. She laughed and jumped a little when it started.

"You're going to be okay, sweetie. Everything is going to be fine," he said to her.

For Rusty, a man who had experienced very little in the way of good fortune go his way for most of his life and had been labeled a born loser by more than one person, he picked the perfect day to get a little lucky. The ambulance crew had just received stock of a synthetic blood substitute as part of an experimental trial program supported by a hospital in Albany.

Every year someone in the Northern Catskill Mountains was involved in a hunting accident. Over the past ten years, seven people had bled out before they even reached the emergency room. Crews couldn't stock blood in the ambulance, as it would not last. The new treatment basically added volume as well as a synthetic oxygenation molecule to the patient's blood system. Because it was synthetic, it could be used without the risk of disease or rejection because of blood type. The biggest advancement was that it had an indefinite shelf life. It was a revolutionary treatment for massive blood loss, and through the trials so far, it had found success. Several cities, where blood banks ran dry regularly or where people preferred bloodless surgery because of their religious beliefs, had been selected for the trial treatment. The hospitals in those cities had just been allowed to begin stocking ambulances with a supply so as to gauge usefulness in the field. Rusty was going to be the first patient to ever receive the synthetic blood substitute en route to the hospital in the history of the United States. He was very lucky indeed.

As soon as they got a pint of the synthetic substance into Rusty's vein, his pulse came back stronger and his blood pressure began to stabilize. He regained consciousness just before they reached the hospital.

"Where am I," he asked, squinting at the light. His voice sounded garbled, as he was still wearing the oxygen mask.

"We're taking you to the hospital. You had an accident and lost a lot of blood. We're going to get you into surgery to sew up that arm," Mikey said, reading his vitals and then looking into his eyes. He shined a penlight into Rusty's eyes and then pointed the beam away, testing the dilation response of his irises.

"Where's Libby?" A wave of panic came over Rusty. He couldn't remember much of anything.

"She's behind us in the police car. She's going to be okay. It looked like just a couple of pretty deep scratches. Do you know what it was that attacked you?"

"Um," Rusty was having some trouble remembering anything beyond the moment. Then it came back to him. "It was like a lion, without a mane. Like uh, mountain lion. Uh, uh, cougar."

"Okay. You're sure? It wasn't a bobcat or bear? Maybe a dog? Pitbull?" Mikey was scribbling down notes on a pad as he asked the questions. Cougars hadn't been in these woods for a couple hundred years.

"I don't know, maybe," Rusty said and drifted off again.

It had taken nearly twenty minutes to get to the hospital, and the two vehicles were flying just about as fast as the roads allowed. Libby was carried in by McMurphy, and she could see over his shoulder her daddy being brought in on the stretcher. His eyes were open now and he spotted his little girl. He raised his good arm to waive at her, but there were tubes and tape all over it, so he put it down again, worried it might scare her.

Rusty was prepped immediately and he headed into surgery. The surgeon had just arrived, so it would only be a half-hour or so before the stitching and reconstruction began. When they peeled back the gauze and bandages and saw the full extent of the injuries, both the surgeon and anesthesiologist commented that Rusty must have been the luckiest man alive. The bite to his arm had come within millimeters of severing an artery. He'd lost a lot of blood, but he would have been dead in two or three minutes if that artery had been hit.

Libby's wounds turned out to be far less serious than they had initially looked: four scratches across her back from the mountain lion's teeth, with very small puncture wounds to the skin. Her puffy pink jacket had probably saved her life. Her wounds were cleaned and dressed by the time her mommy arrived.

McMurphy cleaned himself up as best as possible, but his uniform was finished, perhaps for good. He had blood down the entire front and covering the sleeves. Whenever there was contact with someone else's blood, it was important to wash immediately to remove any chance of infection from blood borne diseases or pathogens. Jack removed his uniform top and saw in the mirror of the hospital washroom that his Kevlar vest had been stained as well. He was down to his white, v-neck tee shirt and his uniform pants as he scrubbed his hands and arms with an antibacterial foam to kill anything on his skin. The hospital staff gave him a plastic bag for his soiled clothing, but he knew he was going to need to purchase a new uniform top to replace this one. He had two additional uniforms, but it would be a forty-five minute ride back to his house, so he thought it best to call in.

He had recorded all of the info he could collect from Libby, then notified Officer Davidson at the DEC that they had a mountain lion attack, and that the DEC should take over the investigation.

McMurphy thought about the accident on Tuesday morning and wondered if maybe the van had been carrying a couple of mountain lions instead of sledding dogs. He had been unable to get anyone on the phone to discuss the accident. No girlfriend, boss, roommate, nothing. It bothered him that a man could be dead and no one seemed to care. The rental company, which was a small, local operation located about an hour north of Charleston, West Virginia, didn't have much to go on. They had rented the van for cash with a big cash security deposit. They didn't ask what the van was for, nor did they think it would end up on the side of the road in the northern Catskill Mountains. For someone who just lost one of their vehicles, they sounded pretty unconcerned.

Before he could spend much time thinking about it, his radio crackled to life.

"McMurphy, this is dispatch, what's your location?" They always called him McMurphy and his father Chief.

"I'm at the hospital, finishing up with the animal attack call from earlier, what's up?"

"We've got an altercation in Coopers Hollow, a fight outside the Peachy Keen, how soon can you get there?"

"I'm about thirty minutes away, anyone closer? See if the Sheriff's department can help out." Jack knew what the answer would be from them. It wasn't really a feud, but the county Sheriff's department and the small three-man Coopers Hollow police department didn't get along very well. There were always complaints leveled at their small village police squad about overstepping their bounds or writing tickets out of their jurisdiction.

"Dispatch, this is the Chief McMurphy," he heard his father's voice over the radio.

"I'm five minutes outside of Coopers Hollow, west bound. I'll take the call, but I'd appreciate any available officers in the area for backup."

"Confirmed. Any available law enforcement officers near Coopers Hollow, please respond for back up request by Chief McMurphy to the Peachy Keen diner on Main Street," the dispatcher said.

Jack cursed under his breath. The old man wasn't in any shape to break up a fight. More than likely he'd end up getting himself hurt.

Who the heck is fighting at ten in the morning on a Thursday?

Chapter 8

It was a complete surprise. To him, the desert was supposed to be sand, heat and camels. He'd gotten the sand part correct, but so far the temperatures weren't much warmer than Parris Island, South Carolina where he'd gone through boot camp, and he could deal with that. As for the camels, he hadn't seen a single one. What he'd seen plenty of, though, were the flies. They were small, annoying insects that were constantly in eyes, noses and especially ears. But the cool weather, sand and flies weren't the most surprising thing for him and the other boys. The border had been secured for days now with air strikes. There hadn't been a viable target since they had taken their position. He had imagined fire fights and hardcore warfare. What they faced was a line of burned out vehicles that had been bombed into oblivion and an opponent that had never shown up.

As a U.S. Marine fresh out of sniper school and now officially a HOG, Michael Cooke was looking for the one thing that newly minted United States Marine Corps snipers wanted: the first kill. It wasn't blood lust in the typical sense. Rather, it was an overwhelming and ardent desire to use all of the skills which had been tattooed on his brain and stitched into his very fabric of being over the past nine months. Until he got the first kill, it was all just theory and practice. After going through the most grueling experience in his entire life and coming out the other end alive, it would kind of be nice for it to mean something and to be able to put to use what he had learned. The only problem was there wasn't a conflict that required his particular skill set. And then the United States of America went from Operation Desert Shield to Desert Storm.

Cooke didn't care about the politics that were causing the largest United States military mobilization since the Vietnam conflict. He had signed up for the Marines because he was from a poor family and he wanted a college education. When he got to sniper school to become a USMC Scout Sniper, he took everything that was thrown at him. They never asked you to leave, you quit of your own choice, they would say.

If a person made it through the twelve week USMC indoctrination, or boot camp, removing all of those undesirable civilian traits like individuality and an aversion to killing, and actually became a Marine, they were still considered a SLUG: Slow, Lazy, Untrained Gunman. Once a Marine was selected for a Scout Sniper platoon, they were given the acronym of PIG: Professionally Instructed Gunman.

Becoming a PIG meant harder work still. But just getting selected for the platoon didn't mean they were considered a USMC Scout Sniper. To receive such a designation, a PIG must attend and pass a USMC division Scout Sniper school. Each school kept a record of those who graduated so there could be unquestioned verification in the future. It's was a very exclusive club and the Marine Corps jealously guarded the list of who could call themselves a sniper.

Sniper school was grueling. Maybe three to four hours of sleep was all that was allowed each day. Everywhere they went, they ran. It was tests all morning, then running, then shooting, then running, then sleep, then running, then more tests and still more running. When they graduated from the thirteen weeks of sniper school, they went from PIG to HOG: Hunter of Gunmen. As a reminder each graduate received what they called a HOG's tooth. It was a rifle cartridge, a full metal jacket cartridge devoid of gun powder, drilled through and slung on a neck chain. They wore them around their necks out of superstition, and a HOG was never caught without his. It was the only bullet that was meant for him, and as long as he had it, he wouldn't catch someone else's bullet.

The perception of a sniper as the lone gunman who instinctively knew how to make the perfect kill shot was only true in Hollywood. The reality was that the instinct was all attributed to training. Sure they were the top of the top and seemed to have a preternatural ability for steady hands and great eyesight. But the training was so intense and was so ingrained that they could do the triangulation equations in their sleep. Scout Sniper teams were some of the best mathematicians in any of the armed forces, and they didn't work alone. Usually they worked in teams of four, two snipers and two scouts. "One is none and two is one" was the sniper motto.

From a personality standpoint, the Marine Corps wanted men who could turn off their emotions like a light switch. They needed to be able to look through the scope, with cold precision work out the geometry and environmental physics of the shot, wait patiently for the go ahead, then pull the trigger and kill whatever or whoever they were looking at. Not everyone could do it. A certain type of personality was necessary, which is why the Marines gave psychological tests to the new recruits to see where they might find the best fit. Cooke fit the psych profile they wanted, they just had to find out if he had the strength and determination which were also a necessary part of the equation.

Everything they threw at him, Cooke absorbed it. He soaked in all the abuse and never cracked. He had a mind that was naturally predisposed to mathematics, a rugged toughness, an insane level of determination, and the precision of a surgeon. He'd gotten the nickname "The Machine" during indoctrination, because he never stopped, and he didn't seem to have any emotions. He went after latrine duty as hard as climbing the wall, focused as much on polishing his boots as cleaning his rifle, and could spend all day behind a scope without losing focus.

It took three years in the Marine Corps before he got his chance to join a sniper platoon. After two years in the platoon he was invited to Scout Sniper school. After the thirteen weeks of intense Scout Sniper training, Cooke became a HOG. He, his rifle and his team were then called out to the Middle East to participate in the conflict with Iraq, removing the Iraqi forces from Kuwait and flushing them back into their own country.

Cooke was on rifle, his scout, Berkley from Newark, was scanning the land out ahead. There was nothing to see. Smoldering wreckage of the fleeing Iraqi army that had been absolutely decimated by the U.S. air strikes stretched on for miles. It was one of the single most decisive military victories in the history of mankind. It had been so one-sided, there wasn't even a straggler to put down.

"Nothing," Berkley said. Cooke responded by taking his eye away from the scope, blinking several times and taking a pull from the straw that was pushed into the drink packet in front of him. Even though it wasn't hot, it was extremely dry, and proper hydration was a fundamental to survival. "We're not going to get one today, sorry pal."

"Figured as much," Cooke replied.

"Not really anything moving at all for practice, even," Berkley said, scanning the landscape in front of them with his binoculars. "Wait, wait. I see something moving out there. Track towards one o'clock, about fifteen hundred meters. There's a burned out truck, movement by the passenger door. Target obscured by the open door. What is that do you think?"

"A dog maybe."

"Whatever it is," Berkley said. "It's got a hold of something out there. Looks like maybe a corpse from that truck. Whatcha think? Fifteen hundred meters. Oh, yeah. It's a dog, I can see it now. Fourteen-eighty?"

"I put it at fourteen-forty."

"Wind is blowing north, nice tail wind at about seven miles per hour."

"Yup," Cooke said.

"Yeah, it's a charred corpse. Looks like it got one of the limbs loose. It's dragging it away. Want to take the shot?"

"Yup." Cooke breathed out. The Machine became one with his rifle. He compensated for the wind and elevation through the scope. The bullet would actually perform an elongated arch into the target. His target was less than a meter square. An impossible shot. The trigger was an extension of his finger now, and he lightly squeezed it back. The rifle fired. Through their scopes they watched the feral dog nearly explode in half. A cloud of dust kicked up eight feet in the air behind the animal, where the bullet had slammed into the desert floor.

"Bingo! You got it!" Berkley reached over and patted Cooke on the helmet.

The dog pulled itself along on its front paws for a few feet, dragging its entrails through the sand. Finally, giving in to its mortal wound moments later, it fell to the ground and died. Berkley put his binoculars down and took a sip from his juice packet. Cooke stayed on scope and watched the dead animal for another five minutes. He felt no remorse, no regret.

"You boys done shooting animals and giving away our position?" A voice came from behind them. Their replacements had arrived and they settled in.

"Giving it away to who? There's nobody out here," Berkley said with noted disappointment in his voice.

The replacement team was Rodriguez and Johnson. They hadn't gotten a kill yet either. They were all just a couple of kill-virgins laying in the sand half way around the world from where each of them had grown up, waiting for some camel jockey to come into range.

"We're on it," Johnson, the scout of the team, said, officially relieving Cooke's team. He looked through his scope at the site of the kill. "Nice, over fourteen hundred meters. Aced him. Maybe we'll get lucky."

"Aw, you killed the puppy," Rodriguez said as he tracked over to the kill with his scope. They all laughed. Some called it gallows humor, others called it just a morbid streak, but one thing was for sure, snipers had their own brand of humor and most of it was a little twisted.

"Happy hunting," Cooke said, slowly backing away from the point on his belly. He paused to fish his HOG's tooth out and plant a dry kiss on it.

Maybe next time.

He cradled his M40a1 rifle like a newborn. The way a sniper cared for his rifle was the stuff of legend. He was constantly cleaning, holding, painting, sleeping with, talking to or otherwise fondling his M40a1. It was a Remington 700 with a 10x Unertl scope and a McMillian fiberglass stock with epoxy. When he'd first gotten her, she was black and he simply called her Beauty. When they received their deployment orders, she was painted for desert combat. Each sniper spent hours perfecting the paint on their rifle, especially since there wasn't much else to do in the giant sandbox.

When they got back to barracks, Cooke walked past the board and took note of the progress from that day. When the battalion had set camp, a cork board had appeared and a collection was made. A picture of each guy's significant other went up on the board and a grid was drawn. The bets began. They all were betting on which wife or girlfriend would end up with another guy before they got back from their tour. As the bets increased for one girl or another, their picture climbed the grid towards the top. The fatties stayed near the bottom, but the hotties shot to the top. It was just a little extra psychological pressure on each of the men. The hotties with kids were especially targeted as cheaters. Each time there was a confirmed break-up, the payouts were made and the pictures were reset to the bottom of the grid.

Cooke's wife of two years had climbed the grid yet again. The boys were enamored with her picture, and he knew some of them would go to sleep at night thinking of her. But she was a good girl, from a simple family in Pennsylvania. They had two kids, a boy and a girl, ages three and five. The kids had come before the marriage, much to the disappointment of the simple family from Pennsylvania. Cooke himself had grown up most of his life in New York City, though he had been born in Knoxville, Tennessee. His mother worked Off-Broadway productions and made just enough to keep food on the table. He was an outcast in school with his southern twang, which he worked hard to hide. He was also quite intelligent, and that made him even more of a target. He hated school in the city, but it made him tough.

A bully had once tried to shake him down for his lunch money. The bully succeeded, but later in the day, after the bully had already forgotten about the conflict, Cooke cracked him across the back of the head with a length of pipe he'd found. After the bully got out of the hospital he was different. He didn't say much to anybody and he never laid a finger on Cooke again. Cooke had escaped getting caught for his revenge, but most of the kids knew who had done the bully in, and they left Cooke alone as well.

It was that toughness that got him through boot camp and then through the hazing when he joined the sniper platoon, and then the sniper school itself. It was that toughness that kept him from breaking when he got the letter from his wife informing him that she was filing for divorce and taking the kids back to live with her parents in Wilkes-Barre, Pennsylvania. The Machine didn't have time to shed a tear, there was a war on.

He decided that he was going to give Berkley, his scout and the closest thing he had to a friend, a little gift. He told his partner that it wasn't going well, and he should bet heavily on that fact. His wife's picture slid up the grid. He figured he'd push it as much as possible to get Berkley a big take. It worked too well. Her picture shot up the grid, and now it might appear like he was sandbagging. He'd have to play a waiting game to not raise suspicion. But she kept going up and up. With another move up the board, he realized they had to pull the trigger on it. They would lose everything if one of the other spouses became a con-firmed cheater before he posted the letter.

Cooke stripped his weapon, cleaned and oiled it care-fully. He always used the good stuff, Q20 oil kept the sand out and the action working smoothly. He carefully reas-sembled the rifle, then marched up to the divorce board and pinned his letter on his wife's picture. He pushed the pin right through her forehead. Headshot. The rest of the guys in his platoon couldn't run fast enough to read it.

The hoots and hollers started, and money changed hands. Berkley took in nearly a thousand dollars. All the pictures were reset at the bottom of the grid to much curs-ing and chest thumping. Cooke's wife's photo was pulled off the board. He tossed it into one of the latrines.

Cooke would never miss a payment for his kids, and he never spoke to his wife after the divorce. He'd just send the money. After getting back from Kuwait he'd called his former father-in-law, just to see how the kids were doing. The man to whose daughter he was once married barely said three syllables. He practically grunted through the whole conversation, and when Cooke asked how his kids were doing, he was told that his ex-wife's kids were fine. Message received loud and clear: you weren't there when they were born, you weren't there when they learned to walk, and you weren't there when they started school. They aren't your kids. Don't even think about coming around now.

· · ·

It had to be at least 90 degrees. The tarred roof absorbed then radiated the sun's heat, making it feel like an oven. It didn't help that the air had stagnated and there wasn't a breeze to be had. August in New York City could be that way.

Cooke was perched on the edge of the building overlooking the bank. It had been surrounded for nearly an hour now, after the silent alarm had automatically dialed into the police station. Two men had entered the bank with handguns, shotguns, masks and a poorly written note that was shoved in front of the teller. The alarm was tripped and police were there within two minutes. Now the would-be bank robbers were trapped, and they did the only thing they thought could save them from a doomed operation: they took hostages and barricaded themselves in.

Michael had decided to move back to New York City and become one of New York's finest after he left the Marine Corps. His combat experience was a plus, and the fact that he had his HOG's tooth helped him get fast tracked into the New York City ESU as a sharpshooter.

It was a good career move. Not only was he set with a good paying job with an exceptional pension plan, but he was also able to enroll in evening classes to earn a degree in forensic science. New York City was a far cry from the sniper perch he manned for eight months on the Kuwaiti border. It took a little time to adjust, but once he did he thoroughly enjoyed it. There was always something to do, and always overtime for which one could volunteer. It turned out that life in the ESU really wasn't much different than the military, as they were constantly training.

The ESU, or Emergency Service Unit, was the multi-faceted team that took on high-risk operations within the New York City metropolitan area. Pretty much anything that went above and beyond the scope of the everyday patrol or criminal investigations unit was handled by ESU. They provided the Special Weapons and Tactical, or SWAT, support for situations like a barricaded suspect or hostage situations and would even respond to hazmat calls. The ESU recruited heavily from the USMC sniper school for its tactical weapons team. So, for Cooke it was a perfect fit: he wanted ESU and ESU wanted him.

When the call came in for the bank robbery, it was going to be Cooke's first chance to get behind the scope for ESU in a real life scenario. His team was briefed on the layout of the bank and the surrounding buildings on their way, and he made the choice to position two blocks away because of the better line of sight through the front doors. Another team was allocated to the building directly across from the bank on the second floor, but Cooke didn't like that angle and opted for his preferred position. He had a fairly good scout in Kolinski, so he was satisfied that if a shot had to be made, his team would take it.

The heat was treacherous, but to Cooke, it was like being back in Kuwait during that summer of '91. He'd sweated off his body weight in water more times than he wished to remember, so it was almost comforting to be back in the saddle with sweat in one eye and the scope in the other.

He'd kept his M40a1 rifle from the USMC at the end of his enlistment. He didn't know a single sniper who didn't do the same thing. He'd gotten it cleared for use on the job within his first week and then meticulously stripped the desert war paint from it and returned it to its natural black. Beauty was back, and she was dialed in to perfection.

"Perps moving at twelve o'clock," Kolinski said.

"I got him," Cooke replied in a hushed voice.

"Command, this is Falcon two. We've got a visual on one of the perps. He's got two female hostages in front of him, using them as shields. It looks like he's duct taped his hand to the handle of the sawed off shotgun and the business end to one of the hostage's neck. Over," Kolinski had broadcast his last bit of information back to command down on the street.

"Falcon two, command copies. We see him. Over." The

reply was curt. They were planning to wait this one out. There hadn't been much indication that those who made such decisions had even considered putting a bullet down there.

"I don't think we're going to get the go ahead for a shot," Kolinski said.

"Probably not. With two perps, we'd have to get a bang-bang shot. No way can I see us getting clearance to move forward with the kill." Despite his doubts, Cooke kept his mind at the ready. As soon as they said shoot, he had to be able to pull the trigger and make the shot.

No sooner had the words of doubt left his lips when a shot rang out, and the hostage who was taped to the shotgun fell to the ground. The other hostage ran out into the street, screaming. The perp was now duct taped to a dead body. Everything had just changed. Even though it looked through the scope like a stupid accident by a stupid criminal, an innocent hostage had just been murdered. ESU wasn't going to allow another one to be harmed. The idiot perp was ripping at the duct tape trying to detach himself from the bloody corpse.

"Falcon one, Falcon two, do you copy?"

"Falcon one here," came the first reply.

"Falcon two copies," Kolinski said.

"This is a command order, shoot to kill, coordinate the shots. We need both perps down, now."

"Copy." The two replies came in rapid succession.

"I've got duct tape guy," Cooke said. "Need to take him now before he gets free."

"We've got a shot," Kolinski said.

"We've got nothing," Falcon one's reply came. "Take it if you got it."

Cooke heard the reply, breathed out, and caressed the trigger. A smooth, even squeeze and the rifle jumped in his hands.

Bang!

The bullet flew out of the end of the rifle at two thousand, five hundred, and fifty-five feet per second. They were approximately one hundred yards away, which meant that in less than a third of a second after leaving the end of the barrel, the bullet shattered the glass window and entered the chest of the perp who had just murdered the innocent hostage. When a bullet strikes a human body with that velocity, it causes an almost supersonic burst within the flesh. It has a ripping, explosive effect that has been known to practically tear a person in half.

What Cooke saw through the scope could only be described as horrific, yet he didn't flinch an eyelash. The bullet entered the perp just below the collar bone, and dropped him to the ground immediately. The bullet proof jacket the perp had been wearing was no match for the sniper's bullet.

Reload.

Re-aim.

As if on cue, the other perp ran over to his partner to investigate. Cooke didn't hesitate for a moment.

Bang!

Dead.

A clean shot through the side just below the shoulder.

The bullet traversed the rib cage ripping out heart and lungs before exiting the other side and burying itself in the marble floor. The scene forty feet below them and a hundred yards away was like a slaughter house. The ESU hazmat team was already mobilizing.

"Command, this is Falcon two, both perps are down, repeat both perps are down," Kolisnki almost cheered into his headset.

"Confirmed, Falcon two. Good shooting, Cooke."

Cooke stayed on scope just in case, but the rest of the ESU tactical team stormed the bank and started escorting the hostages out to safety.

"Not bad for a Monday morning, huh," Kolinski said. "Let's go get some lunch after this, I'm starving."

It had been nearly eleven years to the day since Cooke had become a Marine. Eleven years to get his first kill. Thirteen seconds to get his second. Cooke pulled out his HOG's tooth and gave it a kiss.

• • •

The day the mass-murdering terrorists flew the planes into the Twin Towers, Cooke was in Cozumel, Mexico on vacation. He spent the morning snorkeling on the reef and flirting with two college coeds who were spending a semester abroad. He didn't even hear about the attacks until he got back to the hotel room in the afternoon. He spent the rest of the vacation watching CNN in his room or at the hotel bar with a tall drink in his hand. A week's vacation became two weeks, then three as he couldn't even get on a flight home. He had the money, that wasn't the issue. It was a matter of flights not flying. The airlines had been shut down over the United States affecting most of the air travel around the world. He found a few other Americans who were trapped in paradise just like him, and they would meet daily to see if anyone had gotten lucky and was able to book a flight home. After a week of all planes in the U.S. being grounded, there was a lot of playing catch-up trying to get stranded travelers home. He needed to be with his team.

When he finally did return, it was like going directly into a pressure cooker. Several ESU officers had been killed when they had entered the South Tower and climbed to around the twentieth floor before the building succumbed to the extreme damage and collapsed. The day ended up having the largest number of active duty police deaths from a single force in a single day in the history of the United States. Cooke lost a couple of friends, and he, himself, had actually been counted as one of the dead until he had returned from Cozumel.

After September 11, 2001, life in the ESU changed. He contemplated reenlisting with the Marines, especially after the war in Afghanistan began. However he stayed with the ESU, and eventually retired at a relatively young age of fifty-two. It was just time.

As she aged, his mother began to receive better roles on Broadway. There was no question from where Michael had received his machine-like work ethic. He went to see her many times, now that he was in the city, and was impressed by what he saw. She had become a star. He never told her he was in the audience, and she never knew that he would come almost every Thursday to watch her. His mother worked until the day before she died. Michael got the call and headed down to the hospital. He said a simple goodbye to the woman who gave him life and headed over to her lawyer's office to settle the estate. He was amazed at the wealth she had accumulated over the final years of her life. Within the week Cooke had deposited the money into his account and retired from the NYPD.

He had purchased a small house in the northern Catskills nearly four years before he had retired. The price was right, and it gave him something to do on the weekends. Over the course of those four years he spent as many summer weekends as possible at the house, gutting it right down to the studs and then completely refurbishing it. He promised himself that as soon as the refurbishment was completed, no matter how old or young he still was, he was calling it quits and moving up to his retirement home. It took him two years to finish the house to the point where he called it done. He broke his promise to himself and stayed on the force for another two years. He didn't even go up to the house one whole summer, leaving it winterized for nearly fourteen straight months. It was when his mother died that he suddenly had a feeling of mortality. He decided he didn't want to end up like her, working to the very last day of his life with no time to relax and enjoy himself. Once his mind was made up, there was no turning back and he put in for early retirement. He boxed up his modest apartment and moved up to his new home.

My retirement home. So that's what this is. I'm an old man and I've shuffled myself off to the Catskills to wither and die.

He set the last box on the living room floor. The box was full of DVDs and old VHS tapes. He was going to watch a lot of old movies, drink a lot of beer and read a lot of books. He promised himself he wasn't going to do anything constructive for at least a month. Well besides put things away and organize a little. If there was one thing he couldn't stand it was an unorganized mess.

The first morning in his new permanent home he was up at 4am. He decided to go for a walk around his property. It was fifty acres that stretched back from the road on a gravel driveway. He'd thought about getting it paved, but decided he liked knowing when someone was pulling into the driveway, and tires on gravel gave a distinctive sound. The house itself was roughly 1200 square feet with a large deck and hot tub which he'd installed himself. The yard rolled down towards a meandering creek which ran the entire length of the valley. His property climbed the hill on the opposite side of the creek and terminated at the peak of the hill. One of the reasons he liked the layout so much was that it would allow him to target practice across the valley without fear of a stray bullet going through a windshield or into another retiree sitting on his back porch watching the sunset.

He held a pedometer in his hand and found himself mentally taking stock of notable features of the land that he could use to gauge distance from the back of his house. After nearly an hour of his walk, which included crossing the creek twice, he decided that maybe he should get a dog to keep him company on these morning excursions.

Maybe if I had a dog I wouldn't be triangulating my property in preparation for a kill shot. What am I going to shoot out here, a ground hog?

It wasn't a new problem, though he actually didn't think it was a problem at all. Even after he'd returned from Kuwait and started with the NYPD he would run the calculations in his mind from his position atop steps of the Museum of Natural History to the hotdog vendor down the street. It was in his blood. He was "The Machine." You couldn't just switch it off.

As soon as he got back inside he brewed up a strong cup of coffee and turned on the television. There wasn't much going on at six in the morning. He was only a few chapters away from finishing a novel, so he thought he'd take his coffee and book out to the deck and enjoy the sunrise.

The novel ended with a ridiculous thud and the sunrise, though beautiful, wasn't nearly as inspiring as he'd hoped. The first sunrise of retirement, he'd heard from other retired cops, was one of the most refreshing moments of their lives. Michael didn't feel it. Maybe it wasn't his time yet. Maybe he should have stayed with the ESU for a few more years.

You'll make yourself crazy if you keep thinking like that. It's over. It's time to find something else to do with your life.

Finally, frustrated with the boredom, he decided to hop in his truck and head into town. It was about a ten minute ride. He needed to do some grocery shopping anyway, so it would be a functional trip, not just an excuse to not be alone with himself and his thoughts.

It was just eight in the morning when he parked the car in front of the Peachy Keen diner. He took the steps two at a time and jingled the door chimes loudly as he pulled the door open a bit too aggressively. Everyone in the diner, about six people total, all turned to look at him. He smiled self-consciously and took a seat at the counter.

There was a fella at the other end of the counter who looked like an angry giant in flannel. He was scooping Frosted Flakes into his mouth with a spoon that he held like a baby holds a rattle, full fisted. The milk was dribbling into his beard, and after enough had accumulated, he wiped it away with his flannel sleeve.

"Morning," the guy behind the counter said. He had an ethnicity to his voice that Cooke couldn't quite place. "What can I get you? Coffee to start?"

"Yeah, I'll take a coffee and an orange juice, and some hotcakes with bacon."

"Sure thing. Coming right up for you."

"Do you have a paper," Cooke asked.

"What's that?" The man behind the counter hadn't quite heard him over the din of the television, conversations, clinking of silverware on plates and slurping of Frosted Flakes.

"A newspaper, is there a newspaper?"

"You can buy one off the rack out front, we have The Daily Review from the city, and we have the town paper called *The Mountain Star*." Michael saw the rack just inside the door and went over to grab one of each. They also had *The Wall Street Journal* and *The New York Post*, but he'd read enough of those two publications when he lived in New York. He was hoping for a little local flavor now.

One of the couples in the diner got up to leave, and said goodbye to the man behind the counter and called him "Seemo". Michael made a note of the name. One of the things he did very well is remember names and faces. It wasn't quite a photographic memory, but it was pretty accurate. As his coffee arrived, and he started into the "city" newspaper, he thought about what "Seemo" might possibly be a nickname for.

Being from THE city, Michael thought it comical that the locals used that moniker for the city of Oneonta. Officially it was a city, but a relatively tiny one in the grand scheme of things. The newspaper reflected such. The local news from the previous day was pretty uneventful. A few accidents, a convenience store robbery. A new company was thinking about moving into one of the boarded up buildings downtown. They were an internet start-up company, which meant they would flame out pretty quickly. A drug bust of minimum size occurred, and a whole bunch of old people died. Cooke was amazed at how many of them had gotten over eighty years old and a few were over ninety. If he played his cards right and kept himself healthy, he might have a whole thirty to forty years of retirement to enjoy.

The hotcakes and bacon arrived along with the orange juice, and he dug into it quickly, surprised at how much of an appetite he had been harboring. The gorilla sitting at the end of the counter stood, put money down on the counter and trudged out. A group of elderly women came in dressed up in what looked like their Sunday's finest. They were chattering non-stop with each other as they found a table; everything from grand children to

medication to bowel movements. Michael had to smirk.
He continued on with his reading of the paper from the
"city" then switched over to the local *Mountain Star*. It
wasn't more than eight pages and was a weekly paper apparently. It was truly an old-time local paper. No national
news, just the village of Coopers Hollow and surrounding
villages. Cooke checked and saw that the circulation of the
newspaper was claimed to be 10,000 and the price was two
dollars.

The Mountain Star featured articles about a local artist
who had made a big sale, school events, and news about a
new hair salon that was opening. There was a missing cat,
and a surprising number of items for sale in the small classified section. A few of the local bars ran ads including one
called Taylor's Taproom. He needed to find a good bar. It
only took about ten minutes to finish the whole paper after
reading just about every article and advertisement. He felt
satisfied that he had gottten his two dollars' worth.

The weather came on the news that had been playing
on the television. The station was out of Albany, but the
weatherman indicated that there was going to be some
trouble for the Northern Catskill and Berkshire mountains. A storm was coming up the country, and it looked
like it was going to arrive at night after the higher elevations dropped below the freezing mark.

"For the third year in a row, it looks like snow in
October for the Catskills. And this could be a doozie.
Snow won't start until around ten o'clock tonight, but
when it gets going, it's going to keep going right on
until morning. Up to two inches an hour in some of the
higher elevations. When it's all said and done, we might

be looking at a foot and a half of snow. But don't worry, that snow won't stick around. By Wednesday we will have high temperatures in the fifties, if you can believe that. And then right on through the rest of the week we should have fairly nice and perhaps even a bit seasonally warm weather."

"So it's not all bad news," said the anchor.

"No, but if you're thinking about heading out into the mountains, get there before ten o'clock tonight because it's going to get messy."

"Thanks, Paul," the anchor concluded. He continued on with his broadcast about some politician getting caught in a scandal of infidelity. Cooke wasn't interested. He'd finished his breakfast and pulled out some cash to pay.

"So, Seemo, is it?" Michael asked. "You own this place?"

"Yes sir, for almost thirty years I own this diner," Seemo said.

"You've probably seen just about everything then. You get a real sense of humanity watching so many people," Cooke said.

And lose a sense of humanity watching them through a scope, he thought but didn't say.

"You a cop?"

"Retired. NYPD Emergency Services Unit. How did you know?"

"I seen enough cops in my time to know. You pretty young to be retired, no?"

"Yeah, well, I served in the Marine Corps back in the

first Gulf War, then came back and got a job with the
New York Police Department, and when my mother died
a month ago, well, I had enough money to retire and not
worry about much. I bought the place called the Eagles
Nest just north of town. I've actually been working on it
for a few years now, but I never spent any time in town
here."

"My mother is still alive. Almost one hundred years
old! She drinks a glass of wine and smokes a cigar every
day of her life. If only we could live so good, heh?"

"No kidding." Cooke finished paying, and stood to
leave. "Great breakfast, I'll have to make a habit of coming in here. Really nice to meet you Seemo, I'm Michael
Cooke."

"Mr. Cooke, nice to meet you too." Seemo reached
over and shook the man's hand.

"Come in every day and you will see a different group.
Except for Tubby, he's here every day for his Frosted
Flakes. Today it's the old ladies, tomorrow it could be the
Chief of Police, Jack McMurphy. Then sometimes we get
the preacher man in here. Always somebody to talk to or
watch. You picked a good place to retire."

"Tubby? Was that the big fella who was in here
earlier?"

"Yeah. Sad thing, really. His mama is crazy and he's
a little too. He's good as gold though. Give you the shirt
off his back and help you work all day and never ask for a
penny in return. Good kid. But he's not a kid. He's older
now. He still just acts like one, is all. A little slow in the
head. You know."

"Interesting. Well take care, see you tomorrow if the snow doesn't stop me."

"Take care, Mr. Cooke."

Michael headed back out to his vehicle, a big Ford Super Duty pickup truck that was a couple of years old. It was murder on fuel going up and over these mountains, but he liked the comfort and hauling capacity. It came in handy when he was lugging sheetrock up from the home repair store. Plus the four-wheel-drive would be a necessity once the snow started. If the news was accurate, there would be a pile of it in the morning. He'd hate to be caught out in it with anything less than what he was driving.

By the time he got home, he had decided to chop some wood for the wood stove and settle into the big overstuffed chair and lose himself in one of the books he'd been meaning to finish for months now.

He awoke with a start, his heart pounding in his chest. He looked at his watch and was surprised that it read 3am. The book he'd been reading had slid to the floor. Perhaps that was the noise that woke him, the book slapping down on the hardwood floor. He'd almost finished it. With only but a few chapters left however, sleep had won over. It had been years since he'd fallen asleep doing anything other than trying to fall asleep.

He put the recliner back into the upright position and slowly stood up. His back felt tight after chopping the wood, and falling asleep in the recliner hadn't helped. The fire in the wood stove had long since burned down to ash and a chill had settled onto the room. With a bit of dry mouth, he went to the kitchen, got a glass of water from the fridge and looked out the kitchen window onto the deck. He could hardly believe that there was about eight inches of snow already, and it looked like it wasn't about to let up. Setting the glass down in the sink, he headed off to bed.

As he laid there, staring up at the ceiling, listening to the wind howl outside, he realized that he felt alone. He thought back to his life and what he'd been through and it struck him that he'd never really felt lonely before. He always had a job to do, a duty of some sort, so that all the personal losses he had suffered over the years never had a chance to penetrate his heart.

He missed his mother, though he wasn't much of a son to her. She'd spent her life acting. That was her true love. He was always an afterthought for her, but he still loved her, he guessed. He wouldn't have gone to watch her on stage all those Thursday nights if he hadn't.

He didn't miss his ex-wife at all, but he was curious as to what the kids were up to. He knew she had remarried and he'd signed off on the papers allowing the new husband to officially adopt them and change their names. He had never known them, so it really didn't make much sense to make a fuss about it. They would both be in college now. He entertained the thought of maybe looking them up and going for a visit, but quickly discarded the idea as ludicrous.

He hadn't been with a woman in a long time. Mostly because he didn't have the time. He was always pulling overtime duty when he could, stockpiling his pension, shoving as much money into his savings account as possible. He'd date here and there, but never anything serious, he just didn't have the time to commit to a real relationship. But now, he had the time, now he found himself thinking about family, thinking about children. As he slid off to sleep, he found himself thinking about women.

Outside the bright sun was shining down on the melting snow. It had taken him most of the morning to get everything shoveled out the way he wanted. He'd cleared the driveway with his snow thrower, and then shoveled out the sidewalk and the deck. He finished up by brushing off the hot tub and striping naked right there on the deck and sliding in. The house was secluded and well off the road, so he didn't have anything to worry about. He found it liberating and exciting. The exertion of the morning, the skinny dip in the hot tub, and the welcoming warmth of the sun all put him in a great mood. He decided it was a good day for a trip into town and maybe a stroll and some lunch.

He parked his Ford F-250 in front of the Peachy Keen but decided to go for a walk before he went in for lunch.

Heading up Main Street he looked at the different store fronts, some of which were empty with for rent signs posted. The short stroll led him past a nice little library. He decided then and there that he needed a library card and found his way inside to speak to the librarian about it.

The librarian was nice and helped him find the military and travel section. He wanted to make sure there was something worth borrowing before he went and committed to something like a library card.

Always on reconnaissance, aren't you, Mike. What are you going to do next, use binoculars to check out the video store?

He picked out a couple of books he found interesting and started heading towards the checkout desk with the librarian in tow. He nearly collided with a woman who must have come in while they had been chatting. He stopped short and gave her a once over. She was probably in her mid forties, and was radiant. She had shoulder length brownish blond hair and almond brown eyes. She had a nice figure as well. Her legs looked strong and slender. Though the jacket she was wearing came down to cover her backside, he was sure it was as perky as the rest of her. He found her very attractive.

"Excuse me," he said. "I didn't mean to startle you."

He watched her reaction. She smiled, and then looked down, as if she were embarrassed. Francis, the librarian introduced her as Mrs. Graves.

Married. Too bad. Some lucky guy gets to come home to her every night. Must be nice.

"Oh Francis, just Gloria is fine."

He asked her about her books and what she'd found. For some reason he found himself truly attracted to her. The small talk soon began to wind down, so he continued on with the process of getting registered for his library card and checking out the books.

"So, what's the deal with her? You looked pretty surprised that she spoke to me."

"Surprised doesn't really capture the emotion. Gloria has lived in the area for over a decade now, and I'm probably her closest friend here, and even I have to call her Mrs. Graves. I've never just called her Gloria. And she very rarely talks to people she's never met before. And she never shakes hands or hugs."

"Really? What happened, I mean, to cause her to act that way?"

"I'm not sure. I've never asked and she's never told me. To see her with her daughter, though, is like looking at a completely different person," Francis said as she gave Michael the paperwork to fill out.

"Oh, she has a daughter, too?" He set to filling out his new address and other contact information in the form.

She's locked in. Married with a daughter.

"Her daughter is off to college, and I think she lost her husband years ago. He wasn't with them when they moved up, and she never spoke of him."

"Interesting," Michael said with a smile.

Okay, game change. Single woman, empty nest syndrome. Maybe she's lonely as well. Might be worth asking her for dinner, or starting slow with a cup of coffee at the Peachy Keen.

"She's usually here on Tuesdays, around this time. Just in case you were curious," the librarian said somewhat bashfully. "Sometimes she's back on Thursday's too, if she doesn't like the books she borrowed."

"I appreciate the information," he said, with a wink. Oh, he'd be back on Thursday, and every Tuesday from that point on until he got her to go to dinner with him. He'd just received his new mission.

As he walked out the front door, he thought about his

ex-wife and how unready he was to get married. Truthfully she had been the one to push for it, and when he'd signed up for the Marine Corps, she was completely supportive. Being away for so long, however, changed people. She wasn't the same when he tried to talk to her again. He knew she'd been with other men, but it didn't break his heart. He was disappointed, but he was also realistic. He'd put her in a tough position and she couldn't handle it. You had to know the weaknesses of your personnel. The team was only as strong as the weakest individual. He never saw her under pressure, had never seen how she dealt with adversity. He was just a boy himself, after all, he didn't even know what to look for in a woman. He had fallen into the classic trap of believing that if she was beautiful on the outside, she had to be the same on the inside.

Now, however, there was someone who sparked his curiosity. He'd find out a little more about her and be ready for a potential Thursday encounter. His stomach growled and he decided it was time for a little lunch.

"Good morning, Mr. Cooke. Or should I say, good afternoon."

"Good afternoon, Seemo." Michael said as he took a seat at the food counter. He looked around the diner and saw a different crowd than the previous day. An officer of the law was at the counter. The patch on his shoulder said Coopers Hollow Police Department.

"Officer," Cooke said, giving the man a nod. They made introductions, and idle chit chat for a bit. Then a woman strode in and sat down right between them, blocking his line of sight with the patrolman. It was a pet peeve, but he hated it when people would block his line of sight. He wasn't sure if it irked others the same way, but he felt himself getting a little worked up over it. To top it off, she was really starting to hassle the cop. That pissed him off too.

"Excuse me," he said, after she had just informed the patrolman that she planned to park herself there at the counter and badger him through the rest of his lunch. "I don't want to seem rude, but you kind of interrupted a conversation I was having with Jack here. So, if you would, kindly excuse us."

She tried to stare him down. She was a pretty girl and Cooke imagined that she was used to being aggressive with the men around here, getting her way most of the time. But he was having none of it. He glared right back at her, and she caved. She got her lunch to go, and left them for a bit more conversation before the patrolman stood to leave. The cop argued with Seemo good-naturedly about paying the bill, then dismissed himself and left.

Cooke ate his lunch in silence, watching the news on the television. He asked for a refill on his soda and found himself just sitting there, wasting time. The news went off, and the soap operas started up. He watched about five minutes and had seen enough. He stood, paid his bill, and left.

Content with his morning's excursion, he climbed into his cobalt blue Ford Super Duty truck and headed home.

That's right, this is home now.

Wednesday was uneventful; more chopping wood, more walking the property, this time all the way up to the tree line on the other side of the creek. From that vantage point, you could see the house and the driveway that broke through the trees from the road. If he was hunting himself, this would be the point where he would be stationed. It would make for taking out an easy target. He was perhaps three-hundred meters away. For someone with his abilities it would not be a difficult shot.

By the evening, he found himself getting excited about the prospects of seeing Gloria again the following day. He finished the travel book. It was nearly five-hundred pages about visiting Costa Rica, with a large section on living there permanently. Quite informative, but probably fifteen years old. A lot had changed in the last fifteen years. He'd probably take his laptop into town and do a little more research at one of the high speed connections. He knew the diner didn't have a hotspot, but there was a coffee shop next to the hair salon on Main Street. As he washed his face before bed he took a good look in the mirror and thought maybe he'd get a trim tomorrow too. Clean it up a bit around the ears and neck.

He crawled into bed and found himself thinking about Gloria again. It was stupid. He'd just met her once, but there was something there that caught him just right. He faded off to sleep, dreaming about the woman he'd met at the library.

Thursday morning he was up before dawn. He decided to go for a jog out on the road. After going about a mile and a half, he turned back home. He showered, shaved, splashed on some cologne – but not too much - picked out some casual clothes that were a bit nicer than usual, and got himself ready for another excursion into town.

He was ready to go at seven-thirty and had to keep finding excuses not to leave yet. All of the dishes in the sink were now washed and put away, and he even changed a load of laundry. He looked at the clock again: ten after eight. That was good enough.

Cooke hopped into his truck and headed into town. He parked on Main Street in front of the hair salon. It didn't open until ten, and neither did the library, so he walked back to the Peachy Keen diner for a little breakfast.

The door jingled as he entered, and he found a spot at the counter. Tubby was at the opposite end, shoveling Frosted Flakes into his mouth as he watched the television. There were two women sitting at a table against the far wall. It looked like Gloria from behind, but he wasn't sure. He was probably just starting to obsess over her. That wasn't healthy. She was talking to a younger girl, maybe in her twenties. The younger girl had curly blond hair and wore a vintage style military jacket. She looked at him and caught him staring. He averted his gaze, a little frustrated with himself for getting caught.

He ordered some food from Seemo, and tried to pay attention to the television, but kept stealing glances at the two women. It took just a few minutes for his food to be ready, and Seemo brought it over.

"I didn't get a look at her face when I came in," Michael said in a bit of a hushed tone. "But is that Gloria over there?"

"Yeah," Seemo replied, immediately getting the reason behind the question. "That's her daughter with her. You interested in asking Gloria out for dinner, maybe?"

"Maybe. She's pretty," he said as he took a bite of his French toast after breaking the egg yolk with the piece on his fork.

"Pretty. Smart. She's got money too, I think. Anyway, go for it. You wouldn't be the first guy to get shot down trying to ask Miss Gloria out on a date. Wouldn't even be the first one who got shot down asking her in this diner." Seemo laughed and turned to go back to the kitchen.

"You okay, Thaddeaus?" Cooke heard Seemo ask Tubby. The large, flannel clad man gave no a response. Seemo shrugged his shoulders and went back into the kitchen.

Michael ate his breakfast, and hoped they didn't get up to leave before he was done. They looked like maybe they were in a deep discussion about something. Her daughter had something of a distressed look on her face, but if his lip reading was worth anything, it looked like she was telling her mother that it would be okay. Everything would be fine.

Famous last words, Cooke thought to himself. *Just about the time someone says 'everything will be fine' the perp decides to start shooting hostages.*

He took one last sip of coffee, threw a ten and a few ones onto the counter and stood up. He walked over towards Gloria and her daughter.

"Good morning," he said. Gloria turned to look up at him. Her face was wrought with concern, and then suddenly it softened, brightened almost.

"Oh, hi!" The look of surprise on the daughter's face was unmistakable.

"I guess brilliant minds think alike. Nice morning for a little breakfast out," he said, trying to turn on the charm and hoping that some of his mother's acting ability had somehow made its way into his blood.

"Yes, I guess so. Michael, wasn't it? This is my daughter Starlett. She came up from Binghamton last night. She goes to school there." Starlett extended her hand and he shook it warmly.

"Binghamton University," he asked, getting a nod in response. "Good school, so I've heard. What are you taking there?"

"Business. I'm majoring in business marketing."

"Well, good luck with your studies," he said. "It was really nice seeing you again, Gloria. Really nice. We ought to grab a cup of coffee one of these days. Trade stories."

"Sure, I'd like that," Gloria replied. Starlett nearly spit out the coffee she was sipping.

"Well, ladies. I didn't mean to interrupt your breakfast. Have a nice rest of your day."

"You too, Michael. Or do you prefer Mike?"

"I kind of like the way you say Michael," he gave her a wink and turned for the door.

Always leave them wanting more, like mom used to say.

He overheard Starlett whisper to her mother as he walked out the door.

"Oh my God! Mom, he's hot!"

Michael Cooke walked up Main Street floating on cloud nine. He'd never been much of a ladies' man, but then again, he'd never had trouble talking to women either. He guessed maybe some of his late mother's acting abilities were in his DNA after all.

He walked past a young man who looked a little tired and nervous. The kid started up the steps into the Peachy Keen. Cooke had never seen him before, but he guessed there were a lot of people in town that he hadn't seen before. Even though he'd been coming up for a few years, he'd never spent hardly a moment in town. His previous habit took a different direction of travel when he came and went from New York City, and since he was doing so much repair, he usually would go down to Oneonta or Cobleskill to one of the big box home improvement stores for the needed supplies.

He noted that the hardware store was open, so he decided to poke his nose in and check it out. It was not just a hardware store, but an electronics store too. Cooke was pretty impressed that he could get a cell phone, keyboard, saw blade or stove pipe all in one location. He browsed for awhile, made some small talk with the clerk who looked like he wanted to be anyplace but there, and then checked his watch. It read nine-thirty. It was still a half hour before the library or hair salon opened.

He thought maybe he'd walk the entire Main Street to see what other shops were available. As he walked out the door, he saw what looked like a scuffle going on in front of the Peachy Keen. It looked like two guys were roughing up the nervous kid who'd just gone in. Cooke still had law enforcement in his blood. He couldn't help himself but start walking down the sidewalk towards the fight.

When he was about fifty feet away, Gloria and Starlett

came running out of the diner yelling at the men. One of them turned and pushed Starlett to the ground. Cooke picked up his pace. Suddenly a police car zoomed past, sirens blaring. The tires screeched as it slammed on its brakes and came to a halt by the fight. A silver haired officer in a Coopers Hollow Police uniform hopped out and ran over to the fight.

Cooke was almost to the group, when one of the toughs turned on the cop and hit him hard. The old cop went down and Cooke's blood began to boil. The Machine switched on.

Chapter 9

His son had taken to calling him the Silver Fox, now that his hair was almost completely gray. There were a lot worse things sons called their fathers, he knew, so he didn't mind too much. It was a reminder that he'd gotten quite a bit older, however, and he didn't like that so much. He still had his sharp intellect, it was just that his body wasn't what it used to be. For a man of his age, he was in exceptional shape. He would put men twenty years his junior to shame. In fact it was only recently that his own son outlasted him on their annual trek up to the top of Mt. Pratt. It was a tougher climb than it had ever been, but he didn't give up. He made it to the top, he just had to take a few more breaks than ever before. Getting old sucked.

Jack McMurphy Sr. was sitting in his police cruiser outside the farm equipment store just east of Coopers Hollow as he thought about how old he was getting. His lower back had been hurting for the last few weeks and it didn't seem to be going away. He'd taken most of the easy calls and sent his son and the other Patrolman out on any calls that required anything greater than taking notes.

The reason he was here was because there had been another case of vandalism on the building and some of the equipment out in front of the Elkland Brothers Farm

Equipment dealership over night. The owners, John and Jude Elkland, had just opened the new location. Their father, Roger Elkland, had started Elkland Farm Supply nearly fifty years earlier, and had turned it into a thriving family business. When the old man had died nearly two years ago, a family row had started the likes of which Coopers Hollow hadn't seen in ages.

John and Jude had basically run the store for their father for the last twenty years, and were poised to inherit it. Roger had two other children: daughters named Sabrina and Tatum. The girls wanted nothing to do with working at the store, they preferred to pretend they were high society and run around with the idiots from the city, or cidiots, as Roger liked to call them. He knew he had spoiled the girls rotten, but he still loved them. In his will, he allocated five hundred thousand dollars each for the two girls, and the business to the boys in an even fifty-fifty split ownership.

If old Roger had been around after his death, the feud would have made him sick. Rather than take the half-million dollars each, the girls decided to sue their brothers for a share of the business as well, which they had heard from others in town was worth nearly twenty million dollars. They brought in high end lawyers from New York City who were friends of their cidiot friends. The trial was scheduled to occur just six months later. The lawyers for the two girls started billing before the ink was even dry on their contracts. The girls were so assured of their victory, that they both went out and bought expensive European cars, Sabrina a BMW, Tatum a Mercedes.

When the trial finally occurred, the Elkland Farm

Supply books were opened and all the financial numbers were put on display. The company was doing about three million dollars a year in sales, with a profit of about fifteen percent above operating costs. The money that the girls had gotten in the will had emptied the bank account which had kept the accumulated profits from the previous few years, leaving the company with only about twenty thousand dollars of cash assets. Most of the farm equipment was sold on consignment from the manufacturers, and the building was a simple steel structure without much value.

The lawyers for John and Jude were no match for the slick downstate sharks the girls had brought in. The trial was short and the verdict was in favor of the girls. They were to split all of the assets equally, overriding Roger Elkland's will.

The combined one million dollars the girls were to initially receive from the will were also part of the assets that were to be divided. When it was all said and done, the girls received two hundred fifty thousand dollars and one quarter control of Elkland Farm Supply each. They were then socked with the attorney's fees which totaled one third plus expenses. Those expenses totaled nearly two hundred thousand dollars. This meant that, after all the fees had been extracted from the settlement, the girls walked away with roughly seventy-five thousand dollars each and partial ownership of the business. The lawyers told them that it meant they would make millions of dollars in the years to come.

John and Jude spent a weekend deciding what they were going to do. By Sunday night they had arrived at the decision to take their combined three hundred forty-four thousand dollars, their lawyer had worked for a simple thirty-three percent, and open their own, competing store just on the outskirts of town. They quit their positions at the old store, surrendering their controlling interests to their sisters.

Within three months a new store was constructed and the name Elkland Brothers Farm Equipment went up on the front of the building. The farm equipment industry was still run by people who valued a man's word and were used to dealing with hard working folks. All it took was a few phone calls to their suppliers explaining what had happened, and all of the manufacturers that had worked with the old store pulled their dealership credentials from the sisters and moved them over to the brothers' new operation. The brothers also made an offer to every single one of their previous employees to come work for their new company. They all agreed. In the end, the sisters were left with an old building, sorely in need of repair, no manufacturers to deal with, and no employees. The sisters ended up selling the remaining merchandise to their brothers for another twenty thousand dollars, and were then forced to close the doors of the store they fought so viciously to own.

Just a few months later, the equipment at the new Elkland Brothers location started to be vandalized. It didn't take a master detective to figure out who was behind it. The brothers had no proof at first, but then they got wise and installed a ten thousand dollar video surveillance system. It only took a few weeks before the vandals struck again, but this time John and Jude had the video evidence to nail the culprits.

Police Chief McMurphy got the call around eight in the morning and decided he would go down around nine and review the tape with the boys. The brothers had already pinpointed the portion on the recording where the vandalism had taken place and had it queued up for Jack Sr. when he came in the door.

"See, right there, that's a BMW missing a headlight," Jude said pointing to the vehicle that pulled up into the video frame. "Sabrina hit a deer last week and hasn't gotten the headlight repaired yet. If that's not proof, I don't know what is."

"It gets better," John chimed in. They watched on and two blond haired women got out of the BMW and walked over to one of the big front end loaders. They had what looked like baseball bats. They started hitting the windows of the driver's cab, shattering the safety glass. They then went back to their car and got cans of spray paint. They painted fake gang signs on the side of the building, trying to throw suspicion off themselves. They even gave each other a mistimed high five before getting back into the BMW and speeding away.

"That sure looks like Sabrina and Tatum," Jack said shaking his head. "Have you totaled up the cost of the damages yet?"

"The insurance adjuster is supposed to be out around one today," Jude said.

"Okay, well here's what we're going to do. We aren't going to breathe a word of this to anyone else, got it? Get the total from the insurance adjuster and call my office. Once we have that total we'll know if we're looking at a misdemeanor or a felony. If it's going to be a felony, I'll call Judge Parsons down in Delhi and we'll get a search warrant to go into their homes and look for the baseball bats and the spray cans. We'll rake the two of them over the coals but good."

"Oh, good. This stupidity has to stop," John said. "They are just too greedy and stupid to listen to reason."

"I'll make sure they hear us," Jack Sr. said with a smile. He shook hands with both of the Elkland boys and returned to his patrol car just in time to hear the radio call come through about the disturbance in front of the Peachy Keen. He called in and told dispatch that he was only a few minutes away and would go investigate.

Who the heck is fighting on the street at ten in the morning, Jack Sr. thought to himself.

It was a small police department with just three full time officers and two part time radio dispatchers. They also had a group of about ten people they could count on throughout the year to help with volunteering. They would assist with paperwork, answer phones during the busier summer months, clean the offices on a weekly basis and even help with funding drives. The department was established back in 1933, spearheaded by a couple of local businessmen who were tired of being pushed around by the mob. Back then the mob ran some of the hotels in the region. One of the most famous groups of killers for the mob, dubbed Murder Incorporated, used a lake about seventy miles south of Coopers Hollow to dump bodies of murder victims from New York City.

It was a rough time back then. With Prohibition,

there came speak-easies and moonshine operations. The Catskills made for a nice hideaway for both. The first Police Chief gave his life after fighting the mob element for almost two decades. Then another Police Chief was hired, they called him The Duke, as he resembled John Wayne the famous movie actor of the time. He remained Chief until a heart attack struck him down in 1958. Jack Sr.'s father, Frank McMurphy became the Police Chief next and stayed that way for over thirty years before he passed it on to his son. Now at age sixty, Jack Sr. was thinking it might be a good time to step aside and see if the village wanted to hire his son on as the new Chief of Police.

He hoped that maybe he could hold off retirement for another year or so, however. There had been some recent political problems in the town that he wanted to iron out first. His son had spoken a little too freely with his then girlfriend, Paula Schumann, who was trying desperately to keep the local newspaper afloat. It caused embarrassment for the Mayor who was systematically trying to do all he could to run a religious group out of town. That Mayor lost the next election, and the new Mayor, Theo Patterson, who just happened to be the brother of Sheriff's Deputy Craig Patterson, was elected.

There was no doubt in Chief McMurphy's mind that the Patterson brothers were attempting to knock out the Coopers Hollow department and wrest away the federal aid that they received for the County Sheriff's department instead. The thing that frustrated the Chief was that it really wasn't that much money to begin with. They got about twenty-five thousand dollars a year in Federal aid, fifty thousand in State aid and another twenty thousand dollars a year from the Village budget. All of the rest of the money in the department budget came from a trust fund that had been setup way back in 1933 at the inception of the department. It was a trust that was very well managed and provided nearly one hundred thousand dollars annually to the department. Back in the 70's a non-profit organization was started to support the trust fund, and many of the folks that came up to vacation homes in the area were known to donate quite generously to the fund. What the Patterson boys didn't realize is that if the department no longer existed, the money in the trust would default back to the heirs of the two initial founders, whoever they might be. It wouldn't be going to the Sheriff's department.

Chief McMurphy wanted to make sure that he smoothed it all out before he left the position so Jack Jr. didn't have to deal with it. He would have enough on his plate if and when he took over without having to negotiate the minefield of a hostile relationship with the Sheriff's department.

The Chief drove into town as quickly as possible with sirens blaring. When it came to fist fights, the lights and sirens usually broke things up better than an officer could. Whatever differences the two parties might have, they were usually smart enough to quit fighting when the cops rolled up.

He saw the scuffle on the sidewalk outside of the Peachy Keen: Two men knocking around a third. Chief McMurphy didn't recognize any of them. Then he saw two women join the melee. It was Gloria Graves and her daughter Starlett. Despite the sirens, nobody seemed to be backing down.

The Chief hoped backup arrived soon, as they looked like a couple of pretty tough dudes.

Chapter 10

She settled down into her chair, she was wrapped in a blanket, had her cup of tea, and one of the books from the previous day. The first book she started reading had been a mystery/thriller and it started with a young girl being raped and murdered. She really didn't feel like reading much more of that. She wasn't in the mood to have her sensibilities assaulted.

This book was more of an adventure novel. The back cover described a larger than life hero who faced insurmountable odds to save the world. As she started reading she found herself imagining the main character looking like the man she'd met Tuesday at the library. Michael Cooke was a strong name. He had rugged good looks, dark eyes, graying hair, and he seemed so big and strong. "Solid" was the word came to mind when she thought of him.

She started to lose herself in the book, when the doorbell rang, startling her to the core. It was just after nine at night, and she wasn't expecting visitors, certainly not this late. In fact, she couldn't remember the last time she had invited anyone over at all. The only thing she could think of was that one of the horses had gotten loose again and had wandered down the street.

She pulled her robe tight and went to the door.

Flipping on the porch light, she peeked around the side window cautiously.

"Starlett!" She ripped open the door and threw her arms around her daughter.

"Hi, mom. Sorry about the doorbell. I hope I didn't scare you. I left in such a rush today I forgot my house keys."

"Oh, it takes more than a doorbell to rattle me. Let me help you with your things," Gloria said.

"I didn't bring anything else," Starlett said, as she slid past her mother and went into the house. Gloria stood there for a few moments before she shut the door.

This is worse than I thought. She's more scared than she let on when we spoke on the phone.

"I was just reading a book and having some bedtime tea, would you like me to pour a cup for you?"

"Sure, that would be great," Starlett said. She found her way to the couch and then leaned forward and opened the chest that doubled as a coffee table. Pulling out a big comforter, she closed the lid again and curled up on the couch. She lost herself in the fluffy comforter, as she pulled it close around her.

"Mom, I don't know where to begin," she elevated her voice so her mother could hear her even out in the kitchen.

"Well, just pick a place and then we'll get to the important stuff eventually," Gloria spoke then bit her bottom lip. Her emotions were torn. She was afraid of what her daughter would say next. She half wanted her to say she was pregnant. Being a grandma might be really fun.

"Dalton was arrested, mom. The cops kicked in my door and put both of us in hand cuffs and searched my place. They didn't find anything, so they let me go, but they took him."

"What? What were they looking for?" Gloria came into the living room with the tea, fixed the way her daughter liked it. She handed her the cup, and saw that her daughter's hands were shaking. This was not what she was expecting at all.

"Drugs, mom." She began to cry. "They said that Dalton was dealing drugs on campus."

"Oh, no. Not Dalton. It must be some sort of mistake," Gloria sipped from her cup and then reached forward to touch her daughter's hand, steadying it. No indeed, this was completely unexpected. She had steeled herself to the idea that Starlett had gotten pregnant. She didn't know anything about how to deal with this sort of thing.

"A detective pulled me aside and told me they had pictures and video of him. They took him off to jail."

"Did you know anything about it?"

"Oh, yeah. Of course I knowingly was dating a drug dealer, mom. No! I didn't have any idea. And if he was lying about that, then what else has he been lying to me about?" Starlett was sobbing again. Gloria took the tea out of her daughter's hand and set it on the large steamer chest/coffee table. She then sat next to her daughter on the couch and put her arm around her.

"Everything's going to be okay," Gloria said.

"Mom, he proposed to me on Saturday before all of this happened and I said yes." This caused Starlett to launch into more sobbing. Her entire world had just come crashing down. Gloria knew the feeling. In just a moment everything in life can change. "We were supposed to come up and tell you about it this weekend."

"Well, don't worry about that right now. I think you should stay here for awhile and let Dalton deal with this on his own. He needs to take care of this himself." She stroked her daughter's hair and rocked her gently. "We'll get through this, you and me."

"Anyway, his dad bailed him out. I knew the family had money, but bail was set at five hundred thousand dollars. When he got out, he pretended like nothing had happened, like it wasn't a big deal. We had a big fight and I left and decided to come up here."

"Well," Gloria said. "You made the right choice, honey. You've still got some of the clothes you left behind up in your old room. I'm sure you can find something to wear. In the morning we'll go out for breakfast and then maybe go do a little clothes shopping up in Albany, to take your mind off things."

"Okay," Starlett said, sniffling a little.

"You know, some of your friends will say things like: 'Oh, another guy will come along,' but don't you believe it. Once you give your heart to someone, and it gets broken, it takes a long time to heal. But you know what?"

"What?"

"It does eventually heal. Sometimes when you least expect it. We just have to be strong, that's all." Gloria kissed her daughter on the head and held her close.

"Mom, you were so strong when dad died. How did you do it?" Starlett pulled back and looked into her mother's face. She saw a million different emotions wash across her mother's features in a mere moment's time.

"My heart was broken. But I had to be strong for you, baby. I had to lock away my heart and let it heal on its own. I couldn't use it for a long, long time." Gloria was having a moment of self discovery, realizing what it was that she had done to herself, and recognizing that her heart had healed. The pain wasn't nearly as deep any longer. It made her wonder if she was ready to love again.

"Is it still broken?"

"It's better now. It was really tough when you first left, I kind of felt bitter about your decision."

"I should have never gone," Starlett interrupted.

"I think it was good for me, because it gave me a chance to think about me for a change. You know you've kept me busy for a few years. If it wasn't skinned knees from your bike, it's a boyfriend selling drugs," Gloria said, laughing a little.

"Yeah, I know. I'm such a problem child." Starlett said, pushing against her mother in a playful way. "How's Daisy?"

"Oh, she's good. She misses you though. The ground will be nice and soft with the snow melting, maybe we can take the girls out for a little run tomorrow afternoon. It's supposed to be sunny and warm, temps in the lower fifties."

"I'd like that," Starlett said through a yawn. "I'm exhausted. I'm going to go take a shower and get to bed."

"Okay, sweetie. Listen, everything will work out, you'll see," Gloria said, grabbing her daughter by the hand and giving her a gentle squeeze.

"I know. It just hurts. I love you mom."

"I love you too Starlett."

"That guy is checking you out, mom." They were sitting in the diner, finishing their breakfast.

"What guy?" Gloria asked without turning around to look. Her daughter did this to her all the time, tease her about guys just to see if she could get her flustered.

"The tall guy at the counter. He's been checking you out since he came in. Uh, oh. He knows I just caught him looking." Starlett smiled and took another sip of her coffee. Seemo made the best eggs Benedict anywhere, and they hadn't left very much of it on either of their plates.

"You need to stop. He was probably checking you out. What does anyone want with an old lady like me?"

"Oh, stop it. You're gorgeous mom. Do you remember how I used to have friends over from school? Do you know why the guys always wanted to come too? It was to check you out," Her daughter teased.

"You're ridiculous," Gloria said. Her cheeks flushed a little.

"Ah ha, I got you." Starlett took the last bite of her

meal and washed it down with the coffee. "You know, you're right. Everything is going to be okay. I decided on my drive up that I'm going to take the rest of the semester off. Come home and be with you and try to get my head on straight."

"I think your head is already on straight," Gloria said. Just then Starlett's cell phone chirped with an incoming text message. She didn't like the reaction in her daughter's face.

"It's Dalton. He's here in town looking for me. He says he wants to explain everything," Starlett looked stricken. "What should I tell him?"

"Well, if he wants to talk, he can talk here. I'll be right here too," Gloria said.

"Everything's going to be fine, isn't it?"

"Yes, honey. We'll get through this together." Gloria reached across and patted Starlett on the hand.

"He's coming over here," Starlett said. "The guy who was checking you out."

"What?"

"Good morning," Michael Cooke said.

Oh my God. I can't believe he's talking to me again. He's handsome, and charming. Starlett seems to like him too. Why am I acting this way? I feel like a school girl. I haven't felt this giddy since. . . since Phillip asked me out. That was nearly twenty-five years ago now. My God, has it been that long?

"We ought to grab a cup of coffee one of these days. Trade stories." He said to her.

"Sure, I'd like that," she heard herself say.

Did I just agree to a date? Is it really that easy? And now he's leaving.

"Oh my God, mom. He's hot." Starlett said, as Michael walked out the front door. "How long have you known him?"

"I, uh, what, honey?" Gloria blushed. She wasn't listening to Starlett, she was listening to her heart start beating again. She felt so alive.

"You like him," Starlett said with a grin from ear to ear. "Mom, that is so awesome. You've got a boyfriend!"

"He's not my boyfriend. I just met him. I only agreed to coffee with him, that's all. And it wasn't definite plans. It was indefinite. 'Sometime,' is what he said. We'll get together sometime." She couldn't hide her smile.

"Nice. Here comes Dalton." Starlett's mood immediately changed. She scowled and looked into her cup of coffee.

The next few minutes all seemed like a blur for Gloria. Dalton came in and sat down at their table. He looked awful. He tried to explain what had happened, how he'd gotten caught up in it.

He'd been asked to drive a car, he claimed, for a friend. And it was loaded down with drugs. He didn't know anything about it. When he found out about it, he parked the car and called the police. But the cops came after him. Starlett countered that it didn't make sense, the story he was telling them. Dalton swore it was the truth. Seemo brought over a mug and poured more coffee into each of their mugs.

Two men walked in the door and came right for Dalton. They pulled up chairs and sat on both sides of him. They told him if he didn't get them their stuff, he wasn't going to make it through the day. Dalton said he didn't want anything to do with it. They said it was too late for that now, he was in too deep. They grabbed at his arms, and he fought back. One of the thugs slammed his head down on the table, sending the coffee mugs all over. Gloria heard herself scream and Scarlett jumped up to grab one of the thugs. Seemo yelled that he was calling the cops. The two thugs dragged Dalton outside. He was barely able to stand and blood was flowing freely from his nose.

Gloria sat there in stunned silence.

What just happened?

Starlett ran after Dalton, screaming at the men. Gloria jumped up and grabbed her. She was afraid that it might get more violent than it already was, and the two of them would get caught up in it, getting seriously hurt. The police would be there in a few minutes, and they'd take care of it.

Everything was moving in slow motion, like in a dream. Sounds seemed muffled, except for the thumping of her heartbeat. Gloria could clearly hear that. There were stars at the edges of her vision. She was worried she was about to pass out.

Starlett broke free from her mother's grasp and flew out the front door. She was down the steps and almost on top of one of the thugs. Gloria came out and stood at the top of the steps looking at the commotion on the sidewalk. She grabbed the handrail to steady herself.

One of the thugs was white but deeply tanned, the other Hispanic. The white one had facial hair and a tattoo that ran down the side of his face and into his collar. He was taller than the other, and seemed to be more in charge. He was shouting the orders, and he was the one who had initiated the conversation back in the diner. The Hispanic-looking thug was thicker and shorter. He looked like he was made of pure muscle. He was the one that Starlett jumped on. He pushed her to the ground. Hard.

This seemed to snap Gloria out of the haze she'd been in since the confrontation had begun. She shrieked and came down off the porch of the diner to help her daughter, just as the police car pulled up, screeching to a halt, sirens still blaring.

Oh, thank God, the police are here!

Jack McMurphy Sr. jumped out and ran over to the sidewalk. Gloria wished it was Jack Jr. He was bigger and stronger than his father. No sooner had Jack Sr. put his hands on the white thug, when the Hispanic-looking one hauled back and sucker punched him in the jaw. He went down hard, knocked unconscious before he hit the ground. His head collided with the sidewalk and made a sickening thud. Gloria screamed again. This time she really thought she would faint. Jack Sr. looked dead.

And then, as if in a dream, Michael Cooke was there.

He came in so fast, the Hispanic-looking thug didn't have time to react. He caught a fist right in the side of the head, and it sent him reeling. He stepped awkwardly off the curb and fell against the car. Cooke was then onto the white thug. He grabbed the man by the jacket and brought his forehead into his nose, breaking it. The white thug crumpled to the ground, woozy.

By this time his partner had regained his footing and grabbed Cooke. Michael landed several hard punches in quick succession, but the man shrugged them off. He swung back and punched Michael in the gut which bent him over in agony. Michael tried to fend off the blows, but more were landing than missing. The thug threw him against the car, breaking the window. He pulled something out of his pocket and drew back to strike.

Just then, a giant hand grabbed onto the thug's wrist. Tubby spun him around so that they were eye to eye. In one quick movement Tubby brought his balled up fist down squarely on top of the thug's head. The Hispanic-looking tough guy collapsed in a heap, knocked out cold by the single blow.

"Michael!" Gloria yelled and ran over to her new acquaintance. She helped him up, but he brushed her off. He ran over to Jack Sr. and checked to see if he was okay. It didn't look good. Michael grabbed the radio from the Chief's hip and made the radio call that no police officer ever wants to ever hear.

"We've got an officer down, send back up and an ambulance immediately. I repeat, officer down. On Main Street right in front of the Peachy Keen."

"We need to get him up onto the porch," Gloria said.

"No, don't touch him. If his skull or spine are damaged, we don't want to make it worse by moving him or maybe dropping him. He's breathing okay, and his pulse feels strong, but we need to get him to a hospital quick."

Cooke stood up, clutching his ribs. It felt like maybe they were broken, but the adrenaline was still pumping. The Hispanic-looking thug packed quite a punch. He then walked over to Tubby and extended his hand.

"You saved the day. Tubby, right?"

"Yeah," Tubby said.

"Well, Tubby, you're a hero," Cooke shook the big man's hand, wincing a little from the crush of it. As he drew back his hand, the pain of his ribs struck him, and he suddenly felt his age again. "Even though I had him just where I wanted him."

"Can I ride on the fire truck again?"

Chapter 11

Jack Jr. heard the "officer down" call come across the radio and put his foot into the accelerator a little more. There was no identification as to which officer was down, but if his father was the first to the scene, he was the most likely to have been involved.

"Dispatch, this is Officer Davidson with the DEC. Request a Med-Evac helicopter for head trauma up to Albany Med. I'm going to instruct the ambulance to take the officer down to the school for a football field landing."

"Officer Davidson, this is dispatch. Your request is confirmed." There was a pause. "Is it Jack Sr.?"

The radio was silent. McMurphy knew it was a breach of protocol to announce who was involved in the incident over the open airwaves, but he also understood why the request had come through. If it was his dad, everybody who was anybody in law enforcement within the reach of the radio signal would want to know. Feud or no feud, bad blood or no, when a brother cop went down in the line of duty, other cops would come to help. He was about to pick up the radio and tell Davidson not to say anything over the air, when the radio crackled to life.

"Confirmed, it's Jack Sr." Jack Jr. cursed to himself when he heard Davidson's voice.

"You should have waited for back up, dad. You should

have waited," he said out loud. He knew it wasn't fair to
be angry, but he was anyway. His old man was a stubborn
old cuss, and he knew if there was something going down,
he wasn't about to wait for anyone. Frankly, he knew that
he wasn't much different from his old man in that respect.
After all, where did he think he got it from?

"Officer Davidson, this is dispatch. Med-Evac helicopter is on the way to Coopers Hollow high school football
field. ETA twenty minutes."

"Confirmed," came the reply. "We'll be there."

Jack Jr. had the patrol car almost sideways around
the last corner into town. He came roaring down Main
Street with the lights flashing and siren blaring. He took
Riverbrook Street to the high school and drove around
back to the football field, putting the cruiser right over the
curb and onto the grass. The ambulance was waiting.

He was out of the car and over to the ambulance in
what seemed like two steps.

"How's he doing?"

"He's breathing okay, but he suffered some pretty
substantial head trauma. The witnesses on the scene said
he got punched in the jaw and fell, hitting his head on the
concrete." The name badge on the ambulance crewman's
shirt said Rogers. Jack didn't recognize him. The ambulance looked like it was either from Windham or Oneonta.

"Where did you guys come from?"

"We were over at the retirement home picking up a
deceased woman. She passed last night." Rogers said. "We
heard the call, dropped what we were doing and got over

to the scene ASAP. What's with the tee-shirt?"

"I responded to an animal attack north of town. A man and his little girl. Just got done," McMurphy said. "My uniform and vest got covered with blood and I haven't even had a chance to change yet. It's been a heck of a day."

"I guess so. The Med-Evac can only take him. You won't be able to ride along," Rogers said, looking down. "Sorry."

"Okay, I'll just hang back and make sure he gets off okay." They fell into silence. Jack Sr. had a neck brace on, stabilizing his spine. His forehead was bloodied, as was his nose and mouth. His cheek was already starting to turn a dark purplish hue. They had the oxygen mask on him as well. He looked like he was a hundred years old, to Jack Jr. He was pale and wrinkled. He reached down and took his father's hand in his. He squeezed it gently, trying to fight back tears.

He should have retired this year. Cripes, he's sixty years old!

In just a few moments they heard the beating of the rotor blades. The helicopter circled the area and then came in for a landing at the fifty yard line. The down thrust of the blades kicked up mud, snow and grass. The pilot slowed the engine, and the stretcher was wheeled over to the helicopter. Jack Sr. was in and secured and the bird was back in the air in less than five minutes.

Godspeed, dad.

He went back to his patrol car and noticed all the kids at the windows of their classrooms looking out at the scene that had just unfolded. They had no idea who it was that was flown out, they were just drawn to the spectacle of the helicopter and ambulance. He sat for a moment to collect his thoughts and realized that he had to get back over to the crime scene. As far as he knew a DEC officer was the senior man on the scene.

He led the ambulance back over to Main Street and the Peachy Keen. It looked like a big event. There was a State Trooper vehicle, a DEC SUV, Fire and Rescue had come over with one of their smaller first responder vehicles, and a whole bunch of volunteer fireman had their vehicles there, blue lights flashing. Fortunately the volunteer guys were already directing traffic around the congestion. It would be just a few more minutes, and a couple more Troopers and maybe even a few of the Sheriff's deputies would start showing up. It was going to be a circus. Jack spotted Paula Schumann in the crowd of onlookers. He also saw his new DEC friend, Davidson helping out with crowd control, though in Coopers Hollow, that equated to only ten or twelve people on the sidewalks. They had to worry more about the traffic that came through town. Hundreds of vehicles everyday took the State Route through the small village which became Main Street at each end of the village limits. There was already a line of at least twenty cars backed up in each direction.

This is definitely going to be a circus.

Jack figured that Davidson had been next on the scene after the "officer down" call went out. Fortunately a State Trooper had arrived and relieved Davidson. Jack parked and walked over to the Trooper's car, which held both suspects in the back. He was about to rip the door off its hinges and tear into the thugs when the Trooper interceded.

"Whoa, whoa, take it easy, Jack." The State Trooper was a man named Charlie Loefler. He was a pretty good guy and they had talked a few times in the past. "I'm just as upset with anybody who puts a cop in the hospital, but this isn't the way to take care of it. You hit him while he's in custody and he walks. We do this by the book and we get him on attempted murder."

Jack knew what he was hearing was true, but he wanted to take care of things his way. He took a couple of deep breaths and calmed himself. After a moment he realized he would rather see the guy off the streets for a long time, but the internal pleasure of being able to beat him down to a quivering pile of flesh was cruelly tempting.

"What happened? Who hit my old man?"

"Well, it goes like this. These two characters walk into the diner and start giving this kid Dalton Beckman some grief. Saying he owes them money or something. I really couldn't get a straight answer on that. Anyway they slam him against the table and start dragging him out to their car here. A Mrs. Gloria Graves and her daughter, uh, Starlett, tried to stop the assault. That's when your father showed up. The big guy, Ramirez, struck your father in the face with his fist and knocked him out. He hit his head on the sidewalk after he fell. That's when a bystander named Michael Cooke jumped into it. He took out Mr. Tattoo over there, uh, the name he gave was Smith. Then Cooke and Ramirez exchanged blows and that's when Tubby came out and ended the thing. I guess he just bopped the guy on the top of the head and knocked him out."

"What did he hit him with," Jack asked.

"His fist," Loefler said, raising his eyebrows. "Heck of a fist. Anyway, Ramirez had pulled out a sap of all things. It was a little leather pouch with steel ball bearings in it. So we have assault with a weapon as well. I'm not sure if we can call it a deadly weapon or not. I have to do a little more digging. But at least we've got a weapons charge to go along with everything else."

"Any guns or anything in the car?" Jack asked.

"None that I found. The car looks pretty clean. It's a rental from New York City. I've got a hunch here that this whole thing is a lot bigger than just a couple of guys wanting a couple hundred bucks back." Trooper Loefler said.

"What do you think it is?"

"Well, I ran Dalton Beckman through the system, and he was just picked up in Binghamton three days ago on a drug trafficking charge."

"No kidding. How is he out?"

"His daddy posted bail. Half a mil." This made Jack whistle.

"Best guess then," Jack began. "Dalton gets busted for the drugs, and his suppliers don't want some preppy kid squealing, so they send a couple of toughs to take him out?" This was big time city stuff. Coopers Hollow never had this type of problem before, at least not recently. The worst was usually a couple of local drunks playing fisticuffs at the bowling alley or the Taproom. Heck the biggest thing to happen in Coopers Hollow for the entire last year was the animal attack from which Jack's uniform still bore the stains.

"Okay, well, stop me if you disagree," Jack continued, starting to shiver slightly in his white tee-shirt. "But I think this whole thing is part of the Binghamton investigation. We should probably get a couple of the detectives to come up here to investigate."

"That's what I was going to suggest, but what with your dad getting hurt and all, I didn't want to tell you what to do," Trooper Loefler said.

"No, we need to do this right. This thing is bigger than our little police department can handle. I've got enough things on my plate," McMurphy said.

"What's with the tee-shirt?"

"Just before this went down, I was on a call just north of town. Mountain lion attack, if you can believe that. A guy and his little girl. The guy lost a lot of blood, but the little girl just had a scratch. My uniform was finished, just covered in blood. I didn't get a chance to change before I heard it was dad and had to come down."

"Jeez, you have been busy."

"Yeah," Jack said wearily. "It's always feast or famine around here. I'm going to go talk with some of the witnesses and take some more notes. Thanks for everything." The men shook hands, and McMurphy walked over to get his overcoat out of the trunk of his patrol car before he went to speak with Gloria and her daughter.

"Hey, guys. How are you feeling?" Jack said, trying to break the ice and be less of a cop and more of a friend.

"Not great," was Starlett's reply.

"Do you want to tell me anything that you might have forgotten to tell the Trooper? Like that Dalton was arrested a couple days ago on drug trafficking charges?"

"That's all I know," Starlett said. "I found out about it, and came up here to talk with mom. He followed me, and I guess those two goons followed him. I wish I'd never met him."

"Jack, listen," Gloria said. It was the first time he could remember her using his first name. He kind of liked it. "I think I need to talk to our attorney first. I've got to make sure Starlett is protected. If you would like us to come down and give a full statement, we can do that. But I just think it best if I get her home."

"Are either of you hurt?"

"No, Starlett got a little scrape on her hand when she fell, but it was cleaned up and wrapped by the first responders over there," Gloria indicated the Fire and Rescue crew who were now packing up their gear and heading back to the Fire Department.

"Well that's a relief. I'm really sorry this has happened to you guys. Let me know if there's anything I can do for you two, okay." He reached into his coat pocket, fishing for a business card, but realized they were back in his uniform shirt, probably soaked in blood. "Just call the office and they'll put you right through to me. Okay?"

"Alright, thanks Jack." Gloria said. The two ladies had been sitting on the porch of the Peachy Keen. Gloria extended a hand, and Jack helped her to his feet. Their eyes locked for a moment and then she looked away. Even though she was eight to ten years older than him, she was still very beautiful, and Jack caught himself thinking about her. Of course, her daughter was pretty hot too. There was no denying that. But he was closer to Gloria's age than Starlett's.

McMurphy next walked over to Michael Cooke who looked a little worse for wear.

"Heck of a way to live retirement, Michael," Jack said, extending his hand.

"You're not kidding. How's your dad?"

"I don't know yet. They should be landing in Albany in about fifteen minutes. I'm going to head up there as soon as I wrap things up here. Anything to add to the statement you gave the Trooper?"

"Not really, no. I just saw a fight on the sidewalk, then your dad showed up and took a sucker punch to the jaw, and that's when I jumped in. Truthfully, if it hadn't been for Tubby, I think chunky over there would have gotten the better of me."

"Yeah, I heard Tubby knocked him out with one punch."

"It wasn't even a punch, it was like a kid playing that pop-up gopher game at the mall."

"Like whack a mole?" Jack asked, imagining what it must have looked like.

"Yeah. He just took him and Bop, down the guy went." Michael said, gesturing with his hands to describe how it took place.

"Are you hurt?"

"My gut is sore, my ribs hurt, and my back hurts from where I was thrown into the car, but other than that, I'm okay. I'm just going to go home and soak in the hot tub."

"Sounds like a plan. If you think of anything else, give me a call." Jack said.

"What happened to you?" Cooke asked, indicating Jack's tee-shirt.

"You know, you're like the twelfth person I've had to tell this morning. I should just go over to Paula and get it over with," Jack said, indicating his former girlfriend and part owner of *The Mountain Star*.

"The reporter I was rude to the other day?"

"Yeah," McMurphy replied. "Anyway, there was an animal attack this morning. We're still investigating it. A fella and his daughter. They said it was a mountain lion, but I need to get with DEC and figure out what it actually was. Speaking of which," Jack paused, his mind starting to percolate an idea. "You're a pretty good shot, right?"

"Yeah, I'd say so."

"If it was a mountain lion, and it was responsible, we have to hunt it down. Would you be up for a little hunting expedition?"

"Yeah, maybe."

"Okay, I'm going to coordinate with Davidson over at DEC, but I think it's going to be a reality here in the next day or so. We'll need a couple of good shots, and with dad hurt, I could use some help. We have to do it hush hush and before hunting season starts. If you're up for it, I'll count you in."

"Yeah, do that. I'd like to help out," Michael said. He'd never hunted anything but people before. This could be fun.

"Okay, I'll let you know. Thanks for everything, Michael." Jack was doing a lot of hand shaking this morning. If things didn't go well for his father, the old man might finally take the hint and retire. Jack Jr. could very well be in the running for the next Chief of Police, so it didn't hurt to have a few friends he could count on. He moved on to Tubby, who, he was told, was inside the Peachy Keen, eating another bowl of Frosted Flakes.

"Hey, Tubby, how's it going?" McMurphy didn't get much of a response. "I heard you were quite the hero today."

"They said I could ride on the fire truck for the Halloween parade next week," he said between scoops of milk laden cereal.

"Sure. I think that would be a great idea. So, want to tell me what happened?"

"The guys were out there fighting. Seemo told me to go help, so I did. I didn't mean to hurt anyone."

"You're not in trouble."

"Not even for the freezer?" Tubby asked.

"What freezer?" Jack asked. He hadn't heard anything about a freezer.

"Nothing. Mama said it was okay, but she said I shouldn't talk to nobody about it."

"Okay," Jack realized that Tubby must have been talking about something that happened at home. Maybe he broke something and made a big deal about it. Who knew? It didn't have anything to do with this investigation, though, so Jack let it slide. "She's probably right. If you think of anything else you want to talk to me about, just give me a call, okay?"

"Okay, but Mama doesn't let me use the phone," Tubby said, finishing the last scoop of cereal and picking up the bowl to drink the milk out.

"Well, then just come down and Seemo will let you use his, okay? Or you could just walk over to the station and come see me in person."

"Sure," Seemo chimed in. "Whatever you need, Thaddeus, let Seemo take care of it."

"Thanks, guys." Jack stood to leave.

"Hey, Jack, what happen to you?" Seemo pointed at his shirt. "Where's your uniform?"

"I'll tell you later," Jack said, not wanting to relate the story again. He walked out of the diner and saw that most of the commotion had died down. Trooper Loefler was still there with the handcuffed hooligans in his back seat.

"Did you get a hold of the Detectives in Binghamton?" Jack asked.

"Yeah, they will be up this afternoon. Can we take these two down to the County lockup until they get here?" Loefler asked.

"Sure. Hey, what happened to the Beckman kid, Dalton?"

"Uh, they took him to the hospital in Oneonta. You think I should get a Trooper over there to meet the ambulance?" Loefler was on the same wavelength as Jack.

"Yeah, I think so. If these guys were coming after him to shut him up, it means their friends might try it again. We do need to get these two chuckle heads down to lockup. Why don't you follow me down? In fact, maybe we should separate them. Put one in my car."

"Which one do you want?"

"Well," Jack thought about it.

It sure would be nice to be alone for a bit with the guy who popped dad in the mouth. Show him what happens to guys who want to get tough with a cop. Then again, there was nothing worse than a blown case because of police misconduct.

"Better give me the boy with the dragon tattoo," Jack said. "I just want to go talk with Copper from the fire department before we go."

"Is your car unlocked?"

"Should be."

"Okay, I'll take him over and lock him up for you," Loefler said.

"Thanks." Jack walked across the street to the fire truck which was about ready to pull away. He spotted Copper talking to a couple of the guys from the all volunteer department, and waited until he was done.

"Hey, Jack. I'm so sorry about your dad. Hope he'll be okay. I came as soon as the call went out that it was him. If you need anything from me," Copper said, not finishing his thought. "Your dad and I go way back. If there's anything at all. . ."

"I may need something from you. You're one of the better shots. I don't know if you heard, but we had an animal attack this morning north of town. It might be a mountain lion. We may have to go out and hunt it down. We only have a few weeks before hunting season starts, so it may have to be pretty quick, and I'm a bit shorthanded now."

"Yeah, I'm game. I am a pretty good shot," Copper said. "Actually I could get a couple of the guys I go hunting with together as well, if you want."

"No, not yet. I need to talk to DEC and make sure, but I think that's how this thing is going to go down. Let's keep it under our hats for now. We don't need a panic on our hands, right? Then again, if there is something out there willing to attack people we have to let everyone know that they should be careful. I'll tell you what, I'll call you this afternoon and we can talk about it more."

"Okay, Jack. Sounds good. Good luck with your dad. Give him my best when you see him," Copper shook hands with him and patted him on the shoulder.

"Thanks Copper, I will." As he turned to leave, Jack saw Patrolman Ballard pull up. He was out of the car and over to Jack quickly. Ballard was younger than Jack, just twenty-four, and still learning the ropes. He was smart, though, and picked things up quickly. He was going to make a good cop.

"Jack, jeez, I'm sorry. I was way down near Walton when the call came through. I came as quickly as I could. How is he?" The McMurphy family had kind of adopted Ballard as one of their own. He'd get invited over for dinner four out of seven nights a week. They would always get together Sundays to watch football or NASCAR. They even shared holidays with him. Ballard was single, but had a girlfriend down near the village of Deposit, which was probably where he spent the night, and where he'd been coming from when the "officer down" call went out.

"I'm not sure yet. We've got two guys for assault at least, maybe attempted murder for the guy who hit dad. They may be tied up with something bigger, though. Listen, I've got to change and get up to Albany to be with dad. Do you think you and Trooper Loefler can get the two suspects down to the county lock up and wait for the detectives from Binghamton?"

"Sure, I'm on it. Tell your dad I'm praying for him," Ballard said. "Oh, where's your uniform?"

"Don't ask."

Ballard shrugged and went over to Loefler, who was taking the guy who called himself Ramirez out of the back of the Trooper patrol car. They spoke for a moment and then muscled the suspect over to Ballard's cruiser. They got him in the back, and then Ballard drove off.

It's going to be one long day for paperwork, that's for sure, Jack thought to himself.

Jack went back to the patrol car and sat down for a moment. He took a couple of deep breaths and was about to head home to change, when his cell phone rang.

"Hello, this is Jack," he said.

"Jack, it's Vicki at dispatch. I've got some really awful news," her voice was quivering, and Jack knew immediately what had happened.

"He didn't make it," Jack said. He could tell by the tone in her voice he was right.

"I'm so sorry Jack. I'm so sorry," she began to cry over the phone.

The words didn't seem to register. He felt numb as he closed down the phone.

Chapter 12

Whereas most people unfamiliar with firearms would call the ammunition a bullet, the more accurate description is a cartridge. The cartridge contains the bullet, gunpowder and a primer which, when forced into the gunpowder, ignites, causing an explosion that pushes the bullet out of the cartridge down the barrel and hopefully into the desired target. The spent cartridge is then ejected from the weapon. A rifle's cartridge has a metal casing and a single bullet, whereas a shotgun cartridge is mostly plastic with only a bit of metal at the back end where the primer is located. A shotgun cartridge can have a single slug or shot, which are small pellets and spread as they leave the end of the appropriately named shotgun. The correct ammunition to be selected depends greatly on what the intended target is. Small animals or birds would require shot, but larger game, like a white tailed deer would require a shotgun slug. There are very few places where a rifle can be used for hunting. A rifle bullet can travel ten times the distance of a shotgun slug. That means that a missed shot could travel across a farmer's field and into the livestock or worse, the house. Therefore large caliber rifle hunting is only allowed in very sparsely populated areas, unless the DEC provides a special permit for a specific purpose.

The average hunter would go to their local sporting

goods store and buy cartridges for their rifle or shotgun, and usually receive pretty good results. Michael Cooke preferred to pack, or hand-load, his own ammunition. He created his own workshop when he refurbished the house, and had all the tools and supplies necessary for the undertaking.

After speaking with McMurphy, he started doing research on mountain lions, or as they were often called, cougars. He read an interesting article about the many sightings regularly occurring in the area since 1995. No local attacks, either on people or on livestock, had ever been reported until Thursday's incident. He read another article about numerous attacks on joggers in California as more people moved into the cougars' territory.

The more he read, the more respect and awe he had for the animals. A full grown adult could weight anywhere between eighty to two-hundred twenty-five pounds. They were fiercely territorial, and fed mostly on larger animals like deer or livestock. A kill would last the cougar about a week. If it had tried to make a meal out of that family, it was hungry, and since it didn't succeed, it would either subsist on smaller animals until it could get a bigger kill, or it would go after something bigger right away. Either way there should be tracks and possibly even evidence of a recent kill in the general area. Unless they went in and killed it, the cougar was going to stay and would continue to be a danger to local residents. Cougars had no natural enemies except man.

Cooke did some calculations before he began hand-loading the ammo. He figured the longest distance he would need to shoot would be less than three hundred meters. The chances of actually spotting the animal in the woods at a greater distance than that was slim. Additionally, he wanted a load that would put the animal down in one shot. If it spooked and ran, it would be next to impossible for a clean second shot.

He set to work loading his ammo. When he was done, ten beautiful rifle cartridges sat lined up on his work bench.

One of you is going to get a cougar.

Davidson looked over the wrecked van and sighed. Every single animal that had been in the accident had eventually died, even the Macaw. Except the ones that may have escaped. He popped open the back doors and the smell of animal feces struck his nostrils. Some of the steel cages had been removed, but the large wooden crates were still there. He had a couple of plastic containers that he was going to use for this job. He climbed in and looked for the scat he'd seen that first day. It had dried substantially, but it was still there. He took several samples and popped the tops closed. Climbing back out of the van, he pulled out a permanent black marker, writing on the tops of each container.

He'd gotten budgetary clearance from his superiors to send off the scat to a lab for DNA confirmation. It would take a week or two for results, but it would be worth it to know. He closed the van doors and headed back to his DEC SUV. He threw a wave of thanks to Emilio, who owned the auto repair garage and had agreed to let them store the van there until the rightful owners came for it. If they never picked it up, Emilio could sell it for scrap and maybe make a couple hundred bucks.

Davidson had agreed to go on the hunt, but he was reluctant to admit that it was a cougar attack just yet. He thought it was more likely to have been a bobcat, as they were much more prevalent in the area. The thing that troubled him as he mulled over the story, however, was that the animal had attempted to drag the little girl away. He'd never heard of a bobcat attempting such an attack. There were stories of mountain lions attacking in such a manner out in the mountains of California and Arizona. There was an attack several years back in northern Arizona that shared very similar traits to this attack. He was finding that his opinion could be swayed on the matter.

If it was a cougar, and as cougars were no longer native to this area, he had deduced that it might not have been sled dogs that the van had been carrying, but a couple of cougars. As the driver didn't have the proper paperwork to transport them through New York State, it was no wonder he lied to the Trooper at the road block. It was just a theory right now and one to which he was not yet entirely ready to subscribe. He wanted proof. The DNA test of the scat would support or invalidate his conclusion.

Whatever it was that was out there that attacked the little girl and her father, it was only right to hunt it down and kill it, though he felt it would be a shame to do so. Cougars were beautiful animals, and usually left humans well enough alone. This one must have been either used to people or diseased, as it didn't hesitate to attack. Davidson's money was on the former. There had been several sightings throughout the northeastern United States over the years, and each time a sighting was confirmed with a capture or a kill, DNA testing showed that it was from another area of the world and had probably been transported there as a pet or for a private collection.

As he drove back towards the DEC substation fifteen miles to the east, near the Gilboa Dam, his mind turned towards the hunt that they would face. He wasn't an expert tracker by any means, but he had a fair sense of how to follow an animal, especially a big one like a bear or cougar. He knew that cougars weren't extremely difficult to track, either. They left a lot of tracks and often a mess of a carcass behind. Usually when there was a cougar in the area, livestock or deer carcasses started turning up. However, if the animal had already turned towards people as a potential food source, it was entirely possible that it would try it again.

He felt it was important to get out into the woods and start tracking as soon as possible, but after Chief McMurphy's death, Jack might not be able to make it. It might be better to go out with a smaller group. There were a couple of guys he would trust on a hunt like this. Jack had suggested taking the fella named Cooke who had tried to break up the fight that had killed the Chief, but he didn't know him and didn't feel too comfortable going out on a hunt as important as this with people he didn't know and trust.

He thought it might make sense to run up to the Anders' trailer and just have a quick look around for himself. Hunting an animal like this was far different than deer hunting. Deer weren't known to go from prey to predator. You had to be prepared.

Starlett rode Daisy up over the ridge behind the house. The weather had gotten cold again. That's how it went this time of year. One day it would be fifty degrees and sunny, and the next day it would be below freezing with snow flurries in the air. Daisy had been her horse from the time they had moved up here. For the first few years Starlett was always riding Daisy, or brushing her, or giving her carrots, or rubbing her nose and talking to her. One of the reasons her therapist said she had adjusted so well to the loss of her father and the move to a new town was her relationship with Daisy.

Now, as she leaned forward to get a smell of her mane, she felt like she belonged here, and never wanted to leave again.

"I'm sorry I haven't been home to visit, girl," Starlett said as she patted Daisy's neck. "Life has just gotten so crazy. It was never that way when it was just you and me out here riding. Feel like a run, do you girl? H'yah!" Starlett gave a gentle kick and Daisy sprung forward into a gallop. They road along the spine of the ridge and down into the meadow by the creek. They only covered a few hundred yards, but it was fun.

As they approached the creek, Daisy pulled up short and turned her head. She whinnied loudly and side stepped to the right and back slightly.

"What is it girl? You smell something?" Starlett scanned the woods on the other side of the creek and thought she saw something move, but she wasn't sure. Whatever it was it had stopped. She got a strange feeling in

the pit of her stomach and the hair went up on the nape of
her neck. She didn't like it at all. She turned Daisy around
and gave a short kick to get her back up to a gallop. She
slowed her to a walk as they approached the horse barn behind the house. Starlett dismounted and went through the
process of wiping Daisy down and then giving her some
warm water to drink. She finished her with a vigorous
brushing and then she put a blanket over her for the night.
The sun ducked down over the horizon as she finished and
went into the house to shower and get herself cleaned up
for dinner.

Jack sat at his kitchen table. It was a simple home with
simple furniture, and the kitchen was no exception. The
walnut stained table had been a wedding gift from his dad.
The furniture store in town was closing, and Jack Sr. knew
the owner. He knew everyone. And everyone knew him.

He held a glass of whiskey and ice in his left hand,
swirling it gently, listening to the ice clink against the
glass. He took a sip and winced as it burned all the way
down. He wasn't much of a drinker, but tonight was one of
those nights that it was almost necessary. He took another
gulp and set the glass down.

The funeral was on his mind. He had thought about
having it at the largest funeral home in town, but quickly
realized that the seating would be completely unsuitable.
He called the high school to see about renting out the
auditorium, and they approved it in an emergency board
meeting. The funeral would take place on Monday at 2pm.

The table was covered with paperwork. He was the executor of the will, and had to write up all of the forms for the insurance company. He remembered what his dad had gone through when mom had died nearly ten years earlier. It was months of paperwork. He wasn't looking forward to it. That wasn't the only thing on his mind at the moment.

He looked over the letter from the chairman of the village board. It was a request to place Jack Jr. in the position of chief of police until a thorough review and a permanent recommendation could be made. They were giving themselves six months to make the final decision. If dad had retired and made the recommendation, the board probably would have simply listened and hired Jack Jr. no questions asked. Now they were going to go through a review process which meant that the Patterson brothers would probably try to meddle in it. His father had thought they were trying to shut the department down, but what they were really up to was trying to get Craig Patterson hired on as the new chief of police. With Theo as the mayor and Craig as the police chief, they would be able to just about run the town as their own little fiefdom.

It couldn't have come at a worse time. His world seemed like it had been turned upside down in just a moment's notice. Dad was gone, he was going to have to take over amid the chaos of a funeral and he had to get up in the morning to hunt down the cougar that had attacked that Rusty kid and his little girl. It was a relief to hear they were both doing fine. At least that was one thing that seemed to work out okay.

Jack took a drink from the glass again, and didn't get nearly enough. He looked curiously at the empty glass, and reached for the bottle. He splashed the whiskey into the glass, and a little on the table as well.

Is this three or four? I've probably told a hundred drivers over the years 'if you can't remember how many, it's been too many'. Well, I'm not driving tonight, I'm drinking, so screw it, he thought, throwing the whiskey down his throat again.

And then suddenly, it all came apart. He started weeping, tears welling up in his eyes and then spilling down his face. He couldn't stop.

"Jeez, dad! Why did you have to do that?" He screamed to no one. "Why'd you go and do that? Why did you have to die now?"

He wiped the tears from his face, and forced himself to stop. He was going to be the new Chief, and that meant making decisions and looking after the entire village. It took a real man to do the job, and he might as well start now.

He pushed the glass of whiskey aside and picked up the pen he had been using to fill out and sign the insurance forms. He set to finishing the pile before he went off to bed. His vision was a bit blurry, but it wasn't so blurry as to see where he had to sign his name. The attorney had helpfully flagged each place with a little sticker.

Tubby waited until Mama was asleep before he left. He walked as quietly as he could down the stairs and froze every time they creaked. It was probably almost two o'clock in the morning, but it didn't matter. This was now a nightly ritual.

He was out the front door and down to the sidewalk. He followed the same route every night, the same one he took when he first rolled the freezer over to the storage facility. It was cold, but he had a jacket and his big boots and a hat. The wind was blowing hard, and the air smelled like snow. The weatherman said they might get snow tonight. He liked it when it snowed because it reminded him of Christmas.

As he walked across town, a car drove by slowly. Everything was closed, not even Stewart's was open anymore, they closed at midnight. A few lights were still on in some of the homes, but most of the lights were out. He felt all alone, but that was going to change.

He got to the storage facility and fished the key out from under the collar of his shirt. An old chain necklace dangled from his neck. It was where he had put the key on it so he wouldn't lose it. He bent down to the lock, chain still around his neck, and slid the key in to unlock his unit. The overhead door rolled up with an aluminum rattle. The noise it made caused him to freeze momentarily. When he was sure that no one was coming to investigate, he went inside, closing the door behind him.

Chapter 13

Morning, Seemo," he said as he took a seat at the counter. His head was pounding despite the aspirin he'd taken. "Coffee, eggs and toast, please."

"Sure thing," Seemo said. "So sorry, Jack. So sorry about Jack senior."

"Yeah, me too. It's just one of those things."

"I should have shot those punks myself," Seemo said, his voice a bit shaky with emotion. "Pop, pop."

"No. That's not how to do things. There's laws. We have to live by them. And you can't think like that. It's nobody's fault except the guys who did it."

"It just never shoulda happen. Not in here. Not like that. I'm sorry."

"Seemo, just make my breakfast, okay? I don't blame you, and you shouldn't blame yourself," Jack said with a sense of finality. He couldn't blame the guy for feeling guilty. The fight started right in here, and Seemo did what he should have, he called the police. His dad should have waited for backup or used a more guarded approach to the situation. He never should have gotten within arms' reach. It was a rookie mistake by an old pro.

"Hey, Jack, how you holdin' up?" Davidson slapped a

hand down on his shoulder as he sat down at the counter. "You up for this?"

"Yeah, I'm hanging in there. I figure this might help take my mind off everything." He lied. He couldn't get anything to take his mind off his dad.

"So, I've been reading up on this animal, and it should be pretty straight forward. We start at the location of the attack. It's a very territorial animal, and not too difficult to track. It's heavy and leaves pretty sizable tracks. It's my theory that it was being transported in that van, which means it's used to humans, so it probably won't be as skittish if it catches sight of us. In fact, if it was a pet, it might even think we've got food. It will see us before we see it. So if we do see it, we need to be ready to shoot."

"Right. I've got my shotgun in the car," Jack said. "I have to admit, I haven't been hunting in years."

"Well, we'll see what we can find out there. My guess is we don't see anything. We probably ought to consider bringing in a professional trapper," Davidson said.

"Yeah, I was thinking about that. I'm sure there's a couple of local guys that could handle it, but these things don't live around here. So we'd probably have to bring somebody in from the Rocky Mountains or something. That won't be cheap," Jack said. He had done some snooping around online and saw that there were some guys that claimed to be animal trapping professionals that might be willing to come out for this. None of them listed prices on their websites. As his father used to say, "If you had to ask the price, you couldn't afford it."

"Hello fellow hunters," Cooke said as he came in the

door. He sat down as Seemo brought out Jack's breakfast.

"What can I get you guys," Seemo asked Davidson and Cooke.

"I'll get a western omelet with a coffee," Davidson said.

"That sounds good. I'll have the same. Tall glass of orange juice too. Thanks." Michael turned towards the other two. "So are you guys ready for this? I have to say, I didn't get much sleep."

"Yeah, neither did I," Jack said. "It's been a rough week."

"Hey, how's your dad doing?" Michael asked, oblivious to what had happened.

"He didn't make it," Jack said simply.

"What? Oh, no. I'm so sorry, man."

They sat in silence. There wasn't much else to say at that moment. The news on the television wasn't much of a pick-me-up either. The weather forecast looked fine over the next few days with just clouds and seasonally mild temperatures. On the horizon, however, was the potential for another big storm, with maybe ten to twelve inches of snow possible in their area, just rain everywhere else, of course.

"Great," Davidson said.

"This is my first winter up here, I didn't realize it started in October," Cooke said.

"And goes until April, sometimes May," Jack said sardonically, taking a sip from his coffee.

"I remember when it snowed in June one year," Davidson chimed in.

"Great," Cooke replied. "Guess I should invest in a

snowmobile."

"Not a bad idea. Lots of trails through these mountains. They pulled up the rail lines a decade or so ago. Turned them into bike paths, but in the winter you can run your snowmobiles down them. Miles and miles of trails." Jack finished his breakfast just as the meals arrived for the other two men. They left off the talking and dug into their food.

Copper Owens came in just as the news switched to the story about Jack Sr.'s death. Copper didn't say a word as he took a seat at the counter next to the other men.

"Tragedy has struck in the Northern Catskills as the Chief of the Coopers Hollow Police Department, Jack McMurphy Sr., was killed in the line of duty on Thursday after responding to a call outside of this diner." The reporter was walking in front of the Peachy Keen. They had filmed it Friday afternoon, and had done a few interviews with some of the locals including Seemo and Jack. The reporter continued with the details, and they threw up the pictures of the suspects involved in the altercation. They implicated that Ramirez as the one who threw the punch that killed Jack Sr. The lawyers would now argue that they couldn't get a fair trial in this county, Jack knew. It was probably better off if the trial went down to Binghamton. The news story ended, never running the interviews with Seemo or Jack. The station went to commercial and then switched over to sports.

"Hey, Jack," Copper said quietly. "It's a shame. It truly is. If you need anything, you let Martha and I know first. Your old man was like a brother to me. We view you like family."

"Thanks, Copper. He thought the same of you," Jack sighed heavily. "Well boys, enough about my dad. Let's talk about this cougar we've got on our hands."

"You sure that's what it is? Seemo, I just need a cup of coffee. The wife cooked breakfast for me already," Copper said.

"Well, unless we find it out there today and verify, I won't know for sure until DNA testing comes back from the scat left in the van," Davidson said. "I'm now convinced, though. I spoke with Rusty Anders over the phone and he was certain of what he saw. He said his wife brought her laptop to the hospital and he showed her what type of animal attacked him and his daughter. I'm willing to bet a week's wages that it came from that van. It would have to have traveled nearly two thousand miles on its own for it to be from the wild."

"So what's the plan?" Cooke had powered through his omelet and was finishing his juice. "I've never hunted a cougar before."

"None of us have. I think we start at the trailer where the attack occurred and see if we can pick up the trail from there. I've looked at the map and there's a creek about a half mile away, so it's possible that it frequents the water's edge around that location. If we find evidence of the cougar, like tracks or droppings, then we see if we can track it back to its den. These things will attack people, but usually they'll try to flee first. They will climb a tree to try to get away too."

"I was planning on using my rifle. Do I need a special permit for that?" Cooke figured he'd ask. He'd brought along his shotgun just in case, but he'd prefer to use the rifle.

"That reminds me, I've got some papers for you to sign," Jack said. "Officially you will be acting as a temporary deputy for me on this, so we don't have to worry about permits. Davidson, Copper and I are already authorized for the hunt, but I'll be using a shotgun."

"Just be careful where you aim," Davidson recommended. "We don't want a stray bullet going into one of the houses up there."

"Right. Are there a lot of houses around?"

"Actually, not really, no. There's the Anders's trailer, then another house that's only used in the summer. Most of the houses on the outskirts of town are summer homes for people from New York. Most of that land up there is actually State-owned land, so we shouldn't have too much trouble, I guess," Jack said. He was itching to get out and get this thing over with. He only had two days until the funeral and he had to practice the eulogy. "I think we ride up together to the Anders' trailer and start off. We can split up if necessary, so I got some radios for communication."

A few locals came in, and Jack went quiet. He was nervous about panic setting in. He knew that you couldn't keep something like this quiet, but the fewer people that were aware of it the better. If they didn't kill the cougar today, he'd decided to talk with Paula and get it into the newspaper for this week, warning people to keep their kids in sight and to check on livestock and such. The other thing he was worried about was the number of hunters that would go out into the woods with aspirations of bagging the cougar that attacked Rusty.

He stole a glimpse at the table and saw that it was

a couple of the local boys. They were in their late teens now, but they'd grown up in town. Zach and Tony were brothers and good kids. They worked with their dad, Mitch Trivioli, over at the feed store. They'd turned into pretty big boys, the two of them. Too bad Coopers Hollow didn't have a football program anymore or they might have caught the attention of some college scouts. The school kept the field, but they didn't have the money for a team, not like when he was a kid. Now they had soccer, basket-ball, wrestling and baseball, but no football. The school used the football field for the soccer team, but everybody who had been in town for longer than ten years still called it the football field. They hadn't bothered to take down the goal posts. Jack had heard that the Trivioli boys had signed up to play with the semi-pro football team in Oneonta called the Stallions. He hadn't been to a game yet, and since it was a summer league, the season was already over. He'd missed his opportunity to watch them play. He'd heard they were pretty good.

"Hey, Seemo, can we get two lumberjacks and orange juices?" Zach or Tony said. Jack didn't really know the difference between the two. One was a year older than the other, but he had no idea which was which. Irish twins, despite being Italian.

"Hey, Coach." One of the boys said.

"Hey, Zach. You guys staying out of trouble?" Copper was like every boy's father or grandfather in town. He was old school. He used to coach the boys varsity basketball team for the school, but had given it up a few years back after a winless season. It wasn't like he had much to work with up here in the mountains. The year he went oh and fourteen, he had exactly seven boys on the varsity team. It was a testament to his coaching that they even put points on the board in the second half of each game, as other teams would attempt to run them up and down the court and substitute often. The years the Trivioli boys were on his squad they did pretty well. Those boys were athletes.

"Trying, coach. So, you think it's going to snow enough to take the sleds out next weekend?" Zach asked. He was the youngest of the two, Copper knew, and the more outgoing between them. He wouldn't stay in the small town. He'd be one of the many kids who would forever be from the Catskills but would never look back after he left. He was working for his dad now, but he had aspirations, dreams; and they didn't include Coopers Hollow.

"Last I heard, they're saying at least a foot. That should be enough for some good riding." Copper smiled warmly. "Did you boys get out for the last snow fall?"

"Yeah. Us and Boyd Coffer," Tony answered. "His dad gave him a new sled and we took it out. You should see it."

"Oh, I probably will soon enough. You boys need to stay on the trails now. No more shooting across Mr. Everetts' fields," Copper said. "Jack here doesn't want to get called out at two in the morning again."

"We won't," Tony lied. William Everetts was the biggest land owner in town. He had slowly bought up most of the farms as they began to shut down over the last fifty years and now he owned quite a land empire. He was over eighty years old now, and he wouldn't sell any of his land to developers. Additionally he was trying extremely hard to shut down the hiking trails on the local mountains as well as the snowmobile trails during the winter. He was a hard core environmentalist, bent on returning the land back to its natural state. Though it may have been a noble cause, the kids hated him and most of the adults didn't like him too much either. He didn't come into town too often, but he certainly gave off a creepy vibe when he did.

"Hey, fellas. You didn't happen to see anything out in the woods while you were out riding last week, did you?" Copper figured it couldn't hurt to ask, even if Jack thought it best to keep things hush hush.

"We saw that van just before it got in that accident out on twenty-three," Tony said. This caught Jack's attention.

"What time was that?" Jack swiveled on his stool to look at the boys. He hadn't been paying too much attention to the conversation up until now. "Zach, right?"

"Tony. He's Zach," Tony corrected.

"Well, I had a fifty-fifty chance. What time did you see the van?"

"Jeez, it was late, like two in the morning. We were taking the trails out towards Davenport and then up the power line trails back towards town. We stopped at the road and the van went by. It was kind of slipping and sliding all over. Going way too fast."

"Yeah," Zach chimed in. "After it went by we kept going. We never saw it wreck. I mean, we heard about it a couple days later and put two and two together is all. Maybe it was another white van, though. We can't be sure."

"Yeah, we can't be sure," Tony agreed.

"Did you boys see anything else out in the woods that night?" Jack pressed further. Maybe they had seen the cougar.

"Nope," came the replies from the two boys.

"You talking about the mountain lion?" Zach seemed sharper than his brother. Jack wondered where he would end up in life, probably some desk job in the city. "The one that attacked old Rusty and his little girl?"

"Well, something attacked them. We still think it might have been a coyote or maybe one of the neighbor's dogs. But he claims it was a mountain lion," Jack said. He felt somewhat foolish for believing a story such as this could have been kept under wraps for long in a small town. There simply wasn't anything else to talk about except the weather and the accidents that weather caused. It was a way of life up here. An animal attack story would spread like wildfire during a dry summer heat wave.

"You think it's one of the one's that the DEC stocked in the area?" Tony asked.

"Never happened," Davidson broke in. "I know it's a rumor, but the DEC never released any mountain lions or wolves or black bears into these forests. Truth is we think it came from that van you boys saw. We think maybe it was a pet that was being transported or a zoo animal or something. Anyway, it's used to humans." Davidson shot a glance at Jack. Jack nodded his compliance. The cat was out of the bag, literally.

"That's why we think it attacked the Anders," Jack finished. "So you might want to let your folks and any of your friends know to be careful. I'm going over to the paper shortly to let them know that's what we think is going on."

"Crazy," Zach said.

"Crazy, awesome! We got a mountain lion stalking people," Tony said. Copper had always known Tony was a bit of a meat-head.

"Tell that to the Anders. I was there. He was a couple minutes away from dying. One bite on his arm and the animal nearly ripped it off. Anyway, if you boys see it, you stay the hell away from it and let us know." Jack stood up and brought over some business cards. He passed them out. "Here's a few extras to give to your friends if they see it."

"I didn't know cops had business cards," Tony said, looking it over.

"Well, fellas, we should get going," Copper said. "Time's a wasting."

"Thanks, Seemo." Jack called out.

"You take care, Jack. Be safe," Seemo replied. He was carrying the plates of food over to the boys they'd been talking to. They were both soon distracted by their food as the four men made their way to the door. As they were heading out, Tubby was coming in.

"Hey, Tubby. How's it going?" Jack reached out and patted him on the back.

"It's going," he said quietly, not making eye contact.

"Thanks again for your help the other day. You're a good man for stepping in like that," Jack said.

"And yes, you can ride the fire truck for the Halloween parade," Copper said with a chuckle. "I already checked with the boys over at the fire house. They'd be happy to have you ride along. We'll even let you wear the helmet and jacket if you'd like."

Tubby didn't say another word. He perched himself on his stool and Seemo reached for a cereal bowl and two mini boxes of Frosted Flakes. The four huntsmen left the diner and reconvened on the sidewalk outside. Jack found himself looking at the sidewalk and thinking that the last time his father had been conscious was right here in this very spot. He put the thought out of his mind and tried to focus on the job at hand.

"So, let's make this easy. Let's take two vehicles. Davidson, you and Michael can ride together. I'll take Copper with me." Jack directed them. Nobody balked. They started heading to the vehicles. Copper grabbed his shotgun off the window rack in his truck, while Michael went and retrieved a pretty high-end looking case from his vehicle.

"See you up there," Davidson said to Jack and Copper as he hopped up into the DEC vehicle, buckling his seatbelt and turning the key in the ignition.

"So, where exactly are we heading?" Michael asked as he pulled on his seatbelt.

"It's north of town about seven miles or so. There's a road that shoots off to the west and winds through the mountains and eventually spits out close to Oneonta. There's only like ten or twelve houses on the entire road, and most of those are towards the Oneonta end. It's a pretty rustic area."

"You said you had a map. It's not topographical by any chance, is it?"

"Uh, actually I'm pretty sure I have one of those in the glove box. It's pretty detailed. It even has the hiking trails and stuff drawn in." Davidson said. Michael began rummaging around in the glove box and pulled a few maps out. "That one. That's it."

Michael unfolded the map and traced where they were and then tried to spot where they were going. He found the road that headed west towards Oneonta and studied the topography. A stream ran alongside the road for much of it.

He then took a moment to locate where his house was on the map. The Marine in him took over and he lost himself studying the map, putting into his permanent memory banks the lay of the land surrounding his house for ten miles in each direction.

"By the way, I never did catch your first name," Michael said, breaking from his silence.

"Well, I had a comedian for a father. He named me David."

"David Davidson. At least he didn't name you Sue," Cooke said with a smirk.

"Yeah, well he left me an out. David Jesse Davidson. They called me DJ when I was a kid. Everybody I work with just calls me Davidson. Seems to work better."

"DJ sounds like somebody's punk kid brother," Cooke said. "No offense."

"Yeah, I stopped using it when I started high school. Sometimes I'd tell people my first name was Jesse, but then the stigma of having a girl's name wasn't easy either." Davidson said.

"If you ever have kids, don't saddle them with your name," Cooke said.

"Yeah, like Jack. He's a junior. Poor guy. Losing his dad and then having to deal with this on top of it. Probably the worst week of his life," Davidson said.

"You guys buddies?"

"Not really, no. We actually met for the first time on the scene of the wreck the boys were talking about. I just transferred over to the area. I was over near Kingston for the last five years, but when the position over here opened up, I took it."

"So," Cooke inquired. "What does a DEC cop do?"

"Truthfully? I mostly write tickets for hunting or fishing without a license. You wouldn't believe how many people come up from the city to go camping and have no idea that they can't just throw in a hook without getting their license first. But we also assist with animal calls, like the one earlier in the week. I've been called out to deer strikes to put the animals down, if they're injured and still alive. We also watch over the lakes and reservoirs up here. Especially since 9/11. New York City has the world's largest, unfiltered water supply that's actually safe to drink. It all comes from the reservoirs up here. We're always nervous about somebody pouring a truckload of nerve toxin or something into the water as a terrorist attack."

"I guess I never thought about where the water came from," Michael said. "I lived in the City for most of my life. Retired US Marine Corps, then retired NYPD."

"Pretty young to be retired from two careers," Davidson said.

"Yeah, well the timing was right I guess. My mother passed away and left me some money, so I bought the place up here and decided to get away from the hustle and bustle. I was actually a little long in the tooth for ESU anyway They offered me a desk job and I countered with early retirement. I get half the pension I would have if I stayed on for another ten or fifteen years, but like I said, it wasn't about the money."

"So, what did your parents do?"

"Well, mom was an actress on Broadway. I never knew my dad," Cooke said. "What about yours?"

"Dad was a veterinarian over in the Kingston area. Mom was a stay at home housewife. I went to school to follow in his footsteps, but I just didn't like staying cooped up in the clinic all day. I got an opportunity to join up with the DEC and I took it. Never looked back."

"You like it, then?"

"I love it," Davidson said. "Here we are."

He pulled the SUV in behind McMurphy's patrol car. They got out and retrieved their guns from the trunk. Davidson pulled out his shotgun and loaded shells into it. Cooke took out his trusty rifle, and loaded the cartridges in. He'd field prepped the rifle to hold five cartridges rather than use the combat clip that held twelve rounds. He doubted he'd get a single shot off, let alone twelve. This wasn't war, it was a hunt.

"Jeez, you came ready, didn't you," Davidson said. "Can I take a look?"

Michael checked to make sure the safety was engaged

and cautiously handed over the rifle. In battle, he wouldn't let another man even look at his rifle, let alone touch it. This wasn't battle, he had to remind himself. Davidson peered through the scope and whistled.

"You shouldn't have a problem seeing it with this thing," Davidson said, handing the rifle back. "That's probably too much gun for this. What kind of ammo are you using?"

"I hand loaded ten rounds." He handed one over to Davidson. It was a 7mm full metal jacket with a hollow point tip, an experimental load, for sure. It was meant to hit the animal and then expand brutally inside before making a nice big hole on the other side as it exited. One direct hit would kill the animal. The bullet wouldn't carry as far, as he'd cut back on the gunpowder, but it would still pack a punch. He'd spent Friday zeroing in the rifle sight with the new loads and then hand-loaded another half dozen cartridges in the same way. He had a total of ten cartridges ready to go. Davidson handed back the cartridge as Cooke slung the weapon over his shoulder and joined the others.

"Check out what Rambo's packing," Davidson said to the others. They all took one look at his rifle and laughed. Everyone, that is, except Jack. He'd done a quick check on Mr. Michael Cooke when he'd gotten back to his office after Thursday's street fight, and after just a few phone calls he'd heard about all he needed to know. The man was a master rifleman. If there was one person he trusted to make the kill shot, it was Cooke.

"It's easy to see gun envy. Come on boys, bring your pop guns along and let's start this thing," Cooke said.

Jack shut the trunk to the cruiser and they started into the woods.

They wore camouflage of different prints. Copper's dated back to the early nineties. If he had to think about it, he bought this set of camo in 1993. That was the year he got an eight point buck the first day of hunting season. The camo he wore that day would be his lucky camo for as long as the threads held together.

None of them wore the day-glow orange vests or hats, as they were out in the woods off-season, and theoretically should have been the only people with guns walking around. They planned to stay in a pretty tight group so as to prevent any accidents.

"This was where the attack took place," Davidson said. He'd already been up to scout the area on Friday, and had seen the tracks. He didn't venture out too far by himself and didn't tell the others about his reconnaissance. He knelt next to the tracks. "The animal probably weighs one forty to one hundred sixty pounds. The tracks will be roughly the size of your palm. There aren't too many things in these woods that will have tracks this large."

Davidson took the lead in, as he was really the only one of the group with hunting and tracking experience. They followed the path down to the creek. It was a meandering trail, and the cat had followed its own path back from the attack.

It has already established its territory, Davidson thought. *It will be in the area.*

The creek was only about two feet deep, mostly from the melting snow that had come earlier in the week. In the spring, during the full winter run off, the creek could be up to six feet deep and twice as wide.

"It looks like it crossed the creek here," Davidson said, wading carefully across. It was going to be a lot of fun walking in wet boots for the rest of the hunt. On the other side of the creek, they found a lot more prints. They crossed and re-crossed each other.

"We are definitely in the cougar's territory now. If you look, it has approached this place from several different directions. Everybody needs to keep their eyes open. Cougars are ambush predators, which means they stalk their prey and use stealth right up until the moment they strike. The only thing we may have going for us is that this particular cat may have no experience hunting in the wild. That's a good thing and a bad. It means it's hungry, but it also means that it may have no idea how to sneak up on us without alerting us. Then again, instinct is hardwired. That will come out soon enough."

"Do you think we should split up and track a couple of trails," Cooke asked. Now that he knew what to look for, he was confident he could follow the marks.

"You brought radios, right?" Davidson looked to McMurphy.

"I left them in the cruiser, sorry guys," Jack said.

"I can go back and get them," Copper offered. "You guys figure out which trails we'll follow, and I'll be back in two minutes."

Instinct did indeed take over quickly. Hunger had a

tendency to make animals take greater risks, but it also called up what Davidson had referred to as a "hardwired" response. It had been near the trailer when the vehicles had pulled up, drawn by the scent of garbage. The noise had been enough to push it back into the woods out of sight. It slunk backwards watching as the men gathered their gear, made jokes about each others' guns, and set off into the woods.

Four of them were too many, but if one strayed from the group, it might prove to be a tasty meal. It had learned from the last encounter with humans. The flesh was much thicker and fattier than it had anticipated. It needed a deeper bite for a kill. It wouldn't make the same mistake again. Even though these humans were larger, it was hungrier now and willing to take the risk.

It stalked the group about fifty yards to their left. It stayed low and weaved through the trees with caution and grace. It watched as they stopped at the water. It recognized the spot. It had caught a fish in the shallows there. It had visited several more times but never found a similar meal.

Then one of them split from the group and headed back. It was the slowest of the group. It paused, calculating its next move. Instinct told it to go for the vulnerable prey. It closed in, now only twenty yards away. The prey was oblivious. It was now out of sight of the others of the group, and it could hear the labored breathing of the prey. Suddenly the human stopped. It was resting from exhaustion. The fight would be short. It came in closer. Ten yards. The human began walking again.

The human was leading it back towards the clearing

where it had entered the woods. Instinct said to not have another showdown in the open like it had before. It had lost that prey; it wasn't going to lose this one. It was now following twenty feet behind. The human stopped and turned.

"Jack," Copper called out. His hearing wasn't the best at his age, but he thought he'd heard something. It was a snap of a twig in the woods behind him. It was the type of snap that a person or a large animal would make. He turned around and scanned behind him. He saw no signs of his hunting companions, but of course they were all wearing camouflage, so they'd be difficult to see. "Jack? That you?"

"Did you guys hear that?" Cooke had turned his ear and strained. "I think Copper is calling you Jack."

"Yeah, I think I hear it too," McMurphy said. "He probably can't find the radios. You two stay here, I'll double time it up the hill and be back in a minute." He handed his shotgun to Davidson and started to jog back towards the vehicles and towards Copper.

"He left his gun," Cooke said.

"Yeah," Davidson replied.

"We're in the woods, hunting a deadly cougar and he just gave up the only thing that makes the difference between predator and prey." The Marines had taught Cooke how to hunt men, not animals, but with a target like the one they were hunting, it really wouldn't be much different. One of the things they taught in Scout Sniper school was how to know when the hunter could become the hunted. You never gave up the tactical advantages. That's how you ended up dead.

It was suddenly aware of movement behind it. Heavy footfalls were coming from behind. It crept quietly away from the initial prey, giving up ground as a caution. It waited, crouched low, tail twitching ever so slightly. Its ears were up and it sniffed the air. It could smell one of the other humans now.

Copper thought he saw something in his peripheral vision. He quickly looked over to where he thought he saw the small trees move ever so slightly, even though there wasn't any wind. He brought his shotgun up to his shoulder slowly. He kept his eyes moving. The eye caught movement much better when it was scanning than when it was fixed on one spot. He saw movement again, and slid the safety off.

Suddenly Jack burst through the path and right into Copper's sights. Copper felt his finger press against the trigger for a split second, then release quickly as he realized it was McMurphy.

"Jeez, Jack! I nearly put a bullet in you." Copper was

sweating profusely now. He fingered the safety back into place and pointed the barrel of his shotgun at the ground. "And you nearly gave me a golldarned heart attack."

"Sorry, we thought you were calling me," Jack said. He was angry. He had questioned whether they were all qualified to be out here hunting an animal like this, but having a near miss hadn't even entered his mind. He'd nearly been shot because of sheer stupidity and his forgetfulness. He thought that perhaps they should call this off, end this thing right now. None of them, except for maybe Davidson, were qualified to be out here.

"It's okay, Copper. No harm no foul. Did you think you saw something?"

"Yeah, over there, to the left. I thought I saw something moving," Copper said pointing. They scanned the area he indicated.

"I don't see anything. It could have been a squirrel or bird or something," Jack said. He was sweating now too, despite the cool weather. Double time up the graded hill had him breathing hard.

It's alright, you needed the workout. If you're going to be Police Chief you need to get your butt in shape. A lot of eyes are going to be on you from outside the department, Jacky-boy, he thought to himself. Just finish this thing. It's what the Chief should do.

"Stay here, I'll go get the radios," Jack said. He walked the rest of the way to the vehicle. He could hear his heart pounding in his ears.

You need to get back on the treadmill, you've gotten soft.

He retrieved the four radios and put them in his jacket pockets. As he started walking back, he heard something. It sent a shiver up his spine. It sounded like a wounded animal moaning.

It watched the two humans. They spoke briefly and then the one that had come up on it by surprise headed away. The older, weaker one was alone. It saw its opportunity. It crept in closer. The gap narrowed now. Ten feet. It coiled, and then pounced.

Copper thought he heard something and turned back towards the direction where he knew Cooke and Davidson were. What he saw made him freeze. The cougar was coming straight at him. He tried to bring his shotgun around, but it was on him too quickly. He tried to yell for help, but a hoarse, guttural groan was all that came out. He lifted an arm in self defense and shoved it into the cat's gaping mouth. Teeth crunched down hard, and he felt his forearm break. He fell backwards, as the big cat came down on him, claws digging deeply into his chest.

"Did you hear that," Michael asked.

"Yeah," Davidson said, standing erect. He'd been crouching, looking at the tracks along the creek side.

"That was a man," Cooke remembered stories from some of the boys down at the VFW. Those that had been over in Afghanistan especially had stories that would make you wince. They would talk about the sounds of warfare. It wasn't like in the movies. Often times all you heard was the screams of pain. The closest thing he'd personally experienced was in indoctrination when one of the guys came down the rope too fast and snapped his ankle. It was animalistic in its tone. A wounded human made a horrible sound that you could never forget.

Cooke didn't hesitate. He sprinted up the hill, unslinging his rifle in one swift movement. He'd gone about fifty yards at a dead run when he saw what his eyes couldn't comprehend. The cougar was on top of a man. The man was fighting as best he could, but the cougar had him. It was only seconds away from killing the man. Cooke brought the rifle up and squeezed the trigger.

Bang!

Jack heard the rifle and it was close. He ducked instinctively from the loud report of sound. He realized he didn't have his shotgun, as he'd left it with Davidson. All he had was his sidearm, a 9mm pistol. He unholstered the handgun even as he ran towards the sound.

He was ten steps in when he came upon them. Cooke was racing up the hill towards him, rifle in hand. Copper was absolutely bathed in blood. His face was scratched severely, and he was clutching at his neck with one hand. The other arm was bent at an odd angle halfway up his forearm. Beside him, on the ground, was the cougar. Its chest was blown open, and it's right front leg was barely attached.

"Copper!" Jack was on his knees besides the Fire Chief. Blood was spurting from his neck where a chunk of flesh was missing. Jack could see the cougar had gotten a hold of him and ripped him open viciously. Michael had gotten to the fallen man just a few moments before Jack and was already pressing a hand onto the neck wound, but blood was squirting from between his fingers.

Jack looked Copper in the eyes and saw that he was already fading. It would only be a few more seconds. Copper tried to speak, but he just sputtered blood from his lips. He suddenly reached up for something unseen and then his arm collapsed to the ground. He was dead.

For the second time in a week an ambulance would be called out to the Anders' trailer for an animal attack. For a second time, Jack McMurphy was the first officer on the scene. This time, though, there was a different outcome.

Michael had rushed up to Copper and attempted to staunch the flow, but he realized just as quickly as Jack had, that it was a lost cause. He watched the fragile flicker of life fade from the man's eyes. Looking up he saw Jack turn away, tears welling up in his eyes. Cooke was very much aware that his shot could have passed through the cougar and hit Copper. He checked the wounds and saw that they had all been inflicted by the animal. He had just been a few moments too late.

Davidson came up a few moments later, and dropped to his knees as well. He just hung his head. This was what he was afraid would happen. They'd gotten the cougar, but at what cost? Jack stood and ran back to his car to call the ambulance, and he stayed by the vehicle. He couldn't go back and see his friend laying there in the pool of blood. It was too much for him. First his dad, now this. It was too much for one man to bear in such a short time.

When it was clear that nothing could be done for Copper, and that he was gone, Cooke reached up and closed the man's eyes. He then checked the cougar. The bullet had struck it in the hind quarter and ripped right through its insides. It had exited through the front of the right shoulder, leaving a hole almost ten inches across. The bullet had probably missed Copper's head by less than a foot, not that it mattered now. Cooke had taken the shot he had to take. He'd get credit for killing the cougar, but he took no special satisfaction from the fact. He was late. He took the shot too late.

He thought about that afternoon years before, perched atop the building in New York City, the perpetrator in his sites, the woman cruelly duct taped to a shotgun, her life moments away from a violent end. He had a shot, but he was waiting for the go ahead. Had he pulled the trigger even just twenty seconds sooner, she may have lived. The bullet would have severed the perp's spine, rendering him incapable of pulling the trigger. But he didn't, and she died a cruel death that sweltering afternoon.

Copper Owens lay in the underbrush of the forest, drenched in his own blood. If Cooke's shot had come a moment or two sooner, they might have all been joking about the close call, slapping each other on the backs in congratulatory fashion. Now there were no jokes. No back slapping. No one said a word. He didn't take the shot in time.

The Machine felt broken inside.

Chapter 14

"Are you okay?"

"Yeah, I'll make it," he replied.

He was gingerly getting out of the car. The bright light of the morning hurt his eyes, and it still hurt to squint. He'd been kept under observation for nearly three days. He'd suffered a concussion, broken nose, and possible whiplash to his neck. His neck still hurt, and his nose still throbbed, but the headaches weren't nearly as severe thanks mostly to the pain meds.

His mother and father had hired a full time nurse to get him healthy again, and she was supposed to arrive in just half an hour. That was what life was like in their household. If there was a problem, money could solve it. It made for a very comfortable lifestyle, but it also meant that he had been insulated from his missteps for most of his life. Perhaps that was why he kept pushing his own actions to the very brink of self-destruction.

It was as if he had two completely different persons living inside of him. The one was the well mannered and well manicured son of a wealthy banking magnate and a refined socialite. The other was a morose, self-loathing and very self-destructive young man. He said the right things to get the girl, he did enough to get the grades, and he acted the part of a good son enough to keep the money flowing in from mom and dad. Yet he was also fascinated by the criminal elements, the dregs of society. They seemed to move without the social mores by which he was constrained. They did what they wanted, and nobody told them what to do. It was a power he wanted to possess.

That's how he got mixed up with the wrong crowd. He'd been tempted by curiosity and fascination. He'd been hooked by the danger and intrigue. He'd been reeled in by the prospect of being a real bad guy. Hook, line and sinker, he'd swallowed the bait. Then he'd been caught by the cops.

They'd asked him to drive a car. He didn't ask what was in it, what he'd be carrying, he just did it. The story he'd told Starlett hadn't been one hundred percent accurate. He had seen a police car and had gotten spooked. He parked the car and walked back to their apartment before he made the delivery like he was supposed to. Like an idiot he had parked the car in a tow-away zone. The car was towed and then impounded. A cursory search had turned up the drugs. A security camera had captured Dalton's movements after he had parked the car, so it wasn't difficult for the cops to track him down. They'd handcuffed Starlett as well when they had came to take him away. It scared him, so he told them everything. He wasn't a drug dealer, he was an idiot, and he knew it. From what the family lawyer said, the cops knew it too. It wasn't the first time a spoiled rich kid ended up as a mule for drug dealers. The cops wanted all the details of who he was dealing with. He didn't even cut a deal before he gave them all up. Within hours the cops had made phone calls, they'd snagged several low level dealers, but then the trail ran cold. The family lawyer angled to have him turn State's witness to put away the real dealers. The DA accepted, and he was free on bail. Starlett had been released almost immediately, and had refused to talk to him. That's why he followed her up to Coopers Hollow. The thugs must have followed him.

"Dalton, sweetie, are you going to be okay," his mother was talking to him over the phone. She'd called just before they'd gotten back home. Neither his father nor his mother came to see him while he was in the hospital. The butler and his wife came. They were the ones that gave him a ride home. They'd driven the four hours up to the hospital to pick him up and then four hours home.

"Yeah, mom, I'm going to be fine. I'm going to see if Starlett wants anything to do with me anymore. And if she does, if she wants to talk or something, I'm going to head back up to her mom's place in the Catskills. She's staying there for now. Anyway, I'm going to be fine. Keep soldiering on, right?"

"Do you really think that's a good idea? After all, going up there landed you in the hospital in the first place. You know there are plenty of girls who would just die to go out with you," his mother said. It sounded like she was ordering drinks while she was talking with him.

"I don't want another girl. I'm in love with Starlett."

"Thanks. No, I'm almost done," she said to someone else. "Keep soldiering on, honey. That's all any of us can do." She was in the Bahamas. Dad was in Germany. They were soldiering on in their own ways, in their own little worlds, away from each other. "I love you, honey bun. See you when I get back."

"Love you too, mom. Have fun in the Bahamas." He thumbed the touch screen on his phone to end the call. He walked slowly inside. He was wearing a neck collar to keep his head still and not aggravate the whiplash. He'd have to wear it for a few weeks until everything healed. Especially while riding in a car.

Home was in northern New Jersey. It was close enough to New York for an easy commute for his father, but far enough away to let them have a four thousand square foot house without the multi-million dollar price tag. Last time it was appraised it was only worth $1.2 million, but they hadn't paid that much for it, they were much more frugal.

He went inside and sat down on the overstuffed sectional sofa. He reclined his seat and held up his phone. Thumbing over to Starlett's number, he pressed the talk button. He listened to it ring six times before Starlett's voice came on and told him that she wasn't available but he should leave a message and she'd get back to him. He closed down the connection.

He texted her: "hey. no ur angry. giv me chanc 2 xpln. luv u."

Send.

He turned on the seventy-inch flat screen and kicked off his shoes. Peter, their butler, and more of a father to him than his real dad, came out with a glass of water.

"How are you feeling? Can I get anything for you," Peter asked, concern on his face.

"No, Pete, I'm fine. I'm just tired, is all. Thanks, by the way. Thanks for everything. Everything you've done for me, for us."

"Dalton, it's my job. But it is also my passion. This family has given my family everything. We owe our lifestyle to your mother and father. We're appreciative of what we've been given," Peter said. "Dalton, if I may be so bold, I suggest you think about what you've been given and give thanks as well. I'm not talking about your parents. I'm talking about your second chance at life. You very well could have faced a life in prison. You're not out of the woods yet, but it looks as if you have dodged a significant bullet. Be thankful."

"I get you, Pete. I get what you're saying. I will be. Thanks," Dalton said. He sipped his water and watched the news. His phone beeped as a text message came in.

"Call me again," it read.

He thumbed over to her number again and called her.

"You wanted to see me," she asked as she sat down. She'd put on an outfit that she knew accentuated her curves and showed off more of her figure than normal. She was attractive and she knew it. Most of the unattached guys in town would hit on her when they saw her. Even some of the attached guys would as well. She'd always had her eye on Jack McMurphy, though. She'd actually dated him once, and it had gone well until she ruined it. She'd quoted an unnamed source within the police department who disagreed with what the Mayor of Coopers Hollow was doing about a certain building permit. McMurphy had actually called him a bigot for not letting the religious group build their new meeting hall. The mayor was throwing up every roadblock he could to stop the project. Everyone in town knew that she and McMurphy were an item at the time, and it didn't take a detective to figure out who it was that had called the mayor a bigot. They only had three choices. Needless to say, the mayor lost the election, and she lost Jack.

"Yeah, I do. Thanks for coming in." He looked exhausted. What he'd been through over the last two weeks was enough to make a lesser man snap like a twig. He was bending, but not breaking.

"You look like," she said, pausing. She wanted to say the right things to him. "Like you could use a home cooked meal and a nice shoulder rub." It got a smile out of him.

"That does sound good, Paula. If you keep asking, I might give in one of these days." He was all alone now, with simply no one to talk to and she could see it was difficult for him.

"Well, when do you get off," she pushed.

"At six," he relented.

"I'll have dinner ready, if you want to come over," she leaned in closer. "I won't screw up this time."

"Paula, I'd like to put it behind us, that whole thing that happened with the article. I don't care about it anymore. Life's too short," he said. "It's really too short. But that's not what I wanted to talk to you about. I need your help."

"I'm all yours," she flirted.

"I'm really short on resources right now. With dad gone, I just don't have time to check into a few things that

I need to. There's all this paperwork. And the lawyers. Anyway, you're ten times the investigator I'll ever be."

"What do you need," she asked. This was a completely unexpected development. Jack was usually so tight lipped about investigations these days. Not that there were many true investigations in Coopers Hollow.

"It's the whole cougar fiasco. Nobody wants to do anything about it. Davidson over at the DEC is using all of his resources, but they aren't much. They're running DNA on the dead animal to see if they can trace its origin, but that will only let us know what region of the world it came from. It will just confirm that it was probably trucked in here and not native. We both think that it came in that van that was in the fatal accident over a week ago. Remember, back during the storm? Anyway, I've called the rental company, and they aren't saying anything anymore. Something about breach of privacy or something. I've tried the driver's phone numbers, and there's nothing. Nobody's talking. I'm thinking you might have better luck."

"You want me to investigate where the cougar came from?"

"Yeah. Davidson is certain that it escaped from the van. He thinks it was part of an illegal animal smuggling operation. Well, whoever it was that was shipping that cougar is responsible for Copper's death and the attack on Rusty Anders and his daughter. Somebody should pay."

"Jack, it's been a rough week for you. Losing your dad, watching poor Copper get killed. But you can't blame yourself. None of it was your fault," she reached across his desk and put her hand on his. He didn't pull away.

"It's not about blaming myself. It's about doing my job. If someone was responsible, I need to find out who and do something about it. I'm the Chief of Police now," he said, furrowing his brow. Before his dad died, when he thought about becoming Chief he imagined it would bring with it the ultimate feeling of accomplishment. Instead, it felt like an incredible burden had just been passed to him. The weight of the entire town was on his shoulders.

"I'll do it," she said. "With one condition."

"What's that?"

"You let me snoop around through some of the old records in the basement of this place."

"Why?" Jack thought it an odd request.

"Because I'm a digger, Jack. Not only are there police records here, but old bank records as well. That type of data tells the story of a community like nothing else can. Please?" She used her school girl pouty look.

"Sure, I guess. Everything in the basement is over twenty years old. I don't see the harm in it," Jack relented.

"Well, Chief. I'm your girl. I'll do everything I can to track down that cougar."

"Here's a copy of my investigation up to this point. I have one thing to ask with a promise: If you find out anything, I'll make sure you get the exclusive and I'll only talk to you about it. All the news agencies will have to come through you. But promise me don't breathe a word about this to anyone until we find something. If it got out that I was going outside this office for investigative help, it might not look good. There's already people who would love to see me fall on my face. You treat me fairly on this, and I'll do the same, okay."

The phone rang on his desk and he answered it.

"Coopers Hollow Police Department, this is Chief McMurphy," he said, still not used to saying it. "Oh hey, Jude, can you hang on a second?"

"It's Jude Elkland, I've owed him a call back since before dad died. I need to take this," He explained. "So, you will do it?"

"Absolutely," she said without hesitation.

She took the manila folder he'd held out, and reached over and gave him a quick peck on the cheek. "Six o'clock tonight. Dinner. My place."

"It's a date," he said, with a half smile. He felt a little bit of the weight lift off him as he returned to the phone call with Jude Elkland to talk about the vandalism problem.

She left the Police station and walked down the street towards her office. She had an appointment for a photo shoot with Michael Cooke, the man who shot and killed the cougar. She'd gone back and forth with what she was going to call the animal in her article and finally settled on cougar, as it seemed to fit the easiest. The article was written already, and the entire paper was set, except for the front page photo. She had asked that Cooke bring the rifle that he used to take the shot, and they would get take a few pictures.

This week's paper would be a double issue. They'd been able to sell nearly triple the ads they normally did because of all of the local news. This would be the highest print run of *The Mountain Star* in nearly fifty years. It would be the paper that everyone saved which made the ads all the more valuable. More importantly, it would be the paper that all the other news agencies across the country would pick up. They had decided as a group at *The Mountain Star* that they would release the lead story to the Associated Press, or AP the same morning they published. It would give them a one day lead on the other papers and maybe a forty-five minute lead on the websites and blogs. They'd been monitoring the websites and social networks to see if anyone else was publishing the details of the attack, and so far, there had been very little to get out. Paula had Jack to thank for that. He hadn't said a word to another reporter. He'd really given her the exclusive. Even though she liked the little provincial town, she was now entertaining dreams of being picked up as a writer for a major publication.

She'd wished to get a chance to work for one of the weekly news magazines like *Newsweek* or *Time*, but anymore, the news was not being generated there. What she needed was a big story like this and then once her name was used, she'd push her blog. She'd been updating her personal blog regularly and saw that she had around a thousand people who checked it weekly. That seemed like a lot in a small town, but she knew it was barely scratching the surface of the internet's full potential. She had an ex-boyfriend, once upon a time, who fancied himself an entrepreneur, an internet genius. He would go on and on about how the internet was changing everything. The only thing the internet did for him was support a thousand dollar a day drug and debauchery habit. Last she heard his daddy was paying for yet another stint in rehab.

After the photo shoot, she would finalize the issue. They still had another day until they went to press. The team had talked about going to print a day early, but decided that they could use that extra day to sell a few more ads and maybe add another two pages. They could always enlarge the local sports photos to buy up column inches if they didn't quite have enough ads to fill the extra pages. They also had a couple of seasonal stories ready to go. With Halloween just over a week away, they could always get away with another story featuring the real history behind All Hallows' Eve.

She walked up the front steps and paused, looking up at the old neon sign that said Lexmore Hotel. When she'd done the first floor refurbishing, she'd thought about taking down the sign, but decided she liked it too much to do that. She'd opted instead to have the words *The Mountain Star* painted onto the front window. Besides, she imagined that one day she'd have enough money to convert the old rooms into a couple of nice apartments and the old sign would add some personality to the place. She already had an efficiency apartment on the first floor, which she used for her living quarters. Maybe if she could use the rest of the building to generate additional revenue she could buy out the shares owned by *The Kingston Chronicle* and own the paper free and clear again.

A large blue Ford Super Duty pickup truck was sitting in the gravel parking lot of *The Mountain Star* offices, and she wondered if it was Cooke's vehicle. She checked her reflection in the glass doors to make sure her hair and makeup were still in place and entered the building.

When she walked into the office, she knew something was wrong. Everyone was there, including James Solomon, President of *The Kingston Chronicle*, their partner paper. She also noticed a man sitting in the rather small waiting area, which consisted of just two chairs by a plant in front of Trudy's desk.

"Oh, it's you," she said to Cooke.

"It's me," he replied. "Listen, I was rude when we first met in the diner. I get cranky when I'm hungry. Sorry."

"You must have been really hungry," she said. He apologized for being an jerk, but she didn't have to accept it, at least not right away.

"Trudy, what's going on, why is J.S. here?" Paula asked quietly as she took off her jacket and put it up on the rack.

"I have no idea," Trudy replied, but she looked worried. "He came in and asked where everybody was and then asked when everybody was going to be back. I think he's going to make some kind of announcement."

"If this isn't a good time, I can come back," Michael said. "Or we can just skip this whole photo thing all together. I really wouldn't mind at all."

"No, no. We definitely want a photo of you and your gun," she replied.

"Rifle," he corrected.

"Right," she countered. "You and your rifle. I've seen Full Metal Jacket. I do know the difference." She winked at him and walked back towards her business partner.

"Hey, J.S. What brings you here?" She knew they'd been doing well, which couldn't be said for most newspapers, so she was hoping the visit was for something positive.

"Well, I've got an announcement to make, and I wanted to do it in person," he said with a bit of grandiosity. "Who's that?" He was indicating Cooke.

"He's here for a photo. He's our cover story," Paula said.

"Ok. Well, here it is. You guys have really done a good job over here. I've been impressed with the revenue you've managed to take out of this tiny market, and you've actually increased your circulation. It has to do with your editorial decisions, Paula. It also has to do with the excellent ad designs and the website you guys are running. Articles are updated regularly, and the site looks tight. I'm very happy."

"Thanks," Paula said. "We work really hard over here."

"Yeah, thanks," Toby, the graphic designer, said. He'd taken his oversized earphones off to listen to the conversation. Well, not off, off. They were still around his neck and the music could still be heard.

"So, I hope you'll be excited to hear that we've made a decision. We are going to roll *The Mountain Star* into *The Kingston Chronicle*." He rubbed his hands together and had a look on his face of a kid who was about to draw up the perfect play in a game of back yard football. "We're changing the name of *The Kingston Chronicle* to *The Mountain Chronicle*. We're pulling in *The Catskill Town Crier* as part of this restructuring as well. Rather than a separate weekly paper, you'll have a weekly section. *The Mountain Star*'s section will run Thursdays, and the Town Crier's section will be Tuesdays."

"You can't do that!" Paula felt like she'd just gotten kicked in the stomach.

"Paula, listen. The agreement you signed with us over a year ago was very straightforward. If you didn't meet certain goals, we became the majority owners. That gives us the right to do whatever we need to do to make this paper more profitable," he said matter-of-factly.

"But I won't allow it," Paula countered.

"Then we will buy out your share for the agreed upon ten thousand dollars as stipulated in the contract," J.S. said. Paula was aware of what he was talking about. They had put in a clause that allowed the majority owner to buy out the other party for ten thousand dollars. She had agreed to the terms back when she had been the majority owner. She'd just allowed the paper she had built from practically nothing to be pulled out from under her. J.S. had produced a check from his jacket pocket. He held it out to her, but she didn't take it.

"And what happens if I agree to the move?"

"Like I said, *The Mountain Star* gets its own weekly section under the new *Mountain Chronicle* masthead," he said. He set the check down on the desk.

"So we're being demoted from a paper to a section?" Paula was not happy. She knew that the paper up in Catskill, NY had elbowed out its niche within their market as well, whereas *The Chronicle* was struggling. The lifeboats were being called back in to buoy up the sinking ship. Actually it was more like they were stealing another ship's lifeboats.

"It's not a demotion, it's a restructuring. The advantage

is you'll have more resources at your disposal. You'll get an infusion of new potential customers and broader reach for the articles that you write. Additionally your advertisers should love it! They're going to be able to get advertising all over the region now."

"But rates will go up?" Harry Osterhaut asked. He already knew what was going on. They were in the midst of a hostile takeover. Somebody was looking at the sales in the area and thought it would be a good idea to raid those sales for their own numbers.

"Maybe a little, but the advertisers will get so much more for their money," J. S. explained.

"Realistically, many of our advertisers can't afford higher rates. If you raise rates ten percent, you'll lose thirty percent of the advertisers, especially if their ads are now going to be buried in a back section of the paper," Harry argued.

"So you're saying that all of our jobs are safe if I agree?" Paula interrupted. She was getting the same impression that Harry was. It wasn't a job offer, it was extortion. They'd be forced to turn over all of their client info to the home office and then they'd get the old heave-ho over the railing.

"Sure, we'll have a place for each one of you," J. S. said.

"Here? Will we all still have jobs here?" Harry asked.

"Well," the President of *The Kingston Chronicle* paused. What was he to expect, they were newspaper people. They dug for the meat of the story. "Paula will remain here in Coopers Hollow as the lead reporter for the area if she wishes and will be able to continue with her editorial position for the new section. Trudy and Harry, we have positions available in Catskill for you if you'd like to take them. Toby, we'd like you to come to Kingston and work in the home office."

"Cool," Toby replied. He was a local kid who'd gone to college in Oneonta, received a good degree in art, and promptly moved back into his old room at his mom's house. She'd been trying to kick him out for three years. "I hope that comes with relocation assistance and a bit of a raise."

"We can talk about the details later, but yes, we will be able to offer each of you a little something extra," J. S. said. A very little something extra, he didn't say.

"Well that's fine for Toby, he's got to move, what, a bed and a video game system?" Harry wasn't happy.

"Three video game systems. And a computer," Toby said helpfully.

"We own a house here in Coopers Hollow," Harry continued. "Catskill is a forty-five minute drive on a good day. In the winter it's next to impossible."

"Well, you don't have to take the position. But we're all hoping that you will. Of course it's up to you," J. S. said, as respectfully as he could. What they were really hoping was that Trudy and Harry would reject the offer and find someplace else to work. It would make it so much easier for everybody involved. "Unfortunately, if Miss Schumann rejects our offer and takes the buy-out, we can't really afford to bring any of you on board at all."

"This is extortion, J.S. and it's not fair," Paula said. She already knew what she had to do. She'd accept the terms of the move and keep her forty-nine percent ownership. It would give her a little clout at least.

"Things aren't always fair in life, Paula. I'm sorry that you feel like we're not treating you justly. We are sticking to the contract you signed. When you look at it, the fact that we're willing to keep you all on and give you raises to boot shows that we're being very fair in this. Newspapers across the country are closing down left and right. You all should be glad to have a job in this day and age," J.S. said. He didn't want to trot out the old "you should be thankful to have a job" routine, but sometimes you had to go with what worked. He'd gotten to his position in life by being a shrewd negotiator. He'd purposefully setup the negotiations to put as much pressure on Paula as possible. He wanted to make sure that everyone in *The Mountain Star* office knew that they were following the letter of the contract that she had signed and that if there was anyone to blame for the current situation, it was Paula Schumann. He wanted to erode their loyalty to her.

"What about the logistics? How am I supposed to be editor here when I won't have a designer doing layouts in this office?" Paula was starting to acquiesce to the proposal. She could see no way out of it.

"You can file your stories electronically. We can send emails with PDF files back and forth," J. S. said matter-of-factly. He knew that a PDF was a computer file, and they could look at newspaper pages on the computer screen with them, but he wasn't sure about how they were generated, or why they had to use those over a Word file. He didn't have to know, he figured, that's what he paid people around him to do.

"When does all of this happen," Harry asked. His face had taken on a brighter shade of red than normal. His ears looked absolutely incandescent.

"This week. This issue will be the last to carry *The Mountain Star* masthead. Next week the section will be rolled out under the new *Mountain Chronicle* masthead, and it will be the feature story on the front page, barring any major news. So, wrap up this week and then get things packed up here. Paula, of course you're welcome to stay here, after all, you own the building. Everyone else needs to report to your new positions on Monday." He looked down at his watch in a planned exit strategy. "Oh, is that the time? I need to get back to Kingston. We have a lot of work to do before we make this thing happen next week."

No one else said a word. They mostly looked at the ground. Toby popped his earphones back on and spun back around to his computer where he was working on dropping the last story into place on the front page.

"Well, if any of you have any additional questions, you can call over to Kingston and talk with Davie. He'll make sure everybody makes the transition smoothly. And look at this as a new opportunity. I know change is difficult, but often times, if you embrace it, you might be surprised at how much you actually enjoy it. Take care all!" He pulled on his gray trench coat and left.

"Perfect," Trudy said. Her husband, Harry, stood there, clenching and unclenching his fists. He looked like he was going to punch someone. He turned and, instead, kicked his metal garbage can as hard as he could. It flew against the wall with a loud bang that made everyone jump. Papers and debris went all over, and the can was nearly bent in all the way.

"Well, I've got to go take a few pictures for what is going to be our last issue. If you'll excuse me," Paula said to the others. They didn't make eye contact with her. Both Trudy and Harry blamed her for this. Her inexperience in business negotiations had just cost them their livelihood. This day had not gone nearly as planned.

"I couldn't help but overhear," Cooke said as Paula approached him. "I'm sorry. It sounds like a raw deal."

"For Harry and Trudy more than for me or Toby. Heck, he wanted to move away, he was just too lazy to put out résumés. Let's go get a couple of photos before the sun goes down too far. You did bring your rifle, right?" Paula grabbed the camera as she spoke.

"Yeah, just like you asked on the phone," he replied.

"Good, I'd like you to use it on somebody," she said, only half joking.

They finished taking the shots she wanted, and Cooke said goodbye. He put the rifle back in its case and placed it into the passenger seat of the Ford truck. Then he headed down the street to Taylor's Taproom.

Paula took the camera in to Toby and they went through the photos. They selected two for the front page. One was down the barrel of the rifle, looking at Michael as he had his eye to the scope. It was a very dramatic pose. The hunters would all love it. The liberal city folk who had

moved up here permanently would hate it. The other photo was a waist-up shot that they cropped slightly. Cooke
was standing stone faced holding his rifle across his chest.
They would blow both pictures up as big as possible. This
was the man who killed the cougar that killed Copper
Owens, the fire chief of Coopers Hollow and a pillar of the
community for decades. He'd be a local hero.

After they were done, Paula took the time to look
everything over and give the issue its final approval. It
was a bitter sweet moment. Probably the biggest, most
newsworthy story she'd ever written for the paper and it
was turning out to be her last. Sure there would be more
writing assignments, but they wouldn't be for "her" paper,
as she liked to think of it.

She gave Toby the go-ahead to send off the electronic
files and left for her apartment in the back to start fixing
dinner for Jack. At least maybe she'd have a little fun
tonight.

Chapter 15

So whataya wanna do?" It was the obvious question. What should he do? He could do nothing at all, and just wait for them to come and get him. Or he could take the fight to those that had put him in this position, the people who couldn't keep their mouths shut. And he knew they wouldn't keep 'em shut.

"We shut 'em up," he said simply. There was really only one way for that to be taken. "Make sure they can't talk. We cut 'em off before they can breathe a word. We sever any links."

"We can't get to KayJay or Willow. They're in lock-up."

"Who put them in lock-up?"

"Bull and Shaniqua. But we can't get them 'cause they're in lock-up too."

"And who put them in lock-up?"

"That prep, Dalton Beckman."

"And where's he?"

"Well, they let him out, cause he rolled on everybody else. So he's either at his place on campus, or back at his parents' flat in Princeton."

"Let's take him on campus, finish it there. We make it messy. Everyone else will get the message. They'll do their time and won't breathe a whisper. Find out if they have any kids and take some pictures. Send them the pictures in the joint with circles. Nothing else. Just circles around the kids faces. They'll get the message, awright."

"On the Beckman kid, you want I should maybe take someone or do it alone, boss?"

"I'm going. I'm not going to let some little puissant, college boy run his mouth and make a fool out of me. Before I put a bullet in his head, he'll know who he crossed. El Tigre."

"El Tigre," Ramirez repeated.

"Stand behind that line and face the camera." He did as he was instructed. As of right now, all they had him on was disturbing the peace and maybe a simple assault charge if Dalton was dumb enough to press charges. Ramirez was going to do some time for punching that cop, but that was just a stupid accident. He would get assaulting an officer. Unless Dalton opened his mouth again, there would be nothing to tie them back to anything.

"Take your shirt off," the officer said to him.

"Why?"

"We document tattoos and scars," was the reply. "Please remove your shirt."

He reluctantly complied. He had tats alright. One of his most proud pieces of body art was the Asian styled tiger that went up his neck. He would sometimes cover it with makeup when he dressed in a suit. He was smarter than most dealers. He knew he had to speak respectfully, dress sharply and look like a fine upstanding member of society when he wasn't dealing with his people. People always had and always would judge a book by its cover. That's what book covers were for. Otherwise every single book would just have a plain cover with only the title and author.

"Whoa," the officer said. "Turn around so we can get the ones on your back too."

He had a few nice pieces of art on his well toned chest. A tiger was on his left pectoral and a naked woman with tiger stripes on his right. His back had large tiger stripes all the way down, done in a tribal style. A frequenter of the tanning salon, his skin was a light brown with an orange tint. The dark tiger stripes looked right at home.

"Okay, you can put your shirt back on," the corrections officer said.

He couldn't sleep. The anger was just boiling inside of him. Ramirez had screwed up killing that cop, but that was Ramirez's problem, he wasn't going down for that. He was going to get a simple disturbing the peace and maybe an assault rap as well. Alternatively, Ramirez would get life and maybe worse. They were going to throw the book at Ramirez, he didn't have a prayer.

First things first. As soon as he got out, he was going to make sure Dalton was a dead man. Then he'd get Ramirez the best lawyer money could buy. After that, when the inevitable happened and Ramirez started doing time, he'd make sure they figured out a way to use him to mule into the prison, whichever one he ended up in. It wasn't going to be much of a life, but that's the game they played.

He sat on his bunk, shirtless, and knocked his head against the wall behind him. The rage pulsed through him. He could count on the Fontaine boys coming up, all three of them. T-Mac would come along too. He was going to steer clear of getting any of the Puchka's involved. Those boys were nuts. They'd end up killing everybody else before they put a bullet in Dalton. The new guy, Trig, could make the trip as well. They had to get his hands good and dirty before they could trust him with any of the big moves they had coming up. Maybe he'd bring the surgeon as well. Yes, he would definitely bring along the surgeon. They needed cold, calculated precision.

But it wasn't just Dalton that he was going to finish. The do-gooder who popped him in the face would have to die too. His nose was broken, and once he got out he was going to have to get surgery to correct it. He was a good looking man, and he wanted to make sure he stayed that way. Nobody put a finger on El Tigre and lived to talk about it. For that matter, Dalton's girl and her mother had something coming too. The boys would have fun with them. They would be the bonus.

The rage began to subside. He lay down on his bunk and smiled. He quickly drifted off to sleep to thoughts of death and dismemberment.

"So, they're willing to deal with you," his lawyer said. He was as high priced as they came. Expensive suit, and probably an expensive European car out in the parking lot as well. He was worth every penny. "Ramirez is screwed. He's done. He's getting murder charges, and they aren't going to give him a break down to manslaughter either. Sorry."

"It's a tough break. We can make his life comfortable on the inside and let him know his little girl will get all the best. He can have some value still," El Tigre said.

"For what, I'm sure I don't want to know," the lawyer said. "As for you, they were going to throw accessory to murder at you, but they knew it couldn't stick. Witnesses say you never laid a finger on the cop, so if you're smart, you'll plead guilty to simple assault and creating a public disturbance. Your record as a youth was expunged, so as far as the DA is concerned, you don't have a record. First offense. We're going to be very apologetic. We're going to feel bad for the cop and his family. We're going to say all the right things. Then we're going to get thirty days maximum. We'll get that reduced for time served, which is what, five days already? I know, it must seem like an eternity. By the time we get in front of the judge for sentencing after we plead, you'll have already done your time. This is a small town, I'm going to push for sentencing when we plead."

"What about making bail? It's set at what, fifty grand? I can get that in two hours," he said.

"That might seem like the easy answer, but no. The bail set at that level is a trap. You get that kind of cash and the investigators know they got a fish on the line and you have cops everywhere you look. They'll be in your morning coffee. No, you pay me very well to extract you from sticky situations, and this is the way we play it. We take the thirty days and we melt away afterwards. Let them focus on Ramirez and forget about you. If we're lucky we get less, but expect thirty."

"I can deal with that," El Tigre said.

"How do you plead," the judge asked.

"Guilty, your honor," the lawyer responded.

"Does your client have anything to say before sentencing," the judge asked. It was a small county court, and there wasn't much on the docket for the day. It was amazing that the judge was willing to hand down the sentence so quickly. The DA had told them that they didn't exactly have a lot of room in the county lock-up, so they were going to push this along as quickly as possible.

"Yes, your honor," the lawyer said. He motioned to his client to rise and address the judge.

"Your honor," El Tigre said. "I was involved in a horrible, tragic event. Nobody wanted anyone to get hurt. We was, were," he corrected, having spoken incorrectly on purpose. Everything was scripted. He always took his audience into account when he spoke. "Too aggressive, and now a man is dead. Even though I was not the one responsible for the death of Police Chief McMurphy, my heart is heavy with regret. I can't take back what my friend did, and I can't take back what I did in disturbing the peace and committing actions which have been characterized as assault. I did those things, your honor, and I'm sorry. As you know my record as a youthful offender was expunged. I was a troubled kid, but I tried very hard to change. My record has been clear since I turned eighteen. For ten years I've stayed out of trouble, working for my father at the car dealership he owns in northern New Jersey. I have tried very hard to make my father proud, and now I've let him down." El Tigre paused for effect. He choked on his words, as if he was becoming over taken by emotion. As he continued he let his voice crack and quiver. It was a truly Oscar-worthy performance.

"As you can see, he has not come up here to support me. In his words, I've disgusted him by my actions. Your honor, I'm not sure what your relationship is with your father, but mine means the world to me. Earning back his respect will be my goal. Therefore, I ask that you sentence me in the way you see fit. Once I've paid my debt to society, I can begin to regain the trust I've destroyed. That's all I have to say. Thank you, your honor." He hung his head in perceived shame.

He and his lawyer knew exactly what the judge's relationship with his father was. It was a soft spot that they hoped to exploit. Additionally the judge himself had a boy who had already been arrested three times and he wasn't even seventeen yet. They were hoping that with an artfully contrived speech, they could work on the judge's emotions and get a lighter sentence.

The judge's eyes were wet. They hadn't let a tear go, but if he blinked, one would stream down his face. They'd pushed the buttons. He was eating out of their hands.

"Mr. Smith, I thank you for your candid admission. I wish more young men would own up to what they've done when they come before me. I sentence you to fifteen days in prison, less time served with the balance suspended so long as you stay out of trouble for the length of one year. Son, I hope you realize just how fortunate you are that it was your friend and not you that threw the punch that killed Chief McMurphy. I don't care if that boy owed you a million dollars, there's never an excuse to assault another person. I hope you've learned your lesson and you get back to repairing your reputation with your father."

The judge banged the gavel. Time served plus a one-year probation. The lawyer had earned his paycheck, which would be sizable.

After just five days in the county lock up, he was free. El Tigre was loose. A new hunt would begin.

Chapter 16

Tubby had a pocket full of money that he'd taken out of the back room without Mama knowing about it. He planned to drink until he couldn't remember nothing. He walked into Taylor's Taproom and sat down on a stool. There were the regular faces in the crowd that had gathered on that Tuesday afternoon.

Spike was an old fella who had already suffered a few strokes. He sat at the far end, quietly sipping his drink. He said even less than Tubby, most of the time. Bobby G. was playing keno with a little piece of paper and pencil, watching the little computer ball fall on the numbers on the television screen suspended behind the bar. Darlene had half a beer in her and was already starting to talk silly to Gregor who was behind the bar, paying more attention to the sports report on the TV than anybody sitting there.

"Hey, Tubby," Darlene said. "It was pretty cool what you did last week. Did I tell you that already?" She laughed to herself for no reason.

"Thanks," Tubby said. He'd been saying thanks a lot to people in town. Everybody was treating him different since he knocked that guy out who killed the Chief. He didn't even know the poor Chief had died until a week later when somebody told him.

Then he heard Copper had got killed by that cougar.

And then the guy that was in the fight when the Chief got killed, killed the cougar.

Lots of people are getting killed lately, Tubby thought to himself. It ain't right that so many people are dyin'.

The door opened and in walked that guy. Tubby had seen him a couple of times and even talked to him once or twice, but he didn't know his name. He was the one that killed that cougar that killed Copper.

"Hey there," Gregor said to the guy. "What are you drinking? First one's on me."

"Thanks. I'll just have a light beer, whatever's on tap," Cooke said. He tossed a couple of one dollar bills out onto the bar.

For a time, the bar fell quiet, the only sound was coming from the two sportscasters on the television arguing over who was going to win the games on the upcoming Sunday. Both made good arguments, but Tubby had to side with the guy who was taking the Giants. He sounded a bunch more smarter. A commercial came on, and everyone's attention was broken away from the television.

"You shot that cougar," Tubby said. It wasn't a question but a statement.

"That's right," Cooke replied. "I shot it."

"Was it tough?"

"Well, not really. Once I saw it in my sights I just pulled the trigger."

"Have you ever shot a person?" Tubby asked.

"Yeah," Cooke said after a long pause. "I've shot and killed a person before, Tubby."

"Was it scary?"

"I was too focused to be scared."

"Do you think it was scary for the person you shot?"

"I don't think he knew what hit him. I shot him with a seven millimeter rifle round. He was dead before he hit the ground." Cooke drained his glass. He ordered another beer.

Tubby sat for awhile contemplating the conversation. He sipped his beer quietly. Cooke turned his attention back to the television.

"Do you think they went to heaven," Tubby asked finally.

"That's not for me to say," Cooke answered after a moment. He took a deep drink from his glass before he continued. "Listen, the people I shot were bad people. I like to think that God did with them what he thought was," he paused. "Fair."

"Tubby, what are you talkin' about?" Darlene had switched barstools so as to sit next to Cooke.

"Nothin'," he said, going back to sipping his beer.

"Come on, you can tell me," she finished her beer and put her glass down on the bar. Darlene had blond hair that was obviously out of a bottle. She had five inches of brown roots to prove it. Her clothes were too tight, and she spilled over the top of her blue jeans. She wore a low cut top that showed too much of her cleavage. She pressed up against Cooke's arm. "You don't have to stop. I'm unshockable."

"Jeez, Darlene, give the guy a break," Gregor said, over-hearing her. "Let him enjoy his drink."

"Actually," Cooke said. "We were talking about killing people. You know, like what happens to a person when a sniper round goes through their torso. Have you ever seen the body of a person shot by a sniper? A head shot leaves just about nothing from the shoulders on up. Just splatter. I once saw a guy who got his head blown off and we found parts of his skull forty feet away. It was like somebody threw a big bowl of pasta with red sauce up into the air."

"That's nasty," she said, pulling her breasts off his arm. "God, that's disgusting." She stood up and moved back to her old seat and ordered another beer.

"Unshockable," Cooke said under his breath. He sipped from his beer.

"That wasn't very nice," Tubby said sheepishly.

"What?"

"Being gross like that to Darlene. That was mean," Tubby said quietly.

"Yeah," Cooke said after a few moments. "You're right. I can be a mean old cuss, sometimes." He drained his glass and set it down. Gregor came over and retrieved it.

"Ready for another?"

"Yeah, and get another for Darlene down there too. Tell her no hard feelings," Cooke said. He caught Tubby smiling.

"Is that better," Cooke asked.

"Yeah," Tubby grinned and drank his beer.

A few more patrons came into Taylor's and took stools at the bar. Joe Brach was a Vietnam vet who had found his way up into the mountains when he'd gotten home from the war. He still wore his camouflage jacket with his division's insignia on the shoulder. His jet black hair had faded to gray over the years, but his frame and build had remained the same. He was as gangly as a scarecrow and about as quiet as one as well, unless you got him talking about the war or the government.

He was accompanied by Gary Krakowski, one of his coworkers at the table and bar stool factory in the center of town. It was the biggest employer in town, with forty people on staff. Kracky, as he was known, was only about five feet tall, and about the same in width. He prided himself as a drinker and the unofficial Coopers Hollow historian. Kracky had lived in Coopers Hollow for all of his fifty-seven years of life, and had a memory like an encyclopedia.

"Hey, Gregor. How about a couple of beers," Kracky said. He and Brach were deep in discussion. "So you're saying it's a conspiracy? Big surprise, Brach."

"Listen, you're jaded, I get it. Cynicism is part of the conspiracy. Think about it, how many times are you lied to in a day?" The beers arrived and Brach took a sip, wiping the foam from his gray mustache.

"Every time the boss's lips are moving," Kracky replied, taking a long pull from his drink.

"Besides that. We are lied to literally thousands of times every single day. Think about it, just from the commercials on television alone. I mean, the advertisers call it hyperbole, but if they show you that a truck can drive up a mountain without even getting mud on it or that drinking a certain kind of beer gets you beautiful women, you believe it. Maybe not consciously, but your subconscious takes it all in, man. What about movies? They don't even use real physics! Everything is staged. It's all lies. You see? We're lied to thousands of times every day, and that's the trick. We get numbed to it. We don't detect the lies of the government because they're lost in the lies of Hollywood and advertisers." Brach said. "Look at the television right now. You think that sporting events aren't fixed? Vegas has too much to lose not to have control over the outcomes. They already know who's going to win, they're just going to sit back and collect the money."

"And why are you the only one that knows this?" Kracky asked, humoring his friend.

"I'm not. I just have my eyes open, man. Ever since the war I've been keeping my eyes open. They lied to us big time back then, and they never stopped. And it's gotten worse. Don't even get me started on reality television. There's nothing real about it, it's all rehearsed." Brach paused to watch the game a bit, taking several big gulps from his beer.

"So, what's the end game? What's the point of all the lies?" Kracky asked. Everyone else at the bar was listening as well. Tubby didn't quite understand what they were talking about, but he understood lying. He was all too aware of the lies people told.

"It's not an end game, it's a system. Build a system that self perpetuates. The populace buys into the lies, they stay satiated, opiated, dumbed down. They stay fat and happy. And they pay their money away doing it. It used to be that religion kept people mellowed out. Well, Hollywood has done a very good job of killing off religion and taking over as the opiate of the people. But here's the scary part: One day, something's going to happen and everybody is going to wake up and face reality. And when that happens, look out." Brach took the last swallow of his beer and slid the glass forward for another.

"What happens then? Revolution?" Kracky asked.

"What happens then, is every man for himself. Once the food stops rolling in, people in the cities will panic. Did you know that if the food supply gets shut down to New York City, they've got about two and a half weeks before they run out? Half a month, man."

"That's just food," Kracky chimed in. "Imagine what would happen when the beer runs out. Mass hysteria." He laughed and even got a chuckle out of Brach.

Cooke had been sitting quietly listening to the two of them talk, and couldn't help but get involved in the conversation.

"So, what do you think will be the catalyst? What makes everybody wake up to the lies," Cooke asked. He had read about the police and ESU procedures for what they called "end of world" scenarios. What those end of world scenarios really outlined was the breakdown of society. It wasn't pretty stuff. Cooke himself had taken part in a chemical weapons drill they had role-played in a small town in Kansas. He was still amazed that the people in the town went along with it. The thousand dollars per person might have had something to do with it.

"Well, a natural disaster gets people thinking about the relatively thin veneer that exists between civilization and anarchy. But realistically, a big event, a big reveal would do it. Irrefutable proof of the lies. Then there would be a ground swell of people not happy about it. If enough people rally together, they would overwhelm any police force. Shut down commerce. Once the money stops flowing, then the food stops flowing. Once that happens, it's a snowball rolling down the side of the mountain."

"So what's the irrefutable proof," Cooke asked. "What's the powder keg?"

"Well, let's just say it's revealed that LBJ was behind the JFK assassination? Or that they knew all along that Obama wasn't a legal President and the only reason they let him in was so the greedy Wall Street and international bankers could pocket the government money from all the bail outs? I mean, don't even get me started on Obama! Something that rips apart the confidence the general public has for the government – that's what will light the fuse. But it has to be everybody. Right now it's like half against half. And that's what they want. They can control half against half. They can massage that. They can perpetuate that. People need to rise up, man. Join up. Wake up. Some day it's gonna happen." Brach regarded Cooke for a few moments, then continued. "They know it's going to happen too. Why else do you think they're putting up all the welcome centers at the state borders? It's easier to control a populace that isn't mobile. Once it crashes down, the military will use those welcome centers as border crossing stops between states. Oh it's going to get crazy."

"Well, you've got quite the imagination," Cooke said. "I'll give you that. Heck I'll do you one better. Gregor, next beer is on me."

"You got it," Gregor replied.

"So what's your story," Kracky asked Cooke. "I've heard you moved up here from the city. Former cop, right?"

"Yeah, that's right."

"And word is, you're a crack shot," Kracky added.

"You could say that, yeah."

"You killed the cougar that attacked Copper, and didn't you get mixed up in the fight that killed Chief McMurphy too?" Kracky frowned. "That's a heck of an introduction to the community."

"Yeah, I've kind of been in the right place at the wrong time a few times," Cooke said.

"So is it true that Jack Jr. is going to be the new Police Chief," Kracky asked.

"I don't know. Truthfully I've only talked to him a couple of times."

"A McMurphy has been Police Chief up here for a long time. Maybe it's time for some new blood," Kracky said. No one said anything in response, and they found themselves watching the game for a few minutes. It went to commercial, and the weatherman popped on with a quick update.

"Looks like another bout of snow in the Catskills and Berkshires over the next couple of days, we'll have the full forecast after the game," the weatherman said.

"Perfect," Gregor said. "Just what we need. This is going to be a long winter if we keep getting storms like this."

"They say that ever since that volcano erupted out in

the pacific, it's been a few degrees colder. Colder temps this time of year means more snow. Looks like we're going to be in for it this year," Kracky said.

"I was thinking about getting a snowmobile," Cooke said. "If we keep getting snow like this, I should probably hurry up and go out and get it."

"The best place to go is Coopers Hollow Powersports. They'll fix ya up," Gregor said from behind the bar. "That's where I bought my sled. Tell Phil I sent you over there."

"Okay, I'll do that," Cooke replied.

Tubby finished his second beer and reached into his pocket for more money for another. The book that he had been carrying around in the waistband of his pants was irritating him now that he was perched on the barstool. He slid it out and placed it on the bar.

"Whatcha got ther, Tubby?" Gregor asked.

"Nothin'. Just a book is all," Tubby replied.

"I didn't know you could read," Kracky bellowed. Everyone had a good chuckle at Tubby's expense.

"I can read, I just can't read the cursing writing," Tubby said quietly.

"Cursing?" Kracky pulled his weight off his stool and waddled over to Tubby. Before Tubby could react, Kracky swiped the book and started thumbing through it. "Oh, you meant cursive, you nitwit."

"April twelfth," Kracky read aloud. "Helped Mrs. Josephson with some yard work. She won't give up the idea that the family gold was hidden someplace in the hotel.

Poor old bird has almost completely lost her mind. She told me her husband would be home any minute." Kracky closed the book and looked at the cover. "What is this, some kind of diary?"

"Give it back," Tubby said.

"Sure, it's stupid anyway," Kracky said, tiring of his teasing. "Maybe reading something will make you a little less retarded." He tossed the book back to Tubby and took his wide form to the restroom to relieve himself.

"Alright!" Bobby G had been sitting at the end of the bar, quietly playing Keno on the video screen. "I won!"

"No kidding, let's ring it up," Gregor said, taking Bobby G's card. He ran it through the machine behind the bar and whistled. "Two fifty. Congrats, Bobby G."

"It's about time! Hey give everybody a beer on me," Bobby G exclaimed. This caused everybody to give a hearty cheer. Tubby loved Taylor's, there was always somebody buying drinks. His free beer was placed in front of him, and he gulped down his old one so he could start on the new one. He had already forgotten about Kracky's teasing.

Darlene slid from her seat over to where Bobby G had stationed himself and started flirting with him. She whispered something in his ear and then laughed as his face got red. He pushed her away, but only half-heartedly. Kracky returned from the restroom to see Darlene putting her predictable moves on Bobby G.

"Come on, Darlene," Kracky started in. "Stop being such a whore." The barroom erupted with laughter and derision at the comment.

"Easy, Kracky," Gregor warned with mock seriousness. "She can be vicious."

"That wasn't a nice thing to say," Tubby said, under his breath.

"What's that, Tubby?" Kracky bellowed. He was the type of guy that got louder and meaner the more he drank. There had been more than one occasion in his long and storied history of drinking in Taylor's Taproom, where he'd shot his mouth off and gotten knocked off his bar stool as a reward. "If there's somebody who should know what a whore is, it's you."

"Take it easy, Kracky," Gregor's tone was very serious now.

"Your Mama used to be the town tart, back in the day," Kracky said. "Then she got knocked up with you, found Jesus and went crazy."

"Hey, hey. Kracky, I don't want you picking any fights in here tonight," Gregor warned.

"Jeez, lay off of Tubby," Cooke said. "What the heck, man."

"And what's it to you anyway. You breeze into town, get the Police Chief and the Fire Chief killed and think you have the right to say anything to me?" Kracky's face had grown crimson, and he was almost spitting out his words now. He was a mean drunk, and the alcohol had started to hit his system.

"I think you better take yourself home, pal." Cooke said. Kracky fully turned towards Cooke and sized him up.

"Yeah, is that what you think I should do, old man?"

"I think that's what you should do," Cooke repeated, his voice calm and calculating. Things were about to get ugly if the blowhard didn't back down. After a few beers Cooke was in a good mood for fighting. The fat little toad had said the right things to get him riled up, and now he was ready to take it out on the guy's face.

"Hey, Kracky, let's get outta here," Brach interceded. He stood up and put his hand on Kracky's shoulder. "Let's go get some fresh air. Go for a walk, man. I'll give you a cigarette and we'll chill out, man. Okay? One of my good kind, man."

Tubby stood and threw a couple of dollars onto the bar and walked out. He didn't say a word to anyone, he just grabbed his book and left. If any of them had looked closely, they would have seen his eyes filling with tears.

Jack McMurphy Jr. drove down Main Street in his police cruiser scanning the town as he went. It had gotten dark, and he only had a few minutes before he was due over at Paula's apartment. So he thought he would just make a run through town, fill up the cruiser at Stewart's and maybe see if they had some flowers. Every once in awhile they'd get flower arrangements in, and since the floral shop was already closed, it was this or nothing.

As he pulled into Stewart's convenience store he saw all of the pumps were occupied. He also noticed Cooke's big blue Ford pickup truck. He pulled alongside and put his vehicle in park. Leaving the cruiser running, as he was going to be inside for just a few moments, he headed into the store first, deciding to fill up with gas after dinner. It was just as well, since he was running out of time and didn't want to wait for a vacancy at the pumps.

The electronic door chime rang as he entered. He gave a brief wave to Heather Anders who was behind the counter. He looked around and saw there was one bouquet of flowers left. They were just carnations, but at least it was something. He spotted Michael Cooke in the back of the store picking up a case of beer.

"Hey, Heather. How's Rusty and your little girl doing?" Jack asked as he put the flowers on the counter and fished out his wallet.

"Oh, he's still hurting, but he's home. Baby girl is doing just fine now, though she's still waking up with nightmares. It's just going to take some time. For now, we're just trying to figure out how we're going to make ends meet with him off work. I'm taking as much overtime as I can get," she said.

"I'm sorry to hear that. I hope he heals up quickly," Jack said. He paid for the flowers, and headed out to his cruiser. He sat for a moment and listened to the county dispatch make a call out for a vehicle accident in the southern part of the county. It was near the interstate and out of his jurisdiction, so the State Troopers would grab it. He was officially off the clock, and he had a date to go on.

Jack watched out his windshield as Michael Cooke exited the store with a case of beer under his arm. He took a bit of a misstep off the curb as he headed towards his truck, and then he dropped his keys. He looked a little unsteady as he bent to get them. Jack gave pause, sighed heavily, and then got out of his cruiser to go have a talk.

"Hey, Michael. How's it going?"

"It's going," Cooke replied, spoken like a true local.

"You have anything to drink this evening?"

"Yeah, maybe a few beers over at Taylor's."

"How many?"

"Two or three," he said. "Or maybe four."

"It's not good when you lose track," Jack said. He knew from personal experience. He hadn't found himself at the bottom of a bottle too often, but it had happened before. He thought about his next move and what he should do for the man who, he had to admit, was starting to become a friend. He hadn't officially witnessed Cooke driving, so he didn't have to run him in, not if he didn't insist on driving. "You think maybe you should find somebody to give you a ride home? I wouldn't want to feel obligated to give you a breathalyzer."

"You'd do that? I didn't have too much, I got it under control," Michael said, but he put his keys back into his pocket even as he set the beer down in the truck. He shut the door and turned to face the new chief of police.

"Anybody you can call to give you a ride? I would, but I've got an appointment I've got to keep. Or you can go in, get some coffee and have a seat in there for an hour or two. What are you going to do?" McMurphy wasn't going to leave until he knew Michael wasn't going to be driving drunk, and he could tell that Cooke would blow at least a DUI right now if he put him on the breathalyzer.

Another vehicle, a silver Volvo, pulled up on the other

side of Jack's cruiser. Gloria Graves stepped out of her car and headed towards the store, but stopped short when she saw them standing there.

"Hi," she said, waving to the two men.

"Hey, Mrs. Graves," McMurphy said. Cooke just nodded in her direction. Jack didn't want to embarrass the man. "Are you busy? Michael's having some trouble with his vehicle, and he needs a lift home. I have someplace I've got to be. Do you have time to run him up to his house?"

"Umm, I guess I could do that," she said. "Yes. I can do that. Just let me just run in and grab some milk and I'll be right out. I just have to get some milk. Sorry, I just said that. Sorry, I'll be right out." She had an embarrassed smile on her face as she walked towards the door.

"Thanks. I don't want to be an imposition." Cooke said to her.

"Oh, it's no trouble at all. I'll be right back," she said.

Michael looked at Jack. "I would have been fine."

"Now I know you'll be fine," Jack said and slapped Cooke on the shoulder. "Have a good night, okay?"

"Yeah, alright," Michael said quietly. He kicked at a bottle cap on the pavement and watched it roll away, clenching his jaw.

Jack got back into his cruiser, put it in reverse and pulled out from the convenience store. He promised Paula he'd be there for dinner at six, and he was running late. He hated being late. It was one of those things his father had taught him when he was just a little boy. On time meant ten minutes early. Anything after that was late and inconsiderate. For their first date in nearly a year, Jack didn't want to be late.

He pulled into the gravel parking lot of the former Lexmore Hotel, which was now the office for *The Mountain Star*. There were two entrances to Paula's apartment, one on the side of the building and one through *The Mountain Star* offices. As he walked up the steps to the side door, he found his heart beating fast and his palms a bit sweaty. He took a deep breath and rapped his knuckles on the door. Through the door he heard quick footsteps, a fumbling with the lock and suddenly, there she was.

She wore a dark blue dress that was low cut and came just above her knees. She also wore a white sweater with three-quarter sleeves. Jack noticed she wasn't wearing any hose, and her legs looked smooth and inviting.

"Hey," he said with a smile. He handed her the flowers. "These are for you. They're not much, but I wanted to get you something."

"Oh, they're sweet. Thanks. Come on in." She let him in and closed the door behind him. "So, you decided to wear your uniform."

"Oh, I guess I - Well. Yeah. Sorry. I guess I didn't even think about it."

"Could you at least take off your gun belt?"

"Sure," he complied.

"Keep it handy, we might need the handcuffs," she winked teasingly. "Would you like a drink?"

"Sure," he said again. "What have you got?"

"I have a bottle of wine that's been chilling in the

freezer. I put it in there about ten minutes ago. If you want to pop it open, the glasses are in the center cupboard. I'll finish getting dinner on the table."

"So, how are things?" Jack tried to make small talk as he retrieved the bottle of wine and the glasses.

"Well, it hasn't exactly been a great day for me, actually. They're closing down the paper." She exhaled heavily as she said it. She still was trying to imagine what it was going to be like, working on her own most of the time.

"What? Who's shutting it down? I thought you owned it."

"The paper is now majority owned by *The Kingston Chronicle*, and they're shutting it down and turning it into a weekly section. This week will be our last issue." Even as she said it she couldn't believe it was true. "Jack, I screwed up. I feel horrible."

"Wow. That really - I thought your paper was doing well."

"It was. It's *The Chronicle* that's dying. So they're going to try to capture the advertising dollars and circulation of *The Mountain Star*, but all they're really going to do is kill it. I just can't see how it's going to work out. I guess I had better polish up my résumé and start thinking about moving." She hadn't vocalized that reality yet, but there it was. It simply wasn't realistic to believe that The Chronicle would keep her on for very long. Jack pulled the cork from the wine and poured two glasses. It was a White Zinfandel, and smelled delicious. Paula took her glass from him and then clinked his with hers. "To the future, whatever it brings."

"To the future," Jack echoed. He was still trying to

take in what she'd just told him. He sipped the wine and walked over towards the table. "Whatever it brings."

She brought the dinner plates over to the table, and they sat down. She had prepared lemon chicken over rice. It was a simple dinner, but it was delicious. They ate for a few moments in silence.

"I'm thinking about taking a day or two and going down to southeastern Ohio and do some digging on that animal van accident," Paula said, taking a sip from her wine glass.

"Really? I just figured you could make some phone calls or do an internet search or something. When I asked you to help out I didn't expect you to actually drive down there," Jack put his fork down. He wasn't sure if he liked the idea of having her investigating potential criminals face to face. He was now questioning whether he should have gotten her involved in the investigation at all.

"This whole thing with *The Chronicle* taking over helped make my decision. If I'm going to have any chance getting a job with another publication, I need to have a few solid, investigative stories to my credit. This could turn into something. If it's an animal smuggling ring, it could be a big story, you know? I mean the story about Copper is probably going to get picked up by the AP and Reuters, if I'm lucky. So that would be a good résumé builder, but I need something bigger to have a shot at a major publication. The problem is there are so many writers and editors out there out of a job right now you have to do something really spectacular to get noticed. And even then, there are no guarantees."

Jack picked up his fork again and started pushing the food around his plate. He was trying hard not to get upset by how flippantly she had talked about Copper's death. It was as if she'd slapped him in the face. He knew she didn't mean to hurt his feelings, but it just reminded him of what she'd done to him before. She was more interested in the story than she was in real people.

"What?" Paula was looking at him now. "What did I say?"

"Nothing."

"Nothing? Then why do you look like you just bit into a lemon? Come on, Jack."

"It's nothing. I know you didn't mean anything by it. It's just, I'm still a little raw about Copper. I was there when we lost him. It was horrible, and you treat it just like another story."

"I'm sorry, Jack. I wasn't thinking. Don't be mad at me. Maybe we shouldn't talk about work. Maybe we should just find something else to talk about." She paused for a moment, thinking of a way to change the conversation. "Have you seen any good movies lately?"

"No. I haven't really had the time. What about you?"

"No," Paula laughed. "Neither have I. Well, that worked well."

"Yeah," Jack chuckled too. "Would you like some more wine?"

"Absolutely." She held her glass out to him.

"So, if we don't have anything to talk about, why do we keep ending up together," Jack asked as he poured.

"Well, I think it's obvious," she replied, taking a long sip.

"Yeah?"

"Oh, yeah. We both have super hot bodies and we can't take our eyes off each other," she leaned forward with a tantalizing smile.

"You may be on to something," he smiled in return. She stood quickly and came over behind him, rubbing his shoulders.

"You're seriously wearing your bullet proof vest?"

"I didn't change, I'm sorry. I should have taken it off."

"You still can," she said as she unbuttoned his shirt. "Why are you even wearing a vest?"

"It's that Beckman kid. I don't know, just kind of spooked me. Drug dealers, dad dying. I guess it was silly. I should take it off," he said.

"Oh you most definitely should."

He stood and turned towards her. She pulled him down for a kiss. The first one was brief. They pulled away and looked each other in the eyes. Jack leaned in for a longer kiss, and Paula slipped her hands around his neck. Jack put his arms around her and held her close. For her, it was a kiss she had been dreaming about for nearly a year.

"You taste like wine," she said with a giggle.

"So do you."

"So we're both delicious," she replied. "Let's go over to the other room and continue the taste testing." She led him by the hand to the living room and pulled him down to the couch. She swiveled around and pushed him down.

She straddled him and continued with the task of unbuttoning his shirt. She pulled it out from his pants and then pulled the hook and loop fasteners open on his bullet proof vest. She guided her hands up under the vest, running her fingers through his chest hair. Leaning down, she kissed him hard, lips pressing earnestly against his. Their tongues met, and she suddenly felt a rush through her entire body. He slid her sweater from her shoulders and glided his hands down her curved waist. She started running her hands through his hair when his cell phone vibrated in his pants pocket. She was straddling him, so she felt it as well. With a heavy sigh, he fished it out from his pocket and looked at the number. He sighed again with frustration.

"I've got to take this," he said. He slid his thumb across the phone and opened the connection. "Hello?"

"What? Really? I just saw them, like a half hour ago. Okay, I'm on my way." He closed down the connection.

"Oh, no way. No, no, no. You're not going anywhere," Paula whined. She tugged at his belt and stuck out her lip in a pout.

"I've got to get over to Gloria Graves' place," he said as he refastened his vest and began buttoning his shirt.

"Seriously?"

"Seriously," he said, leaning over and kissing her on the lips. "Let's pick this up again really soon."

He got to the door and turned to look at her sitting on the couch, sweater off her shoulders, dress up over her thighs. She stuck out her bottom lip even further and gave him the puppy dog eyes.

"Duty calls," he said, strapping on his gun belt.

"I know," her voice full of disappointment. "I know."

Gloria's heart was beating fast in her chest. She was just buying milk and then giving Michael Cooke a ride home, yet she was suddenly feeling as giddy as a junior high girl going to her first school dance. A scenario such as this did not happen in real life. Real life was full of disappointment, missed opportunities and regrets. Perfect coincidences didn't happen to her. It was more like something out of one of the romance novels she read as a guilty pleasure.

"Is that it?" The girl behind the check-out counter looked like she was ready to go home. She looked exhausted.

"Yes, just the milk," Gloria answered. The total rang up and she paid in cash. Starlett was already home fixing dinner for the two of them, and they had run out of milk, thus the unplanned trip into town. Suddenly the thought struck her. An idea. It was something she would have thoroughly dismissed even three months ago, but something was different now. She thought about it, and it made perfect sense. She left the store and walked over to where Michael Cooke was standing.

"Listen, I really appreciate the gesture, but you don't have to do this. I'm sure I can get my vehicle started in a bit," he said.

"Nonsense," Gloria stated. "It's no trouble at all. In

fact, my daughter and I were preparing dinner, and if you haven't eaten yet, I'd love to have you join us."

"Oh," was all he could say.

"Unless you've already eaten, in which case I can run you home. I don't think you live too far away."

"No, I don't. But yes, I'd love to have dinner with you," he said. "And your daughter."

"Okay, it's settled then. Let's get going, Starlett needs this milk to finish." They got into Gloria's Volvo and headed out of town.

Michael was a little nervous about appearing drunk, or smelling of alcohol, but so far, Gloria had been oblivious. He'd always been able to handle his booze, and he knew he would have gotten home just fine, but he couldn't deny that he may have been over the limit. A DWI wasn't a slap on the wrist like it used to be. He knew why. Too many innocent people had been killed by drunk drivers over the years. It made sense, but it still frustrated him a little. His plan had been to go home and get proper drunk. Falling down, black out drunk. He hadn't done it in awhile, and figured now would be a good time. The loneliness had started in again. He thought he could fix it by hanging out in the local bar, but it descended pretty quickly into a squabble that would have gotten physical if it hadn't ended when it did. He didn't have the patience to stick around to see if anyone more interesting showed up. Plus, the more drinks he had, the more reasonable an option Darlene had seemed. He knew he had to call it a night before he went and did something stupid like that.

As they drove, Michael tried to get his bearings. The

roads in the mountains twisted and wound around, often following streams and creeks. He forced himself to pay attention to the compass display on the rear view mirror of Gloria's Volvo and remember the map he had studied while riding along with Davidson before the hunt. They were following the same road he would have taken home, but then they took a left off the State Route and followed Brick House Road up over the hill. The road had probably been named after a long since demolished house made of bricks, as there was none in sight now. They drove for another three or four minutes and then pulled into a long driveway that wound back to a ranch house with a horse barn behind it. It was a very nice home, in Cooke's opinion, and from his calculations, only about three or four miles away from his place, as the crow flies. They lived just over the mountain from each other.

"Oh, it looks like we have another guest as well," Gloria said, indicating the Mercedes parked in front of the garage. She didn't sound happy about the discovery. "It has to be Dalton. I don't know what to tell Starlett about him. He seemed like such a nice guy, and then out of the blue this whole thing happened."

"I know about the guys jumping him, heck, I caught a couple punches because of it. What is he involved in?" Michael had mostly healed from the encounter, but it was still fresh in his mind. His ribs had just been bruised, not broken. Gloria sighed heavily before she replied.

"According to Dalton, he was just helping out a friend. He drove a car from New York up to Binghamton. The car happened to be carrying drugs. Dalton was caught and he turned in everyone he knew to be involved. I'd like to

think that he was just a naïve rich kid who didn't put two
and two together. I know his type. We used to live in New
Jersey and my late husband worked in the city. We were
surrounded by kids and families that had book smarts, but
lacked any common sense. Truthfully, I was one of those
people. So was my husband."

"Well, I guess time will tell. Why is Starlett still letting
him hang around?" Michael would have kicked the kid out
on his ear if it was his daughter's boyfriend.

"She broke it off, and then he called and wanted
to talk. She relented, said yes, and that's when he was
attacked in the diner. She's torn. He had just proposed to
her, you know, and she had said yes," Gloria said.

"Oh, man."

"I know."

"So what happened to your husband?"

"Well, he - " Gloria paused for a long while. "He was
killed in the World Trade Center attacks on nine-eleven."
She hadn't told anyone in the area about her husband since
they'd moved up to Coopers Hollow. She had kept it secret
for Starlett's sake. She had wanted to be treated normally
and not as the child of a 9/11 victim. For some reason,
however, Gloria needed Michael to know.

"Oh, Gloria. I'm so sorry," he said. He reached over
and grabbed her hand and gave it a squeeze without even
realizing he was doing it. Had he been stone cold sober,
he would never have made such a gesture. "I was on the
NYPD force at the time. I lost a couple of good friends in
the attacks. I could have been killed that day if I hadn't

been out of the country. For awhile afterwards I kept wishing that I was killed instead of some of the guys on the force who had families. Survivor's guilt."

"I know what you're talking about. Some days I wished it had been me who had been killed and Philip had survived. But it's a long time ago now, and I've learned to deal with it. Slowly, I've learned." They fell quiet for a moment, still sitting in the vehicle in Gloria's driveway. They could hear music coming from inside the house. It was loud enough that they could clearly hear the lyrics to the song.

"Maybe we should go in," Michael suggested.

"Yes, how silly of us."

"It's not silly at all," he said. "I'd love to stay out here and talk some more, but I have to make a confession about something."

"What's that," she asked.

"I need to use your bathroom." There was an uncomfortable pause for a moment, and then Gloria started laughing.

"Okay, let's go inside."

When they got inside the music was almost deafening. The stereo in the living room was going almost full blast. Starlett and Dalton were in the kitchen but were oblivious to Gloria and Michael.

"The bathroom is just down the hallway, first door on the right," Gloria had to practically yell. "Let me take your coat and turn down the music"

"Thanks," he mouthed rather than try to make himself heard, excusing himself to use the facilities. The bathroom was spotless. It was obvious that Gloria didn't have a man around. The potpourri and fragranced hand soaps were a dead giveaway. Michael emptied his bladder and felt better instantly. He also felt like he'd sobered up a bit. The music dropped down to a normal decibel level as he washed his hands, splashed some cold water on his face, and toweled off. When he came out, Gloria was waiting for him with a glass of wine.

"Dalton, Starlett. This is Mr. Michael Cooke. You may remember he stepped in to lend a hand back during the little sidewalk scuffle. He was having some car trouble in town, so I thought, what a great opportunity to have him over to dinner as a thank you."

"Hello," Michael said with a nod. He took a sip from his wine glass.

"What type of car trouble," Dalton asked as he shook Michael's hand.

"Uh, it wouldn't start. I'm sure it will be fine if we just let it sit for a little while," he replied.

"Dinner will be ready in about fifteen minutes," Gloria said. "We could sit in the living room or maybe go out and see the horses."

"You've got horses?"

"Two of them. Well, one belongs to Starlett. Daisy is her name. Mine is Chestnut. Do you ride?"

"I've never had the chance to try it, but I've always wanted to," he said, taking another sip from the wine glass. He wasn't much of a wine drinker, he preferred beer, but this was tasty.

"Well let's get our jackets on and I can introduce you," she said with a smile.

Back on the jackets went, and Gloria slipped on a pair of gloves as well. She took her wine glass, and led Michael by the hand out towards the horse barn.

"We moved up here shortly after the attacks, and I decided to get a couple of horses for Starlett and me. It really made a difference. It helped with the healing process. Now they're like family," she said. As they walked towards the barn, Gloria noticed that the barn door was slid partially open. "That's odd, Starlett must have been out here, the door's open."

Gloria reached around the corner and switched on the light. As she turned she saw it. Her world began to spin, and her knees buckled. She dropped the wine glass from her hand and it shattered on the concrete floor. Michael caught her before she fell. He assessed the scene quickly, and knew he had to get them both back into the house as fast as possible. He scooped Gloria up in his arms and ran as fast as he could back to the house.

"Call the police," he shouted to Starlett and Dalton, as he came through the door and gently laid Gloria onto the couch.

Police Chief Jack McMurphy Jr. pulled up in his cruiser and saw Michael Cooke standing with a cup of coffee waiting for him.

"Jeez, Michael. This has been a heck of a couple of

weeks, hasn't it," Jack said as he shook his hand and took the cup of coffee that was offered.

"Yeah. I have to say, though. I'm glad I was up here with her. She fainted and I had to carry her into the house," Cooke said. "I guess I have you to thank for that. She offered me dinner after you left. Starlett is here and her boyfriend Dalton is here too."

"Where is it?"

"Around back, in the horse barn. I'll show you," Cooke said. They walked around the side of the house and back towards the barn. The light was still on within the barn, and Jack could see something on the concrete floor just within the doors. When they got closer, he realized what it was.

Jack swore under his breath as he took it in.

"The head is here, and the rest of the body is back in the stall. It's been shredded and eaten, it looks like," Michael said. They stood over the horse's head which was in a pool of blood. The blood was seeping out from under the stall door as well and flowed to the drain in the center of the concrete floor. The horse in the other stall was still kicking against the door and whinnying loudly. It hadn't stopped since Gloria had shattered the wine glass on the floor.

"Another cougar?"

"That's what I thought too. But when I told Dalton, he kind of freaked out. He said it was just like in the movie The Godfather. He's positive it was a message from the guys he's going to testify against. Did you know about all the crap he's mixed up in?"

"I got the rough picture from the Binghamton detectives, yeah. Maybe it is a message. Look at the paw prints, though. An animal was definitely in here eating the dead body. You think maybe somebody cut off the horse's head then the smell drew in scavengers?" Jack knelt down and looked at the bloody paw prints. He put up his hand next to one. "Jeez, it would have to be a bear. I don't think cougar paws get this big. I need somebody that would know more about this. Let's not jump to conclusions just yet. It could be a bear attack. I've never heard of a bear attacking livestock up here before, especially a horse in a barn, but it's possible. Davidson is going to hate me calling him out in the middle of the night like this."

It took almost an hour for the DEC officer to arrive at Gloria's house. He shook hands with Michael and Jack as they headed back to the barn. He'd already been briefed by Jack on the phone, so he wasn't as shocked when he saw the carnage.

"Together again, huh?" Davidson wasn't happy to be called out at night, but as soon as he saw the scene he was glad they called him.

"So, two theories right now," Jack said. "One, a straight animal attack. Based on the paw prints, maybe a bear. Two, the horse was killed by someone trying to send a message to Dalton in there and then an animal smelled the blood and came in to have a meal."

"Any human tracks?" Davidson was already down looking at the paw prints Jack had studied.

"Not that we found. I don't even know what someone would use to cut off a horse's head. A power tool like a chainsaw or circular saw would have put blood splatter everywhere. That's not what we see. It looks like maybe there was some arterial spray, but nothing like we'd expect to see if somebody had taken the head off with a power tool. Which leaves a large knife and hand tools. Maybe a machete. I would think that a person couldn't avoid leaving tracks with the amount of blood around, though," Jack was talking out loud as he tried to piece together a theory that fit the facts at the scene.

"The wound to the neck looks like it was ripped, not cut. I think this was all animal attack. But truthfully, I don't have a clue what could have done this. They're definitely not bear tracks. My first guess would be another cougar, but look at these paw prints," Davidson said, spreading his hand out next to one of the bloody prints. "Didn't anyone hear a commotion? The other horse is still spooked."

"They had the music blaring," Cooke said. "They didn't hear a thing."

"Probably for the best," Davidson continued. "It would have to be one huge cougar. I mean, like a four hundred pounder. I don't think they get that big, but maybe. If they heard the horses making a fuss and came out to investigate, they could have been killed as well."

"Well, let's just say that this was the other animal from that van accident. It's possible that it was a big one, and that's why it was in captivity and being transferred. Maybe it was being sold. I still don't have anything to go on in that investigation. It's been frustrating," Jack stated.

"Jack, I think that's the best explanation we have right now. I think we've got a big problem on our hands. This cougar took down a horse. It was strong enough to rip its head off. Jack this is one big cat. It's an imminent danger to the community," Davidson said.

"I agree. There's nothing we can do about it tonight, but I think I need to call a news conference tomorrow and go public with this," Jack said, adding a few choice curse words as well. He'd found himself doing a lot more cursing as of late. He had to get that under control.

"Listen, if there's another hunt, I'm in," Michael said.

"I will take you up on that, Michael," Jack replied.

"I need to take some samples here to see if the animal that killed this horse had rabies. Nobody should touch any of the animal remains without proper protection. Make sure the owners know. Once I have my samples, I would suggest pulling the carcass out and burning it just to be sure. The sooner the better, so it doesn't attract any other scavengers. These hills are full of coyotes and bears."

"And cougars," Michael said.

"And apparently cougars," Davidson agreed.

Chapter 17

This is the biggest cat we have," he said. "It's more powerful than anything else and fast too." The two men stood back and took in its beauty. They were both quiet for a moment. They were sizing each other up as they both knew they were about to begin a negotiation.

"It's pretty expensive, though. Not that price is the final determining factor, mind you. I'm just not sure if I should get one so big for my first. It might be difficult to tame."

"No, she's a pussycat. Listen. You're a pretty big guy. You're not going to want to buy a smaller one and then regret your decision. I've seen it before. People buy something too small and they end up regretting it down the road."

"Could you knock a couple hundred off the price?"

"This is the top of the line here. She's high quality. You won't find a cat like this anywhere else around here. But listen, I can throw in a helmet and a gas card for Stewart's here in town."

"You drive a hard bargain," Michael said, furrowing his brow slightly. He had already made up his mind he was going to buy it. He just enjoyed the back and forth of negotiations. "Let's talk about accessories. I'll want a trailer as well.

"Let's go get you sized for the helmet, then I can show you the options we have for trailers," Phil Coffer, owner of Coopers Hollow Powersports, said. "You know, besides the helmet, you'll want a full outfit. Being out in the snow is one thing, being out on one of these Arctic Cat's going sixty miles per hour in the snow is quite another. Do you have proper riding gear?"

"Uh, no. Let's take a look," Michael said. The price tag kept going up and up.

If you can't spend money and enjoy your retirement, when can you?

After a half hour, Michael had his new Arctic Cat 1100 on a trailer hooked to the back of his Ford F250 Duper Duty, with the passenger seat loaded with a helmet, gloves, boots, jacket and snow bibs. He'd dropped a lot of money on the ensemble, but he was determined he was going to have the time of his life for the first winter of his retirement; kick boredom right in the teeth.

As he climbed up into his vehicle, he checked his watch. He still had time to catch a late breakfast over at the Peachy Keen. He'd been subsisting on just a cup of coffee and some toast all morning as he ran errands and went all-in on the snowmmobile.

Pulling the trailer, he was going to have to park further up the street and then walk back to the diner. It seemed like it had gotten colder since he'd started out in the morning, and he noticed there was a light flurry in the air. He'd looked into the volcano theory that he'd heard in the bar the other day, and sure enough, there had been a large eruption in the Pacific, and the ash that was spewed into the air was having a dramatic cooling effect on the northern hemisphere. The northeastern United States was in for a long cold winter.

"Morning, Seemo," Michael said as he entered the diner. He had started to become something of a regular over the last few weeks. "Cup of coffee and one of your western omelets, please."

"Sure thing, Mr. Cooke. Coming right up," Seemo answered from behind the counter.

Tubby was in his usual location eating his Frosted Flakes and watching the television. Cooke wondered just how many bowls of the stuff Tubby packed away on a daily basis. There was an old couple at one of the tables, but other than Tubby and them, the place was empty. It was usually busier at nine in the morning on a Wednesday.

Michael went out front and grabbed the new issue of *The Mountain Star* off the rack. He sat back down at the counter and saw his own face staring back at him on the cover of the paper. There was a full color picture of him standing with his rifle, and then another image from the barrel end of the gun looking back towards the scope. His face was mostly obscured by the scope. Cooke began reading the article. It didn't read like a normal, small town news story. It was polished, had a defined voice and gave him all the details he hoped for. He was so engrossed in the article he didn't notice the other people who came into the diner.

"Nice picture in the paper there," one of the new patrons said. He was an older gentleman with thinning gray hair and liver spots on his face and hands. He looked like he was probably close to ninety years old.

"Thanks," Cooke replied. "Michael Cooke." He extended his hand to shake with the elderly man.

"Tom Street. I own the floral shop, video store and storage garages here in town. I've been here all my life and I've never seen this town in such a state as it has been the last couple of weeks." The old man sat down at the counter next to Michael and asked for a coffee.

"So it's not always like this?"

"Nope. Can't say that it is. I've got my notions that it's all the out-of-towners moving in and causing the ruckus," he said matter-of-factly.

"I'm an out-of-towner," Cooke said.

"Like I said," the old man replied, sipping his black coffee. There was no sense of sarcasm in his voice. "People come up here to the mountains to get away from their troubles, but the reality is, you can't run away from your problems. They always follow you."

"I can't disagree with that," Cooke said. "But it's a different world these days. A place like this isn't as secluded as it used to be. This article here is probably on the newspaper's website, which means that it can be read all over the world."

"Yes sir, it's a sad state we're in, Mr. Cooke." Tom Street said. He picked up a menu and started looking it over.

"I think it's awesome," someone said from behind them.

"Bah," Mr. Street replied.

"Mr. Cooke, I think what this town needs is more outsiders. For the longest time the only people with any say around here are the people who have lived here their entire lives. I think it's about time we had a change," the young man said. He was probably eighteen or nineteen years old, had dark hair and looked like he was trying desperately to grow a mustache, but wasn't doing so well with the project.

"What's your name," Cooke asked.

"Boyd Coffer," said the teen. He stood from his seat at the table where two other teens sat and walked over to Cooke. He shook hands.

"Coffer, huh? Does your dad own Coopers Hollow Powersports?"

"Yeah, that's him. Is that your new Arctic Cat out there?"

"Yes, sir. I just bought it from him this morning. Can't wait for it to snow so I can try it out," Michael said.

"Have you ever gone snowmobiling before?"

"A couple years back I went up to Vermont with a couple of guys on the force and we rode for about a week. I had a blast."

"Well it doesn't compare to up here in the Catskills. There are literally hundreds of miles of trails up here. You can ride all night. And you never know what you're going to see out there on the trails," Boyd said.

"Yeah," said one of the other guys with Boyd. "Tell him what you saw last week."

"Shut up," Boyd said. "You're an idiot."

"Tell him," the other teen chimed in.

"What did you see out there?" Cooke had swiveled around on his stool and leaned back casually, resting his elbows on the counter.

"Nothing. I don't know what it was. It was dark."

"That's not what you told us when you saw it," the first teen continued.

"He says he saw a tiger out there," the other youth said. This caused the two of them to start into hysterics, laughing and snickering at their friend.

"I don't know what it was," Boyd argued.

"When did you see it?" Michael rose up on his elbows slightly.

"When it snowed last. I don't know. What was it ten, twelve days ago? We were out and riding the trails late at night. We saw that van that was in that accident, then headed up the valley. We circled back towards town and that's when I saw it. I was going pretty fast and it just flashed across my headlight, but it wasn't a deer."

Cooke leaned forward as he listened to the young man's story. He wondered if maybe what he'd actually seen that night was one of the cougars.

"What did you see? Describe it to me," Cooke said.

"It was huge, like maybe eight or nine feet long. Orangey-brown and striped, with white paws and a belly. It cleared the trail in one leap in front of me. I didn't stop to find out what it was and the other guys didn't see it," Boyd said. "I had ridden way ahead of them."

"Did you tell anybody else about this? Your dad? The police chief?"

"No. Who would have believed me? I thought maybe it was the cougar that you shot. When I saw a picture of it, though, I don't think it's what I saw on the trail. It was late, though. And dark. Maybe the shadows played tricks on me," he said, shrugging his shoulders.

"I think the Chief should hear about this," Cooke said, turning back to his breakfast as Seemo deposited it on the counter. "I'll give him a call after breakfast and see what he has to say about it."

"He's not going to believe me."

"We'll see," Cooke said. From what he understood of the van that had wrecked, it had a bunch of animals in it. They had just assumed it was another cougar. When Davidson had seen the tracks of the animal that had killed Starlett's horse, he said they were too big to be a cougar. If they had a tiger running around in the woods, then they had real problems. Tigers were man eaters. Of course everything he knew about them came from his enormous experience watching the nature channel in the comfort of his living room. As embellished as those shows might be, he didn't want to come face to face with one in the wild.

"Like I said, a bunch of outsiders coming into town making a big stink about things," Tom Street said. "Speaking of stinks, Tubby whatever you've got in your storage unit has got to go. It's stinking to high heaven over there."

"Sorry," Tubby said. He'd been quietly finishing his Frosted Flakes and watching the television.

"If you don't get it taken care of by this afternoon, I'm going to cut the lock off and spray it out with a fire hose," Mr. Street continued.

"Don't," Tubby said simply.

"I'll cut that lock off," he repeated, with a bit more gusto.

None of them had time to react to what happened next. Tubby leapt off his stool and grabbed Tom Street by the front of the shirt. He ripped him off the stool and held him up in the air, feet dangling off the ground. The buttons popped off Tom's shirt, and he went white as a ghost.

"Don't you go in there," Tubby said, nose to nose with the older man. He didn't yell, he just said it, calm and direct.

"Tubby!" Cooke jumped up and grabbed the mountain of a man and tried to loosen his grip on old man Street. It was like wrestling with a bear. Tubby was as strong as a Clydesdale. "Put him down!"

"Okay," Tubby said simply. He set Street down on one of the stools, and then looked around. Everyone was frozen in shock in the diner. Tubby ran out the front door.

"Are you okay," Cooke asked, checking the old man over.

"Yeah, I'm fine. He ruined my shirt. He'll have to pay for that," Street said.

"I'm sure he will. Do you want me to call the police?"

"I don't think so, I'm okay." Tom Street said. His neck was getting red from where the shirt had bound against it. His shirt was now without buttons and untucked from his pants. The old man was trying to save face, as he was embarrassed by the confrontation, but Cooke was worried that he needed medical attention.

"Seemo, why don't you call 911. I'd feel better if somebody checked him out to make sure he was okay," Cooke said. He was back in cop mode for a moment. He'd just witnessed an assault, and he couldn't just let it go.

"Okay, Mr. Cooke. Okay," Seemo said. He got the phone and dialed.

Tom Street was starting to get pale. Cooke was worried he was about to faint. He put his hand on the old man's back and took his wrist to check his pulse. It was going a mile a minute.

"Let's get you off this stool and into a chair with a back," Cooke said. He helped the older man over to a chair. "Seemo can you get a glass of water for him?"

"I'm fine," Street said, but he was short of breath now.

"Get an ambulance," Cooke said. "And a couple of aspirin."

"Okay, this is starting to get ridiculous," McMurphy said to Cooke as he entered the diner. "Have you been involved in every bit of drama that's gone down in this town in the last month or what?"

"Wrong place, right time, I guess," Cooke said.

"I guess," McMurphy said with eyes narrowed. "So, would you like to tell me what happened here?"

Cooke told him about the outburst by Tubby and the assault. It only took a few moments. McMurphy scribbled furiously in his notebook.

"How's the old man doing," Cooke asked.

"They have him in the ambulance. They're giving him oxygen. He doesn't want to go to the hospital, but they're trying to talk him into it. Is that everything?" McMurphy paused with his writing and looked up at Michael after posing the question.

"Yeah. No, wait. I think you should talk to the Coffer kid. He says he saw something in the woods the night of the animal van accident. I think you need to hear it," Cooke said.

"What do you think?" He was on the phone with Davidson at the DEC. At first he didn't believe what he was hearing. But after thinking about the carnage back at Gloria Graves' horse barn, it wasn't that big of a stretch to think that the van had been transporting a tiger as well as a cougar. "Yeah, me too. Well, see if they're done with the DNA testing and call me back. I'd like to have something a little more concrete than just a kid's late night story. I've already called a press conference for three o'clock this afternoon. I'd like to be able to notify the public of exactly what we're dealing with. Okay thanks for all your help, Davidson. Take care."

He closed down the mobile phone and turned to Cooke. Jack had a look on his face that vacillated between frustration and panic.

"Davidson said that the size of the tracks fit an adult tiger much better than a cougar. He had taken some samples of the droppings from the van back when we investigated the accident. He's going to call the lab to see if they have any results yet. I have to say, after what happened with the cougar, I'm not inclined to head out into the wood to hunt a tiger. I think we need to get an expert in here," McMurphy said.

"Yeah, I agree. We're gonna need a bigger boat," Michael said. McMurphy didn't laugh.

"I'm feeling a little like Chief Brody at the moment," McMurphy said, referencing the movie *Jaws*. It was one of his favorite movies. "I just hope I don't find myself face to face with this thing hoping for a miracle shot."

"Naw. That stuff only happens in the movies," Cooke said. He hoped he was right.

"I need to go find Tubby before he does something stupid. I've been meaning to talk to him, he hasn't been acting right lately," Jack said. "It's been kind of crazy, though. Hectic."

"I'll say. I think it's going to get worse before it gets better."

"God, I hope not." Jack wasn't sure if he could take anymore. After his dad passed away, and he took on the mantle of Chief of Police, it seemed like the problems of the town were just snowballing out of control. The position, with all of its responsibilities, was much more than he had ever anticipated. As Chief he should have had one of his patrolmen out here investigating such a minor thing, but he was in the area. He had stopped over to *The*

Mountain Star to congratulate Paula on a well written
article and on her final issue. He'd gotten her some real
flowers from Tom Street's floral shop not twenty minutes
before he received the call over the radio about the disturbance and possible heart attack victim at the Peachy Keen.
He'd arrived in just minutes. The ambulance wasn't far
behind. He was going to go see if he could talk to Tubby
and then get back to his office on Main Street. The mountain of paperwork wasn't going away, and he had to prepare
for his press conference which would be held out in front
of the Police station on the granite steps. Not to mention
his father's funeral, which had been postponed to Friday
after Copper had been killed. Jack was under an enormous
amount of pressure, but he couldn't let it get to him. He
needed to start acting like a Police Chief now, and not like
a patrolman.

"Mind if I tag along when you talk to Tubby?" Cooke
was worried about the guy. He'd been there when the guys
had given him too much grief at the bar the other day, and
thought maybe the poor fella felt like the entire town was
coming down on him. "I feel like I kind of owe him one,
you know."

"Sure, why not."

They pulled up in front of Tubby's house on Oak Hill
Road, just off Main Street. It was a large Victorian style
house, but it had fallen into severe disrepair. It had been
pink and white at one time, and was probably very attractive. Now some of the shutters had fallen off, the paint was

peeling, and the porch was leaning dangerously on one corner.

"Stay here, I'm going to go up and see if he's inside or not," Jack said, exiting the vehicle and leaving his door open.

He follows procedure pretty well. Michael thought. Closing a door could alert a suspect to police presence, giving them the opportunity to arm themselves or escape.

Jack cautiously walked up onto the porch, making sure of his footing on the wooden planks which were starting to rot. He rang the doorbell then knocked heavily on the old door.

"Tubby, it's Jack McMurphy," he yelled. "Why don't you come on out so we can talk about what happened over at the Peachy Keen just now."

The door opened suddenly and Tubby came out aiming what looked like a small caliber rifle right at Jack's forehead. Jack had his gun out and pointing at Tubby in a flash.

"Tubby, don't do this," Jack said in a calm voice. "This is no way to solve anything. Put your gun down and I'll put mine down and we'll talk. Something's bugging you and we can work it out."

Michael saw Tubby with the gun and he immediately went into action. He grabbed the radio in Jack's vehicle and put a call in to dispatch for backup. He gave them the address and told them who he was. The call went out county wide for assistance.

A shotgun that was sitting at the ready in a holster by

the dashboard. Michael took it off the vertical rack and checked to make sure it was loaded. He stepped out of the vehicle and aimed it at Tubby. He slowly walked up the sidewalk.

"I've got you covered, Jack," he called out. "Tubby, we're all friends here, don't do this."

"I got this Michael," Jack said tensely. "Tubby, come on. We've known each other since we were just kids. We were in school together, remember? We can talk this out."

"Tell him he can't go and get in my garage," Tubby said.

"Who, Tubby? Who's getting into your garage?"

"Old man Street. He said he was going to go in and wash it out with a hose. Tell him he can't do that!"

"Okay, okay. I'll tell him. Put the gun down," Jack said. "I'll go talk to him as soon as we're done here, okay?"

"Jack," Michael said.

"What?" he was annoyed that the older man was here now. He had told him to stay in the vehicle. He figured he had his shotgun trained on Tubby, and Jack wasn't too pleased that his gun was in the hands of someone else, either.

"It's a pellet gun," Michael said. He lowered his shotgun and thumbed on the safety. "It's an air rifle." Jack looked and saw that Cooke was correct. He lowered his hand gun and put it back in his holster.

"What's wrong with you, Tubby? Are you trying to get yourself killed? I've got to take you in now, you understand that? You've assaulted Mr. Street and now you've pulled a gun on an officer of the law. You understand we have to go to the police station to solve this now?" Jack asked calmly, trying to control his temper.

"I'm not going nowhere," Tubby turned and ran back into the house slamming the heavy door behind him.

"Great. Michael, can you cover me? You're still deputized," Jack called out. It had probably been a hundred years since a citizen was deputized in such a fashion in these parts. It was still legal for a Sheriff to do it, but it was just never done. Jack hadn't really been sure if he had the authority to deputize Michael back when they were hunting the cougar, but he figured it was easier to ask for forgiveness than permission if anyone made a fuss about it.

"Yes, sir. I told you I've got your back."

"Stand down as soon as back up arrives, I don't want you getting yourself shot by accident," Jack said. He was going into the house. It was against protocol, but he was worried Tubby was going to hurt himself.

He tried the doorknob and found it unlocked. He entered the house and called for Tubby. The television was blaring in the other room and he wasn't sure if his voice could even be heard over it. The smell was pungent. There were cats everywhere, and probably cat feces as well.

"Tubby, come on out. We need to get this fixed. It's only going to get worse if you don't let me help you," Jack yelled.

Suddenly there was a pink flash of fabric in front of him. Tubby's mother, standing in a stained pink bathrobe was pointing a medium caliber pistol at him. It was an old .38 Smith & Wesson Special from the looks of it.

"You leave my boy alone," she screeched at him.

"Mrs. McIntyre, put the gun down now. Don't make it worse. We can work this out. Put your gun down," he said sternly but as calmly as possible. He didn't want her to flinch and pull the trigger accidentally.

"My boy ain't hurt nobody. You leave him alone! It weren't his fault," Just as she finished, a hand clamped down on her wrist from behind, forcing the gun's barrel down towards the ground. She pulled the trigger and it fired into the floorboards. Michael had circled around the back of the house and had come in through the rear door. He'd taken the opportunity to sneak up on her from behind, using the noise of the television to conceal his approach.

In one swift motion he bent her wrist and pulled the gun away. She screamed like a trapped animal. He spun her around and Jack was there with his handcuffs. They got her chubby arms behind her back and got her onto the ground without being too rough. She was wailing and kicking her feet, and the two men stood there and let her have her tantrum. Finally she wore herself out and just sobbed.

"I think he went right out the back door," Michael said a little out of breath. "I heard footsteps running through the woods as I came around back and the door was open."

"Oh, Tubby, you idiot," Jack said under his breath. "Let's get her out to the back of my cruiser and wait for backup."

"Okay," Michael said, helping get Mrs. McIntyre to her feet.

"And thanks. I appreciate the help," Jack said.

"No problem, Jack."

"Are you sure you're okay?"

"Yeah, I'm tougher than I look," Tom Street said. "I didn't make it to ninety by being a pansy."

"Well, let's take a look at what he's got in there," McMurphy said. He'd let Michael go home as soon as Patrolman Ballard had arrived. After Old Tom Street had refused to go to the hospital, they had no choice but to let him go home as well. Jack had talked to him, however, and asked if they could get into the locked storage unit that belonged to Tubby. He now had probable cause, and could get a warrant if he needed to. Street had told him that the contract was written in such a way that he could allow access to officers of the law if it was suspected that there was any illegal activity going on within the unit, which included the storing of stolen goods. At this point, everybody agreed that Tubby was hiding something, whether it was illegal or not was still of question. None of them believed Tubby was smart enough to lawyer up and give them any hassle if they didn't find anything illegal. They would just let him ride on the fire truck in the next parade and he'd be as happy as a kid in a candy store.

Street took the small circular saw in hand and cut through the lock. It fell away, and Jack opened up the unit. The foul stench that hit them was staggering. Street, covering his mouth and nose with his handkerchief, reached in and flipped on the light switch. None of them could fathom what they saw.

It took a moment for the sight to register. It wasn't what any of them were expecting and it gave them all a jolt.

A decomposing corpse sat upright at a card table, holding five cards in its hand. It was dressed in a business suit out of the seventies, with a hat, tie, and what was probably a white shirt once upon a time. The eyes were open and jaw was slack. There was a puddle of decomposing fluids beneath the chair.

The body had been bound to the chair using bungee cables and rope. The flesh on the face and hands looked like it had been frozen and was now thawing. It was too cold for flies and maggots, but the rot had definitely begun. The suit was tan with a large collar. A wide striped tie was around the neck and brown stains had soiled the shirt; an unmistakable ensemble from the seventies or early eighties if one was fashionably tardy.

No one said a word. Besides the hum of the freezer in the back of the unit, all that could be heard were the drips of decomposing fluids as they fell from the body and splashed into the puddle on the floor.

Patrolman Ballard started to gag, while Tom Street turned white as a sheet. Jack looked at the scene in shock. He was not expecting to find a corpse.

Jack broke his promise to himself and cursed. Just then his phone buzzed in his pocket. He fished it out and looked at the number. It was Paula. He didn't answer it. He cautiously entered the storage unit. It looked as if someone else had been playing cards with the dead man. Another hand of cards was laid down on the table. Two jacks, two threes and a ten of clubs. Jack walked around to the corpse. His hand was three aces and two kings. A full house.

He looked closer at the face. He didn't recognize who it was, though it was tough to see the features clearly, as some of the flesh had dropped off onto the table and the corpse's lap. If it wasn't for the incredible stench, Jack would have guessed that it was a Halloween decoration rather than a real dead body. After a few moments the smell finally got to him, and he felt the bile rising in his throat. He had to get out of the enclosure into some fresh air.

"We're going to have to get a clean up team in here," Jack said. His phone buzzed again, this time it was Davidson. "Listen, close this door. Don't tell anyone about this. I'm calling in the county hazmat team to wrap up the body and get it down to the medical examiner's office. For now, we're treating this as a homicide."

He finished with Ballard and opened the connection with Davidson.

"This is Jack," he said.

"Davidson here. I got the results back from the lab."

"And?"

"We've got ourselves a full grown adult male Siberian Tiger wandering in the woods around Coopers Hollow."

"Thank you all for coming on such short notice. We don't usually call affiliates in Albany or Binghamton for news conferences, but we felt it was important enough to try to reach as many people in our community through as many news outlets as possible.

"It's been a tumultuous month for the Coopers Hollow Police department. As most of you know, Chief Jack McMurphy Senior, my father, passed away in the line of duty earlier this month. Not a week later, the community lost another leader, Fire Chief Copper Owens who was killed while trying to hunt down an escaped cougar. Our investigation has led us to believe that the cougar was being transported in a white rental van which was involved in a single vehicle accident early on the morning of October fifteenth during a snowstorm. The driver was killed in the accident. The vehicle was transporting many species of exotic animals. We believe one of those animals was an adult male Siberian Tiger. I repeat: we believe that there is an adult male Siberian Tiger loose in the woods around Coopers Hollow. David Davidson of the Department of Environmental Conservation retrieved droppings from the van and had them analyzed for DNA. The results were conclusive. Additionally, the night of the accident there was an eye witness who saw the animal running through the forest. Last night the horse of a local woman was attacked and killed by the tiger. There were no eye witnesses to the attack, however paw prints were found and photographed. When those prints were analyzed by an expert, she concluded that they were the prints of a Siberian Tiger.

"This is a highly irregular occurrence, and it merits special consideration. I have contacted the United States Department of Fish and Wildlife and they have specialists en route even as we are having this press conference. I have consulted with them and they agree that the following provisions for public safety should be put in place:

"We are canceling any and all outdoor youth sports

and practices for schools in the northern part of the county. Additionally we are suspending the Halloween parade planned for Saturday as well as all trick or treating on Halloween. Now if we are able to find and capture the tiger, we will lift these bans. But for right now, for the safety of everyone and especially the children, we are putting these bans into effect. Also, recess at all area schools will be held indoors and we strongly suggest that children be driven to school and not allowed to walk to school or wait at a bus stop unprotected.

"Also, I need to make this strong admonition: Siberian Tigers can be man eaters. If this one is, as we suspect, used to human interaction due to its captivity, it will have no fear of humans. This means that it very well may attack a person. No one should attempt to go into the woods during this time, nor should anyone attempt to hunt and kill this animal themselves. Additionally, please take all precautions necessary to protect your pets and farm animals. This tiger has already gone into a closed barn and killed livestock. The experts I have talked to say this is a very disturbing development, as it means that the animal has now adapted and may repeat this behavior.

As I said before, we have experts coming from the U.S. Department of Fish and Wildlife to help us capture, and if necessary, kill this animal. Thank you all for your cooperation. Now, are there any questions?"

The reporters all started shouting their questions. Jack surveyed the group of about eighteen reporters. Some he recognized from the television stations in Binghamton and Albany. Others he figured wrote for the papers throughout the region.

"One at a time. I'll get to everyone's questions. Let's start up here, Paula."

"Paula Schumann with *The Mountain Star* and *Kingston Chronicle.* Do you have any indication of how large this tiger is, and you did say it was a Siberian and not a Bengal tiger, correct?"

"Yes, it's a Siberian tiger which is indigenous to northern Asia. They aren't normally as aggressive in the wild as Bengal tigers, but we don't know the background of this animal, so it must be considered extremely dangerous. The only thing we have to go on right now is the size of the paw print and the brief eye witness encounter. Our estimates are that it's about 110 to 130 inches in length, that's nose to tail, and probably around four hundred pounds. That's about average for a full grown adult male, so I'm told," Jack said. "Next question. You in the red."

"Amber Heyman, channel thirty-seven in Utica. Why has it taken nearly two weeks to inform the public that there is a dangerous animal lurking in the woods that could easily maim or kill an individual?"

"Well, as I stated, we believe this animal, along with a cougar which was killed earlier this week, were being transported through the area when the vehicle they were in was in an accident and they escaped. The vehicle wasn't discovered for nearly five hours, and unfortunately the driver was killed in the accident. No paperwork of any kind was found indicating what animals were being carried and all attempts to contact anyone who might have additional information garnered no results. We took DNA samples and it took this long to get confirmation. The eye witness didn't come forward until this morning, as the individual wasn't sure what they had seen. Also, our initial investigation into the van didn't turn up much. It was rented out of state, in Ohio to be precise, and there was very little paper trail. We've done all we could to investigate and keep the public safe." Jack nodded to another reporter for their question.

"Timothy Cooley channel six. Are you going to try to trap the tiger, or just go out and ruthlessly kill it?"

"I will follow the direction of the U.S. Department of Fish and Wildlife. They're the experts. If they feel that the tiger is too much of a threat and cannot be safely captured, we will kill it. Obviously, we don't want to harm an animal unnecessarily, but we will do what needs to be done to keep people safe. Yes," he said indicating another reporter.

"Patrick Fleischer, *Cobleskill Gazette.* On our way in, we picked up the police band and a call for a hazmat team. Does this have anything to do with the tiger, and if not, what does it have to do with?"

"Yes, a call was put out for a hazmat team to clean up a scene that our office deemed to have what might have been hazardous material. It is not related to the tiger or the investigation into how it got here. I don't have any additional information for you on that at this time. Any other questions? Yes, Paula."

"How are you doing? You've lost your father and one of your mentors in the last few weeks. How are you handling the sudden responsibilities that have been thrown onto your shoulders?"

"It's not easy. From a personal standpoint, it's been extremely difficult. But the Coopers Hollow police department has a duty to be fulfilled. Our department has a

responsibility to the people of this village to keep them safe
and serve them in a professional manner. Yes I've suffered
a loss, but with the threat to the community, I'm working
hard to make sure that this doesn't end up in additional
losses for anyone else. If there are no further questions, I'd
like to thank you all for coming. We will send out updates
as they occur. Thank you."

Chapter 18

Two black Lincoln Navigators with dark tinted windows and low profile tires drove up the driveway and parked in front of the door. A man stepped out of the first vehicle and looked around to see if anyone was watching him. Satisfied that he wasn't being observed, he walked up and rang the doorbell. The door opened and Peter stood there for a moment looking at the man at their door. It took only a moment for him to realize what was unfolding. He thanked God that his wife was off buying groceries. He knew why the men in the black vehicles were there and he knew he probably wouldn't live to tell anyone about them. His time had come. He'd spent much of his life serving the Beckmans, and he'd finish his duty. Dalton really had no idea what type of people he had gotten involved with, that was obvious. He was a good kid, but sometimes he was just dumb as a box of rocks.

The questions started, Peter deflected. He did know where Dalton had gone, but he wasn't going to tell these men. They clearly wanted him dead. If they had anything to do with it, Dalton was never going to testify in Binghamton.

They made it painful for him. They bound him to a dining room chair and placed it in the center of the living room. First they broke his hands, then his legs midway up his shins. Peter knew that he was slipping into shock and his heart wasn't going to be able to take the abuse. He died quickly and with a smile on his lips, numb to the pain. He died thinking about the last thing he'd said to his wife and how they'd parted that morning with a kiss.

The men poured gasoline over his dead body and around the house and one of them threw a Molotov cocktail back through the front door. The gasoline ignited immediately and flames engulfed the home in moments. The black SUVs pulled away from the Beckman's house and headed towards their next stop.

Paula had more luck with the phone numbers from the van driver than Jack had. There were some tricks she had used before to get reluctant sources to talk, and they proved highly successful. One of the numbers in the phone that was simply labeled "Tam" provided some tangible information. The list of names Jack had investigated from the driver's cell phone had notes next to them. Most said "No answer, no call-back." Jack didn't quite understand how much of the population viewed police officers. He'd grown up in a family of cops and all of his friends from his youth came from respectable families, never having any trouble with the law. Everyone had caller ID now, and if Jack had called from his office in the Sheriff's department, it would have read Coopers Hollow Police. Based on the driver's license being from Coopers Hollow, Ohio, whoever saw the caller ID would have had to assume that it was local police calling. Her guess was that the type of people the van driver had been involved with did not want to talk to anyone from any police department.

Tam was probably short for Tammy or Tamara, and probably was a current or ex-girlfriend. Paula went with that assumption and bluffed her way into getting as much info as possible.

"Is this Tamara?" Paula guessed.

"Yes, who's this?"

"My name is Paula, I found a cell phone and your number was in it. I was thinking maybe you could help me return it to the owner, do you know who it belongs to?" Paula read off the cell phone number to the woman on the other end of the call.

"Yeah, it's my brother, Tommy's phone."

"Oh, should I send it to you or to Tommy or his work, maybe? I'll want to ship it where I can make sure there's a signature for it."

"Um, where is it? I haven't heard from Tommy in a couple weeks. Where did he lose it?"

"New York, up in the mountains."

"Oh, he must be out of town working, then. He drives all over the country for his work."

"Maybe I should ship it to his work then. He might need it and they might know where he is and can get it to him."

"Um, let me see if I have that address, hang on a second."

And just like that, Paula had the address to Ohio Exotics. The hunt was on.

"I've got something," she said over the phone to Jack.

"Really? What?"

"Next of kin and an address to his place of work, a place called Ohio Exotics, Incorporated. Listen, I did a quick search for them online and I found their website. They specialize in locating exotic animals around the world and are willing to buy and sell just about anything. They reference a whole bunch of zoos they've dealt with and seem like a legitimate business. They even have the Better Business Bureau logo on their website," she sighed as she said this. She was hoping it was going to be a big story, a smuggling ring or something. "I called the number provided on the website and I got a girl who was very open about what they did. I asked her about a shipment that contained an adult cougar and tiger and she said that she could not discuss other transactions, and then she was quiet. She said she was going to put me through to the owner."

"What did he have to say?"

"The guy's name is Marcus Higgs. He sounds like a real sleaze ball on the phone. Real used car salesman type. Anyway, he says that yes, Tommy worked for him, but he took off and stole some animals from him a couple weeks ago. He said he didn't report it to the authorities because he liked the kid. Didn't want to get him into trouble. He says he was trying to help him out, as the kid didn't have much of a family. Only a sister was still alive. He confirmed that a Siberian Tiger was one of the animals that among those stolen. Anyway, he asked if I knew what happened to Tommy. I gave him your name and number and told him he'd have to call you. I hope that was okay," Paula said.

"Yeah, that was good. I don't know, maybe this guy Tommy was a thief. It would make sense why he didn't have the paperwork and was trying to drive through a snowstorm. He was running, or maybe trying to cash in on a deal before anybody knew the animals were missing. Whatever the case, I guess we have our lead. I've got to turn this info over to the Fish and Wildlife guys. Thanks for your work. Sorry it wasn't a big story for you." She could hear it in his voice, he really was sorry for her.

"It's okay. Now that we have the tiger loose in town, the AP picked up my story on Michael Cooke. I'm going to get a little bonus for it. It's my first national story," she said. It would have been nice to follow it up with a second. It wasn't everyday that a big story of national or maybe international interest fell in her lap.

"Well, in that case we should celebrate," Jack said. "I'm finishing up here, clearing out the paperwork from the last week. I could be up there in about an hour and a half. We could go out for dinner. I'll change this time. No uniform, I promise."

"Okay, where do you want to go?"

"We could go up to Schenectady and have a real dinner out. If it gets too late, we could find a place to stay up there," he said. Her heart skipped a beat with excitement. "I'm taking tomorrow off for the funeral, so we just have to be back in town by two. The guys from Fish and Wildlife won't be here until Saturday. What do you think?"

"Yeah, I'd like that. I'll pack a bag," she replied, grinning from ear to ear. "See you in an hour and a half."

"Is that enough time?"

"I'll be ready," she said.

"Okay, see you then."

She closed down her cell phone and just sat there for a moment. She thought back on their relationship, if you could call it that. They'd gone out to dinner a couple of times, and then he'd let slip about the Mayor and she'd written about it and it wasn't the same after that. Not until three nights ago, when they'd almost gotten intimate. Almost.

"Well, tonight's the night," she said out loud to the empty room. She tilted back in her office chair and scissor kicked her feet back and forth in the air like a kid on a swing in the park.

The two black SUVs traveled from New Jersey north on Interstate 87. It was about a four hour drive taking into account the New Jersey traffic. They hadn't gotten what they wanted from the butler, and his heart gave out before they could get to any of the really interesting methods for extracting information. They weren't just a rag tag bunch of misfits from the streets. Some of them were former military. A few of them even had college degrees. They ran this operation like a business. A brutal business. El Tigre hadn't risen to the top and kept his organization in line by being passive.

Every once in awhile he liked to get his claws dirty and make an example. That's what he had planned on doing with Dalton. It was going to be a nice little intimate affair in the mountains. Something from which the rest of the organization, especially the lower level guys, would be able to learn a valuable lesson. You don't even think about turning over on the organization. They wouldn't stop with just the snitch. They'd finish the girlfriend, parents and even close friends or kids. A message would be sent. It would have gone smoothly if it hadn't been for that do-gooder stepping in. They would have been long gone with the Beckman kid. It was his own, stupid fault for doing it in person. He took it personally when someone tried to hurt his organization. Now it was even more personal.

The guy, Michael Cooke was his name, was going to pay as well. El Tigre had gotten the name from his lawyer. They knew that the girlfriend and her mother lived in or around Coopers Hollow, as did Cooke. It would only take a matter of asking around a bit to find out where they could be found. They'd be done with it in just a matter of hours and then hunt down the Beckman kid. It was preferable to El Tigre that Dalton know his girlfriend died because of him. He liked the hopeless look in their eyes just before the flicker of life was extinguished. He'd feel cheated if he didn't get to see that in Dalton's eyes.

They pulled off in Kingston and filled the vehicles with fuel. It would give them at least four hundred miles of travel. He didn't want to stop anywhere else when they got there. Gas stations, especially, had security cameras. One of the guys went inside to get a drink and came back with the local newspaper. El Tigre was watching out his window

when he saw his man stop cold in his tracks. He suddenly
rushed over to the vehicle and tapped on the window.

"Boss, look at this," he handed the paper through the
window.

It was an article on Michael Cooke. He'd apparently
shot and killed a cougar up in the woods. There he was
standing with a rifle in his hands, looking all tough. He
was going to shove that rifle up his back side so far he'd
choke on it. El Tigre scanned the article but saw no mention of an address. It only said he was a new transplant
to Coopers Hollow. At the bottom of the article it said,
"Paula Schumann is *The Kingston Chronicle* affiliate in
Coopers Hollow and the surrounding area. If you have a
story of interest, contact her." It gave her phone number. El
Tigre dialed the number.

She was alone in the former offices of *The Mountain
Star*. The only company she had now was her cell phone
and laptop. The other employees were gone, as was most of
the furniture. Pretty much everything that needed to be,
had already been boxed up and shipped over to Kingston
for storage. They had run an ad in their own last edition in
the classifieds for the office furniture. It was disheartening.
She'd received a few calls during the day, some were locals
asking about the paper and the news they had heard about
it closing down. Most of the callers had just wanted to
know the location of the office so they could come by and
take a look at the furniture. She'd already sold off some
of the chairs and desks. Not much was left, a few of the

old heavy desks, a couple of filing cabinets, stuff that she probably wouldn't be able to give away.

The merger wasn't all bad, though. They had run her article in *The Kingston Chronicle* the day after it ran in *The Mountain Star*. It wasn't front page news, but it was on the front page of the local section. She would put her time in for another six months or year, but she wasn't going to pass up any opportunities that might come along. She had nothing keeping her in the area anymore, unless this thing with Jack took off. She knew if she got into anything with him they'd never leave. They would be lifers. At first the thought had scared her, but as she thought about it over the last couple of days she had warmed to the idea.

Paula was about to head into her apartment through the adjoining door, but stopped short. She thought she heard something in the rooms above. It wasn't the sound of a mouse or squirrel, it was heavy footfalls. Someone was upstairs. She had a TASER device for personal protection, and she retrieved it from her purse.

Holding the devise in front of her, she started up the steps to the second floor.

"Who's up here?" she called out. "I have a gun," she lied. There it was again, someone was walking around in one of the rooms. It was at the end of the hallway, room 213. She cautiously walked down the corridor towards the room.

"I've already called the police," she said. "You might as well come out. Listen, you don't want to get shot by accident, do you?"

Suddenly the door opened.

He was scared. If what Mama said was true, then they were going to lock him up forever. They might even put him in the 'lectric chair. She had told him that the man in the freezer was his daddy. She told him that Tubby didn't remember, but when he was a little boy, he took his great grampa's gun and shot him. She said that it was just an accident, but she didn't want anybody to take him away, 'cause he was just little when it happened. So she put his daddy in the freezer so Tubby wouldn't get in trouble.

And then he messed it all up when he opened the freezer. The secret she was trying to protect him from was now out in the open, and if he wasn't smart and kept it to himself, he was going to get in trouble and now that he was older, they wouldn't treat him nice like they would have if he was little. They'd treat him like a killer now, a murderer. And they put murderers in the 'lectric chair and sent a million volts through them until they sizzled. He didn't want to die like that. Plus God sent murders to Hell and the Devil would burn murderers in Hell forever and they were there with people who killed babies. Tubby didn't want to go to Hell, neither. He didn't want nobody finding out about it.

So when Old Man Street had said he was going to open the storage garage, Tubby couldn't let him. And then Chief Jack Junior had come looking for him, and he tried to scare him off with his gun, but it didn't work. It only made things worse. He ran into the woods behind his house and hid. There was a hollowed out tree that had been struck by lightning. Tubby used to hide in the hollowed out section when he didn't want nobody finding him. That's where he hid when Chief Jack Junior came looking for him. Then it got cold. So cold.

He couldn't go back home. He couldn't go back to the storage garage to talk to his daddy nomore. He had to find someplace else to hide. He waited until it was late, late at night. He could hardly feel his toes or fingers when he first came out from the tree, but then as he started walking they warmed up a little.

He kept thinking that his daddy was talking to him. Telling him what to do. But he knew his daddy wasn't really alive no more. But he was just 'pertendin'. Now his daddy was tellin' him to go find someplace warm. And to go stay at the hotel. But he couldn't tell if it was his own idea or his daddy's. It was weird because it kinda sounded like his own idea, but it was in his daddy's voice, even though he didn't know what his daddy's voice was like. He didn't remember his daddy's voice.

When he was younger, before Miss Paula had bought it, he had gone exploring in the old hotel. One time he climbed up the metal fire escape and went in through a broken window. He stayed there all night, then. So he thought maybe he could do that again. It only took a few minutes to get there, and nobody saw him. He climbed up the metal ladder like he had before and opened the window. He was bigger now than when he was here last time and he barely fit through the open window.

Once he was inside, he saw that there was an old bed and blanket. He was so tired. And cold. So cold. He climbed into the bed. It smelled bad, but it was warm.

In his dream he was talking to his daddy again. They were playing cards and laughing. In his dream he wasn't dumb, and he kept telling jokes and it made his daddy laugh and laugh. Then there was somebody yelling. They were saying they had a gun and they were going to call the police. And that they weren't gonna touch the boy no more. The boy weren't gonna get touched no more. Not no more. In his dream his daddy suddenly died and started to rot. It scared him awake.

"What are you doing here, Tubby?" Paula asked him. She was pointing something like a gun at him. He was scared, and didn't know what to do. He thought about running again, but he had no place else to go. She had always been nice to him, so he decided to tell her.

"I don't want to go in the 'lectric chair," he said.

"Tubby, it's okay. Nobody is going to put you in the electric chair. Everybody just wants to make sure you're okay. Now I need to go call Jack and have him come and see you. Just to talk. You stay right here, okay?"

"Okay," he replied.

"Promise?"

"I promise."

She turned and headed back downstairs. Adrenaline was still pumping through her veins. Her heart had been nearly in her throat when the door had opened. She was relieved that it was just Tubby. What he was doing in a room on the second floor was a little disconcerting, but at least he looked like he was okay. He was just scared.

Paula grabbed her cell phone off the desk and dialed Jack's number. It rang four times and then went to voicemail. She didn't leave a message. He was probably getting ready to come get her. As long as Tubby stayed put, Jack would be there in just a few minutes anyway. It looked like their night on the town was off. Again.

Maybe it was for the best, as she looked out the front window of the office, she saw snow beginning to fall. She'd heard they might be getting another storm. Two big storms before Halloween. It wasn't the first time it had happened in the history of the town, but it was extremely rare. Forecasters were expecting another ten inches, though it would be back in the forties by the end of the following week, so it would all melt off again.

As she walked over to her desk she took a moment to look around. She was suddenly struck by how the place looked so lonely and depressing now. Only two of the big heavy desks were left, along with their chairs. The cubicle walls that cordoned off the front waiting area were also still in place. She looked over at where the Osterhauts used to sit, and was amazed at how large the office looked without their desks. She missed the little arguments they'd get into as much as she used to loath them back when they happened. They'd worked together for several years, and it would be strange not to see them every day. The last she'd heard from them, they were contemplating selling their home and moving south and retiring early.

Good for them, if they can do it. It was a raw deal for them, she thought to herself. *I really messed this thing up.*

The front door opened, and she looked at her watch. He was always early.

"Hey, Jack. You're not going to believe who I found," she said.

"Oh yeah? Who's that, sweetheart?" came the gruff reply with a chuckle. She turned to see four men, the size of football players, standing in front of her. A thinner white guy stepped forward. He was extremely tanned and he had a tattoo on his neck. She knew him from his police booking photo. It was the guy who got in the fight in front of the Peachy Keen. He smiled at her with bright white teeth that contrasted dramatically with his artificially orange tan.

"What do you guys want," she asked. She tried to sound tough, but the hairs on the back of her neck were standing on end. It didn't take a sixth sense to know that the group had trouble in mind. She had set the TASER devise on the desk by the stairs. She would never reach it before they got to her.

"Just some information. That's all. I was very interested in your article this week, about Michael Cooke. Where can I find him?"

"I don't know. He came here for the interview."

"And you never asked for his address? What about Dalton Beckman's girlfriend?"

"Starlett? I don't know that either. I know she goes to school in Binghamton."

"Her mother lives around here someplace, we'd like to talk to her as well," the man approached her. "That's a pretty dress you're wearing. It sure would be a shame to disappoint - Jack, wasn't that his name?"

"Listen, I don't know any of the addresses of the people you're asking about. I don't know where they are. I'm just a small town reporter," she said as convincingly as possible. He stopped and thought about her response. She could tell he was trying to decide whether to believe her or not.

"Okay, we'll do it the hard way. Boys." They came forward and grabbed her forcefully by the arms. She screamed and one of the four clamped a massive hand over her mouth. He followed it with a gag which he fastened over her mouth and around the back of her neck. They threw her into a chair and bound one of her wrists and both ankles with plastic pull ties.

"We're going to make this quick. For every minute you don't tell me what I want to know, I cut off a finger," he produced a large knife which he brought up to her nose. "You'll be surprised how much it's going to hurt. The one thing I've always found interesting is how willing people are to talk after they lose that first finger. If only they realized they could have saved themselves all the pain by just talking in the first place."

Her eyes were fixated on the enormous knife. It looked extremely sharp, and the way he held it, she imagined he'd used it many times before. She'd never been this scared in her entire life. She kept hoping that Jack would come through the door and rescue her. The knife was coming down away from her face. He grabbed her wrists and pulled her towards the desk. He pressed her hand flat on the desktop and singled out one of her fingers, the pinky on her left hand. He brought the knife down slowly and pressed the blade against her finger. She yelled as best she could through the gag.

"Are you going to tell us what we want to know?" He looked her in the eyes. She looked at them and they seemed empty, devoid of life. They were the eyes of a heartless killer. She nodded her head in compliance.

"Good. I knew you were a smart girl, just by the look of you," he said. "Take the gag off so she can talk." One of his men grabbed her roughly and pushed her chin to her chest and undid the gag.

"It's in my computer," she said, gasping. "I kept notes on everybody that was involved. I have all their home addresses, phone numbers, email addresses, everything."

"Get on the computer," he said to one of his men. "What's the password?"

"It's HappyJack," she said. "All one word, the H and J are capitalized."

"I'm in," the goon said.

"Open my contacts. Everything is alphabetical," she hung her head. It was the ultimate sin for a reporter to give up a source. They would have found it anyway, she figured, and by then she'd be missing fingers or dead. She might as well tell them and hope Jack arrived before they could hurt anybody else. She thought about ways to stall, but she couldn't take her eyes off the knife.

"Got it," the goon said. By the way he typed, fingers flying over the keys, she could tell he knew his way around the computer. Even criminals had to have IT guys. He printed out the two addresses and handed them to the boss man.

"Well, that was easy," the leader said. "I'll go talk with Mr. Cooke. Two of you stay here and finish up, then meet us at the mother's house. The rest come with me. It was a pleasure working with you Ms. Schumann. I wish you all the best."

"Go to hell," she spat after him.

As soon as the front door shut, the two goons were on her. They put the gag back in place, cut her restraints from the chair and pushed her to the floor. They pulled the two remaining desks closer together, so there was about four feet between them as they faced each other. One goon fastened plastic pull ties around the legs of the desk and then dragged her across the floor so he could fasten her to them. He used additional plastic quick ties to bind her to the desk legs. When they were done, she was laid out, spread-eagled on her back. She fought and bucked as best she could, but they were big guys and were simply too strong and heavy.

"Who goes first," the shorter of the two asked.

"Flip you for it," the other replied. "Heads you go first, tails I do."

"No. I'll call it in the air. I win I'm in. I lose you go first."

"Fine." He flipped the coin, caught it in his hand and slapped it onto the back of his other hand.

"Heads." The coin was revealed. It was heads. The loser spat out an expletive.

"Go watch the front until I'm done. Let Trig know I'm going to be a minute."

The loser relented and walked towards the front of the office. He exited through the front door to go tell the driver who had been left behind that they were going to take their time with her. It had started to get dark and the snow was beginning to fall harder. Paula could just see out a portion of the front window from beneath the desk. It was strange to her how peaceful the falling snow looked outside while something so violent was about to take place inside.

The thug came closer as Paula fought and wriggled as best she could. He bent down and kissed her. She winced and tried to pull away, writhing in agony against her restraints. She felt the warmth of blood beginning to flow on her wrists and ankles from where the plastic ties were gouging into her flesh. She began to go numb, as if she wasn't there at all. She could feel him on her, pressing himself against her, but it was as if she was watching herself in a movie, or in a bad dream, and it was all just a made up thing. As if from the other side of the world, she heard the front door open, and she was suddenly back in her body, hoping against hope that it was Jack, come to rescue her.

"Come on T-Mac," the thug yelled. "Boss says we gotta torch it and go."

"I'm not done," said the one on top of her, annoyance in his voice. "I haven't even started."

"He just sent me a text. It said: 'If you're not out of there yet, hurry up and torch it.' So much for love, Casanova. I'll get the gas cans."

The one that was on top of her, T-Mac, he'd been called, strung together a paragraph's worth of obscenities as he slowly pushed himself off of her. As he got up, he looked down with menace and hatred. With a twisted smile, he leaned over and let a large drop of spit fall from his mouth. It struck her in the face and she whipped her head back and forth to try to get it off.

The thug slunk out the front door, continuing his stream of profanities. She heard a trunk lid or door slam closed from a vehicle outside, then she heard the splashing of liquid on the floor, and the smell of gasoline assaulted her nose. Now that he wasn't on top of her, she had a little more leverage. She pulled as hard as she could and got the desk to slide a few inches. She inched it closer and closer. The splashing liquid sounds stopped. They had just laid it down in the front of the offices. There were raised voices, as if an argument was taking place. She had been afraid they would splash her with the gas as well. Then she wouldn't have had a chance. She had once seen a newsreel of someone who had poured gasoline on himself and self-immolated in protest. It looked agonizing.

"Sweet dreams, princess. Sorry it didn't work out," T-Mac called to her, making kissing noises.

Suddenly there was a whooshing noise and an explosion of heat. The concussion knocked the wind out of her. She yanked at the desk as hard as she could and pulled it close enough to wedge her shin under it and use her leg as a lever to lift it upward. The desk tipped up just enough so she could slide her hand free. The ties were still biting into her wrist, but at least she was free. She slid over and tried to perform the same maneuver to free her other hand, but the desk was just too heavy. It was one of those old steel desks and must have weighed at least two hundred pounds. She just didn't have the right leverage to get it up. Reaching behind her head she removed the gag. She started screaming, while continuing to yank at her bonds. The heat was intense and she suddenly realized she was going to die.

"Help! Somebody help me!" She was screaming with all of her might. She started to sob. "Jack! Tubby! Help!"

"Please God," she cried out loud. "Please help me!" She hadn't been much of a religious person growing up, but she did believe in God, and even though it was desperation, she cried out to him as earnestly as she knew how.

The smoke began to fill the room and the heat seemed to intensify. She could hear the crackling of the wooden timbers. She was going to die. She screamed out in even greater desperation, and then suddenly there was a large man standing over her.

"Miss Paula, we need to get out of here," Tubby McIntyre said. "Everything's on fire."

"I'm stuck, Tubby, please help me!"

With one hand he lifted the desk and practically tossed it across the room. He helped her to her feet and she turned to look at the flames. They were licking the ceiling, and completely blocked off their exit through the front.

"Paula!" The voice was distinct. It was Jack, calling through the flames!

"Jack!" She yelled as loud as she could. "We're going to try to get out the back way!"

"Who's in there with you?"

"Tubby McIntyre! We'll try to make it out through my apartment!"

"Tubby we need to go through my apartment to get out," she said, racing over to the door. It was locked, and her keys were in her jacket which was now engulfed in flames. There was no other way out.

"Tubby, can you knock down this door?"

"Okay," he said. He took two steps back and launched his entire bulk at the door. It gave slightly, breaking away the frame. He stepped back again and charged, this time splintering the door off its frame and giving them access to her apartment. She didn't hesitate, grabbing him by the hand, she ran for the side exit.

As she ran out of the inferno, she saw Jack and he saw her. She ran to him through the snow, bare feet and all. She jumped into his arms and kissed him all over his face. He almost lost his footing, but managed to keep his balance.

"What happened?"

"These guys, they busted in and threatened to cut off my fingers if I didn't give them the addresses of Michael Cooke and Starlett Graves," she sobbed. The reality of her escape was starting to sink in, and she suddenly felt weak and dizzy. "Jack, I gave it to them. They're going to kill them. You have to do something."

"Okay, I'll take care of it." By that time the fire and rescue squad had started to show up and he carried her over to one of the trucks. They wrapped her in a blanket and let her sit in the truck. Jack ran to his cruiser and called out to the county dispatcher. This was an absolute emergency, and he made sure the dispatcher understood it. Not moments later he heard the call go out for any and all

officers to report to the addresses of Michael Cooke and
Gloria Graves.

Jack ran back to the fire truck and reached up to kiss
Paula hard on the lips.

"Duty calls," he said.

"Jack," she said, grabbing hold of him as he tried to
leave. "I want you to kill them."

As he turned to leave, Paula watched from the fire
truck as flames burst from the windows of the old Lexmore
Hotel, thoroughly engulfing the structure. The fire department could not even hope to rescue the structure now.
They were just going to control the blaze and make sure
it didn't spread to other nearby structures. Paula hung her
head and began to cry. All of her dreams were literally
going up in flames.

Jack didn't see her pained expression as he ran back
to his police cruiser and tore out of town going way too
fast for the now snowy roads. He was too focused on
what needed to be done. Everyone was being called in for
backup. He knew Ballard would be on his way as would
the State Troopers who heard the call. Anyone from the
County Sheriff's department would also respond. He
called dispatch again and filled them in on what had happened at *The Mountain Star* office. The perpetrators were
to be considered armed and highly dangerous. He feared
that this was going to get very ugly.

He fought in his mind over who he should go after to
assist, Michael or Gloria. He knew what Michael would
want. He figured he only had a few minutes until he had
to decide. If he went straight it would be about five more

minutes to Michael's house. If he took a left up ahead, it would take four minutes to get to Gloria's. It really wasn't a decision at all.

He slammed on the brakes and cranked the wheel to the left, fish-tailing the cruiser around the corner and storming up the hill towards Gloria Graves' house. He'd further instructed dispatch to call both of their houses and warn them if they could. He hoped they got through.

Jack pushed his cruiser well above safe speeds for the conditions. He almost lost control a couple of times, but each time he was able to correct the maneuver and get the vehicle heading straight down the road again. If they had a more robust budget, he would have purchased a four-wheel drive vehicle like the Chevy Tahoes that the State Troopers had, but he just didn't have the money.

As he crested the final hill, it happened. He lost control of the car. It lurched left then right and spun out in the snow. Trees flashed by through the windshield, and he knew he wasn't going to rescue the spin. The cruiser slid sideways down the road and then slammed hard backwards into a ditch. The impact rattled him, but he wasn't seriously injured. The snow was coming down much heavier up here, and he'd misjudged his speed and the traction.

He swore under his breath as he tried to get the vehicle unstuck. He mashed on the accelerator, but the wheels were just spinning. It was no use. The car was tilting at a thirty degree angle down into the ditch. The passenger side wheels were actually suspended in the air, as the undercarriage of the vehicle was resting on the edge of the ditch. It would take a wrecker with a winch to pull it out. He couldn't even open his door, as it was jammed fast against

the embankment. He crawled across the car to the passenger side door and forced it open. It was about another
mile to Gloria's house. Grabbing his shotgun, he radioed in
his situation. He hoped to God dispatch was able to warn
everyone. It would take him about fifteen minutes on foot.
Maybe less if he cut through the woods. Shotgun in hand,
Jack started to run, heading into the woods.

Chapter 19

The Chinese culture holds the Siberian Tiger in special reverence. The Tungusic people view the Siberian Tiger as a god, while one of the most elite military battalions in the Chinese army goes by the name of Hu Shen Ying or The Tiger God Battalion. Yet throughout much of the late Nineteenth and early Twentieth Centuries the tiger was hunted to near extinction due to the international value of its hide and other body parts.

In 1986 the Chinese government began the first breeding park for the Siberian Tiger, called Heilongjiang Northeast Tiger Forest Park. It was here that the Chinese began to ensure genetic diversity in the tiger population. When it began, there were but eight tigers in captivity in the park. By the time Tommy was driving through the Catskill Mountains with the Siberian Tiger sedated in its crate, there were nearly a thousand healthy tigers in the Heilongjiang Northeast Tiger Forest Park. Tommy had no idea that the cargo he was transporting for a sale just across the Vermont border had begun its life nearly twelve years earlier on the other side of the globe.

It was one of three cubs that were born in the litter. It already had a buyer as soon as it had been born, but wouldn't be shipped for another eight months. The agreement that the breeders had with the government outlined that they would be free to sell one third of the tiger litters they received, but not until they were checked to be defect and disease free. After eight months the cubs received their shots and were then shipped all over the world. Once they left the breeding facility, the breeders washed their hands of them. They knew that some would be grown into adults and then be butchered for their parts and hides, while others would live for a long time in relative luxury in zoos or private collections. Still others might find their way into circus acts or road side menageries. During the 1990's, hundreds of tigers were transported around the globe, netting the breeding facility millions of dollars. The money went to support further research and daily upkeep for the growing tiger population in the park. The sales were a means to an end. The tiger population was now more robust than it had been in centuries and by selling through legal avenues the market for poachers was drying up. Overall, it was good for the tigers.

The breeders would often name the cubs from the litter. This one started with the name Sweet Baby, but after receiving its immunization shots, it became much more aggressive. By the time it was placed into the shipping crate to head off to the United States, they had renamed it Little Fighter, referencing a beat 'em up video game that was popular at the time.

Little Fighter was flying into Seattle and would then be transported southeast to Henderson, Nevada, just outside the city limits of Las Vegas. A small casino had decided it would be a nice attraction to add a tiger sanctuary in the center of the casino floor. They hired a former zoo keeper out of California to come and oversee the sanctuary. Little Fighter would be the first tiger, with plans to introduce at least two more in the next few years.

Almost immediately the tiger handler found working with Little Fighter to be much more difficult than her previous experience. She had always found the Siberian Tiger species, Panthera Tigris Altaica, to be much more docile than its cousin, the Bengal Tiger. Whereas Bengals came from India, and were known to attack in the wild with regularity, the Siberian Tiger lived in the forests of northern China and eastern Russia. They rarely attacked, and when there were documented cases of Siberian Tiger attacks, it usually proved that there had been some sort of provocation on the part of the attack victim.

Little Fighter, however, would constantly nip at her fingers as she fed him, and would sometimes lie in wait for her around feeding time and attack her legs. She received more than a few puncture wounds in her legs and arms from his constant scratching and biting. The casino management was slow to listen to her recommendation to find another tiger, as Little Fighter was also very active in his enclosure, much to the delight of the casino patrons. He was always climbing and jumping and playing. He was doing exactly what the casino owners were hoping he would do, attract more business. Finally, the handler quit after Little Fighter slashed at her leg and damaged her right thigh. It took over thirty stitches to close up the wound.

Because of the attack, the casino's insurance company would no longer cover the animal, so they had to get rid of it. The tiger was transported to an animal trader in northern Nevada, outside of Reno. It was now nearly full grown at two years old, and quite aggressive. It needed to be fed through the bars of its enclosure and could not be allowed to be in the company of other tigers. When Little Fighter had first arrived at the trader's facilities, they had hoped it would breed with their female, so they placed them together in the larger enclosure. Rather than mate, Little Fighter attacked the female and nearly killed her. They were able to get him to halt the attack by spraying him with a fire hose.

The trader made the tiger available for sale and was very clear about its aggressive nature. It took nearly eighteen months to find a buyer. A private company in Utah, which had a roadside zoo, was looking for a replacement for their Bengal tiger, which had died of old age earlier in the year. They were fine with the aggressive nature, as part of the attraction for families stopping at the tourist trap on their way to Salt Lake City was the spectacle of feeding time. At first they would toss in large portions of beef, but eventually they found that releasing live chickens into the enclosure with Little Fighter gave the audiences what they wanted. Sure there were laws against such things, but in that part of Utah, there wasn't much in the way of animal rights people around to blow the whistle.

For eight years Little Fighter made Utah his home, growing large with the regular feedings, and staying in a fighting mood most of the time. Then one night the owner's son had too much to drink before he went out for the night feeding, and got too close to the bars when he tossed in the leftovers from the snack counter. Little Fighter reached through the bars and swiped at the young man, slicing his jugular and killing him. The family was extremely distraught and looked to sell Little Fighter as quickly as possible.

The owner was familiar with many different animal traders and brokers across the country, as he had purchased hundreds of animals over the thirty years of being in business. He finally got in touch with Ohio Exotics and Marcus Higgs. They closed their deal. Little Fighter was moving to Ohio.

Higgs was a careful man. He knew that any injury or death on his property would bring the authorities storming in. He'd been cited several times over the years, and had done everything in his power to fix the problems and make sure the fines weren't repeated. However, in the animal trading business, there was always a fine line between legal and illegal, and Higgs balanced on that line like a tightrope walker at one of the small time circuses he would provide with exotic animals.

Big cats were an especially lucrative trade, though the market for tigers particularly had decreased substantially in the U.S. after the U.S. Fish and Wildlife Service had made it legal to transport "generic" tigers without permits starting in 1998. Generic tigers were considered to be cross breeds, not purebreds, which meant that all a dealer had to do was "lose" his paperwork when it came time to sell the animal and he could do so without so much as a sniff by government officials. They could be advertised as purebreds, but the transaction paperwork would have to list the breed as unknown. Dealers could talk their way around this little detail with a customer and still demand the higher prices for purebred animals.

Higgs followed the paper trail of Little Fighter and realized that he had purchased an excellent animal that would have a higher value on the east coast of the United States, especially in the Asian markets. There was a farmer in Vermont who butchered his own cows and hogs, and was also known to butcher exotic animals, portioning off the parts for sale in New York City.

"Tommy, listen. I've got a job for you that will probably take a couple days," Higgs said as Tommy walked in.

"What about Colby?"

"He's sick. Normally it would be Colby's turn, but I need to make sure this shipment gets where it's supposed to go, and I can't risk having a sick driver make it late."

"Okay, but I want more this time," Tommy said. He had seen how much money was being spent on some of the cargo he was driving around the country, so he figured he should get more than his hundred bucks a day.

"What did you have in mind," Higgs was a business man, and was always willing to negotiate, but he wasn't going to bend over and drop trou for a driver.

"I want double my old rate plus money for food and hotel. I hate sleeping in the van," Tommy said.

Higgs did some mental calculations. The job should take two days of driving, one overnight at a hotel, and six meals. "I'll give you two hundred a day for driving, and a hundred for expenses. That's it."

"A hundred for expenses? That won't even get me a room," Tommy whined.

"Sure it will. Don't think I'm putting you up in a Marriot or something. Get one of those cheaper places. You're just there to sleep and get a shower. Those places are like thirty bucks a night."

"Two hundred a day, plus one-fifty for expenses and you got a deal," Tommy countered. He'd been watching a reality TV show about a pawn shop, and had picked up some negotiating tactics of his own.

"Okay, but just this once," Higgs said, though he knew that Tommy had finally wised up and would never go back to the cheap rates he used to work for. One of the reasons Higgs had decided to use Tommy instead of Colby was the fact that he was usually cheaper. Colby wasn't really sick. So much for that plan.

The last time Higgs saw Tommy, he was hopping up into the white rental van which had been filled to capacity with animals. He hadn't even made it out of the parking lot before it looked like he was lighting up a cigarette.

The last meal it had been fed had been laced with a light sedative. It would make it far less agitated during the trip. It found sleep to come easily in the tight wooden enclosure. Suddenly it was awoken with a crash, and found the small world it was in was being literally turned upside down. The walls around it crumbled, and it was hit hard by something in its hind quarter. As the van came to a rest, the animals around it started into a chorus of chortles and squawks. It turned itself to lick the gash that was now bleeding quite a bit. After a few moments, the wound stopped bleeding, and it decided to try the confines of its enclosure. It pressed a large paw against the end of the crate and felt it give immediately.

In just a few moments, Little Fighter was out of the van and into the snow. It was cautious at first, never having experienced snow before. It bent and licked at the snow and found it to be quite refreshing. It couldn't know, it didn't have the capability to have such a thought, but it had been built for this type of environment. Its coat would protect it from the cold, and its orange and black stripes would blend well with the trees, even as the white under-belly matched the snow.

It found itself hungry, and turned back towards the van, entertaining the thought of trying to get at one of the other animals, or perhaps the driver. It caught sight of the escaped enclosure, however, and decided to get as far away as quickly as possible.

Little Fighter had never been in the wide open during its life. It had never known the freedom of running, and suddenly found that it liked it. In just a few leaping bounds, it was across the road and into the field, with an eye towards the woods. The snow was coming down heavily, and it instinctively knew that it should find shelter first and food later. It found the same stream that the cougar had stopped at, not ten minutes earlier. It caught the scent of the cougar, recognizing it from the van. It followed the scent for a bit, and then broke off as it grew tired.

Suddenly it caught a sound in the air, something was approaching. It crouched low, but as the noise approached, it panicked and ran at top speed through the woods. It was narrowly missed by something with a bright light, and it didn't stop to investigate. It ran for miles before it finally stopped to rest. It cautiously wandered back towards the stream and followed it until it found what it had been looking for.

About six miles away from the crash site, it discovered a small rocky cave next to the stream. It forced its way inside, and was surprised to find a family of raccoons hibernating. With just a few quick bites, it killed them, allowing it to dine in leisure. After the meal, Little Fighter coiled up and went to sleep.

Over the next few days it foraged for food, finding small game like rabbits and squirrels. After meandering through the mountains another seven miles, it sensed other animals in the air. The manure smell lured it closer to the homes, until it found itself curiously digging at the back side of a building, trying to get at the animals it knew were inside. It grew bored and went back into the woods to look for an easier meal.

It felt the impact of the hooves on the ground even before it saw the horse and its rider. It followed stealthily, tracking the new prey. It had not been satisfied on the light meals it had found. It was used to multiple feedings a day without much effort. It needed a big kill to give it the energy it needed to put on a heavier coat for the winter. It stalked the horse for nearly a mile before it was put into the barn. The rider exited awhile later and went into the house. Little Fighter now knew where it would get its next meal.

It had been just a couple of days since it had killed Starlett's horse and devoured it. The meal had contented Little Fighter for a long time. It slept in its den and didn't venture out much, conserving its energy and building a nice layer of fatty tissue even as its fur thickened to combat the colder environment. A distant crash awakened it from its slumber, and it cautiously left the small cave. It crossed the creek and headed towards where it believed it had heard the crashing noise.

It was suddenly aware of a presence in the woods. Something was running. It could hear the heavy breathing and feel the footfalls with its paws on the ground. It was a man, and it knew from experience that a man had soft skin and could make an easy meal, if it could just get a hold of one. It picked up its pace and began to hunt.

Chapter 20

He had to admit, it had been an extremely interesting retirement so far. He recounted in his mind all the things that had occurred since he'd moved up to his new home in the Catskills permanently. The fist fight, the cougar hunt, the showdown with Tubby on his front porch and then his mother inside. Not to mention meeting Gloria and the whole dead horse thing.

If I didn't know any better, I'd say a person had to be crazy to live up here.

He was excited to hear the forecast for the weekend: snow. He'd timed his purchase perfectly. The Arctic Cat was a beautiful black with green stripes. He'd backed it into the garage, leaving his the Ford truck parked out front. The forecast said snow could start as early as 4pm. He looked at his watch, it was nearing five now. The sky had grown almost completely dark already, the clouds were thick and there was a chill in the air. As he stood on his front porch, cup of coffee in hand, he noticed the first few snowflakes descending from the sky. It was deathly quiet, next to no wind was stirring at all. He could almost hear the snowflakes as they struck the ground.

The quiet unsettled him slightly. He'd been used to the constant noise of the city for most of his life. Even when he was serving in Kuwait during Gulf War I, there were always trucks or choppers going by in the middle of the night. True absolute silence was foreign to him, and it made him realize just how alone he was.

He thought about Gloria and what she was doing this evening. Their last dinner had been ruined by the grisly discovery of Starlett's horse. She had told him she'd give him a rain check for another dinner in the future. He wondered if he should be the one to initiate the dinner or if he should leave it up to her. As he sipped his coffee again he thought he heard his phone ringing inside. He reached it just as it went to the recorded message.

"Hello?"

"No one is available to take your call," the mechanical messenger said.

"I'm here," he countered. "Just hang on a minute." He fought with the controls of the machine to try to get it to stop recording.

"Michael Cooke?"

"Yes."

"This is Vicki with the Delaware County Sheriff's Department. We've received notice that there was an attack in Coopers Hollow today by several men. They tried to kill Paula Schumann."

"Oh my God, is she okay?"

"She's okay at last report, but that's not why I'm calling you. She indicated that the men were actually looking for you and Gloria Graves. These men, they have your addresses. Please leave the house immediately and do not return until you've contacted law enforcement. Do you understand?"

Michael turned towards the front window as he heard tires on the gravel driveway. If it had been someone just stopping by, or the UPS driver making a late delivery, he knew there would be headlights, but there were none. Whoever it was that just pulled into the driveway didn't want to be seen.

"They're already here," he said. He set the phone down, but didn't disengage the line.

Dalton watched television, aimlessly flipping between the channels on the satellite feed. There were two hundred channels with nothing worth watching. He checked his phone again. Four-thirty. Starlett and Mrs. Graves were due home any time. They had gone out for lunch and they decided to catch a matinee at the theater in Oneonta. It was about a forty minute drive, and the movie should have let out around three-thirty. He wondered what was for dinner.

He'd spent the entire day doing nothing. He and Starlett had slept in until about ten. She'd gotten up and showered and left with her mother, while he slept past noon. He'd then risen, eaten some toast and coffee and dropped onto the couch. He really hadn't moved since, except to use the bathroom. His neck still hurt as did his nose, but he was feeling better. The doctor had said he needed to rest, so that's what he was going to do.

Standing and stretching, he decided to take a quick shower before the girls got back. He trotted barefoot towards the bedroom where he had a change of clothes. He didn't want to get caught by Mrs. Graves in just a towel making a dash for Starlett's room.

Retrieving everything he needed, he went into the guest bathroom and started the water. He waited until it was good and hot before he got in. The shower stung his skin, but he liked it that way. It helped get his blood flowing.

He shampooed his hair and then used Starlett's body wash. He loved the way she smelled, like vanilla and strawberries. He took his time, soaping up and then letting the hot water wash it away. Gingerly, he washed his face. His nose was still healing, and was tender to the touch. His doctor said it would take a couple of weeks before the pain went away completely. Luckily the family doctor had given him some strong pain medication. The effects of the last dose were starting to wear off, but he was enjoying the hot shower too much to end it. He lost track of time, and thought he heard the phone ring.

The machine will get it, he thought to himself.

His cell phone rang on the edge of the sink. He'd been in the shower long enough, so he cut off the water, stepped out and grabbed his phone. It was Starlett.

"Hello?"

"Hey, just wanted to let you know we're running a bit late, we'll be home in about twenty minutes," she said.

"What time is it now?"

"Just about five."

"Okay," he said to her. "Love you." There was a long

pause. He hadn't tried the "L" word on her since all the trouble had started.

"Love you too," she said, finally, after several moments of silence. It made him smile, nonetheless. Maybe she was going to forgive him after all. He closed down the connection, hitting the touch screen with his thumb. He finished drying himself and then started getting dressed: Blue jeans and a yellow collared shirt over a long sleeve thermal shirt.

He tossed the towel in the hamper and walked out into the living room. The television was still on, and he noticed the phone was blinking with one message. He was feeling restless and bored, and he needed a drink. He popped one of his pain pills and turned on the television, which was switching over to a news program. He listened as he went to seek out the liquor cabinet. He was pouring a shot of whiskey for himself when he heard a car pull up. It sounded like Gloria's Volvo. They were quicker than he thought they would be. He downed the whiskey and put the bottle back. He grabbed a beer from the fridge and popped the top. The house phone rang again.

The caller ID said "Del Co Sheriff". He scowled as he looked at it, wondering if he should pick up. He decided to let the automatic answering machine take the call. It rang three more times before the recording engaged and informed the caller that no one was home.

"Mrs. Graves. This is Vicki with the Delaware County Sheriff's department. We are concerned for your safety. We need you to leave your house immediately and seek out a law enforcement officer. This is a life and death situation, Mrs. Graves. Don't stop to call us back until you are out of your house."

"What the heck," Dalton said to himself. He picked up the phone. "Hello?"

Just then the front door burst in, and three large men dressed all in black and holding pistols came at him. He had no time to react. He tried to turn and run, but they were on him in a flash. Two of them muscled him to the ground, guns pointed at his head, while the third hung up the phone.

"Payback time, rich boy."

Michael didn't pause a moment. He realized he probably didn't have too many of them to spare. His rifle case was on the table, and he grabbed it as he headed out the back door. He launched himself into a run off the deck and down through the yard in his stocking feet. He splashed nearly knee deep in the creek before he started up the back hill. It was another fifty yards before he dropped to the ground and turned to watch his house. He slowly opened the rifle case and retrieved his M40a1 sniper rifle, flipping open the covers to the scope as he brought it up. The scope could magnify up to ten times, and he was barely a hundred yards from his back porch, elevated by maybe twenty feet. He could see right through the large sliding glass doors and into the house, with a clear view of the front door. It was now open and four men, each carrying what looked liked high powered hand guns, stalked through his home. Two disappeared down the hallway and out of his line of sight. He saw the bedroom light come on. Moments later it went out again.

What are you guys looking for, Michael thought. *And how is Gloria involved in this?*

The snow was coming down with such ferocity that, at times, he had difficulty seeing the house from the distance. It was nearly white-out conditions due to the wind which was blowing and gusting. They had wandered through his house now for almost five minutes. They had arbitrarily knocked over chairs and broken whatever they wanted to. He felt his rage starting to build. As he looked through the scope he suddenly realized that he might not be able to just lay in wait until they left. He had left tracks through the snow right to his location. Slowly he reached into the rifle case and retrieved several cartridges. He loaded each one into the rifle. He only needed four, as there were only four targets. As long as they didn't open the back door, he was sure he would be relatively safe.

They moved about in the kitchen, and then he saw the garage light blink on through its back door. Shadows moved across the window as they searched for him. No doubt they had found the basement door and were searching there as well. He was happy that he'd remembered to lock the gun cabinet. His scope was trained on the garage when he heard the glass door to the deck slide open. He quickly refocused on the back door and saw one of the home invaders looking at the fresh tracks across the deck and out into the yard.

"Ignore them, they don't mean anything," Michael said. He chambered a cartridge in the rifle and thumbed off the safety. He saw the man signal for the others. Two of them stepped out onto the deck. Michael waited. He slowed his breathing. They started following the tracks.

The other two stood at the door, watching.

"Who are you guys?" He said this out loud as he took the scope away from the men following his trail and went back to the glass doors. There were three of them now instead of just two, and he recognized the newcomer. It was the punk who had jumped Starlett's boyfriend back at the diner. It all came together for him in that instant. They were here for payback, they intended to kill him, and if the phone call was correct, they intended to kill Gloria too. He only hoped they had come here first.

He aimed at the two thugs heading towards the creek. He breathed out and squeezed the trigger.

Bang! The first one was down. Cooke had put a bullet right through his chest.

He reloaded and aimed at the second figure who had frozen in place.

Bang! That was two. Headshot.

He brought the rifle back up to bear on the house, but the three figures were gone. They were smart enough to realize what was happening. They had gone from the hunters to the hunted. They didn't know who they were messing with. Michael stood, eye still to scope, and slowly came down the hill. He was now about seventy yards away and had a lower vantage point through the house. He couldn't see anyone. They must have made a run for it. He took the rifle down just in time to see the flames erupt in the living room. They were torching the house!

He swore through his teeth as he ran at an angle down the hill, planning to navigate around the edge of his property and get a view of the front. He heard an engine start and then another fireball erupted in front of the house. They'd set his truck on fire as well. As he came within sight of his driveway, he saw headlights come on and begin rapidly backing away. The vehicle was out onto the road and speeding away.

Cooke turned back towards the house and saw it was hopeless. They'd obviously poured gasoline or some sort of accelerant in the living room. Without his truck, he was stranded. His feet were wet and freezing. His adrenaline had been pumping so hard he had barely realized how cold they had become. He couldn't get back into the house for shoes, but he had left his boots in the garage. The flames hadn't reached there yet.

Then he realized that he might not be completely stranded. He ran to the garage and opened it. They'd left the snowmobile intact, and the keys were still in the ignition. He pulled on his boots and jacket that had been hanging on the peg by the door. He slung his rifle over his back and got on the sled. It started with one turn of the key. He powered it out of the garage and around the side of the house. He headed back up the hill to where he'd taken the shots. In just moments he was there, grabbing the few remaining cartridges from his rifle case and stuffing them into his jacket pockets. He headed back towards the house again, stopping by the dead men. Searching their bodies, he grabbed their hand guns and extra clips. They had both been carrying 9mm pistols. Those weren't pop guns, they could do some real damage.

He took a quick moment to admire his handy work. One through the chest, one through the head. Clean kills.

The men were dead before they hit the ground. Steam still rose from the bodies in the cold snowy air.

When you go out hunting Marines, be careful. You might actually find one.

Back on the sled he took a moment to get his bearings. If his memory was correct, he could head across the road and up over the hill and from there it was just a few miles to Gloria's house. He had no choice but to go. He hit the accelerator and created a rooster tail of snow, grass and mud behind him. He only hoped he could get there in time. He couldn't afford to be late. Not this time. The Machine was needed once again.

"Listen, we can work this out," Dalton said. He received a crack across the cheek from a balled up fist.

"Shut up," said the thug. Dalton had never seen these guys before, but he had no doubt why they were here. He was going to die. It was over. "When we want you to talk, you'll talk. When we're done with your talking, we'll cut out your tongue."

Dalton hung his head. They had stripped him down to his boxers and forced him into one of Gloria's high backed dining room chairs. They'd tied his wrists together behind the chair with plastic pull ties and then they'd strapped his ankles to the chair legs. They'd smacked him around some in the process as well. He was bleeding from four or five places on his face, and his ribs on his right side hurt and made it difficult to breathe. The way his nose throbbed, it felt like they had re-broken it. He heard two of them talking to each other.

"What should we do?"

"Boss says hold tight. He wants to do this one himself."

"Where's he at?"

"He's taking care of the Cooke dude. He'll be here in a minute. We're just supposed to keep him tied up. If his girlfriend shows up, we're supposed to do her too. You cool?"

"Awright, I'm cool."

Dalton pulled against his restraints, but it was no use. He would need to be cut free, the plastic strips were too tough and they'd pulled them so tight they were cutting off circulation. His feet and hands were going numb. Then a vehicle pulled up outside.

"I don't know mom, the ending was a little contrived, wasn't it? I mean coming in, guns blazing and none of the hostages got shot?"

"It's just a movie," Gloria said. They hadn't done a mother-daughter movie night in ages. The one they'd chosen was supposed to be one of the year's best. It had a pretty good story line and a steamy love scene which had made both of them squirm a little in their seats.

"I know, but why can't they make movies more realistic? The good guys always arrive just in time. It never happens that way in real life. And why do they always have to be about cops or ex-cops?" Starlett leaned her head against the cold window. The snow was coming down hard now, and it was getting difficult to see the road.

"I guess they're the only characters that can end a movie with a shootout," Gloria said. "As soon as they can figure out how to have a banker or architect finish off the bad guys with explosions and flying bullets, they'll probably do it." They both laughed at this. It felt good to laugh. They had been through so much over the last couple of weeks, and it had made them both exhausted. Laughing was cathartic for them.

"Thanks for taking me out, I had fun," Starlett said.

"I did too, sweetie. I hope Dalton didn't mind."

"I think he wanted to go back to sleep. He's depressed. He didn't mean for any of this to happen. He feels guilty that Chief McMurphy was killed. Even though he hasn't said anything, I can tell," Starlett said quietly. A few hours at the movies was nice as an escape, but once the theater lights went up and the credits rolled, it was back to real life.

"It's just going to take some time. It was a tragedy. As long as he does everything the cops ask him to do, he'll be alright. You'll see. Everything's going to be fine."

They pulled onto their road, and Gloria engaged the four-wheel drive, one of the main reasons she'd purchased the Volvo. It was a twisting road up the back side of the mountain and then down into their valley. On a good day they could take it at forty-five miles per hour, but tonight it would be a bit sketchy. As they pressed on, they both grew quiet. Gloria was concentrating and Starlett liked it that way, she didn't want to be a distraction.

They crested the hill and started down the other side. The four-wheel drive worked perfectly and guided them down the inclined roadway with ease. They pulled into the driveway and the headlights shown on the back of a black Lincoln Navigator.

"Who's that, I wonder," Gloria said. "I don't think its Michael's, he drives a pickup truck."

"Mom, back up. Go. This isn't good," Starlett said. Before Gloria could react, there were headlights on them from behind. They were blocked in. Suddenly there was a knock at Gloria's window. A tall figure, dressed in black was rapping the tip of a pistol against her window.

"Mom, what do we do?"

"Just be calm and do what they say, we'll get through this," Gloria said. The doors were opened and both women were pulled out and pushed roughly towards the house. As they came through the door they saw Dalton, bloodied, naked, except for his boxers, and tied to the chair. His head was down, chin to his chest. Blood was streaming from his face down his chest, soaking into the boxers. He looked half dead.

"So glad you could join us," said one of the men. It took a moment for Starlett to recognize him. It was the same one that had attacked Dalton in the diner. "Allow me to intro-duce myself. They call me El Tigre, the tiger. They call me that because I'm the biggest cat in the jungle. Tigers are very territorial, did you know that? In India they will kill a man just for walking through their territory. It's been known for tigers to track a man for miles and then drag him out of his bed as he sleeps just to seek revenge for the perceived slight. You see, the scent stays with them, it sticks in their noses, and they can't get rid of it until they kill."

"Thanks for the lesson in animal science, but you're just a drug dealer. You use people to do your dirty work. You're not a tiger you're a cockroach, and these are all your cockroach friends. And as soon as the cops get here and you see the flashing lights outside, you'll scurry back into the darkness, afraid of-" Starlett didn't get a chance to finish the insult. The man who called himself El Tigre slapped her across the face so hard it knocked her to the ground. Dalton yelled and wriggled against his restraints, but he was helpless.

"You think I need other people to do my dirty work?" He was yelling at her as he stood over her. He took the gun out of his waistband and pointed it at her head as she cowered on the floor. He brought it right down to her face and jammed the barrel cruelly into her eye.

"You see this? Or are you blind and stupid? You're going to die tonight. The only thing you get to decide is if it's fast and relatively painless or if we should have our fun with you and let you watch your boyfriend and mother die first."

"Leave her alone!" Dalton yelled at him.

"We've gotten all we needed out of him," El Tigre said. He'd brought along the man he called The Surgeon for this very moment. "Cut out his tongue. Strap the girlfriend and mommy dearest to chairs first so they can watch." The men started immediately, dragging two more dining room chairs out into the living room and roughly binding their wrists and ankles in the same fashion as they had done with Dalton. The Surgeon opened his bag.

Michael rode the snowmobile as fast as he could through the woods. Surprisingly there seemed to be quite a few trails that snaked up over the mountain. He was at the crest in what seemed like just minutes. His face and hands were bloody with scrapes from the tree branches as they whipped at him in passing. He could see lights down below in the valley and hoped he was going the right direction. His instinct told him he was.

He followed the trail down through the trees until he came out onto a clearing that overlooked the valley. Continuing across the field and down the hill, he rode at top speed, trying to make out the details of the few houses along the road below, trying to see if he recognized any of them. The skis of the Arctic Cat snowmobile cut twin grooves through the fresh snow, even as the drive belt sent the snow up into the air behind him in a high arc.

Michael stopped and pulled his rifle from his back and held up the scope, carefully training it on each house. The two closest weren't Gloria's. Down the road another half mile he saw a house with a horse barn out back. That one had to be hers. He slung the rifle back into place, blew a quick hot breath onto his ungloved hands and hit the accelerator, sending the sled full speed down the hill towards Gloria's house.

The snow that was falling was whipping against his

cheeks, numbing them. It was like a million little pin-
pricks slashing at his skin all over. The relentless nature
of it bordered on torture. He squinted to see the terrain
ahead, but his eyes still stung from the wind and the snow.
He was only about two hundred yards away when he killed
the headlight on the snowmobile and brought it to a stop.
He lifted the rifle and looked through the scope right
through the large glass doors on the back of Gloria's house.
He saw six men standing around three people tied to
chairs. Gloria and her daughter were facing him. Two men
were doing something to the third person while holding
him down.

Michael cursed under his breath. With a regular
cartridge, he would have had no problem taking a shot
from here, but he had used a light load for the rounds he
carried. They were the ones he hand-loaded for the cougar
hunt. They were hollow points, not as accurate, would not
travel as far. Without the extra velocity, the shots might
not stay true through the glass. He needed at least another
hundred yards to make sure the bullet would punch
through the tempered glass and into the target. He rode
the snowmobile through the snow as fast as he could push
the machine.

Without warning he was suddenly ripped off the snowmobile and thrown violently into the snow. His chest felt like
it was on fire from the pain. Had he been shot? It was like
someone pounded a nail into his chest and then dragged it
across. He saw the snowmobile had continued on without him
about ten feet and then was ripped off its skis onto its side.
As he tried to stand he realized he was connected to a barbed
wire fence. It had imbedded into his chest, having gone right

through the jacket. As he looked down he saw the white insulation bursting out from where the jacket was torn open. Even in the dim light he could see the white stuffing turning dark as the blood began to soak in.

He was fortunate it was an old fence and the wire gave upon impact. Had it been just ten inches higher, the rusty wire very well may have decapitated him. As it was, he knew he had gouges in his chest that were now bleeding heavily. His left shoulder didn't feel quite right as if something had been torn. His leg had bent awkwardly beneath him and his knee felt as if it were on fire. The wind was knocked from him, but he recovered quickly. Giving a tug on the wire, Cooke pulled out the barbs and extracted himself from the steel entrapment. The sled had been overturned and also looked entangled in the barbed wire, upon quick inspection.

Time was simply too precious to lose trying to untangle the vehicle, so he proceeded on foot. Trudging through the snow with a knee that wouldn't cooperate, Cooke willed himself closer towards the house. A clock was ticking in his head. It was counting down the time he had left. The sickening shock of electricity that shot through his leg with every step, the searing pain of his shredded chest; he pushed it all out of his mind.

He was back in boot camp on Parris Island, and his drill instructor was barking orders at him, telling him to get his pansy butt up and keep going. He wasn't a quitter, was he? Every ounce of his being told him to stop, but there was no quit in the Machine. With each step he let out an audible grunt to combat the pain.

A growl started deep down inside of him. It built up and

burst forth from his lips as he brought the M40a1 rifle up to his eye. He saw that they had taken Gloria out of the chair and had her on the floor. They were holding her down, and there was no question what their intentions were.

He thumbed off the safety and aimed for the one who had positioned himself to violate her.

"I will be the one doing the violating," Cooke said out loud.

Bang! Dead. Neck shot.

Reload. Re-aim.

Bang! Dead. Square of the back.

Reload. Re-aim.

Bang! Dead. Head shot.

The rest of the men in the room ran for the front door and just beyond his line of sight. He broke into a limping run, pushing himself as fast as his failing leg would go, stumbling twice as it gave out. In a leap with his good leg he was up on the back deck. He paused just out of the light and brought the rifle up again. He looked over the scope now, using the notches on the end of the rifle to align with his target. He stepped into the house. Gloria was trying to free Starlett. They both looked to be in shock and were disoriented, while Dalton looked like he was dead. Michael barely acknowledged them. The Machine was in tracking and targeting mode.

"Where did they go?" he asked.

"Out the front," Gloria said. Michael didn't pause. He followed the prey. He heard the rev of an engine and walked faster, though he was now practically dragging his damaged leg. He fired again, aiming just above the retreating headlights, where a driver would be. The vehicle continued backwards and slid out onto the road. Michael hobbled down the driveway, trying to get another shot, but there were trees lining the driveway back to the road and he wasn't fast enough. He pressed on through the trees to try to cut it off, but he simply didn't have a shot. His legs couldn't carry him any faster. He hurled curses at his fleeing targets, angry at himself for not being twenty years younger with a body that could take a fall from a snowmobile without such incapacitating results.

Suddenly, about twenty feet in front of him, at the road's edge, another weapon discharged with a thunderous report. It was the loud blast of a shotgun. It fired again and again as the black Lincoln Navigator drove past. Michael continued towards the sound. The SUV swerved in the snow, went off the road and into the ditch, rolling up onto its roof.

Michael didn't know who was shooting, if it was a neighbor who'd heard the ruckus or the police.

"Hey! Who's up there?" Michael called ahead.

"Coopers Hollow Police department, put down your weapon," was the reply in a familiar voice.

"Jack! Hey, Jack! It's me Michael Cooke!"

"You've got to be kidding me." The voice was filled with incredulity. The sirens could be heard from further down the valley. It was a sweet sound to Michael's ears.

"Cooke, get over here and help me cover these guys," Jack yelled. Michael limped towards him as fast as he could, gun lowered. They got out onto the road and slowly approached the inverted SUV. The wheels were still spinning and the engine was still running somehow.

"If anybody is still alive in there, you'd better let us know if you don't want a bullet in your head," Jack yelled. He wished he had been wearing his uniform. There was a small flashlight that he always kept on his belt and it would have been extremely useful right now. He lowered himself down to peer into the smashed out window. He saw two men in the front seats, both of them were dead from bullet wounds.

"How many were in there?"

"I counted three that ran out of the house," Michael replied.

"There's only two in the truck," Jack said. Michael slowly angled around to the other side of the vehicle, steadying himself against it as he went. The window in the rear door of the SUV was smashed out, and there were signs that someone had pulled himself out. The tracks lead off into the woods, and it looked like he was bleeding pretty badly.

"We got one on the run," Michael said.

"Great," Jack replied as he hustled around to Michael's side. "These guys are both dead. You're still on the clock as far as I'm concerned. Are you up for this?"

"Till the job's done," Cooke said, heading out into the snow after the trail. His knee was tightening up and his leg was weak, but it was still marginally functional. He wouldn't be running any marathons, but he could track a bleeding suspect through the snow. Jack let him take the lead, knowing that he had the military training and quite a few more years experience. They followed the trail out into the woods, even as the sirens grew louder.

It was impossible. It didn't register as reality, but more like a bad trip or a sick nightmare. As the glass exploded and he watched his men fall to the ground with bloody, gaping wounds, he knew it had to be Cooke. How Cooke had managed to get over here from his house, he didn't know. They had burned his truck and there wasn't another vehicle in sight. However he'd gotten here, El Tigre was wise enough to know not to stick around. Killers recognized killers, and Cooke had already taken down five of his men with just five shots. Retreat was a completely acceptable tactic.

He and two of his men made it out to the SUV, and had it in reverse, when he saw Cooke step out the front door of the house and aim at them.

"Get down!"

The windshield shattered, and the driver's chin disappeared in an explosion of blood and bone. El Tigre's other man, the Surgeon, was in the front passenger seat. He grabbed the wheel and reached his leg over, keeping his foot on the accelerator. They swerved out onto the road, scraping against trees as they went. The passenger side mirror was sheared off and went skittering across the road in the pool of light splashed down from the vehicle's headlights. The Surgeon put the vehicle in drive and punched it, sending the SUV into a bit of a fishtail.

El Tigre told himself that if they made it out of
here, he'd found himself a new driver. No sooner had he
thought it, than the windshield exploded from a gunshot
in front of them. The Surgeon jerked back from the blast,
catching the brunt of it in his face and shoulder. Another
blast, then another hit the side of the vehicle and he felt
metal tear into his flesh. The SUV went off the road and
rolled onto its roof. He was tossed about in the back seat
and lost his bearings from the shock of the impact.

He knew he only had moments to escape. He slithered
through the shattered window of the tailgate and tried to
run, but his leg weren't responding. He reached down and
felt warm wetness on his left thigh where he'd been struck
by the shotgun blast. He reached down to his waistband
for his gun, but it wasn't there. He didn't have a chance out
here in a showdown without a weapon. His only option
was to flee. If he could find another vehicle he could make
still make it out alive. He'd seen other houses when they'd
driven up. All he had to do was bust down one of their
doors and take their keys, and he'd be on his way.

He cut a path back, parallel to the road, and headed
in the direction where he remembered seeing the houses.
There were sirens in the distance, and they were growing
louder. The net was closing. Even in the trees the snow was
coming down hard, and he had to brush it from his face.
He would not let himself be defeated, not yet.

Suddenly a chill came over him as he heard rustling
through the trees behind him. It sounded like something
was coming up on him fast. He turned and felt the quick
adrenaline of panic and impending death. It was as if his

worst nightmare had come horribly true. A scream of terror left his lips.

Little Fighter was on the hunt now. It had followed the man through the woods for nearly ten minutes. It knew from experience that humans were soft and easily killed. It had gotten little tastes of human blood over the years, but had never gotten the chance to eat one. The human it was tracking had just about exhausted itself from the run it had undertaken. The kill would be quick and easy. Slowly it stalked him, closing to within twenty feet.

Suddenly there was the crack of gun fire, and it startled the tiger. It gave up the chase and ran back into the shadows of the woods, a good hundred yards away from the house, on the opposite side of the road. It paced slowly, waiting for the prey to show itself.

Three humans ran from the front door and into a vehicle. Thunder struck the tiger's ears again, and it fell back further into the woods. There was a loud crashing noise, and then voices.

Moments later, it sensed prey. Heavy breathing and irregular footfalls through the snow tingled its senses. Instinct told it that the prey was wounded, and the scent of blood in the air confirmed it. It began to stalk the wounded man. In mere moments it was on his trail, the unmistakable smell of blood now in its nostrils. Saliva built in its mouth. Adrenaline built in its veins. It started to close the distance between predator and prey. There was no hesitation, no caution. The prey was alone, wounded, defenseless. Little Fighter leapt through the underbrush springing the ambush in full. At the last moment, the prey turned and recognized the danger. In desperation the man let out a scream.

Little Fighter leapt and attacked El Tigre, sinking claws into his chest and biting him in the face. The scream turned to a guttural moan. El Tigre struggled against the four hundred pound animal, but was no match. Little Fighter released its bite on his face, and bit down hard on his neck, severing an artery. The fight left the prey. The blows the man struck were without force, and then stopped all together. Finally the man was motionless, and the meal could begin.

Michael and Jack both heard the scream up ahead. The tracks they had been following made a slow turn back towards the road. It was difficult to see in the dim light. Neither of them had a flashlight, but the snow reflected the ambient light, and they could just make out the areas of disturbed snow in the form of footprints. As they pressed on they heard the sounds of ripping and tearing.

Michael stopped short as he saw the silhouette ahead in the snow. Jack came up next to Cooke, as the animal lifted its enormous head and looked back at them. The green eyes reflected off a distant light and appeared to glow with menace. It must have regarded them as not much of a threat, as it put its head back down and continued to eat its meal.

The man who had called himself El Tigre was now

nothing more than a piece of meat to another predator. His flesh had been torn away by the ravenous beast, steam rising from the horrific scene even as heavy snowflakes continued to fall.

Michael slowly lifted his rifle. He paused.

"What are you waiting for," Jack asked in a hushed voice.

"Even the condemned get a last meal," Michael said. He gave the big cat another moment and then pulled the trigger. The bullet pierced the great Siberian Tiger's heart and killed it immediately. Michael fished his HOG's tooth out from under his torn jacket and brought it up to his lips.

Chapter 21

I t was a clean shot, right through the heart."

"Really?"

"No doubt about it."

"Can you place the time of death?"

"We'd be lucky to get the year of death. I'm guessing over two decades ago," the county medical examiner said. "Probably right around the time I became medical examiner."

"You think the body was stored in the freezer we found, then." It was more of a statement than a question. McMurphy was taking notes in his small spiral bound pad.

Patrick Fuller had been the county medical examiner for close to thirty years. In that time he had overseen the autopsies of fourteen homicides. A few of those were murder-suicides. He'd investigated suspected homicides that were later classified as accidents, as in the case of the apartment fire that killed two people in 1988. It turned out to be a faulty electrical conduit that had ignited newspaper which had been stuffed in the wall for insulation.

Patrick was a fastidious man, very focused, with an acute attention to detail. He wasn't very tall, almost a full foot shorter than Jack. His hair had slowly retreated until he was now almost completely bald. He sported a mustache which he'd taken to dying now that he was in his fifties. He smelled of formaldehyde and aftershave. Jack liked the man and trusted him implicitly.

He had his own private practice in Coopers Hollow but would travel to Delhi when necessary, as the medical examiner's lab was in the basement of the same building where the Sheriff's office and the DMV were located. They had room for six bodies in cold storage, which meant that they had to double stack a few of the drug dealers who had been killed by Jack and Michael.

"As I understand it, frozen body fluids were found in the freezer, yes? Based on that and the current condition of the body, I think that he was placed into the freezer shortly after he was killed."

"Tell me about the bullet that killed him," Jack asked.

"It was a medium caliber. Looked very similar to an older standard issue police round, maybe a .38. The bullet was in pristine condition. I think we should be able to get a pretty good ballistics match if we have a gun," the examiner said.

"We might have a weapon to compare it to," Jack confirmed. "Any indication of who he might be?"

"No identification on the body. We took fingerprints, which I was amazed to see intact, and I took some molds of the dental work for comparisons, should we get the chance. I'd suggest looking into missing persons cases back in the 1980's. Based on the outfit he was wearing and the hairstyle I might even say late seventies, early eighties. Wish I had more for you." Fuller closed his file and simply shrugged his shoulders. He'd come up from the lab to talk to Jack in the Sheriff's office. The County Sheriff had been kind enough to loan Jack the use of a room for the purposes of this meeting. It wasn't often that they had a homicide in these parts, and especially one that dated back nearly thirty years, if his guess was correct. Of course it wasn't often that the Police Chief of Coopers Hollow was involved in a shootout that made the OK Corral seem tame, either. Though it wasn't the first time that violence had come to the small town in the form of organized crime, it had been decades since there had been such a bloody spectacle. Cities a hundred times the size of Coopers Hollow didn't have shootouts the likes of which had transpired. Needless to say, Chief McMurphy had gained quite a bit of respect from the Sheriff's department.

Fuller sat back in his chair and studied the young Chief. McMurphy had a lot heaped on his plate in a very short time, and it looked like the stress was starting to get to him.

"Jack, have you thought about taking a vacation?"

"I don't have time for a vacation," McMurphy said with a laugh. "You're aware of what's going on around here, there's too much for me to do. Heck we've had to postpone dad's funeral twice!"

"Then I think you need to get some help," Fuller said.

"Really? What kind of help would you suggest? Psychotherapy or maybe a nice prescription to take the edge off? If I needed to take the edge off I could drown myself in a glass of whiskey," Jack snapped at the doctor.

"That's not what I meant Jack. I meant help around the office. Have you considered hiring an assistant for clerical work? Maybe somebody with some investigative experience," Fuller offered. "Being understaffed along with all the other stress you're facing just exacerbates the situation."

"I could use the help," Jack said, putting his pencil down and sitting back in his chair. "I'm sorry I snapped at you. It has been a crazy month. You know, it doesn't feel like he's gone."

"Your father?"

"Yeah. I keep feeling like he's going to walk through that door and tell me to get the heck out of his chair and then take over the meeting. And to lose Copper too -"

"Copper and I were good friends. It's been a tragic month for all of us, Jack, but especially for you. Normally when an officer is involved in a shooting, they are put on paid leave for awhile until the investigation is concluded. Killing a man takes something out of you. Your dad went through it," Fuller said.

"What? Dad never killed anybody."

"Oh, yes, he did. It was back in the eighties I think, you were probably just four or five years old. Your father was a patrolman at the time. Your grandfather was the chief of police. Anyway, your father was doing a routine traffic stop right on Main Street in Coopers Hollow. It was back before you had those computers in your cars, so he radioed in the license and then went to check on the driver. It was a stolen car from New Jersey. An eighteen year old kid had stolen it. The kid decided it was a good idea to pull a gun and try to shoot it out with your father. Your dad was a pretty good shot and put two in the kid's chest.

Killed him right there on the street. It shook him up pretty good. Your grandfather gave him a month off during the investigation."

"I remember that. I was five. Dad took me and mom down to Disney World. We spent like the whole month in Florida. He'd always been so serious about me not missing school, and then, all of a sudden, he just took me out for the month and didn't think anything of it. He never told me he had been on leave for shooting a kid," Jack furrowed his brow in thought. He remembered that vacation. It was one of the greatest times he had ever had with his mom and dad. His dad seemed so mellow during the whole thing. Normally the family vacations were like time trials with specific daily objectives and arrival times. That time, though, Jack Sr. had come home, told his wife and son that they were going on a trip, packed up and headed to Florida. He'd spent most of the time reading by the pool at their hotel, except for the few days they went to Disney World.

"Well, anyway, I thought you might want to know. There's no shame in taking some time off to get your head together. It is normal, Jack. I'm sure the Sheriff's department would lend out a couple of deputies to help with things until you returned. Just think about it, okay?"

"I will," Jack replied.

"Listen, I've got to get going. You'll have my full report typed up and in the system by tomorrow, noon at the latest," Fuller stood and reached his hand across the table. Jack did the same.

"Thanks, Patrick."

After Fuller left, Jack thought about the next step in the investigation. They were holding Mrs. McIntyre on charges of assault of an officer already, and it looked very realistic that a new charge of first degree murder would be following. The gun she had was indeed an old police issue. Her grandfather had been the first chief of police in the history of Coopers Hollow. More than likely it was his gun.

Jack had an afternoon appointment with the district attorney, and he would be making the recommendation to formally charge her for the murder of the frozen John Doe.

The thing that bothered him right now about the case was the whereabouts of Tubby. Nobody had seen any signs of him since he'd shown up out of nowhere and rescued Paula from the burning building. What he was doing in *The Mountain Star* building in the first place was a mystery as well. Jack had talked to Paula and she had told him that she had found him upstairs, in room 213. Perhaps that's where he had been hiding after he fled his mother's house.

Tubby wasn't the brightest guy in the world. He'd heard rumors that Tubby had been dropped when he was just a baby and suffered some brain damage as a result. One of the guys, Krakowski, at Taylor's Taproom had even said that it was the delivery doctor who had dropped him, and that Tubby was worth millions from the trust fund which was set up for him as a result. Tubby wouldn't be the first millionaire to walk around in tattered clothing and act like he didn't have two nickels to rub together. But nobody believed Kracky. The guy was a know-it-all blowhard.

Jack had finished what he'd needed to do for the time

being, and left the small room in the Sheriff's department building. He found his way to the Sheriff's office and poked his head in to say thank you. The Sheriff was on the phone, but he saw Jack. He barely acknowledged him, just giving a nod and a curt wave before swiveling his chair around and continuing his phone conversation. It was still going to be a prickly relationship. Jack left the building, got into his dad's police cruiser, as his was still in the repair shop, and headed back to Coopers Hollow.

The smell of smoke still hung in the air, even though any remaining live ember had been extinguished days ago. Michael Cooke walked around the blackened remains of his retirement home, searching for anything worth salvaging. So far he'd found nothing. Not a scrap of anything usable had escaped the blaze. Most of the local fire departments had been busy fighting the Lexmore Hotel blaze. The Cobleskill fire department had finally arrived to put out the fire at his house, but by the time they had gotten there, it was fully engulfed, as was his truck. All they could do was try to keep it from igniting the surrounding trees. They got the flames under control after battling the blaze for nearly four hours. The roof collapsed and the pressure of the collapse extinguished some of the flames. It had given the firefighters a chance to get closer with their hoses to put it out.

He knew from his forensic training that jewelry including gold and precious stones could be recovered from a blaze, but usually not much else was left. He didn't own much jewelry, preferring to sink his money into guns.

Once he cleared some of the debris he would be able to get down to the basement level to see if any of his weapons were able to be salvaged. They had been locked in a large steel cabinet as had the ammunition, fortunately. During the blaze none of the ammo ignited. This gave him hope that the guns had survived. It was going to take a lot of work just to get down to the gun cabinet. He would need to rest up a bit more before he could start tackling such a project. At least he still had his black beauty.

He required forty-one stitches in his chest from where the barbed wire tore into his flesh. He couldn't lift his left arm above his head from a torn rotator cuff. His right knee had suffered the most damage, however. He'd torn his medial collateral ligament or MCL as well as split the meniscus cartilage. It was a common sports related injury, and would require surgery and several months of rehab. His body wasn't what it used to be, but it had done the job it needed to.

Cooke was surprised at how quickly his insurance company had jumped to help him out. He'd gotten a rental vehicle the very next morning after the shootout and received a full reimbursement check for his truck four hours later. The house insurance company had put him up in a hotel in Oneonta indefinitely until they had the full police report. His agent had promised him that he would have a check for his full amount the same day they received the report. The expensive part was going to be the health costs. It was going to eat into his retirement savings to the tune of thirty thousand dollars. The reconstructive surgery to his knee ligaments and cartilage would be the most expensive part. For the time being he had to deal with a leg brace and crutches. It wasn't exactly easy getting around, even driving was a chore, but just like everything else, he would endure.

A vehicle pulled into his driveway, a silver colored Volvo. He recognized it immediately as Gloria's. She pulled up and parked next to his new Ford F250, which he had purchased that very morning. He'd opted for the deep black paint with tan interior. She hopped out and looked surprisingly refreshed and vibrant.

"Hey," he called to her.

"Hey yourself," she said with a cheery smile. She walked over to him. He held out his crutch-wielding arm and she slid under it and encircled him for a hug. He returned the gesture and found himself feeling very comfortable. She left her arm around him as she spoke.

"So, is there anything left?"

"Nothing. Some of my guns in the basement might be salvageable, but I can't get down to them in this state," he said gesturing down to his battered body. "At least my rifle made it."

"Yes, thank God for your rifle. And thank God for you, Michael." She gave him another squeeze.

"How did the surgery go with Dalton?"

"He's recovering. They were able to reattach his tongue and the doctor is actually optimistic that he'll regain full muscle control of it. He's not sure if he'll have any taste or not, only time will tell. Nerve regeneration is still a bit of a tricky business," she said. "Starlett's doing better. She was in a pretty serious state of shock for seventy-two hours or so, but she's recovering now. She didn't want to stay in the house, and I can't say that I blame her. She's in a hotel across the street from Dalton's hospital up in Albany. I'm going up again today to be with her."

"How are you doing?" He looked into her eyes, and whereas when they'd first met he'd seen a nervousness and uncertainty, he now saw strength and determination.

"I'm good. You know, my doctor told me that one day I might have a breakdown over the whole ordeal, but I don't think so. I've been through just about everything a grown woman can go through, and I've survived. I've had to come face to face with my biggest fears, and I'm still here. I don't think I have to be afraid of anything anymore," she smiled as she looked back into his eyes and saw warmth and concern.

"That's good. You're a strong woman. I'm just sorry I got there too late to stop them from hurting Dalton," he said, looking away. He'd been late, again.

"But you came and saved us. Michael, they were going to kill us. You stopped them. You saved us. I love you for it, Michael, and I always will." She stepped in front of him and reached up with both hands, pulling him down to her. She kissed him on the lips. She had intended it to be a simple, short kiss, but he leaned into it more. Dropping his crutches, he slid his arms around her. She hadn't kissed a man since she'd said goodbye to her husband that horrible Tuesday over a decade ago. It felt nice.

"Hi there," the US Fish and Wildlife officer said as he

walked in the entrance to Ohio Exotics, Inc. "Can I speak to Mr. Marcus Higgs?"

"Can I tell him who's asking for him?" The girl behind the desk was cute and young, maybe twenty one. She smacked her gum as she chewed. The officer told her his name and why he was there. In a few moments, Marcus Higgs came out, wearing blue jeans, alligator skin boots, a cowboy shirt with a huge, shiny metal belt buckle. He was in his fifties, and his love of steak and beer had pushed his stomach out well beyond the belt buckle.

"Come on in, what can I do for ya?" Higgs was nervous. He had read all the articles and seen all the news stories about the cougar and tiger that had gotten loose in the Catskill Mountains, and he knew that they were the ones Tommy had been tasked to deliver. He'd also found out that Tommy was dead, poor sucker. The kid had been a screw up since the day he'd met him.

"Well, we have reason to believe that one John Thomas Bartlett was employed by you, is that correct?" The officer was looking at a notebook and appeared somewhat bored.

"Tommy, yeah. He did. I reported a few weeks ago that he had stolen some of the animals I owned here and disappeared. I told the cops, er, officers, that if he just returned what was mine I wouldn't press charges. Did you find him?" Higgs was going to play this as naïvely as possible. He would take a beating if he was forced to pay any damages for what had happened.

"Well, Mr. Higgs, I hate to be the one to break the bad news to you, but Tommy is dead. He was killed in an accident. It looks like he was trying to steal the animals alright. They found him up in the Catskill Mountains of New York State. Maybe you saw the news," the officer said.

"I caught something about it. I thought they had escaped from a zoo or something up there. I didn't put two and two together, I guess," Higgs said, continuing his dumb charade.

"I guess," the officer echoed. He knew what was going on, but he was helpless to do anything about it. "Well, anyway, I just wanted to see if you had anything else to add to our investigation."

"Not that I can think of," said Higgs. "Did any of the animals survive?"

"No. Not a single one. In fact, two people were killed and two were seriously injured from your animals, Mr. Higgs. We're currently investigating all the details, but there may be charges from this."

"I'm just as innocent a victim here as anyone else. They were stolen from me. I take all the proper precautions whenever I transport animals. This is a dangerous business, and it takes a real professional to prevent disaster. I guess Tommy just didn't get it. I can't say he was the smartest guy I'd ever met. I'm more than willing to assist in any further investigation, but I have to take issue with your implicating me in any of this," Higgs protested.

"I figured you'd say something like that," the officer said. He scribbled a few more notes in his notebook.

"Is that everything then? I'm a busy man, I need to get back to work," Higgs said.

"You don't have anything else to add? You say this was all Tommy's fault then?"

"Yes, I don't have anything else to add."

"Didn't think so," the officer said. "Well, have a nice day. I'm sure we'll run into each other again sometime."

"Uh, okay. Thanks." Higgs knew they would be out here checking up on him now. He was going to have to lay low and play by the book for awhile until memory of this blew over. Higgs went over to the window and sighed with relief as the U.S. Fish and Wildlife officer climbed back into his truck and backed out of the parking lot.

The officer paused to look at the steel building with the sign Ohio Exotics. Some day life would catch up to guys like Higgs. But as far as he was concerned, this whole fiasco was now officially over. He headed back to his office to type up the report.

The funeral finally took place nearly two weeks after Jack McMurphy Sr. had been killed in the line of duty. There had been a private memorial for the family and close friends, and then a public memorial at the Coopers Hollow High School auditorium. The service incorporated a memorial for Copper Owens as well.

Copper's son, Eric, Eric's wife Sylvia and their two children were there. Eric was an architect in New York City, but now with the death of his father, he was talking of moving up to help take care of his mother. Jack made small talk with him and tried to be positive, but he couldn't help but feel guilty.

The community turned out almost in its entirety to show their support. The gun battle that had occurred was a sobering reminder that the police were willing to put their lives on the line for the people they swore to serve and protect.

The Delaware County Sheriff's department had most of its officers on hand for the memorial, and many State Troopers came to give pay their respects.

Jack Jr. said a few words in memory of his father, and only had to stop twice to wipe away tears.

Finally the two community leaders were laid to rest in the Coopers Hollow Cemetery, with another short grave side prayer ceremony for each.

Jack said his final goodbye to his father, tossing a handful of dirt down onto the casket as it was being lowered. He wiped his hands together and turned to walk back to his car, with Paula by his side.

Chapter 22

"It's a travesty."

She stood with her hands on her hips looking at the remnants of the Lexmore Hotel. The building had been insured quite responsibly, so she would end up with a nice payout, but she had fallen in love with the century-old hotel for a reason, it had character. Now it was a pile of scorched wood and smoldering ash.

She knew she wasn't the only one picking up the pieces from a fire. Michael Cooke's place had been torched as well. The only difference was he had gotten the satisfaction of killing the men who had done it. She would have loved to have taken at least one of the shots. The thug who had attacked her was dead, she knew, which meant that there was still some semblance of justice in the world. Once upon a time she had been very anti-gun, but after this experience she could see that, on occasion, they could be useful.

She heard footsteps behind her, and she felt an instant rush of fear induced adrenaline course through her veins. It would take a long time before she wouldn't jump when someone came up behind her. Turning quickly she saw that it was Tubby McIntyre. He looked like he'd been sleeping outside since he'd rescued her two days before. He literally had leaves in his hair and beard.

"Hey there, Tubby."

"Hi, Miss Paula. I'm sorry your hotel burned down," he said.

"Tubby, thank you for saving my life. You ran off before I got a chance to tell you." She reached up her arms and gave him a big hug. He smelled like cats, but she endured the smell and gave him a good squeeze. After a moment of uncertainty, he hugged her back.

"Now you listen to me, I know your Mama is in some trouble, I talked to Jack and he told me about it. We are going to get you cleaned up and then we're going to go talk to Jack and get everything straightened out, okay?" She felt somewhat responsible for him now. He was like a big stray puppy that just needed a good home.

"Okay," he complied.

Paula had asked Jack if she could stay with him until the insurance company paid out, and he had agreed. He had a three bedroom, two bathroom house, so there was plenty of room for her. She had hoped that maybe he wouldn't force her to use the spare bedroom, but when she'd gotten to his house he made a fuss about getting the room in order for her, so she didn't make a big deal of it. Additionally she had been so exhausted she didn't have any energy for any level of hanky panky. Over the next few days, he got her a key, and she made herself at home.

Now she took Tubby over to Jack's place and forced him into the shower. She gave him a washcloth and a big bottle of body wash. She told him that she expected him to wash everything at least three times over. She hoped that would get rid of the stink. She also demanded that he hand out his dirty clothes. She didn't even bother washing them, but rather, after checking the size put them right into a garbage bag and put it out in the big bin in Jack's garage. She told Tubby through the bathroom door that she was going to go get him some new clothes and instructed him to wrap in one of the big towels when he was done and he could watch television in the living room until she got back. He acknowledged her instructions, so she left for Cobleskill where there was a SuperStore that she knew had a big and tall section.

She picked out a triple-extra large colored polo shirt, and a pair of cargo khakis. She also bought him socks and underwear. Shoes were next, and she picked out black work boots in his size. Finally she selected a triple-extra large jacket with a warm liner. The total for the outfit came to over a hundred fifty dollars. The boots were the most expensive part.

When she returned to Jack's house nearly an hour and a half later, Tubby was wrapped in one of the large towels and sitting on the couch watching a movie on the big screen television. The towel barely covered him, and she could tell he was embarrassed when she came in.

"Here, I got you some clothes. Go put them on. When you're done we're going over to the salon in town to take care of that hair of yours," Paula said. She wasn't going to take no for an answer. He dutifully complied and went into the bathroom to get dressed. When he came out he looked almost presentable. The clothes, as large as they were, just barely fit Tubby. He seemed to be pleased with them, and thanked her.

"We're not done yet," she informed him. "Come on, we're going over to see my friend Melanie."

Despite having washed his hair in the shower, Melanie insisted on doing a thorough shampooing before she cut his hair. It took her nearly forty-five minutes to complete the haircut, which included shaving his beard. When she was done, she swiveled the chair around so he could see himself in the mirror. He ran his hand over his smoothly shaved face and through his short hair. Paula couldn't tell if he was pleased or in shock. His washed and conditioned hair caught the light with gentle tints of red.

"Do you like it," she asked as she paid for the services.

"I don't know, it doesn't look like me in the mirror," he replied.

"Well I think you look handsome, Tubby," Melanie said.

"Me too," Paula echoed. They both laughed as Tubby's cheeks flushed red. "Don't be embarrassed, you're a good looking man, you just need to take care of yourself."

"I'll try," he promised.

When they walked into the Peachy Keen, Seemo didn't even recognize Tubby. Not until he took his regular seat and asked for some Frosted Flakes.

"Thaddeus, is that you?" Seemo was nearly speechless at the transformation.

"Yeah, Miss Paula got me these new clothes and Miss Melanie cut my hair and shaved off my beard," he said sheepishly.

"Well you look like a million bucks! They did a good job," Seemo said admiringly. "Frosted Flakes coming right up! And what can I get for you Paula?"

"I'd just like one of your grilled turkey sandwiches with fries on the side," Paula said, sitting on a swivel stool next to Tubby.

"Okay, I make it just how you like it," Seemo said and went in to tell Poppi about the new development of Tubby's changed appearance.

As Seemo retrieved the food for his customers, Tubby took a book out of the back of his pants. He set it on the counter and turned to Paula.

"Can I ask you something, Miss Paula?"

"Sure, what is it?"

"I can't read this, because it's written in cursing."

"You mean cursive?"

"Yeah. I'm not good at reading that kind of writing. Could you read it and tell me what it says?" He slid the book over to her. The cover read "Officer James McIntyre".

"Sure, I could do that, Tubby. Where did you get it from?"

"It was in Mama's back room. I think it belonged to somebody related to me because the last name on it is the same as my last name. See," he pointed to the front cover.

"Sure, okay. Let me take a look," she replied, taking the book off the counter. She opened the cover and began to read. "Tubby, do you know what this is?"

"No. Well, maybe. I think it's a diary. Kracky said it was a diary."

"Based on the dates, it looks like it's the journal your

great-grandfather kept. He was the first police chief in this town. I don't know if you know that or not. If I remember correctly, he was gunned down by some mobsters. He had killed more than twelve of their hired guns before they got him. I remember reading about it in some of the old newspaper files when I was researching the history of the Lexmore. This is quite a find. Do you mind if I hang on to it and read the whole thing?"

"Okay, but just to borrow, not to keep," Tubby said.

"Just to borrow, not to keep," she promised.

"Jack, go easy on him, okay?" After their lunch, Paula had brought the cleaned up Tubby in to the police station to talk with Chief McMurphy.

"Paula, I know how you feel, I'm indebted to him as well, but the law is the law. He pointed a gun at me. Not only that, he had a corpse in a storage facility. We can't just ignore that stuff."

"I know. But listen, he hasn't had anybody looking out for him. His Mama mistreated him, and everybody treats him like an imbecile. We've got to watch out for him now," Paula said.

"Okay, I'll try to help him out, but he's broken the law, there's only so much I can do," Jack said. He was the Chief of Police, after all. He couldn't afford to allow an accusation of favoritism to be leveled at his office. He had the public trust to uphold. Deep down inside, though, he thought that if the law couldn't make room to protect people like Tubby, then there was no point in writing laws in the first place.

"So, what do you think?" Jack was speaking to the district attorney, Dean Wagner.

"Jack, it's up to you. I won't press charges if you don't want me to. Based on the psychological work up on him, though, I think he will need to have a guardian assigned by the state. I don't think he should be allowed to be on his own. At least not with a gun in the house."

"Dean, I don't want to press charges against him. That's decided. What do you think about his mother?"

"She's a fruitcake. She's gone mentally. She thinks she's on a TV show right now. I think she killed the man, stuffed him in the freezer and slowly went mad over the years. She probably would have been institutionalized a long time ago if she hadn't been such a recluse and had Tubby around to keep bringing her food and such. She's got a state appointed attorney, Jamerson from Delhi. Jamerson has already told me he's going to go for innocent by reason of insanity. He also says that she claims the dead man raped her and that's why she killed him."

"So she admitted to killing him, but is pleading insanity and self defense," Jack stated. "Well, I can't say I'm surprised. Did she say who the guy was?"

"No, it's a mystery."

"A mystery, huh?"

"Yes," Paula said. She and Jack were having dinner at his place. Tubby was at a state facility for a few days as they sent someone to his Mama's house and cleaned out the cats and tried to make it livable for him once again. People from the congregation that Tubby had started attending with Anton were also pitching in to help. They were giving the house a thorough cleaning top to bottom. So, for the time being, they were alone. "Look, right here he says that the last words from Josephson's mouth were 'Gold, room, great.' McIntyre spends several pages talking about what it could all mean. After talking to his widow, McIntyre believed that Josephson had hidden gold someplace, perhaps in the hotel in one of the rooms."

"And why would the widow think that," Jack asked, only somewhat interested in the story. He was thoroughly exhausted. It had been three weeks of nonstop paperwork and interviews. The FBI had sent agents up to discuss the shootout, and they hadn't exactly been complementary in the way he handled it. They were especially interested in why Michael Cooke had been so involved. They had informed Jack that despite what he thought, only the county Sheriff had the power to deputize a citizen, and then only in extreme cases. They informed Jack that they were considering bringing him up on charges for the act. The FBI's investigation was ongoing.

As soon as they left, Jack had called Dean Wagner to discuss it. Wagner said that if they wanted to charge him, they could, but it was probably just a scare tactic to make sure he never did it again. That's all he hoped it was.

She was reading from the journal Tubby had let her borrow.

"Listen to this section:

> Mrs. Josephson said that she knew her husband had kept gold in several banks in New York City. When she called the banks after his death, they all said the same thing: Mr. Josephson had come in and taken the contents of his safe deposit boxes and terminated the box rentals. She remembered that it was the day he had gone to the city and returned after she had gone to bed. The next morning she had found tracks of sawdust in the hallway on the second floor. She never asked him about it, but she imagined that he'd gotten the gold and hid it someplace. I promised her I wouldn't tell a soul and even helped her pull up some of the floor boards looking for her treasure. She died in May, though, by the end she had pretty much gone senile. I don't know if he hid the gold or if he was just having a vision of grandeur in his last seconds on this earth. I guess I'll never really know."

"What happens to gold in a fire," Paula asked.

"It might get blackened a little from soot, but a house fire doesn't burn hot enough to melt it. A house fire usually maxes out at around fourteen hundred degrees Fahrenheit. Gold melts at a higher temperature," Jack said. He'd studied up on the subject when he was helping Copper Owens with a few arson investigations a few years back. He missed that old man.

"So what you're saying is that the gold could still be there," Paula said with a bit of excitement in her voice.

"In theory, if there was gold hidden in the floor of the old hotel, it would now be in the pile of debris, yes," Jack answered.

"We've got to find it, Jack. It could be our ticket out of here," she said excitedly, not thinking about her words.

"Why would we want to get out of here," Jack replied, a bit irritated by her embracing the fantasy. "What's wrong with living here?"

"Nothing. I don't know, I don't have anything keeping me here anymore. My company has been taken over, my home and the office I spent so much energy refurbishing are all gone. What else do I have to keep me here," she asked, hoping he would take the bait.

"Well I've got too much going on to just leave it. I've got to stay," he said. He saw her reaction, putting her head down and scowling slightly. He reached across the table and took her hand. "But I'd like you to be here with me."

"And what am I supposed to do? Where am I supposed to work?" She pushed the food around on her plate with her fork. She'd lost her appetite.

"Well, you could work on your writing and you could help out at the station for awhile. I could really use someone," he said. "What I meant to say is, I need you."

She was quiet for a moment thinking about his words. She didn't want to read too much into them, but she liked what it meant.

"Yeah, okay," she said after a moment. "Only if you

help me look for the gold, though." She finished with a laugh.

"Okay, I'll help you look for the gold," he said laughing at her. "We're never going to find it you know."

"You don't know that. We might get lucky," she said.

"So you've got the results from the test?"

"Yes," Fuller said. "I do."

"Is it a match?" Jack hoped to put this case to bed. If the DNA matched Tubby, it was fair to say that the story that she was raped by the man in the freezer and killed him, would hold water. It was also fair to say that she had been driven insane by the whole ordeal. They wouldn't get a conviction, but they could get her institutionalized and maybe get her some help.

"Yes, Jack, it's a match."

"So it's Tubby's father."

"It's a match to Tubby and it's a match to Eloise McIntyre as well."

"Wait, what? What does that mean?" Jack didn't understand what he was being told. DNA was shared by relatives.

"The man in the freezer, the John Doe, he has enough DNA in common with Eloise McIntyre that I believe they were siblings. Also, it's conclusive that Tubby is their child."

"Oh, jeez." Jack put his face in his hands. "Have you told this to Dean yet?"

"Yes, about twenty minutes before I came to see you," Fuller said evenly.

"What did he say?"

"I think the exact same thing you just did," Fuller laughed.

"If we go public with this, Tubby won't be able to live in Coopers Hollow anymore. The guys he knows at the Taproom will be merciless. It's a small town. News like that is too juicy not to get repeated all over."

"Wagner agrees. He's leaning in the direction of dropping charges and having you press to have her committed instead," Fuller said. "If we go to trial, all the gory details will come out and everyone will know about it. News like that would travel like wildfire across a dry prairie."

"He said that? Drop the charges and have her committed?"

"Yes."

"Well, I agree. I think we have to give poor Tubby a break, here." News like this might wreck the poor guy. He might end up like his mother, completely crazy.

"Listen, I'm not going to tell anybody about this, Jack. I'm going to make a written report on this. I'm not going to file it digitally. Someone will have to actually get into my filing cabinet or yours to read about it."

"I agree," Jack said. "The only people that know about this are you, me and Wagner. At least we know who the John Doe is now."

"Case closed?" Fuller asked.

"Case closed," Jack replied with finality.

"Good morning," Seemo said as they came in and sat at the table. "You know what you want, or you need menus?"

"Menus, please," said Gloria.

"I know what I want, but I'll wait to order when she does," Michael said.

"Okay," Seemo replied, handing a menu to Gloria. "Just let me know when you ready."

"Morning, Tubby," Seemo said as the large man walked over to his place at the counter. Without even asking, Seemo produced a bowl of Frosted Flakes and poured on the milk just how Tubby liked it. Tubby smiled and looked rather charming with his short hair and no beard. Paula had gone out and purchased more clothes for him so he had something nice to wear each day of the week, and a suit for Sunday.

"Hey, good morning," Jack said to Michael and Gloria as he walked in to the diner, accompanied by the jingle of door chimes. "How are you?"

He walked over and shook both of their hands. He wasn't in uniform. He wore a pair of jeans, a flannel shirt and a work jacket. Paula came in a few moments later, dressed in similar work clothes.

"So, meeting here for a little breakfast?" Jack smiled at the two of them.

"Actually, uh," Michael stammered.

"Michael's staying at my place for awhile. He's helping with the repairs and such. I had the spare bedroom, so I figured, why not." Jack was surprised at the news but he was also happy for her. "But we thought we'd come down for a little breakfast before we left. He's taking me on a cruise!"

"Wow, that's great. I hope you guys have fun. How's Starlett and Dalton?"

"They're doing well. Dalton's mother came and got him out of the hospital three days ago. She was going to take him on their yacht down to their chalet in the Bahamas to recuperate since their home in New Jersey won't be finished until the spring. He's still really sore, but they're very happy with his recovery. He's still eating through a straw, but in another week or so, he'll be able to start on mushy foods and such.

"Starlett is doing much better," Gloria continued. "She's going back to school next semester. I think the two of them are going to take a break for awhile and see how the next couple of months go."

"And what about you?" Jack smiled. It was good news all around and it made him happy.

"Oh, I'm doing well," Gloria said, reaching across the table and squeezing Michael's hand.

"Yeah, we're doing pretty good," Michael echoed. He was beaming, with a grin ear to ear. Jack thought about it and couldn't remember if he'd ever seen the man smile. "Everything is healing up pretty good. Hopefully this old fart will be healthy enough for a little shuffleboard on the cruise."

They all had a good laugh at that. Michael had been able to get rid of the crutches, but he still had a brace and a cane to get around. His shoulder still wasn't working right, but the gash across his chest was healing well. He'd gotten the stitches out weeks before, and the scabs were almost ready to come off. The surgery had gone smoothly and, though it would take time to rehabilitate the knee, he was going to have full use of it.

"That's great," he slapped Michael lightly on the shoulder. "Well, I'll let you two get back to your breakfast. We've got to eat and run too."

"Oh, yeah? What are you two up to?" Michael nodded to Paula. She smiled and nodded back.

"We're going to grab some breakfast and then head over to the remains of Paula's place. We're going to dig around and see if the old place held any secrets," Jack said.

"Ugh. We had clean up duty at Michael's place too. Good luck with that," Gloria replied.

"Thanks. Good luck on your cruise. I hope you have fun." Jack smiled at them. "When you get back let's get together for dinner, the four of us."

"Sounds good," she said looking at Michael. "We'll look forward to it."

Jack and Paula got breakfast sandwiches and coffee to go and headed over to the site of the burned down Lexmore Hotel.

The wind had picked up slightly, but it was still relatively warm for a late November day. They had purchased a metal detector for their project, but Jack was skeptical they would find anything. He'd promised to humor her, though, so he was going to try to stay positive during their search.

"We need to be very careful," Jack said. "It could still cave into the basement." He'd brought along an extension ladder that he planned on stretching across the blackened debris so there would be a level of stability as they searched.

He dropped the ladder down in place, and held it steady as Paula climbed out with the metal detector over the debris. She made sweeping arcs as she slowly progressed out onto the ladder. She had been crawling along on hands and knees when she stopped in one location and continued sweeping over it.

"Jack," she exclaimed, rising to her knees and turning to call out to him. "I think I found something!"

Suddenly there was a loud crack and the burned timbers gave with a crash, sending Paula and the ladder down into the basement of the burned hotel. Jack watched in horror as she disappeared in a cloud of ashen dust.

He called out to her, but she didn't answer. He swung himself onto the ladder and began to climb down. He pulled the flashlight out from his coat pocket and pointed the beam down into the hole.

"Paula! Are you okay?!"

"Jack! Can you come down? I think I broke my ankle!" She coughed out the reply. He came down the ladder cautiously. The burned wood that the ladder was now leaning on continued to crack and pop under his weight. Finally he made it down to the basement level. The air was thick with sooty dust, and Paula was covered in it. She was on the ground, digging through the debris.

"Paula, come on. That's enough. Let's get you out of here."

She kept digging, pawing at a pile of ash. He felt bad for her. She was trying so hard, but there was nothing here. There was nothing left of her treasured building. Her dreams had been diminished to ash.

"Okay. Okay. Stop. That's enough," he said forcefully. He had humored her little treasure hunt for as long as he could. He bent down to grab her by the arm when she turned and held something up.

"Look Jack," she said, with eyes beaming. "Gold!"

Tubby had been staying with Mr. Anton since his mother went away to the hospital for good. The old man had heard through the grapevine that Tubby needed to have a guardian or else he was going to have to go live in an assisted living home. So he volunteered to take Tubby in. Anton Oleksandr's house was quite small, so Tubby had to sleep on the couch for the time being.

They were almost done cleaning out his Mama's house, so they were all going to move in there when it was done: Tubby, Mr. Anton and Mr. Anton's wife. But not Mama.

The doctors told Tubby that Mama was going to get help now and that she would be much happier. It made Tubby feel good to know that. Mr. Anton had said that he would help Tubby out, and he was really nice. He understood him.

Mr. Anton made Tubby take a shower every day, and shave too. He also made him get a haircut every two weeks from Melanie. They went shopping and got a whole bunch of new clothes for Tubby, and he liked the way they made him look. Mr. Anton didn't like him going to Taylor's Taproom, though. Tubby told him he was just going to go one more time, and then he wouldn't go back ever again.

Tubby walked into Taylor's and smiled at everyone he knew. He saw his friend Rusty. His arm still wasn't strong enough for working or anything, so he spent most of his days here in the Taproom.

"Hey! Tubby!" Rusty pushed out a bar stool for his friend.

"I'm not drinking anymore," Tubby said.

"Really? What, did you find religion or something?" Rusty laughed. Tubby didn't say anything. He knew Rusty didn't mean nothing by it.

"I have a present for you, Rusty," Tubby said.

"You're not going to fart, are ya?" Rusty socked him in the arm with his good fist.

"No. It's an envelope. So you can take your wife and your little girl to Florida and open your tattoo place. And maybe I can come and visit sometimes," Tubby said. He handed the envelope to Rusty.

"What the heck are you talking about, Tubby," Rusty asked. He set down his beer and took the envelope from

Tubby. He opened it and pulled out a check. He almost fell off his bar stool. "Tubby, this isn't real, is it?"

"Yeah, it is."

"How – but – where?" Rusty couldn't spit out the words.

"I saved it up. I want you to go have your tattoo place, Rusty."

It had been a horrible two months. The cougar attack had left him probably permanently disabled. His wife had to work overtime at Stewart's just so they could make ends meet. Disability finally kicked in, but it wasn't enough. They were falling more and more behind on their bills. It looked like they were going to have to move in with her parents if things didn't change. Truthfully, Rusty had thought about putting a gun in his mouth and pulling the trigger, just so Heather and Libby could have the small life insurance policy money. But he loved them both too much to do that.

"I can't take this, Tubby."

"Yes you can. It's for you."

"I don't know what to say," Rusty stammered. He felt like crying, but he didn't want to do it in front of the guys at the bar. He stood up and gave his big friend a hug. "Thanks man, I'll never forget this."

"Okay. You're welcome. Send me a letter when you get moved so I can come and visit. I'll take a bus because I don't like airplanes."

"You can count on it, Tubby."

"And call me Thaddeus, now. I like that name. It's from the Bible, Mr. Anton says. It's a good name."

"Okay, Tu – Thaddeus. I won't call you anything else anymore."

He turned and walked out of Taylor's Taproom for the last time. Rusty just looked at the check he was holding and couldn't believe it. Forty thousand dollars.

Thaddeus McIntyre had thought about moving too, but he didn't know where he would go. He liked Mr. Anton very much, and thought maybe they could move to Florida too, but Mr. Anton said he was too old to move. The lady that came to help him with his money told him that he had several hundred thousand dollars all over the house and that he should put it in the bank. So he did. She helped him with all the paperwork, and so did Mr. Anton. He knew that it would be enough for him and Mr. Anton and Mr. Anton's wife, and they could be like a family.

Miss Paula and the Chief checked in on him too just to make sure he was okay. Chief Jack Junior had told him that Mama shot the man in the freezer, and yes it was his daddy. It made him sad, but he was glad that it wasn't his fault like Mama had told him.

Paula had found a whole bunch of gold in the ashes of the hotel that burned down, so she and Jack were very happy and were getting married in just a few months. They were really nice to him and he liked them very much.

He would go to see Mama at the home where she stayed, but she wasn't very nice to him when he came for visits. So after going there three or four times, he decided he wasn't going to go back. It made him sad, but he hoped the Lord would forgive him. Mr. Anton said that the Lord would understand just fine.

The people at the congregation were really helpful too. They liked him good. They helped him learn how to read. And helped him learn that he weren't goin' to Hell even if he was a sinner, no matter what Mama said.

He was the happiest he'd ever been ever.

He walked down the street away from Taylor's Taproom and back towards Mr. Anton's house. As the sun shown down on his face, Thaddeus Cornelius McIntyre looked up and down Main Street of Coopers Hollow and smiled.

"This is a good place to live," he said.

A Sneak Preview

of

Hollow Pointe

Coming Soon

Prologue • Autumn 1947

He hurt all over. Even sitting in the wooden swivel chair, which he'd found so comfortable for so many years now made his back ache after just a short time. They had never been able to dig out some of the bullets that were lodged in his body. His left leg still ached from when it had been crushed between the bumper of his cruiser and a 1939 Ford with a dead driver behind the wheel.

Coopers Hollow had seen a rash of violence since his shootout with mob goons back in 1933. Organized crime syndicates had long memories. The fact that he had killed one of the mob's favorite trigger men brought with it a wave of vengeance.

In the fall of 1933 a lone gunman shot at him while he sat in his patrol car in front of the hardware store. Two bullets had struck him in his side, but he was still able to return fire, killing the mob thug in the middle of the street. He was stuck recovering in the hospital for three weeks after the surgery to remove the bullets.

In 1935 it was an all out war. Four of the mob's men were sent to Coopers Hollow to put an end to him for good. They had caught him in his office, which, at that time, was in the same building as the fire department. He heard the commotion as several of the volunteer firemen challenged the would-be assassins. They lost their lives for their bravery. He took out two of the thugs before they even had a chance to raise their weapons. The other two took the better part of an hour fight it out. It was a bloody battle. The fire station looked like Swiss cheese and he ended up with six bullets lodged in his body and, what seemed like, most of his blood on the concrete floor of truck bays. He was in the hospital for three months that time, and nearly died of pneumonia during his recovery.

It was quiet for half a decade, and he thought that perhaps the grudge against him had burned down and extinguished. Coopers Hollow was facing other problems, however. The small town lost much of the tourist business due to a shift in habits of people from the big city. Fewer individuals rode the train up from the city for their summer vacations, and instead, drove their new family automobiles all across the country. Everyone wanted to see Niagara Falls or the Thousand Islands. Sure there were still vacationers, and seasonal farm workers rode the trains up during apple picking season or strawberry season, but it wasn't like it used to be.

The Lexmore Hotel hadn't been the same since Jacobson had been killed. The poor man's wife tried to keep it running, but a man was needed to make the repairs that were necessary. He tried to help her as best he could, but he had his own house and family to look after.

Money in the town was drying up. Farms were shutting down. The banks were foreclosing on families. It wasn't just Coopers Hollow, the whole country had it tough. They weren't calling it the Great Depression for nothing. But the Catskills were taking a beating. McIntyre didn't know if they'd ever recover.

He married in 1934 to a local farmer's daughter. She was a hard worker but a bit daft at times. Their first child had been born the following year. He was a weak child, he didn't have his father's size or countenance. He was constantly sick, and preferred to play with the girls and help his mother around the house rather than play sports. They'd named him Thomas James McIntyre, but the kids in town took to calling him TJ.

He tried to teach TJ how to be a man, but it was a struggle. They'd gone hunting when TJ was just eight years old. He shot a four point buck on their first day out. It meant venison for the winter. As he began to field dress the felled deer, TJ began to cry. Great, heaving sobs. Finally he sent TJ back to the car. After dragging the carcass back to the vehicle and draping it over the fender, they started home. TJ didn't say a word for nearly two days, and refused to eat any of the venison all winter.

Three weeks after the deer incident, the mob came calling once again. He was struck by a bullet in the back and left for dead. They couldn't remove this bullet, as it was too close to his spine. Every once in awhile, especially after he'd been sitting for two long, his left leg would go numb.

It was the fact that the leg had gone numb, and he had no strength in it that caused him to be unable to leap out of the way of the 1939 Ford which was bearing down on him. He put a bullet in the driver's head, but couldn't leap out of the way before his leg was crushed between the bumpers of the colliding vehicles. This injury landed him in the hospital for a month, and after three surgeries, he was deemed healthy enough to go back to work. He needed a cane for five months as he built the strength back in the leg. But he was stubborn, and even if it locked up on him every now and again, he refused to use the cane.

When the violence in the small town finally subsided during the second world war, it was because the mob families had suffered severe losses due to a government crack down during the previous ten years. A small town cop in the northern Catskill mountains no longer merited much attention. There were bigger fish to fry.

In all, Chief James McIntyre had put seven mafia assassins in the ground. Of course rumors persisted that he was responsible for another half dozen, but according to his count, it was seven. Watching seven men die was plenty for him.

1942 was an especially painful year. Their second child, a girl named Elizabeth McIntyre was born. She was a healthy and happy baby, and James and his wife Ellen were pleased, even if TJ was upset that it wasn't a baby brother. When Josephine was two, she fell down the steps leading to the second floor of the house. She was in a coma for several days before she died. TJ claimed to have seen the accident, and he said that one of the cats had tripped his little sister causing her to take the horrific tumble. James and Ellen mourned their loss, and TJ became even more sullen.

The boys came home from war in 1945 and the town was abuzz with pride over several of the heroes. Of course the town was stinging from the fact that some of the boys were never coming home. They'd poured out their blood on the battlefields of Europe pushing back the evil that was the Nazi regime.

Chief McIntyre was forced to deal with a new problem. Some of the boys who had returned had young wives, and many of the children that they'd fathered before they left were now school age. The rigors of war and the stresses of family life led many a returning soldier to the bottle. The bottle led them to violence. All too often that violence was aimed at wife or child.

John Everett was especially mean to his son, Billy. Like TJ, Billy was a soft spoken, more tender-hearted boy, even if he did exhibit his father's mean streak every now and again. Chief McIntyre had once caught the boy drowning kittens in the brook. It was a common way to get rid of a litter in those days, but Billy was handling the task in a cruel way. He would hold the struggling kitten underwater and then bring it back up, letting it gasp and choke for air. Then he would repeat the plunge for longer and longer periods until the kitten finally drowned. Chief McIntyre put a stop to it and then used his .22 pistol he kept in the trunk of his patrol car to finish off the three remaining kittens. He promised not to tell Billy's father, as he knew the boy would have been beaten to within an inch of his life.

Though Billy was three years older than TJ, they were the only friends each other had. They would go off into the woods and play until dark. As they grew older, they both became more secretive. Coopers Hollow had a theater at the time and spy films were all the rage. The theater rarely ran the newer movies, but the boys did get to see Casablanca when it came out. From that point on the two boys were French and American spies, dodging Nazis at every corner. They were always carrying on secretively, passing secret codes to each other which only they could

decipher and so on. It was the type of thing that boys their
age should have already grown out of, but their families
were happy that they both had friends, so no one said anything to them and just let them be.

In 1947 it had been something of a dry year in the
Northern Catskills. It certainly wasn't as bad as the
drought of '34, but it was dry enough for the forest rangers
to declare a moratorium on open burning in the state forests during the autumn season.

People would still burn their leaves in their backyards,
and there was little Chief McIntyre could do about that.
But in the woods, the rangers were keeping a look out for
anyone who was camping or cooking without a proper fire
ring to protect from the spread of the flames and perhaps
spark a forest fire.

So on October 2nd, Chief McIntyre, his leg throbbing
and his back hurting from the long since healed wound,
wasn't surprised when his phone rang and it was Timothy
Parks, the forest ranger currently assigned as lookout on
the peak of Mt. Pratt.

"Hey, Chief. Sorry to bother you," Parks said. "I spotted a small fire over on Hollow Pointe. Can't leave my post.
Was wondering if you could go have a look-see."

"Alright, I'll drive over and take a look," McIntyre said
reluctantly. "You owe me one, Parks." McIntyre cradled the
phone, pulled himself to his feet and willed his left leg to
unkink and function the way he needed it to. He limped
the first few steps towards the door, but by the time he
pulled on his fleece lined patrol jacket, it had loosened up
enough for him to take the front steps with ease.

The way the hills were situated, Mt. Pratt was the tallest of the surrounding hills and mountains. It stood at roughly 3,200 feet above sea level. It sloped from its peak down to what was called, "the saddle" and then the ridge climbed again to 2,900 feet to Hollow Pointe.

Whereas Mt. Pratt held a fire tower that could oversee the surrounding terrain in all directions for nearly twenty miles on a clear day, Hollow Pointe was where many of the locals went for picnics and such. A dirt road, which had once been used for logging, stretched from Saddle Brook Road nearly up to the peak of Hollow Pointe. A large, bare rock outcropping at the peak provided a forty foot drop to the trees and vegetation below. Many a couple had spoken their nuptials at this point, and several depressed souls had taken their lives by diving off the granite platform.

Chief McIntyre turned his patrol car onto the bumpy dirt road and peered through the darkness ahead. There were plenty of tire tracks on the dry dirt, as many people had come and gone that day. The fall foliage was still quite spectacular. Usually by this time of year, a strong rain storm had already swept in and taken all the leaves down. But this year, the sun had stayed with them longer and the leaves had clung tightly to the trees. It had been a pleasant autumn. Hopefully it meant that a gentle winter was ahead.

At this height, McIntyre wondered if he could catch the World Series game on his radio. He tuned it in for one of the stations out of Binghamton or Oneonta and was surprised at how clear and crisp the signal came in. The Yankees were up to bat, and they were putting in a pinch hitter. Yogi Berra was facing Ralph Branca on the mound. The pitch was made and Yogi put it out of the park. McIntyre made a fist in the air in silent victory. Even though he was from Boston, the Yankees were his team. Heck, they were most of America's team this year.

Up ahead McIntyre could see a rather large fire burning. The trail ended, so he was going to have to walk the rest of the way. He took his flashlight with him and started through the trees towards the flames. He could hear voices. Giggles. It was probably just a couple of teenagers necking, he thought to himself.

As he neared the clearing of Hollow Pointe, he stopped short. In the light of the flames he recognized one of the faces. He'd stopped dead in his tracks as a chill went down his spine as he saw the other face. Once his brain registered what his eyes were telling him, he flew into a rage.

He burst forth from the trees and grabbed Billy Everett by the hair, pulling him to his feet. The boy was naked except for his stocking feet. McIntyre reeled back and put the back of his hand across the boy's face, knocking him to the ground. Next he turned to his son, TJ.

"Put your clothes back on and get in the car," he barked at him.

"Dad, we weren't doin' nuthin'. We were just wrestlin' around, like in gym class," TJ said in his defense. He too only wore his white gym socks. This sent McIntyre into a rage. He slapped his boy to the ground, then commenced raining down open handed slaps on him. He connected hard with the boy's back and rear. He then grabbed him by the hair and pulled him to his feet. He slapped him across his face, bloodying the boy's nose.

Chief McIntyre turned towards Billy, when suddenly he felt the familiar stabbing pain of a bullet entering his body. He felt it before he heard the gun blast. Billy held his father's pistol from the war with both hands. Smoke was still rolling out of the barrel.

"Billy, no!" TJ called. Billy didn't listen. He pulled the trigger again and again, each bullet tearing into Chief McIntyre's chest.

The big Chief stumbled backwards, and fumbled for his own revolver, but his hand couldn't manage the snap. He felt weak, cold and confused. The adrenaline that he'd been pumping while enraged at the boys now left him thoroughly exhausted. Another shot hit him in the chest, this one knocked him down.

He lay on his back looking up at the stars, his breathing labored. He suddenly had a vision. He was standing over his own body. It was a crime scene, and he was both the victim and the investigator. He was looking down at himself, sprawled out on the granite of Hollow Pointe. He was staring into his own lifeless face, taking notes in his little notebook. The light all around was a sicky-green hue, like in the basement of the hospital where they kept all the dead bodies. His perspective jumped back and forth. He was the investigator; he was the corpse. He drew a blanket over the body; the blanket was drawn over his head. It was the last thought he would have.

The boys stood in shock. TJ couldn't move. He had just witnessed his father being murdered. Billy was awestruck by what had just happened. He'd brought along the gun just in case there was a bear or coyote. He never planned to shoot anyone.

"What do we do?" TJ cried. He was sobbing. Billy hated it when the younger boy cried.

"Listen, nobody knows it was us. It was just an accident," Billy said.

"You kept shooting him," TJ wailed.

"I was scared, my finger slipped," Billy countered.

"But he's dead. You killed him!"

"Nobody else knows that, TJ," Billy said, a plan hatching in his teenage mind. "If we take off and take all of our stuff, people will think it was somebody from the mob. They've been trying to kill him for years. If we just keep our mouths shut, nobody will ever know."

"I don't know if I can do that," TJ said, still sobbing.

"Here." Billy gave him the flask they had been sharing. The whiskey was sharp in TJ's throat, and it warmed his stomach. "Take another drink," Billy ordered.

TJ immediately felt warmer, and started to believe that Billy's plan could really work. Billy put his arm around TJ and gave him a squeeze.

"We just have to think like gangsters. What would gangsters do if they just shot a guy they'd been trying to kill for a long time?" Billy asked.

"They'd probably push him over the edge," TJ said, the alcohol working fast on his twelve year old body. He'd had a few drinks already, so his head was starting to swim.

"You're right, good idea," Billy said. "You push him over the edge, and I'll sweep up our tracks with a branch. That way nobody will know it was us."

TJ walked towards the body of his father. He didn't hate the man, but he didn't really love him like some boys loved their father. He just felt like he never really measured up to the man's standards, to his ideals. Whereas James McIntyre was a larger than life man, TJ was small and thin, taking more after his mother. TJ always felt that he was somehow a disappointment. Especially after Elizabeth had died.

The cat hadn't done it. TJ had gotten angry at Elizabeth for taking one of his toy soldiers and chewing off its head. It was his favorite, a general leading the charge. He'd pushed his baby sister expecting her to fall immediately. But she just kept stumbling and stumbling, trying to catch her balance, but she didn't. She went over the edge of the stairs, tumbling all the way to the bottom, hitting her head on just about every step.

This was like that time. It wasn't really his fault, and if he kept to the story, no one would blame him.

TJ bent low and put all of his strength into it. He pushed Chief James McIntyre, his father, over the edge of Hollow Pointe.

Chapter 1 • Present Day

"So what have you got for me?" His cigarette was burning down to his fingers. He'd been waiting for a long time for his contact to arrive. A drizzle began to fall from the gray sky, and this dampened his spirits even more. This time of year always made him melancholy. The trees were bare of leaves, the wind was full of chill, and the days were shorter and shorter. Though he was a man who liked to travel in shadows, he hated the gloom of autumn and winter.

"Well you're not going to like it," the contact said. The contact's name was Howard Dimmler and he was middle aged, balding, wore thick glasses and a thick middle, as well as a rumpled trench coat. He looked like an unpolished salesman or a government bureaucrat who had climbed about as high as he was going to climb and was now finding his way back down the ladder.

Dimmler handed him a manila envelope. Within was a tablet computer which contained all of the photographs, reports and dossiers on project Tiger Trap.

"Why am I not going to like it?" He was a man of particulars. Details. He was excellent at reviewing data and picking out the aberrations, the anomalies, the inconsistencies.

"Well, it's all been blown up. The whole thing. All of

our contacts, all the inroads, even the tiger cub himself.
Gone. We lost an agent too," the contact said. He brought
his fat hands together into a ball and then exploded them
out, wiggling his fingers as he brought his hands down.
He made an exploding noise with his plump cheeks just
for the right effect. He always found a certain amount
of joy in being the bearer of bad news. All these smarty-
pants federal investigators with their perfectly orchestrated
stings, their iron clad convictions and their well tailored
and pressed suits; they were humans just like everybody
else. They had to be brought back to reality every now and
again, and Dimmler was more than happy to be the one to
do it.

"So it's a total loss, then?" He asked. Some called him
Mr. Shadow, others called him the Shadow Man. When
he was home, his children called him daddy and his wife
called him dear. They didn't understand what daddy
dearest did for a living. He infiltrated the organizations
of the bad guys. He played by his own rules, and worked
outside of the major government agencies. His was a small
team, just nine players. They would sometimes spend years
infiltrating an organization just for that small snippet of
information that would bring down the whole house of
cards.

His team was called off the terrorist cell eighteen
months before the World Trade Center buildings were
taken down. They were close. They knew the players, they
knew the plot, they even knew the month. But it was a
different time then. The men he reported to didn't take the
threats seriously. They were drunk on the profits of their
stock portfolios and didn't want to upset the apple cart.

When the apple cart exploded they were quick to point the
fingers and allocate the blame. Mr. Shadow simply closed
the case and filed his information away. He would never be
called in front of a Congressional Inquiry or have a news
microphone shoved in his face. Then again, he wouldn't
be asked to assist with international matters again. They
didn't blame him per se, but he got a little black mark next
to his name. He was out of the terrorist game for awhile. If
he was going to work, it would be at home, in the good old
U. S. of A.

It was a good thing that there was plenty of work to be
had at home. The war on drugs was faltering. The moral
high ground had been lost, and the enemy had even gained
an advantage by utilizing all of the new technology which
was readily available in the form of hand-held devices or
internet connectivity. It still called for good old fashioned
investigation and even some undercover work. Mr. Shadow
had several members of his team currently working undercover. Deep undercover. They were cleared to cooperate
with and or participate in any manner of law breaking in
order to keep their cover concealed. The assignment was
more important than adhering to the laws. If you wanted
to catch the dirtiest of the dirty, you had to expect to get a
little dirty yourself. It had become bad business to let the
war continue south of the border. Legalization and regu-
lation was about to be on the table. But before that could
happen, you had to remove the major players.

"Is the information complete, have we got the full story
here?" Mr. Shadow took one last puff on his cigarette and
then flicked it out into the drizzle of rainfall.

"Not exactly. The reports encompass what could be

gleaned from the state police and sheriff's reports. Those were all kept on their network drives. Very easy to punch into. The bulk of the investigation went through the local police chief, though. All of his files are still hard copies and locked away in steel filing cabinets in his office," Dimmler said.

"And?"

"And what? I don't do B and E. I hack. These are my lock picks," Dimmler said, wiggling his fat fingers again.

"Then I guess our business is done," Mr. Shadow said with a level of finality. He reached into his jacket, causing Dimmler to stand quickly and flinch. Mr. Shadow began to laugh in a gravely voice. He put the new cigarette he'd retrieved up to his lips. He fished a lighter from his pocket and lit up with a quick puff.

"Did you think I was going to shoot you?" Mr. Shadow asked with a chuckle.

"I didn't - I mean, of course not. I just have to go is all," Dimmler said quickly. He turned and walked briskly back towards the sounds of traffic at the edge of the park.

Mr. Shadow enjoyed his cigarette for several more minutes. It looked like he and his team needed to pay a visit to the town of Coopers Hollow, New York and one Police Chief Jack McMurphy Jr.

Author's Sketches for *The Catskills*

While writing I sometimes sketch out characters or scenes as they pop into my head. I thought you might enjoy seeing some of the rough sketches I made while writing *The Catskills*. Some were made while talking on the phone, others were done because I was frustrated and couldn't write. The one below was made because I wanted to see Michael Cooke with his rifle.

A very rough and scowling Jack McMurphy Jr. The
character was so put-upon through the book, so over his
head. He started off being older, but the more I wrote
him, the younger I needed him to be. Once his father was
killed, he needed to seem completely overwhelmed. His
growth as a character was about learning how to manage
life out from under his father's and grandfather's shadow.
By the end of the book, he was just starting to learn how.

Gloria was a fun character. She was pretty, but closed
up. I'm a people watcher. I love going to the mall and
watching shoppers and imagining their stories based on
their body language. The character of Gloria grew out
of one shopper's body language. I wanted to make sure I
remembered it in a sketch.

Thaddeus "Tubby" McIntyre in his natural environment. I hope I don't get in trouble by Kellogg's for so many Frosted Flakes® references. I stand at 6'5" if *The Catskills* is ever made into a movie I totally want to play Tubby!

This is just horrible. I included it so I could stay humble. If you ever catch me getting too full of myself, flip open a copy of this book, point to this illustration and remind me of how much of a talentless hack I really am. I thank you in advance for your help!

Though many liked the previous cover, I felt it was too ambiguous. It will always have a special place in my heart, so I thought I would give it an honorable mention here in the closing pages of the revised edition.

Acknowledgments

I would first like to thank my wonderful wife Belinda and my three children for supporting me so completely throughout the process of writing this novel. Without you, this never could have happened. I would also like to thank all of the people who encouraged me to write. You really have no idea how much you helped to make this novel a reality. Lastly, I would like to thank all of the organizers and supporters of National Novel Writing Month. This novel began on a November 1st just like many others, I'm sure. Support the cause and donate at nanowrimo.org.

About the Author

Adam Cornell was born in upstate New York but spent some of his life in Louisiana, which he considers his second home. He began writing in grade school and could never kick the habit. He has previously written a screenplay and television pilot, both of which never got past the first stages of production. Adam has previously worked on the air as a radio personality utilizing the name Adam Speed while in Baton Rouge and New Orleans, LA as well as Elmira, NY. He has also made a career in the field of graphic design, working at several ad agencies along with other companies in the printing, housewares and automotive industries. Adam currently lives with his wife and three children in Watertown, NY.